The Edgar Allan Poe Collection

The Edgar Allan Poe Collection

Edgar Allan Poe

MINT EDITIONS

The Edgar Allan Poe Collection features short stories and poetry first published between 1839–1849.

This edition published by Mint Editions 2021.

ISBN 9781513269184 | E-ISBN 9781513274188

Published by Mint Editions®

MINT
EDITIONS

minteditionbooks.com

Publishing Director: Jennifer Newens
Design & Production: Rachel Lopez Metzger
Project Manager: Micaela Clark
Typesetting: Westchester Publishing Services

Contents

Tales

The Cask of Amontillado 9

A Descent Into the Maelstrom 16

The Fall of the House of Usher 31

The Gold-Bug 48

The Masque of the Red Death 81

The Murders in the Rue Morgue 87

The Mystery of Marie Roget 118

The Purloined Letter 161

The Tell-Tale Heart 178

Poems

The Bells 185

The City in the Sea 186

The Conqueror Worm 188

A Dream Within a Dream 190

Dreamland 191

Fairyland 193

The Haunted Palace 195

The Raven 197

Romance 201

Silence 202

The Sleeper 203

Song 205

Spirits of the Dead 206

Ulalame 207

Prose

Eureka: A Prose Poem 213

The Power of Words 298

Shadow: A Parable 302

Silence: A Fable 305

TALES

The Cask of Amontillado

The thousand injuries of Fortunato I had borne as I best could, but when he ventured upon insult, I vowed revenge. You, who so well know the nature of my soul, will not suppose, however, that I gave utterance to a threat. *At length* I would be avenged; this was a point definitely settled—but the very definitiveness with which it was resolved, precluded the idea of risk. I must not only punish, but punish with impunity. A wrong is unredressed when retribution overtakes its redresser. It is equally unredressed when the avenger fails to make himself felt as such to him who has done the wrong.

It must be understood that neither by word nor deed had I given Fortunato cause to doubt my good will. I continued, as was my wont, to smile in his face, and he did not perceive that my smile *now* was at the thought of his immolation.

He had a weak point—this Fortunato—although in other regards he was a man to be respected and even feared. He prided himself on his connoisseurship in wine. Few Italians have the true virtuoso spirit. For the most part their enthusiasm is adopted to suit the time and opportunity—to practise imposture upon the British and Austrian *millionaires*. In painting and gemmary, Fortunato, like his countrymen, was a quack—but in the matter of old wines he was sincere. In this respect I did not differ from him materially: I was skillful in the Italian vintages myself, and bought largely whenever I could.

It was about dusk, one evening during the supreme madness of the carnival season, that I encountered my friend. He accosted me with excessive warmth, for he had been drinking much. The man wore motley. He had on a tight-fitting parti-striped dress, and his head was surmounted by the conical cap and bells. I was so pleased to see him, that I thought I should never have done wringing his hand.

I said to him—"My dear Fortunato, you are luckily met. How remarkably well you are looking to-day! But I have received a pipe of what passes for Amontillado, and I have my doubts."

"How?" said he. "Amontillado? A pipe? Impossible! And in the middle of the carnival!"

"I have my doubts," I replied; "and I was silly enough to pay the full Amontillado price without consulting you in the matter. You were not to be found, and I was fearful of losing a bargain."

"Amontillado!"

"I have my doubts."

"Amontillado!"

"And I must satisfy them."

"Amontillado!"

"As you are engaged, I am on my way to Luchesi. If any one has a critical turn, it is he. He will tell me—"

"Luchesi cannot tell Amontillado from Sherry."

"And yet some fools will have it that his taste is a match for your own."

"Come, let us go."

"Whither?"

"To your vaults."

"My friend, no; I will not impose upon your good nature. I perceive you have an engagement. Luchesi—"

"I have no engagement;—come."

"My friend, no. It is not the engagement, but the severe cold with which I perceive you are afflicted. The vaults are insufferably damp. They are encrusted with nitre."

"Let us go, nevertheless. The cold is merely nothing. Amontillado! You have been imposed upon. And as for Luchesi, he cannot distinguish Sherry from Amontillado."

Thus speaking, Fortunato possessed himself of my arm. Putting on a mask of black silk, and drawing a *roquelaire* closely about my person, I suffered him to hurry me to my palazzo.

There were no attendants at home; they had absconded to make merry in honour of the time. I had told them that I should not return until the morning, and had given them explicit orders not to stir from the house. These orders were sufficient, I well knew, to insure their immediate disappearance, one and all, as soon as my back was turned.

I took from their sconces two flambeaux, and giving one to Fortunato, bowed him through several suites of rooms to the archway that led into the vaults. I passed down a long and winding staircase, requesting him to be cautious as he followed. We came at length to the foot of the descent, and stood together on the damp ground of the catacombs of the Montresors.

The gait of my friend was unsteady, and the bells upon his cap jingled as he strode.

"The pipe," said he.

"It is farther on," said I; "but observe the white web-work which gleams from these cavern walls."

He turned towards me, and looked into my eyes with two filmy orbs that distilled the rheum of intoxication.

"Nitre?" he asked, at length.

"Nitre," I replied. "How long have you had that cough?"

"Ugh! ugh! ugh!—ugh! ugh! ugh!—ugh! ugh! ugh!—ugh! ugh! ugh!—ugh! ugh! ugh!"

My poor friend found it impossible to reply for many minutes.

"It is nothing," he said, at last.

"Come," I said, with decision, "we will go back; your health is precious. You are rich, respected, admired, beloved; you are happy, as once I was. You are a man to be missed. For me it is no matter. We will go back; you will be ill, and I cannot be responsible. Besides, there is Luchesi—"

"Enough," he said; "the cough is a mere nothing; it will not kill me. I shall not die of a cough."

"True—true," I replied; "and, indeed, I had no intention of alarming you unnecessarily—but you should use all proper caution. A draught of this Medoc will defend us from the damps."

Here I knocked off the neck of a bottle which I drew from a long row of its fellows that lay upon the mould.

"Drink," I said, presenting him the wine.

He raised it to his lips with a leer. He paused and nodded to me familiarly, while his bells jingled.

"I drink," he said, "to the buried that repose around us."

"And I to your long life."

He again took my arm, and we proceeded.

"These vaults," he said, "are extensive."

"The Montresors," I replied, "were a great and numerous family."

"I forget your arms."

"A huge human foot d'or, in a field azure; the foot crushes a serpent rampant whose fangs are imbedded in the heel."

"And the motto?"

"*Nemo me impune lacessit*."

"Good!" he said.

The wine sparkled in his eyes and the bells jingled. My own fancy grew warm with the Medoc. We had passed through walls of piled bones, with casks and puncheons intermingling, into the inmost recesses of catacombs. I paused again, and this time I made bold to seize Fortunato by an arm above the elbow.

"The nitre!" I said; "see, it increases. It hangs like moss upon the vaults. We are below the river's bed. The drops of moisture trickle among the bones. Come, we will go back ere it is too late. Your cough—"

"It is nothing," he said; "let us go on. But first, another draught of the Medoc."

I broke and reached him a flagon of De Grave. He emptied it at a breath. His eyes flashed with a fierce light. He laughed and threw the bottle upwards with a gesticulation I did not understand.

I looked at him in surprise. He repeated the movement—a grotesque one.

"You do not comprehend?" he said.

"Not I," I replied.

"Then you are not of the brotherhood."

"How?"

"You are not of the masons."

"Yes, yes," I said; "yes, yes."

"You? Impossible! A mason?"

"A mason," I replied.

"A sign," he said, "a sign."

"It is this," I answered, producing a trowel from beneath the folds of my *roquelaire*.

"You jest," he exclaimed, recoiling a few paces. "But let us proceed to the Amontillado."

"Be it so," I said, replacing the tool beneath the cloak and again offering him my arm. He leaned upon it heavily. We continued our route in search of the Amontillado. We passed through a range of low arches, descended, passed on, and descending again, arrived at a deep crypt, in which the foulness of the air caused our flambeaux rather to glow than flame.

At the most remote end of the crypt there appeared another less spacious. Its walls had been lined with human remains, piled to the vault overhead, in the fashion of the great catacombs of Paris. Three sides of this interior crypt were still ornamented in this manner. From the fourth side the bones had been thrown down, and lay promiscuously upon the earth, forming at one point a mound of some size. Within the wall thus exposed by the displacing of the bones, we perceived a still interior recess, in depth about four feet in width three, in height six or seven. It seemed to have been constructed for no especial use within itself, but formed merely the interval between two of the colossal supports of the roof of the catacombs, and was backed by one of their circumscribing walls of solid granite.

It was in vain that Fortunato, uplifting his dull torch, endeavoured to pry into the depth of the recess. Its termination the feeble light did not enable us to see.

"Proceed," I said; "herein is the Amontillado. As for Luchesi—"

"He is an ignoramus," interrupted my friend, as he stepped unsteadily forward, while I followed immediately at his heels. In an instant he had reached the extremity of the niche, and finding his progress arrested by the rock, stood stupidly bewildered. A moment more and I had fettered him to the granite. In its surface were two iron staples, distant from each other about two feet, horizontally. From one of these depended a short chain, from the other a padlock. Throwing the links about his waist, it was but the work of a few seconds to secure it. He was too much astounded to resist. Withdrawing the key I stepped back from the recess.

"Pass your hand," I said, "over the wall; you cannot help feeling the nitre. Indeed, it is *very* damp. Once more let me *implore* you to return. No? Then I must positively leave you. But I must first render you all the little attentions in my power."

"The Amontillado!" exclaimed my friend, not yet recovered from his astonishment.

"True," I replied; "the Amontillado."

As I said these words I busied myself among the pile of bones of which I have before spoken. Throwing them aside, I soon uncovered a quantity of building stone and mortar. With these materials and with the aid of my trowel, I began vigorously to wall up the entrance of the niche.

I had scarcely laid the first tier of the masonry when I discovered that the intoxication of Fortunato had in a great measure worn off. The earliest indication I had of this was a low moaning cry from the depth of the recess. It was *not* the cry of a drunken man. There was then a long and obstinate silence. I laid the second tier, and the third, and the fourth; and then I heard the furious vibrations of the chain. The noise lasted for several minutes, during which, that I might hearken to it with the more satisfaction, I ceased my labours and sat down upon the bones. When at last the clanking subsided, I resumed the trowel, and finished without interruption the fifth, the sixth, and the seventh tier. The wall was now nearly upon a level with my breast. I again paused, and holding the flambeaux over the mason-work, threw a few feeble rays upon the figure within.

A succession of loud and shrill screams, bursting suddenly from the throat of the chained form, seemed to thrust me violently back. For a brief moment I hesitated—I trembled. Unsheathing my rapier, I began to grope with it about the recess; but the thought of an instant reassured me. I placed my hand upon the solid fabric of the catacombs, and felt satisfied. I reapproached the wall; I replied to the yells of him who clamoured. I re-echoed—I aided—I surpassed them in volume and in strength. I did this, and the clamourer grew still.

It was now midnight, and my task was drawing to a close. I had completed the eighth, the ninth, and the tenth tier. I had finished a portion of the last and the eleventh; there remained but a single stone to be fitted and plastered in. I struggled with its weight; I placed it partially in its destined position. But now there came from out the niche a low laugh that erected the hairs upon my head. It was succeeded by a sad voice, which I had difficulty in recognizing as that of the noble Fortunato. The voice said—

"Ha! ha! ha!—he! he! he!—a very good joke indeed—an excellent jest. We shall have many a rich laugh about it at the palazzo—he! he! he!—over our wine—he! he! he!"

"The Amontillado!" I said.

"He! he! he!—he! he! he!—yes, the Amontillado. But is it not getting late? Will not they be awaiting us at the palazzo, the Lady Fortunato and the rest? Let us be gone."

"Yes," I said, "let us be gone."

"*For the love of God, Montresor!*"

"Yes," I said, "for the love of God!"

But to these words I hearkened in vain for a reply. I grew impatient. I called aloud—

"Fortunato!"

No answer. I called again—

"Fortunato—"

No answer still. I thrust a torch through the remaining aperture and let it fall within. There came forth in reply only a jingling of the bells. My heart grew sick on account of the dampness of the catacombs.

I hastened to make an end of my labour. I forced the last stone into its position; I plastered it up. Against the new masonry I re-erected the old rampart of bones. For the half of a century no mortal has disturbed them. *In pace requiescat!*

A Descent Into the Maelstrom

The ways of God in Nature, as in Providence, are not as our ways; nor are the models that we frame any way commensurate to the vastness, profundity, and unsearchableness of His works, which have a depth in them greater than the well of Democritus.

—Joseph Glanville

We had now reached the summit of the loftiest crag. For some minutes the old man seemed too much exhausted to speak.

"Not long ago," said he at length, "and I could have guided you on this route as well as the youngest of my sons; but, about three years past, there happened to me an event such as never happened to mortal man—or at least such as no man ever survived to tell of—and the six hours of deadly terror which I then endured have broken me up body and soul. You suppose me a *very* old man—but I am not. It took less than a single day to change these hairs from a jetty black to white, to weaken my limbs, and to unstring my nerves, so that I tremble at the least exertion, and am frightened at a shadow. Do you know I can scarcely look over this little cliff without getting giddy?"

The "little cliff," upon whose edge he had so carelessly thrown himself down to rest that the weightier portion of his body hung over it, while he was only kept from falling by the tenure of his elbow on its extreme and slippery edge—this "little cliff" arose, a sheer unobstructed precipice of black shining rock, some fifteen or sixteen hundred feet from the world of crags beneath us. Nothing would have tempted me to within half a dozen yards of its brink. In truth so deeply was I excited by the perilous position of my companion, that I fell at full length upon the ground, clung to the shrubs around me, and dared not even glance upward at the sky—while I struggled in vain to divest myself of the idea that the very foundations of the mountain were in danger from the fury of the winds. It was long before I could reason myself into sufficient courage to sit up and look out into the distance.

"You must get over these fancies," said the guide, "for I have brought you here that you might have the best possible view of the scene of that event I mentioned—and to tell you the whole story with the spot just under your eye."

"We are now," he continued, in that particularizing manner which distinguished him—"we are now close upon the Norwegian coast—in the sixty-eighth degree of latitude—in the great province of Nordland—and in the dreary district of Lofoden. The mountain upon whose top we sit is Helseggen, the Cloudy. Now raise yourself up a little higher—hold on to the grass if you feel giddy—so—and look out, beyond the belt of vapor beneath us, into the sea."

I looked dizzily, and beheld a wide expanse of ocean, whose waters wore so inky a hue as to bring at once to my mind the Nubian geographer's account of the *Mare Tenebrarum*. A panorama more deplorably desolate no human imagination can conceive. To the right and left, as far as the eye could reach, there lay outstretched, like ramparts of the world, lines of horridly black and beetling cliff, whose character of gloom was but the more forcibly illustrated by the surf which reared high up against its white and ghastly crest, howling and shrieking forever. Just opposite the promontory upon whose apex we were placed, and at a distance of some five or six miles out at sea, there was visible a small, bleak-looking island; or, more properly, its position was discernible through the wilderness of surge in which it was enveloped. About two miles nearer the land, arose another of smaller size, hideously craggy and barren, and encompassed at various intervals by a cluster of dark rocks.

The appearance of the ocean, in the space between the more distant island and the shore, had something very unusual about it. Although, at the time, so strong a gale was blowing landward that a brig in the remote offing lay to under a double-reefed trysail, and constantly plunged her whole hull out of sight, still there was here nothing like a regular swell, but only a short, quick, angry cross dashing of water in every direction—as well in the teeth of the wind as otherwise. Of foam there was little except in the immediate vicinity of the rocks.

"The island in the distance," resumed the old man, "is called by the Norwegians Vurrgh. The one midway is Moskoe. That a mile to the northward is Ambaaren. Yonder are Islesen, Hotholm, Keildhelm, Suarven, and Buckholm. Farther off—between Moskoe and Vurrgh—are Otterholm, Flimen, Sandflesen, and Stockholm. These are the true names of the places—but why it has been thought necessary to name them at all, is more than either you or I can understand. Do you hear anything? Do you see any change in the water?"

We had now been about ten minutes upon the top of Helseggen, to which we had ascended from the interior of Lofoden, so that we had caught no glimpse of the sea until it had burst upon us from the summit. As the old man spoke, I became aware of a loud and gradually increasing sound, like the moaning of a vast herd of buffaloes upon an American prairie; and at the same moment I perceived that what seamen term the *chopping* character of the ocean beneath us, was rapidly changing into a current which set to the eastward. Even while I gazed, this current acquired a monstrous velocity. Each moment added to its speed—to its headlong impetuosity. In five minutes the whole sea, as far as Vurrgh, was lashed into ungovernable fury; but it was between Moskoe and the coast that the main uproar held its sway. Here the vast bed of the waters, seamed and scarred into a thousand conflicting channels, burst suddenly into phrensied convulsion—heaving, boiling, hissing—gyrating in gigantic and innumerable vortices, and all whirling and plunging on to the eastward with a rapidity which water never elsewhere assumes except in precipitous descents.

In a few minutes more, there came over the scene another radical alteration. The general surface grew somewhat more smooth, and the whirlpools, one by one, disappeared, while prodigious streaks of foam became apparent where none had been seen before. These streaks, at length, spreading out to a great distance, and entering into combination, took unto themselves the gyratory motion of the subsided vortices, and seemed to form the germ of another more vast. Suddenly—very suddenly—this assumed a distinct and definite existence, in a circle of more than a mile in diameter. The edge of the whirl was represented by a broad belt of gleaming spray; but no particle of this slipped into the mouth of the terrific funnel, whose interior, as far as the eye could fathom it, was a smooth, shining, and jet-black wall of water, inclined to the horizon at an angle of some forty-five degrees, speeding dizzily round and round with a swaying and sweltering motion, and sending forth to the winds an appalling voice, half shriek, half roar, such as not even the mighty cataract of Niagara ever lifts up in its agony to Heaven.

The mountain trembled to its very base, and the rock rocked. I threw myself upon my face, and clung to the scant herbage in an excess of nervous agitation.

"This," said I at length, to the old man—"this *can* be nothing else than the great whirlpool of the Maelström."

"So it is sometimes termed," said he. "We Norwegians call it the Moskoe-ström, from the island of Moskoe in the midway."

The ordinary accounts of this vortex had by no means prepared me for what I saw. That of Jonas Ramus, which is perhaps the most circumstantial of any, cannot impart the faintest conception either of the magnificence, or of the horror of the scene—or of the wild bewildering sense of *the novel* which confounds the beholder. I am not sure from what point of view the writer in question surveyed it, nor at what time; but it could neither have been from the summit of Helseggen, nor during a storm. There are some passages of his description, nevertheless, which may be quoted for their details, although their effect is exceedingly feeble in conveying an impression of the spectacle.

"Between Lofoden and Moskoe," he says, "the depth of the water is between thirty-six and forty fathoms; but on the other side, toward Ver (Vurrgh) this depth decreases so as not to afford a convenient passage for a vessel, without the risk of splitting on the rocks, which happens even in the calmest weather. When it is flood, the stream runs up the country between Lofoden and Moskoe with a boisterous rapidity; but the roar of its impetuous ebb to the sea is scarce equalled by the loudest and most dreadful cataracts; the noise being heard several leagues off, and the vortices or pits are of such an extent and depth, that if a ship comes within its attraction, it is inevitably absorbed and carried down to the bottom, and there beat to pieces against the rocks; and when the water relaxes, the fragments thereof are thrown up again. But these intervals of tranquility are only at the turn of the ebb and flood, and in calm weather, and last but a quarter of an hour, its violence gradually returning. When the stream is most boisterous, and its fury heightened by a storm, it is dangerous to come within a Norway mile of it. Boats, yachts, and ships have been carried away by not guarding against it before they were within its reach. It likewise happens frequently, that whales come too near the stream, and are overpowered by its violence; and then it is impossible to describe their howlings and bellowings in their fruitless struggles to disengage themselves. A bear once, attempting to swim from Lofoden to Moskoe, was caught by the stream and borne down, while he roared terribly, so as to be heard on shore. Large stocks of firs and pine trees, after being absorbed by the current, rise again broken and torn to such a degree as if bristles grew upon them. This plainly shows the bottom to consist of craggy rocks, among which they are whirled to and fro. This stream is regulated by the flux and reflux of the sea—it being constantly high and low water every six hours. In the year 1645, early in the morning of Sexagesima Sunday, it raged with such noise and impetuosity that the very stones of the houses on the coast fell to the ground."

In regard to the depth of the water, I could not see how this could have been ascertained at all in the immediate vicinity of the vortex. The "forty fathoms" must have reference only to portions of the channel close upon the shore either of Moskoe or Lofoden. The depth in the centre of the Moskoe-ström must be immeasurably greater; and no better proof of this fact is necessary than can be obtained from even the sidelong glance into the abyss of the whirl which may be had from the highest crag of Helseggen. Looking down from this pinnacle upon the howling Phlegethon below, I could not help smiling at the simplicity with which the honest Jonas Ramus records, as a matter difficult of belief, the anecdotes of the whales and the bears; for it appeared to me, in fact, a self-evident thing, that the largest ship of the line in existence, coming within the influence of that deadly attraction, could resist it as little as a feather the hurricane, and must disappear bodily and at once.

The attempts to account for the phenomenon—some of which, I remember, seemed to me sufficiently plausible in perusal—now wore a very different and unsatisfactory aspect. The idea generally received is that this, as well as three smaller vortices among the Ferroe islands, "have no other cause than the collision of waves rising and falling, at flux and reflux, against a ridge of rocks and shelves, which confines the water so that it precipitates itself like a cataract; and thus the higher the flood rises, the deeper must the fall be, and the natural result of all is a whirlpool or vortex, the prodigious suction of which is sufficiently known by lesser experiments."—These are the words of the Encyclopædia Britannica. Kircher and others imagine that in the centre of the channel of the Maelström is an abyss penetrating the globe, and issuing in some very remote part—the Gulf of Bothnia being somewhat decidedly named in one instance. This opinion, idle in itself, was the one to which, as I gazed, my imagination most readily assented; and, mentioning it to the guide, I was rather surprised to hear him say that, although it was the view almost universally entertained of the subject by the Norwegians, it nevertheless was not his own. As to the former notion he confessed his inability to comprehend it; and here I agreed with him—for, however conclusive on paper, it becomes altogether unintelligible, and even absurd, amid the thunder of the abyss.

"You have had a good look at the whirl now," said the old man, "and if you will creep round this crag, so as to get in its lee, and deaden the roar of the water, I will tell you a story that will convince you I ought to know something of the Moskoe-ström."

I placed myself as desired, and he proceeded.

"Myself and my two brothers once owned a schooner-rigged smack of about seventy tons burthen, with which we were in the habit of fishing among the islands beyond Moskoe, nearly to Vurrgh. In all violent eddies at sea there is good fishing, at proper opportunities, if one has only the courage to attempt it; but among the whole of the Lofoden coastmen, we three were the only ones who made a regular business of going out to the islands, as I tell you. The usual grounds are a great way lower down to the southward. There fish can be got at all hours, without much risk, and therefore these places are preferred. The choice spots over here among the rocks, however, not only yield the finest variety, but in far greater abundance; so that we often got in a single day, what the more timid of the craft could not scrape together in a week. In fact, we made it a matter of desperate speculation—the risk of life standing instead of labor, and courage answering for capital.

"We kept the smack in a cove about five miles higher up the coast than this; and it was our practice, in fine weather, to take advantage of the fifteen minutes' slack to push across the main channel of the Moskoe-ström, far above the pool, and then drop down upon anchorage somewhere near Otterholm, or Sandflesen, where the eddies are not so violent as elsewhere. Here we used to remain until nearly time for slack-water again, when we weighed and made for home. We never set out upon this expedition without a steady side wind for going and coming—one that we felt sure would not fail us before our return—and we seldom made a mis-calculation upon this point. Twice, during six years, we were forced to stay all night at anchor on account of a dead calm, which is a rare thing indeed just about here; and once we had to remain on the grounds nearly a week, starving to death, owing to a gale which blew up shortly after our arrival, and made the channel too boisterous to be thought of. Upon this occasion we should have been driven out to sea in spite of everything, (for the whirlpools threw us round and round so violently, that, at length, we fouled our anchor and dragged it) if it had not been that we drifted into one of the innumerable cross currents—here to-day and gone to-morrow—which drove us under the lee of Flimen, where, by good luck, we brought up.

"I could not tell you the twentieth part of the difficulties we encountered 'on the grounds'—it is a bad spot to be in, even in good weather—but we made shift always to run the gauntlet of the Moskoe-ström itself without accident; although at times my heart has been in my mouth when we happened to be a minute or so behind or before the slack. The wind sometimes was not as strong as we thought it at starting, and then we made rather less way than we could wish, while the current rendered the smack unmanageable. My eldest brother had a son eighteen years old, and I had two stout boys of my own. These would have been of great assistance at such times, in using the sweeps, as well as afterward in fishing—but, somehow, although we ran the risk ourselves, we had not the heart to let the young ones get into the danger—for, after all is said and done, it *was* a horrible danger, and that is the truth.

"It is now within a few days of three years since what I am going to tell you occurred. It was on the tenth day of July, 18-, a day which the people of this part of the world will never forget—for it was one in which blew the most terrible hurricane that ever came out of the heavens. And yet all the morning, and indeed until late in the afternoon, there was a gentle and steady breeze from the south-west, while the sun shone brightly, so that the oldest seaman among us could not have foreseen what was to follow.

"The three of us—my two brothers and myself—had crossed over to the islands about two o'clock P. M., and had soon nearly loaded the smack with fine fish, which, we all remarked, were more plenty that day than we had ever known them. It was just seven, *by my watch*, when we weighed and started for home, so as to make the worst of the Ström at slack water, which we knew would be at eight.

"We set out with a fresh wind on our starboard quarter, and for some time spanked along at a great rate, never dreaming of danger, for indeed we saw not the slightest reason to apprehend it. All at once we were taken aback by a breeze from over Helseggen. This was most unusual—something that had never happened to us before—and I began to feel a little uneasy, without exactly knowing why. We put the boat on the wind, but could make no headway at all for the eddies, and I was upon the point of proposing to return to the anchorage, when, looking astern, we saw the whole horizon covered with a singular copper-colored cloud that rose with the most amazing velocity.

"In the meantime the breeze that had headed us off fell away, and we were dead becalmed, drifting about in every direction. This state of things, however, did not last long enough to give us time to think about it. In less than a minute the storm was upon us—in less than two the sky was entirely overcast—and what with this and the driving spray, it became suddenly so dark that we could not see each other in the smack.

"Such a hurricane as then blew it is folly to attempt describing. The oldest seaman in Norway never experienced any thing like it. We had let our sails go by the run before it cleverly took us; but, at the first puff, both our masts went by the board as if they had been sawed off—the mainmast taking with it my youngest brother, who had lashed himself to it for safety.

"Our boat was the lightest feather of a thing that ever sat upon water. It had a complete flush deck, with only a small hatch near the bow, and this hatch it had always been our custom to batten down when about to cross the Ström, by way of precaution against the chopping seas. But for this circumstance we should have foundered at once—for we lay entirely buried for some moments. How my elder brother escaped destruction I cannot say, for I never had an opportunity of ascertaining. For my part, as soon as I had let the foresail run, I threw myself flat on deck, with my feet against the narrow gunwale of the bow, and with my hands grasping a ring-bolt near the foot of the fore-mast. It was mere instinct that prompted me to do this—which was undoubtedly the very best thing I could have done—for I was too much flurried to think.

"For some moments we were completely deluged, as I say, and all this time I held my breath, and clung to the bolt. When I could stand it no longer I raised myself upon my knees, still keeping hold with my hands, and thus got my head clear. Presently our little boat gave herself a shake, just as a dog does in coming out of the water, and thus rid herself, in some measure, of the seas. I was now trying to get the better of the stupor that had come over me, and to collect my senses so as to see what was to be done, when I felt somebody grasp my arm. It was my elder brother, and my heart leaped for joy, for I had made sure that he was overboard—but the next moment all this joy was turned into horror—for he put his mouth close to my ear, and screamed out the word '*Moskoe-ström!*'

"No one ever will know what my feelings were at that moment. I shook from head to foot as if I had had the most violent fit of the ague. I knew what he meant by that one word well enough—I knew what he wished to make me understand. With the wind that now drove us on, we were bound for the whirl of the Ström, and nothing could save us!

"You perceive that in crossing the Ström *channel*, we always went a long way up above the whirl, even in the calmest weather, and then had to wait and watch carefully for the slack—but now we were driving right upon the pool itself, and in such a hurricane as this! 'To be sure,' I thought, 'we shall get there just about the slack—there is some little hope in that'—but in the next moment I cursed myself for being so great a fool as to dream of hope at all. I knew very well that we were doomed, had we been ten times a ninety-gun ship.

"By this time the first fury of the tempest had spent itself, or perhaps we did not feel it so much, as we scudded before it, but at all events the seas, which at first had been kept down by the wind, and lay flat and frothing, now got up into absolute mountains. A singular change, too, had come over the heavens. Around in every direction it was still as black as pitch, but nearly overhead there burst out, all at once, a circular rift of clear sky—as clear as I ever saw—and of a deep bright blue—and through it there blazed forth the full moon with a lustre that I never before knew her to wear. She lit up every thing about us with the greatest distinctness—but, oh God, what a scene it was to light up!

"I now made one or two attempts to speak to my brother—but, in some manner which I could not understand, the din had so increased that I could not make him hear a single word, although I screamed at the top of my voice in his ear. Presently he shook his head, looking as pale as death, and held up one of his fingers, as if to say *'listen!* '

"At first I could not make out what he meant—but soon a hideous thought flashed upon me. I dragged my watch from its fob. It was not going. I glanced at its face by the moonlight, and then burst into tears as I flung it far away into the ocean. *It had run down at seven o'clock! We were behind the time of the slack, and the whirl of the Ström was in full fury!*

"When a boat is well built, properly trimmed, and not deep laden, the waves in a strong gale, when she is going large, seem always to slip from beneath her—which appears very strange to a landsman—and this is what is called *riding*, in sea phrase. Well, so far we had ridden the swells very cleverly; but presently a gigantic sea happened to take us right under the counter, and bore us with it as it rose—up—up—as if into the sky. I would not have believed that any wave could rise so high. And then down we came with a sweep, a slide, and a plunge, that made me feel sick and dizzy, as if I was falling from some lofty mountain-top in a dream. But while we were up I had thrown a quick glance around—and that one glance was all sufficient. I saw our exact position in an instant. The Moskoe-Ström whirlpool was about a quarter of a mile dead ahead—but no more like the every-day Moskoe-Ström, than the whirl as you now see it is like a mill-race. If I had not known where we were, and what we had to expect, I should not have recognised the place at all. As it was, I involuntarily closed my eyes in horror. The lids clenched themselves together as if in a spasm.

"It could not have been more than two minutes afterward until we suddenly felt the waves subside, and were enveloped in foam. The boat made a sharp half turn to larboard, and then shot off in its new direction like a thunderbolt. At the same moment the roaring noise of the water was completely drowned in a kind of shrill shriek—such a sound as you might imagine given out by the waste-pipes of many thousand steam-vessels, letting off their steam all together. We were now in the belt of surf that always surrounds the whirl; and I thought, of course, that another moment would plunge us into the abyss—down which we could only see indistinctly on account of the amazing velocity with which we wore borne along. The boat did not seem to sink into the water at all, but to skim like an air-bubble upon the surface of the surge. Her starboard side was next the whirl, and on the larboard arose the world of ocean we had left. It stood like a huge writhing wall between us and the horizon.

"It may appear strange, but now, when we were in the very jaws of the gulf, I felt more composed than when we were only approaching it. Having made up my mind to hope no more, I got rid of a great deal of that terror which unmanned me at first. I suppose it was despair that strung my nerves.

"It may look like boasting—but what I tell you is truth—I began to reflect how magnificent a thing it was to die in such a manner, and how foolish it was in me to think of so paltry a consideration as my own individual life, in view of so wonderful a manifestation of God's power. I do believe that I blushed with shame when this idea crossed my mind. After a little while I became possessed with the keenest curiosity about the whirl itself. I positively felt a *wish* to explore its depths, even at the sacrifice I was going to make; and my principal grief was that I should never be able to tell my old companions on shore about the mysteries I should see. These, no doubt, were singular fancies to occupy a man's mind in such extremity—and I have often thought since, that the revolutions of the boat around the pool might have rendered me a little light-headed.

"There was another circumstance which tended to restore my self-possession; and this was the cessation of the wind, which could not reach us in our present situation—for, as you saw yourself, the belt of surf is considerably lower than the general bed of the ocean, and this latter now towered above us, a high, black, mountainous ridge. If you have never been at sea in a heavy gale, you can form no idea of the confusion of mind occasioned by the wind and spray together. They blind, deafen, and strangle you, and take away all power of action or reflection. But we were now, in a great measure, rid of these annoyances—just as death-condemned felons in prison are allowed petty indulgences, forbidden them while their doom is yet uncertain.

"How often we made the circuit of the belt it is impossible to say. We careered round and round for perhaps an hour, flying rather than floating, getting gradually more and more into the middle of the surge, and then nearer and nearer to its horrible inner edge. All this time I had never let go of the ring-bolt. My brother was at the stern, holding on to a small empty water-cask which had been securely lashed under the coop of the counter, and was the only thing on deck that had not been swept overboard when the gale first took us. As we approached the brink of the pit he let go his hold upon this, and made for the ring, from which, in the agony of his terror, he endeavored to force my hands, as it was not large enough to afford us both a secure grasp. I never felt deeper grief than when I saw him attempt this act—although I knew he was a madman when he did it—a raving maniac through sheer fright. I did not care, however, to contest the point with him. I knew it could make no difference whether either of us held on at all; so I let him have the bolt, and went astern to the cask. This there was no great difficulty in doing; for the smack flew round steadily enough, and upon an even keel—only swaying to and fro, with the immense sweeps and swelters of the whirl. Scarcely had I secured myself in my new position, when we gave a wild lurch to starboard, and rushed headlong into the abyss. I muttered a hurried prayer to God, and thought all was over.

"As I felt the sickening sweep of the descent, I had instinctively tightened my hold upon the barrel, and closed my eyes. For some seconds I dared not open them—while I expected instant destruction, and wondered that I was not already in my death-struggles with the water. But moment after moment elapsed. I still lived. The sense of falling had ceased; and the motion of the vessel seemed much as it had been before, while in the belt of foam, with the exception that she now lay more along. I took courage, and looked once again upon the scene.

"Never shall I forget the sensations of awe, horror, and admiration with which I gazed about me. The boat appeared to be hanging, as if by magic, midway down, upon the interior surface of a funnel vast in circumference, prodigious in depth, and whose perfectly smooth sides might have been mistaken for ebony, but for the bewildering rapidity with which they spun around, and for the gleaming and ghastly radiance they shot forth, as the rays of the full moon, from that circular rift amid the clouds which I have already described, streamed in a flood of golden glory along the black walls, and far away down into the inmost recesses of the abyss.

"At first I was too much confused to observe anything accurately. The general burst of terrific grandeur was all that I beheld. When I recovered myself a little, however, my gaze fell instinctively downward. In this direction I was able to obtain an unobstructed view, from the manner in which the smack hung on the inclined surface of the pool. She was quite upon an even keel—that is to say, her deck lay in a plane parallel with that of the water—but this latter sloped at an angle of more than forty-five degrees, so that we seemed to be lying upon our beam-ends. I could not help observing, nevertheless, that I had scarcely more difficulty in maintaining my hold and footing in this situation, than if we had been upon a dead level; and this, I suppose, was owing to the speed at which we revolved.

"The rays of the moon seemed to search the very bottom of the profound gulf; but still I could make out nothing distinctly, on account of a thick mist in which everything there was enveloped, and over which there hung a magnificent rainbow, like that narrow and tottering bridge which Mussulmen say is the only pathway between Time and Eternity. This mist, or spray, was no doubt occasioned by the clashing of the great walls of the funnel, as they all met together at the bottom—but the yell that went up to the Heavens from out of that mist, I dare not attempt to describe.

"Our first slide into the abyss itself, from the belt of foam above, had carried us a great distance down the slope; but our farther descent was by no means proportionate. Round and round we swept—not with any uniform movement—but in dizzying swings and jerks, that sent us sometimes only a few hundred yards—sometimes nearly the complete circuit of the whirl. Our progress downward, at each revolution, was slow, but very perceptible.

"Looking about me upon the wide waste of liquid ebony on which we were thus borne, I perceived that our boat was not the only object in the embrace of the whirl. Both above and below us were visible fragments of vessels, large masses of building timber and trunks of trees, with many smaller articles, such as pieces of house furniture, broken boxes, barrels and staves. I have already described the unnatural curiosity which had taken the place of my original terrors. It appeared to grow upon me as I drew nearer and nearer to my dreadful doom. I now began to watch, with a strange interest, the numerous things that floated in our company. I *must* have been delirious—for I even sought *amusement* in speculating upon the relative velocities of their several descents toward the foam below. 'This fir tree,' I found myself at one time saying, 'will certainly be the next thing that takes the awful plunge and disappears,'—and then I was disappointed to find that the wreck of a Dutch merchant ship overtook it and went down before. At length, after making several guesses of this nature, and being deceived in all—this fact—the fact of my invariable miscalculation—set me upon a train of reflection that made my limbs again tremble, and my heart beat heavily once more.

"It was not a new terror that thus affected me, but the dawn of a more exciting *hope*. This hope arose partly from memory, and partly from present observation. I called to mind the great variety of buoyant matter that strewed the coast of Lofoden, having been absorbed and then thrown forth by the Moskoe-ström. By far the greater number of the articles were shattered in the most extraordinary way—so chafed and roughened as to have the appearance of being stuck full of splinters—but then I distinctly recollected that there were *some* of them which were not disfigured at all. Now I could not account for this difference except by supposing that the roughened fragments were the only ones which had been *completely absorbed*—that the others had entered the whirl at so late a period of the tide, or, for some reason, had descended so slowly after entering, that they did not reach the bottom before the turn of the flood came, or of the ebb, as the case might be. I conceived it possible, in either instance, that they might thus be whirled up again to the level of the ocean, without undergoing the fate of those which had been drawn in more early, or absorbed more rapidly. I made, also, three important observations. The first was, that, as a general rule, the larger the bodies were, the more rapid their descent—the second, that, between two masses of equal extent, the one spherical, and the other *of any other shape*, the superiority in speed of descent was with the sphere—the third, that, between two masses of equal size, the one cylindrical, and the other of any other shape, the cylinder was absorbed the more slowly. Since my escape, I have had several conversations on this subject with an old school-master of the district; and it was from him that I learned the use of the words 'cylinder' and 'sphere.' He explained to me—although I have forgotten the explanation—how what I observed was, in fact, the natural consequence of the forms of the floating fragments—and showed me how it happened that a cylinder, swimming in a vortex, offered more resistance to its suction, and was drawn in with greater difficulty than an equally bulky body, of any form whatever.

"There was one startling circumstance which went a great way in enforcing these observations, and rendering me anxious to turn them to account, and this was that, at every revolution, we passed something like a barrel, or else the yard or the mast of a vessel, while many of these things, which had been on our level when I first opened my eyes upon the wonders of the whirlpool, were now high up above us, and seemed to have moved but little from their original station.

"I no longer hesitated what to do. I resolved to lash myself securely to the water cask upon which I now held, to cut it loose from the counter, and to throw myself with it into the water. I attracted my brother's attention by signs, pointed to the floating barrels that came near us, and did everything in my power to make him understand what I was about to do. I thought at length that he comprehended my design—but, whether this was the case or not, he shook his head despairingly, and refused to move from his station by the ring-bolt. It was impossible to reach him; the emergency admitted of no delay; and so, with a bitter struggle, I resigned him to his fate, fastened myself to the cask by means of the lashings which secured it to the counter, and precipitated myself with it into the sea, without another moment's hesitation.

"The result was precisely what I had hoped it might be. As it is myself who now tell you this tale—as you see that I *did* escape—and as you are already in possession of the mode in which this escape was effected, and must therefore anticipate all that I have farther to say—I will bring my story quickly to conclusion. It might have been an hour, or thereabout, after my quitting the smack, when, having descended to a vast distance beneath me, it made three or four wild gyrations in rapid succession, and, bearing my loved brother with it, plunged headlong, at once and forever, into the chaos of foam below. The barrel to which I was attached sunk very little farther than half the distance between the bottom of the gulf and the spot at which I leaped overboard, before a great change took place in the character of the whirlpool. The slope of the sides of the vast funnel became momently less and less steep. The gyrations of the whirl grew, gradually, less and less violent. By degrees, the froth and the rainbow disappeared, and the bottom of the gulf seemed slowly to uprise. The sky was clear, the winds had gone down, and the full moon was setting radiantly in the west, when I found myself on the surface of the ocean, in full view of the shores of Lofoden, and above the spot where the pool of the Moskoe-ström *had been*. It was the hour of the slack—but the sea still heaved in mountainous waves from the effects of the hurricane. I was borne violently into the channel of the Ström, and in a few minutes was hurried down the coast into the 'grounds' of the fishermen. A boat picked me up—exhausted from fatigue—and (now that the danger was removed) speechless from the memory of its horror. Those who drew me on board were my old mates and daily companions—but they knew me no more than they would have known a traveller from the spirit-land. My hair which had been raven-black the day before, was as white as you see it now. They say too that the whole expression of my countenance had changed. I told them my story—they did not believe it. I now tell it to *you*—and I can scarcely expect you to put more faith in it than did the merry fishermen of Lofoden."

The Fall of the House of Usher

Son coeur est un luth suspendu;
Sitot qu'on le touche il resonne.

—De Beranger

During the whole of a dull, dark, and soundless day in the autumn of the year, when the clouds hung oppressively low in the heavens, I had been passing alone, on horseback, through a singularly dreary tract of country; and at length found myself, as the shades of the evening drew on, within view of the melancholy House of Usher. I know not how it was—but, with the first glimpse of the building, a sense of insufferable gloom pervaded my spirit. I say insufferable; for the feeling was unrelieved by any of that half-pleasureable, because poetic, sentiment, with which the mind usually receives even the sternest natural images of the desolate or terrible. I looked upon the scene before me—upon the mere house, and the simple landscape features of the domain—upon the bleak walls—upon the vacant eye-like windows—upon a few rank sedges—and upon a few white trunks of decayed trees—with an utter depression of soul which I can compare to no earthly sensation more properly than to the after-dream of the reveller upon opium—the bitter lapse into everyday life—the hideous dropping off of the veil. There was an iciness, a sinking, a sickening of the heart—an unredeemed dreariness of thought which no goading of the imagination could torture into aught of the sublime. What was it—I paused to think—what was it that so unnerved me in the contemplation of the House of Usher? It was a mystery all insoluble; nor could I grapple with the shadowy fancies that crowded upon me as I pondered. I was forced to fall back upon the unsatisfactory conclusion, that while, beyond doubt, there are combinations of very simple natural objects which have the power of thus affecting us, still the analysis of this power lies among considerations beyond our depth. It was possible, I reflected, that a mere different arrangement of the particulars of the scene, of the details of the picture, would be sufficient to modify, or perhaps to annihilate its capacity for sorrowful impression; and, acting upon this idea, I reined my horse to the precipitous brink of a black and lurid tarn that lay in unruffled lustre by the dwelling, and gazed down—but with a shudder even more thrilling than before—upon the remodelled and inverted images of the grey sedge, and the ghastly tree-stems, and the vacant and eye-like windows.

Nevertheless, in this mansion of gloom I now proposed to myself a sojourn of some weeks. Its proprietor, Roderick Usher, had been one of my boon companions in boyhood; but many years had elapsed since our last meeting. A letter, however, had lately reached me in a distant part of the country—a letter from him—which, in its wildly importunate nature, had admitted of no other than a personal reply. The MS gave evidence of nervous agitation. The writer spoke of acute bodily illness—of a mental disorder which oppressed him—and of an earnest desire to see me, as his best, and indeed his only personal friend, with a view of attempting, by the cheerfulness of my society, some alleviation of his malady. It was the manner in which all this, and much more, was said—it was the apparent heart that went with his request—which allowed me no room for hesitation; and I accordingly obeyed forthwith what I still considered a very singular summons.

Although, as boys, we had been even intimate associates, yet I really knew little of my friend. His reserve had been always excessive and habitual. I was aware, however, that his very ancient family had been noted, time out of mind, for a peculiar sensibility of temperament, displaying itself, through long ages, in many works of exalted art, and manifested, of late, in repeated deeds of munificent yet unobtrusive charity, as well as in a passionate devotion to the intricacies, perhaps even more than to the orthodox and easily recognisable beauties of musical science. I had learned, too, the very remarkable fact, that the stem of the Usher race, all time-honoured as it was, had put forth, at no period, any enduring branch; in other words, that the entire family lay in the direct line of descent, and had always, with very trifling and very temporary variation, so lain. It was this deficiency, I considered, while running over in thought the perfect keeping of the character of the premises with the accredited character of the people, and while speculating upon the possible influence which the one, in the long lapse of centuries, might have exercised upon the other—it was this deficiency, perhaps, of collateral issue, and the consequent undeviating transmission, from sire to son, of the patrimony with the name, which had, at length, so identified the two as to merge the original title of the estate in the quaint and equivocal appellation of the "House of Usher"—an appellation which seemed to include, in the minds of the peasantry who used it, both the family and the family mansion.

I have said that the sole effect of my somewhat childish experiment—that of looking down within the tarn—had been to deepen the first singular impression. There can be no doubt that the consciousness of the rapid increase of my superstition—for why should I not so term it?—served mainly to accelerate the increase itself. Such, I have long known, is the paradoxical law of all sentiments having terror as a basis. And it might have been for this reason only, that, when I again uplifted my eyes to the house itself, from its image in the pool, there grew in my mind a strange fancy—a fancy so ridiculous, indeed, that I but mention it to show the vivid force of the sensations which oppressed me. I had so worked upon my imagination as really to believe that about the whole mansion and domain there hung an atmosphere peculiar to themselves and their immediate vicinity—an atmosphere which had no affinity with the air of heaven, but which had reeked up from the decayed trees, and the grey wall, and the silent tarn—a pestilent and mystic vapour, dull, sluggish, faintly discernible, and leaden-hued.

Shaking off from my spirit what must have been a dream, I scanned more narrowly the real aspect of the building. Its principal feature seemed to be that of an excessive antiquity. The discoloration of ages had been great. Minute fungi overspread the whole exterior, hanging in a fine tangled web-work from the eaves. Yet all this was apart from any extraordinary dilapidation. No portion of the masonry had fallen; and there appeared to be a wild inconsistency between its still perfect adaptation of parts, and the crumbling condition of the individual stones. In this there was much that reminded me of the specious totality of old wood-work which has rotted for long years in some neglected vault, with no disturbance from the breath of the external air. Beyond this indication of extensive decay, however, the fabric gave little token of instability. Perhaps the eye of a scrutinizing observer might have discovered a barely perceptible fissure, which, extending from the roof of the building in front, made its way down the wall in a zigzag direction, until it became lost in the sullen waters of the tarn.

Noticing these things, I rode over a short causeway to the house. A servant in waiting took my horse, and I entered the Gothic archway of the hall. A valet, of stealthy step, thence conducted me, in silence, through many dark and intricate passages in my progress to the studio of his master. Much that I encountered on the way contributed, I know not how, to heighten the vague sentiments of which I have already spoken. While the objects around me—while the carvings of the ceilings, the sombre tapestries of the walls, the ebony blackness of the floors, and the phantasmagoric armorial trophies which rattled as I strode, were but matters to which, or to such as which, I had been accustomed from my infancy—while I hesitated not to acknowledge how familiar was all this—I still wondered to find how unfamiliar were the fancies which ordinary images were stirring up. On one of the staircases, I met the physician of the family. His countenance, I thought, wore a mingled expression of low cunning and perplexity. He accosted me with trepidation and passed on. The valet now threw open a door and ushered me into the presence of his master.

The room in which I found myself was very large and lofty. The windows were long, narrow, and pointed, and at so vast a distance from the black oaken floor as to be altogether inaccessible from within. Feeble gleams of encrimsoned light made their way through the trellised panes, and served to render sufficiently distinct the more prominent objects around; the eye, however, struggled in vain to reach the remoter angles of the chamber, or the recesses of the vaulted and fretted ceiling. Dark draperies hung upon the walls. The general furniture was profuse, comfortless, antique, and tattered. Many books and musical instruments lay scattered about, but failed to give any vitality to the scene. I felt that I breathed an atmosphere of sorrow. An air of stern, deep, and irredeemable gloom hung over and pervaded all.

Upon my entrance, Usher rose from a sofa on which he had been lying at full length, and greeted me with a vivacious warmth which had much in it, I at first thought, of an overdone cordiality—of the constrained effort of the ennuye man of the world. A glance, however, at his countenance, convinced me of his perfect sincerity. We sat down; and for some moments, while he spoke not, I gazed upon him with a feeling half of pity, half of awe. Surely, man had never before so terribly altered, in so brief a period, as had Roderick Usher! It was with difficulty that I could bring myself to admit the identity of the man being before me with the companion of my early boyhood. Yet the character of his face had been at all times remarkable. A cadaverousness of complexion; an eye large, liquid, and luminous beyond comparison; lips somewhat thin and very pallid, but of a surpassingly beautiful curve; a nose of a delicate Hebrew model, but with a breadth of nostril unusual in similar formations; a finely-moulded chin, speaking, in its want of prominence, of a want of moral energy; hair of a more than web-like softness and tenuity; these features, with an inordinate expansion above the regions of the temple, made up altogether a countenance not easily to be forgotten. And now in the mere exaggeration of the prevailing character of these features, and of the expression they were wont to convey, lay so much of change that I doubted to whom I spoke. The now ghastly pallor of the skin, and the now miraculous lustre of the eye, above all things startled and even awed me. The silken hair, too, had been suffered to grow all unheeded, and as, in its wild gossamer texture, it floated rather than fell about the face, I could not, even with effort, connect its Arabesque expression with any idea of simple humanity.

In the manner of my friend I was at once struck with an incoherence—an inconsistency; and I soon found this to arise from a series of feeble and futile struggles to overcome an habitual trepidancy—an excessive nervous agitation. For something of this nature I had indeed been prepared, no less by his letter, than by reminiscences of certain boyish traits, and by conclusions deduced from his peculiar physical conformation and temperament. His action was alternately vivacious and sullen. His voice varied rapidly from a tremulous indecision (when the animal spirits seemed utterly in abeyance) to that species of energetic concision—that abrupt, weighty, unhurried, and hollow-sounding enunciation—that leaden, self-balanced and perfectly modulated guttural utterance, which may be observed in the lost drunkard, or the irreclaimable eater of opium, during the periods of his most intense excitement.

It was thus that he spoke of the object of my visit, of his earnest desire to see me, and of the solace he expected me to afford him. He entered, at some length, into what he conceived to be the nature of his malady. It was, he said, a constitutional and a family evil, and one for which he despaired to find a remedy—a mere nervous affection, he immediately added, which would undoubtedly soon pass off. It displayed itself in a host of unnatural sensations. Some of these, as he detailed them, interested and bewildered me; although, perhaps, the terms, and the general manner of the narration had their weight. He suffered much from a morbid acuteness of the senses; the most insipid food was alone endurable; he could wear only garments of certain texture; the odours of all flowers were oppressive; his eyes were tortured by even a faint light; and there were but peculiar sounds, and these from stringed instruments, which did not inspire him with horror.

To an anomalous species of terror I found him a bounden slave. "I shall perish," said he, "I must perish in this deplorable folly. Thus, thus, and not otherwise, shall I be lost. I dread the events of the future, not in themselves, but in their results. I shudder at the thought of any, even the most trivial, incident, which may operate upon this intolerable agitation of soul. I have, indeed, no abhorrence of danger, except in its absolute effect—in terror. In this unnerved—in this pitiable condition—I feel that the period will sooner or later arrive when I must abandon life and reason together, in some struggle with the grim phantasm, FEAR."

I learned, moreover, at intervals, and through broken and equivocal hints, another singular feature of his mental condition. He was enchained by certain superstitious impressions in regard to the dwelling which he tenanted, and whence, for many years, he had never ventured forth—in regard to an influence whose supposititious force was conveyed in terms too shadowy here to be re-stated—an influence which some peculiarities in the mere form and substance of his family mansion, had, by dint of long sufferance, he said, obtained over his spirit—an effect which the physique of the grey walls and turrets, and of the dim tarn into which they all looked down, had, at length, brought about upon the morale of his existence.

He admitted, however, although with hesitation, that much of the peculiar gloom which thus afflicted him could be traced to a more natural and far more palpable origin—to the severe and long-continued illness—indeed to the evidently approaching dissolution—of a tenderly beloved sister—his sole companion for long years—his last and only relative on earth. "Her decease," he said, with a bitterness which I can never forget, "would leave him (him the hopeless and the frail) the last of the ancient race of the Ushers." While he spoke, the lady Madeline (for so was she called) passed slowly through a remote portion of the apartment, and, without having noticed my presence, disappeared. I regarded her with an utter astonishment not unmingled with dread—and yet I found it impossible to account for such feelings. A sensation of stupor oppressed me, as my eyes followed her retreating steps. When a door, at length, closed upon her, my glance sought instinctively and eagerly the countenance of the brother—but he had buried his face in his hands, and I could only perceive that a far more than ordinary wanness had overspread the emaciated fingers through which trickled many passionate tears.

The disease of the lady Madeline had long baffled the skill of her physicians. A settled apathy, a gradual wasting away of the person, and frequent although transient affections of a partially cataleptical character, were the unusual diagnosis. Hitherto she had steadily borne up against the pressure of her malady, and had not betaken herself finally to bed; but, on the closing in of the evening of my arrival at the house, she succumbed (as her brother told me at night with inexpressible agitation) to the prostrating power of the destroyer; and I learned that the glimpse I had obtained of her person would thus probably be the last I should obtain—that the lady, at least while living, would be seen by me no more.

For several days ensuing, her name was unmentioned by either Usher or myself: and during this period I was busied in earnest endeavours to alleviate the melancholy of my friend. We painted and read together; or I listened, as if in a dream, to the wild improvisations of his speaking guitar. And thus, as a closer and still closer intimacy admitted me more unreservedly into the recesses of his spirit, the more bitterly did I perceive the futility of all attempt at cheering a mind from which darkness, as if an inherent positive quality, poured forth upon all objects of the moral and physical universe, in one unceasing radiation of gloom.

I shall ever bear about me a memory of the many solemn hours I thus spent alone with the master of the House of Usher. Yet I should fail in any attempt to convey an idea of the exact character of the studies, or of the occupations, in which he involved me, or led me the way. An excited and highly distempered ideality threw a sulphureous lustre over all. His long improvised dirges will ring for ever in my ears. Among other things, I hold painfully in mind a certain singular perversion and amplification of the wild air of the last waltz of Von Weber. From the paintings over which his elaborate fancy brooded, and which grew, touch by touch, into vagueness at which I shuddered the more thrillingly, because I shuddered knowing not why;—from these paintings (vivid as their images now are before me) I would in vain endeavour to educe more than a small portion which should lie within the compass of merely written words. By the utter simplicity, by the nakedness of his designs, he arrested and overawed attention. If ever mortal painted an idea, that mortal was Roderick Usher. For me at least—in the circumstances then surrounding me—there arose out of the pure abstractions which the hypochondriac contrived to throw upon his canvas, an intensity of intolerable awe, no shadow of which felt I ever yet in the contemplation of the certainly glowing yet too concrete reveries of Fuseli.

One of the phantasmagoric conceptions of my friend, partaking not so rigidly of the spirit of abstraction, may be shadowed forth, although feebly, in words. A small picture presented the interior of an immensely long and rectangular vault or tunnel, with low walls, smooth, white, and without interruption or device. Certain accessory points of the design served well to convey the idea that this excavation lay at an exceeding depth below the surface of the earth. No outlet was observed in any portion of its vast extent, and no torch, or other artificial source of light was discernible; yet a flood of intense rays rolled throughout, and bathed the whole in a ghastly and inappropriate splendour.

I have just spoken of that morbid condition of the auditory nerve which rendered all music intolerable to the sufferer, with the exception of certain effects of stringed instruments. It was, perhaps, the narrow limits to which he thus confined himself upon the guitar, which gave birth, in great measure, to the fantastic character of the performances. But the fervid facility of his impromptus could not be so accounted for. They must have been, and were, in the notes, as well as in the words of his wild fantasias (for he not unfrequently accompanied himself with rhymed verbal improvisations), the result of that intense mental collectedness and concentration to which I have previously alluded as observable only in particular moments of the highest artificial excitement. The words of one of these rhapsodies I have easily remembered. I was, perhaps, the more forcibly impressed with it, as he gave it, because, in the under or mystic current of its meaning, I fancied that I perceived, and for the first time, a full consciousness on the part of Usher, of the tottering of his lofty reason upon her throne. The verses, which were entitled "The Haunted Palace," ran very nearly, if not accurately, thus:

I

In the greenest of our valleys,
By good angels tenanted,
Once a fair and stately palace—
Radiant palace—reared its head.
In the monarch Thought's dominion—
It stood there!
Never seraph spread a pinion
Over fabric half so fair.

II

Banners yellow, glorious, golden,
On its roof did float and flow;
(This—all this—was in the olden Time long ago)
And every gentle air that dallied,
In that sweet day,
Along the ramparts plumed and pallid,
A winged odour went away.

III

Wanderers in that happy valley
Through two luminous windows saw
Spirits moving musically
To a lute's well tuned law,
Round about a throne, where sitting (Porphyrogene!)
In state his glory well befitting,
The ruler of the realm was seen.

IV

And all with pearl and ruby glowing
Was the fair palace door,
Through which came flowing, flowing, flowing
And sparkling evermore,
A troop of Echoes whose sweet duty
Was but to sing,
In voices of surpassing beauty,
The wit and wisdom of their king.

V

But evil things, in robes of sorrow,
Assailed the monarch's high estate;
(Ah, let us mourn, for never morrow
Shall dawn upon him, desolate!)
And, round about his home, the glory
That blushed and bloomed

Is but a dim-remembered story,
Of the old time entombed.

VI

And travellers now within that valley,
Through the red-litten windows, see
Vast forms that move fantastically
To a discordant melody;
While, like a rapid ghastly river,
Through the pale door,
A hideous throng rush out forever,
And laugh—but smile no more.

I well remember that suggestions arising from this ballad, led us into a train of thought wherein there became manifest an opinion of Usher's which I mention not so much on account of its novelty (for other men* have thought thus,) as on account of the pertinacity with which he maintained it. This opinion, in its general form, was that of the sentience of all vegetable things. But, in his disordered fancy, the idea had assumed a more daring character, and trespassed, under certain conditions, upon the kingdom of inorganization. I lack words to express the full extent, or the earnest abandon of his persuasion. The belief, however, was connected (as I have previously hinted) with the gray stones of the home of his forefathers. The conditions of the sentience had been here, he imagined, fulfilled in the method of collocation of these stones—in the order of their arrangement, as well as in that of the many fungi which overspread them, and of the decayed trees which stood around—above all, in the long undisturbed endurance of this arrangement, and in its reduplication in the still waters of the tarn. Its evidence—the evidence of the sentience—was to be seen, he said, (and I here started as he spoke,) in the gradual yet certain condensation of an atmosphere of their own about the waters and the walls. The result was discoverable, he added, in that silent, yet importunate and terrible influence which for centuries had moulded the destinies of his family, and which made him what I now saw him—what he was. Such opinions need no comment, and I will make none.

Our books—the books which, for years, had formed no small portion of the mental existence of the invalid—were, as might be supposed, in strict keeping with this character of phantasm. We pored together over such works as the Ververt et Chartreuse of Gresset; the Belphegor of Machiavelli; the Heaven and Hell of Swedenborg; the Subterranean Voyage of Nicholas Klimm by Holberg; the Chiromancy of Robert Flud, of Jean D'Indagine, and of De la Chambre; the Journey into the Blue Distance of Tieck; and the City of the Sun by Campanella. One favourite volume was a small octavo edition of the Directorium Inquisitorum, by the Dominican Eymeric de Gironne; and there were passages in Pomponius Mela, about the old African Satyrs and OEgipans, over which Usher would sit dreaming for hours. His chief delight, however, was found in the perusal of an exceedingly rare and curious book in quarto Gothic—the manual of a forgotten church—the Vigiliae Mortuorum Secundum Chorum Ecclesiae Maguntinae.

I could not help thinking of the wild ritual of this work, and of its probable influence upon the hypochondriac, when, one evening, having informed me abruptly that the lady Madeline was no more, he stated his intention of preserving her corpse for a fortnight, (previously to its final interment), in one of the numerous vaults within the main walls of the building. The worldly reason, however, assigned for this singular proceeding, was one which I did not feel at liberty to dispute. The brother had been led to his resolution (so he told me) by consideration of the unusual character of the malady of the deceased, of certain obtrusive and eager inquiries on the part of her medical men, and of the remote and exposed situation of the burial-ground of the family. I will not deny that when I called to mind the sinister countenance of the person whom I met upon the staircase, on the day of my arrival at the house, I had no desire to oppose what I regarded as at best but a harmless, and by no means an unnatural, precaution.

At the request of Usher, I personally aided him in the arrangements for the temporary entombment. The body having been encoffined, we two alone bore it to its rest. The vault in which we placed it (and which had been so long unopened that our torches, half smothered in its oppressive atmosphere, gave us little opportunity for investigation) was small, damp, and entirely without means of admission for light; lying, at great depth, immediately beneath that portion of the building in which was my own sleeping apartment. It had been used, apparently, in remote feudal times, for the worst purposes of a donjon-keep, and, in later days, as a place of deposit for powder, or some other highly combustible substance, as a portion of its floor, and the whole interior of a long archway through which we reached it, were carefully sheathed with copper. The door, of massive iron, had been, also, similarly protected. Its immense weight caused an unusually sharp grating sound, as it moved upon its hinges.

Having deposited our mournful burden upon tressels within this region of horror, we partially turned aside the yet unscrewed lid of the coffin, and looked upon the face of the tenant. A striking similitude between the brother and sister now first arrested my attention; and Usher, divining, perhaps, my thoughts, murmured out some few words from which I learned that the deceased and himself had been twins, and that sympathies of a scarcely intelligible nature had always existed between them. Our glances, however, rested not long upon the dead—for we could not regard her unawed. The disease which had thus entombed the lady in the maturity of youth, had left, as usual in all maladies of a strictly cataleptical character, the mockery of a faint blush upon the bosom and the face, and that suspiciously lingering smile upon the lip which is so terrible in death. We replaced and screwed down the lid, and, having secured the door of iron, made our way, with toil, into the scarcely less gloomy apartments of the upper portion of the house.

And now, some days of bitter grief having elapsed, an observable change came over the features of the mental disorder of my friend. His ordinary manner had vanished. His ordinary occupations were neglected or forgotten. He roamed from chamber to chamber with hurried, unequal, and objectless step. The pallor of his countenance had assumed, if possible, a more ghastly hue—but the luminousness of his eye had utterly gone out. The once occasional huskiness of his tone was heard no more; and a tremulous quaver, as if of extreme terror, habitually characterized his utterance. There were times, indeed, when I thought his unceasingly agitated mind was labouring with some oppressive secret, to divulge which he struggled for the necessary courage. At times, again, I was obliged to resolve all into the mere inexplicable vagaries of madness, for I beheld him gazing upon vacancy for long hours, in an attitude of the profoundest attention, as if listening to some imaginary sound. It was no wonder that his condition terrified—that it infected me. I felt creeping upon me, by slow yet certain degrees, the wild influences of his own fantastic yet impressive superstitions.

It was, especially, upon retiring to bed late in the night of the seventh or eighth day after the placing of the lady Madeline within the donjon, that I experienced the full power of such feelings. Sleep came not near my couch—while the hours waned and waned away. I struggled to reason off the nervousness which had dominion over me. I endeavoured to believe that much, if not all of what I felt, was due to the bewildering influence of the gloomy furniture of the room—of the dark and tattered draperies, which, tortured into motion by the breath of a rising tempest, swayed fitfully to and fro upon the walls, and rustled uneasily about the decorations of the bed. But my efforts were fruitless. An irrepressible tremor gradually pervaded my frame; and, at length, there sat upon my very heart an incubus of utterly causeless alarm. Shaking this off with a gasp and a struggle, I uplifted myself upon the pillows, and, peering earnestly within the intense darkness of the chamber, hearkened—I know not why, except that an instinctive spirit prompted me—to certain low and indefinite sounds which came, through the pauses of the storm, at long intervals, I knew not whence. Overpowered by an intense sentiment of horror, unaccountable yet unendurable, I threw on my clothes with haste (for I felt that I should sleep no more during the night,) and endeavoured to arouse myself from the pitiable condition into which I had fallen, by pacing rapidly to and fro through the apartment.

I had taken but few turns in this manner, when a light step on an adjoining staircase arrested my attention. I presently recognized it as that of Usher. In an instant afterwards he rapped, with a gentle touch, at my door, and entered, bearing a lamp. His countenance was, as usual, cadaverously wan—but, moreover, there was a species of mad hilarity in his eyes—an evidently restrained hysteria in his whole demeanour. His air appalled me—but anything was preferable to the solitude which I had so long endured, and I even welcomed his presence as a relief.

"And you have not seen it?" he said abruptly, after having stared about him for some moments in silence—"you have not then seen it?—but, stay! you shall." Thus speaking, and having carefully shaded his lamp, he hurried to one of the casements, and threw it freely open to the storm.

The impetuous fury of the entering gust nearly lifted us from our feet. It was, indeed, a tempestuous yet sternly beautiful night, and one wildly singular in its terror and its beauty. A whirlwind had apparently collected its force in our vicinity; for there were frequent and violent alterations in the direction of the wind; and the exceeding density of the clouds (which hung so low as to press upon the turrets of the house) did not prevent our perceiving the lifelike velocity with which they flew careering from all points against each other, without passing away into the distance. I say that even their exceeding density did not prevent our perceiving this—yet we had no glimpse of the moon or stars—nor was there any flashing forth of the lightning. But the under surfaces of the huge masses of agitated vapor, as well as all terrestrial objects immediately around us, were glowing in the unnatural light of a faintly luminous and distinctly visible gaseous exhalation which hung about and enshrouded the mansion.

"You must not—you shall not behold this!" said I, shudderingly, to Usher, as I led him, with a gentle violence, from the window to a seat. "These appearances, which bewilder you, are merely electrical phenomena not uncommon—or it may be that they have their ghastly origin in the rank miasma of the tarn. Let us close this casement;—the air is chilling and dangerous to your frame. Here is one of your favourite romances. I will read, and you shall listen;—and so we will pass away this terrible night together."

The antique volume which I had taken up was the "Mad Trist" of Sir Launcelot Canning; but I had called it a favourite of Usher's more in sad jest than in earnest; for, in truth, there is little in its uncouth and unimaginative prolixity which could have had interest for the lofty and spiritual ideality of my friend. It was, however, the only book immediately at hand; and I indulged a vague hope that the excitement which now agitated the hypochondriac, might find relief (for the history of mental disorder is full of similar anomalies) even in the extremeness of the folly which I should read. Could I have judged, indeed, by the wild overstrained air of vivacity with which he hearkened, or apparently hearkened, to the words of the tale, I might well have congratulated myself upon the success of my design.

I had arrived at that well-known portion of the story where Ethelred, the hero of the Trist, having sought in vain for peaceable admission into the dwelling of the hermit, proceeds to make good an entrance by force. Here, it will be remembered, the words of the narrative run thus:

"And Ethelred, who was by nature of a doughty heart, and who was now mighty withal, on account of the powerfulness of the wine which he had drunken, waited no longer to hold parley with the hermit, who, in sooth, was of an obstinate and maliceful turn, but, feeling the rain upon his shoulders, and fearing the rising of the tempest, uplifted his mace outright, and, with blows, made quickly room in the plankings of the door for his gauntleted hand; and now pulling therewith sturdily, he so cracked, and ripped, and tore all asunder, that the noise of the dry and hollow-sounding wood alarmed and reverberated throughout the forest."

At the termination of this sentence I started, and for a moment, paused; for it appeared to me (although I at once concluded that my excited fancy had deceived me)—it appeared to me that, from some very remote portion of the mansion, there came, indistinctly, to my ears, what might have been, in its exact similarity of character, the echo (but a stifled and dull one certainly) of the very cracking and ripping sound which Sir Launcelot had so particularly described. It was, beyond doubt, the coincidence alone which had arrested my attention; for, amid the rattling of the sashes of the casements, and the ordinary commingled noises of the still increasing storm, the sound, in itself, had nothing, surely, which should have interested or disturbed me. I continued the story:

"But the good champion Ethelred, now entering within the door, was sore enraged and amazed to perceive no signal of the maliceful hermit; but, in the stead thereof, a dragon of a scaly and prodigious demeanour, and of a fiery tongue, which sat in guard before a palace of gold, with a floor of silver; and upon the wall there hung a shield of shining brass with this legend enwritten—

Who entereth herein, a conquerer hath bin;
Who slayeth the dragon, the shield he shall win;

and Ethelred uplifted his mace, and struck upon the head of the dragon, which fell before him, and gave up his pesty breath, with a shriek so horrid and harsh, and withal so piercing, that Ethelred had fain to close his ears with his hands against the dreadful noise of it, the like whereof was never before heard."

Here again I paused abruptly, and now with a feeling of wild amazement—for there could be no doubt whatever that, in this instance, I did actually hear (although from what direction it proceeded I found it impossible to say) a low and apparently distant, but harsh, protracted, and most unusual screaming or grating sound—the exact counterpart of what my fancy had already conjured up for the dragon's unnatural shriek as described by the romancer.

Oppressed, as I certainly was, upon the occurrence of the second and most extraordinary coincidence, by a thousand conflicting sensations, in which wonder and extreme terror were predominant, I still retained sufficient presence of mind to avoid exciting, by any observation, the sensitive nervousness of my companion. I was by no means certain that he had noticed the sounds in question; although, assuredly, a strange alteration had, during the last few minutes, taken place in his demeanour. From a position fronting my own, he had gradually brought round his chair, so as to sit with his face to the door of the chamber; and thus I could but partially perceive his features, although I saw that his lips trembled as if he were murmuring inaudibly. His head had dropped upon his breast—yet I knew that he was not asleep, from the wide and rigid opening of the eye as I caught a glance of it in profile. The motion of his body, too, was at variance with this idea—for he rocked from side to side with a gentle yet constant and uniform sway. Having rapidly taken notice of all this, I resumed the narrative of Sir Launcelot, which thus proceeded:

"And now, the champion, having escaped from the terrible fury of the dragon, bethinking himself of the brazen shield, and of the breaking up of the enchantment which was upon it, removed the carcass from out of the way before him, and approached valorously over the silver pavement of the castle to where the shield was upon the wall; which in sooth tarried not for his full coming, but fell down at his feet upon the silver floor, with a mighty great and terrible ringing sound."

No sooner had these syllables passed my lips, than—as if a shield of brass had indeed, at the moment, fallen heavily upon a floor of silver—I became aware of a distinct, hollow, metallic, and clangorous, yet apparently muffled reverberation. Completely unnerved, I leaped to my feet; but the measured rocking movement of Usher was undisturbed. I rushed to the chair in which he sat. His eyes were bent fixedly before him, and throughout his whole countenance there reigned a stony rigidity. But, as I placed my hand upon his shoulder, there came a strong shudder over his whole person; a sickly smile quivered about his lips; and I saw that he spoke in a low, hurried, and gibbering murmur, as if unconscious of my presence. Bending closely over him, I at length drank in the hideous import of his words.

"Not hear it?—yes, I hear it, and have heard it. Long—long—long—many minutes, many hours, many days, have I heard it—yet I dared not—oh, pity me, miserable wretch that I am!—I dared not—I dared not speak! We have put her living in the tomb! Said I not that my senses were acute? I now tell you that I heard her first feeble movements in the hollow coffin. I heard them—many, many days ago—yet I dared not—I dared not speak! And now—to-night—Ethelred—ha! ha!—the breaking of the hermit's door, and the death-cry of the dragon, and the clangour of the shield!—say, rather, the rending of her coffin, and the grating of the iron hinges of her prison, and her struggles within the coppered archway of the vault! Oh whither shall I fly? Will she not be here anon? Is she not hurrying to upbraid me for my haste? Have I not heard her footsteps on the stair? Do I not distinguish that heavy and horrible beating of her heart? Madman!" here he sprang furiously to his feet, and shrieked out his syllables, as if in the effort he were giving up his soul—"Madman! I tell you that she now stands without the door!"

As if in the superhuman energy of his utterance there had been found the potency of a spell—the huge antique panels to which the speaker pointed, threw slowly back, upon the instant, their ponderous and ebony jaws. It was the work of the rushing gust—but then without those doors there DID stand the lofty and enshrouded figure of the lady Madeline of Usher. There was blood upon her white robes, and the evidence of some bitter struggle upon every portion of her emaciated frame. For a moment she remained trembling and reeling to and fro upon the threshold,—then, with a low moaning cry, fell heavily inward upon the person of her brother, and in her violent and now final death-agonies, bore him to the floor a corpse, and a victim to the terrors he had anticipated.

From that chamber, and from that mansion, I fled aghast. The storm was still abroad in all its wrath as I found myself crossing the old causeway. Suddenly there shot along the path a wild light, and I turned to see whence a gleam so unusual could have issued; for the vast house and its shadows were alone behind me. The radiance was that of the full, setting, and blood-red moon which now shone vividly through that once barely-discernible fissure of which I have before spoken as extending from the roof of the building, in a zigzag direction, to the base. While I gazed, this fissure rapidly widened—there came a fierce breath of the whirlwind—the entire orb of the satellite burst at once upon my sight—my brain reeled as I saw the mighty walls rushing asunder—there was a long tumultuous shouting sound like the voice of a thousand waters—and the deep and dank tarn at my feet closed sullenly and silently over the fragments of the "House of Usher".

The Gold-Bug

What ho! what ho! this fellow is dancing mad!
He hath been bitten by the Tarantula.

—All in the Wrong

Many years ago, I contracted an intimacy with a Mr. William Legrand. He was of an ancient Huguenot family, and had once been wealthy; but a series of misfortunes had reduced him to want. To avoid the mortification consequent upon his disasters, he left New Orleans, the city of his fore-fathers, and took up his residence at Sullivan's Island, near Charleston, South Carolina.

This island is a very singular one. It consists of little else than the sea sand, and is about three miles long. Its breadth at no point exceeds a quarter of a mile. It is separated from the mainland by a scarcely perceptible creek, oozing its way through a wilderness of reeds and slime, a favorite resort of the marsh-hen. The vegetation, as might be supposed, is scant, or at least dwarfish. No trees of any magnitude are to be seen. Near the western extremity, where Fort Moultrie stands, and where are some miserable frame buildings, tenanted during summer by the fugitives from Charleston dust and fever, may be found, indeed, the bristly palmetto; but the whole island, with the exception of this western point, and a line of hard white beach on the seacoast, is covered with a dense undergrowth of the sweet myrtle, so much prized by the horticulturists of England. The shrub here often attains the height of fifteen or twenty feet, and forms an almost impenetrable coppice, burdening the air with its fragrance.

In the utmost recesses of this coppice, not far from the eastern or more remote end of the island, Legrand had built himself a small hut, which he occupied when I first, by mere accident, made his acquaintance. This soon ripened into, friendship—for there was much in the recluse to excite interest and esteem. I found him well educated, with unusual powers of mind, but infected with misanthropy, and subject to perverse moods of alternate enthusiasm and melancholy. He had with him many books, but rarely employed them. His chief amusements were gunning and fishing, or sauntering along the beach and through the myrtles in quest of shells or entomological specimens;—his collection of the latter might have been envied by a Swammerdamm. In these excursions he was usually accompanied by an old negro, called Jupiter, who had been manumitted before the reverses of the family, but who could be induced, neither by threats nor by promises, to abandon what he considered his right of attendance upon the footsteps of his young "Massa Will." It is not improbable that the relatives of Legrand, conceiving him to be somewhat unsettled in intellect, had contrived to instil this obstinacy into Jupiter, with a view to the supervision and guardianship of the wanderer.

The winters in the latitude of Sullivan's Island are seldom very severe, and in the fall of the year it is a rare event indeed when a fire is considered necessary. About the middle of October, 18—, there occurred, however, a day of remarkable chilliness. Just before sunset I scrambled my way through the evergreens to the hut of my friend, whom I had not visited for several weeks—my residence being at that time in Charleston, a distance of nine miles from the island, while the facilities of passage and re-passage were very far behind those of the present day. Upon reaching the hut I rapped, as was my custom, and, getting no reply, sought for the key where I knew it was secreted, unlocked the door and went in. A fine fire was blazing upon the hearth. It was a novelty, and by no means an ungrateful one. I threw off an overcoat, took an armchair by the crackling logs, and awaited patiently the arrival of my hosts.

Soon after dark they arrived, and gave me a most cordial welcome. Jupiter, grinning from ear to ear, bustled about to prepare some marsh-hens for supper. Legrand was in one of his fits—how else shall I term them?—of enthusiasm. He had found an unknown bivalve, forming a new genus, and, more than this, he had hunted down and secured, with Jupiter's assistance, a *scarabæus* which he believed to be totally new, but in respect to which he wished to have my opinion on the morrow.

"And why not to-night?" I asked, rubbing my hands over the blaze, and wishing the whole tribe of *scarabæi* at the devil.

"Ah, if I had only known you were here!" said Legrand, "but it's so long since I saw you; and how could I foresee that you would pay me a visit this very night of all others? As I was coming home I met Lieutenant G——, from the fort, and, very foolishly, I lent him the bug; so it will be impossible for you to see it until the morning. Stay here to-night, and I will send Jup down for it at sunrise. It is the loveliest thing in creation!"

"What?—sunrise?"

"Nonsense! no!—the bug. It is of a brilliant gold color—about the size of a large hickory-nut—with two jet black spots near one extremity of the back, and another, somewhat longer, at the other. The *antennæ* are—"

"Dey aint *no* tin in him, Massa Will, I keep a tellin on you," here interrupted Jupiter; "de bug is a goole-bug, solid, ebery bit of him, inside and all, sep him wing—neber-feel half so hebby a bug in my life."

"Well, suppose it is, Jup," replied Legrand, somewhat more earnestly, it seemed to me, than the case demanded, "is that any reason for your letting the birds burn? The color"—here he turned to me—"is really almost enough to warrant Jupiter's idea. You never saw a more brilliant metallic lustre than the scales emit—but of this you cannot judge till to-morrow. In the meantime I can give you some idea of the shape." Saying this, he seated himself at a small table, on which were a pen and ink, but no paper. He looked for some in a drawer, but found none.

"Never mind," said he at length, "this will answer;" and he drew from his waistcoat pocket a scrap of what I took to be very dirty foolscap, and made upon it a rough drawing with the pen. While he did this, I retained my seat by the fire, for I was still chilly. When the design was complete, he handed it to me without rising. As I received it, a low growl was heard, succeeded by a scratching at the door. Jupiter opened it, and a large Newfoundland, belonging to Legrand, rushed in, leaped upon my shoulders, and loaded me with caresses; for I had shown him much attention during previous visits. When his gambols were over, I looked at the paper, and, to speak the truth, found myself not a little puzzled at what my friend had depicted.

"Well!" I said, after contemplating it for some minutes, "this *is* a strange *scarabæus*, I must confess; new to me: never saw anything like it before—unless it was a skull, or a death's-head, which it more nearly resembles than anything else that has come under *my* observation."

"A death's-head!" echoed Legrand—"oh—yes—well, it has something of that appearance upon paper, no doubt. The two upper black spots look like eyes, eh? and the longer one at the bottom like a mouth—and then the shape of the whole is oval."

"Perhaps so," said I; "but, Legrand, I fear you are no artist. I must wait until I see the beetle itself, if I am to form any idea of its personal appearance."

"We'll, I don't know," said he, a little nettled, "I draw tolerably—*should* do it at least—have had good masters, and flatter myself that I am not quite a blockhead."

"But, my dear fellow, you are joking then," said I; "this is a very passable *skull*,—indeed, I may say that it is a very *excellent* skull, according to the vulgar notions about such specimens of physiology—and your *scarabæus* must be the queerest *scarabæus* in the world if it resembles it. Why, we may get up a very thrilling bit of superstition upon this hint. I presume you will call the bug *scarabæus caput hominis*, or something of that kind—there are many similar titles in the Natural Histories. But where are the *antennae* you spoke of?" "The *antennae*!" said Legrand, who seemed to be getting unaccountably warm upon the subject; "I am sure you must see the *antennae*. I made them as distinct as they are in the original insect, and I presume that is sufficient."

"Well, well," I said, "perhaps you have—still I don't see them;" and I handed him the paper without additional remark, not wishing to ruffle his temper, but I was much surprised at the turn affairs had taken; his ill humor puzzled me—and as for the drawing of the beetle, there were positively *no antennae* visible, and the whole *did* bear a very close resemblance to the ordinary cuts of a death's-head.

He received the paper very peevishly, and was about to crumple it, apparently to throw it in the fire, when a casual glance at the design seemed suddenly to rivet his attention. In an instant his face grew violently red—in another as excessively pale. For some minutes he continued to scrutinize the drawing minutely where he sat. At length he arose, took a candle from the table, and proceeded to seat himself upon a sea-chest in the farthest corner of the room. Here again he made an anxious examination of the paper; turning it in all directions. He said nothing, however, and his conduct greatly astonished me; yet I thought it prudent not to exacerbate the growing moodiness of his temper by any comment. Presently he took from his coat pocket a wallet, placed the paper carefully in it, and deposited both in a writing-desk, which he locked. He now grew more composed in his demeanor; but his original air of enthusiasm had quite disappeared. Yet he seemed not so much sulky as abstracted. As the evening wore away he became more and more absorbed in revery, from which no sallies of mine could arouse him. It had been my intention to pass the night at the hut, as I had frequently done before, but, seeing my host in this mood, I deemed it proper to take leave. He did not press me to remain, but, as I departed, he shook my hand with even more than his usual cordiality.

It was about a month after this (and during the interval I had seen nothing of Legrand) when I received a visit, at Charleston, from his man, Jupiter. I had never seen the good old negro look so dispirited, and I feared that some serious disaster had befallen my friend.

"Well, Jup," said I, "what is the matter now?—how is your master?"

"Why, to speak de troof, massa, him not so berry well as mought be."

"Not well! I am truly sorry to hear it. What does he complain of?"

"Dar! dat's it!—him neber plain of notin—but him berry sick for all dat."

"*Very* sick, Jupiter!—why didn't you say so at once? Is he confined to bed?"

"No, dat he aint!—he aint find nowhar—dat's just whar de shoe pinch—my mind is got to be berry hebby bout poor Massa Will."

"Jupiter, I should like to understand what it is you are talking about. You say your master is sick. Hasn't he told you what ails him?"

"Why, massa, taint worf while for to git mad bout de matter—Massa Will say noffin at all aint de matter wid him—but den what make him go about looking dis here way, wid he head down and he soldiers up, and as white as a gose? And den he keep a syphon all de time—"

"Keeps a what, Jupiter?"

"Keeps a syphon wid de figgurs on de slate—de queerest figgurs I ebber did see. Ise gittin to be skeered, I tell you. Hab for to keep mighty tight eye pon him noovers. Todder day he gib me slip fore de sun up and was gone de whole ob de blessed day. I had a big stick ready cut for to gib him d——d good beating when he did come—but Ise sich a fool dat I hadn't de heart arter all—he look so berry poorly."

"Eh?—what?—ah yes!—upon the whole I think you had better not be too severe with the poor fellow—don't flog him, Jupiter—he can't very well stand it—but can you form no idea of what has occasioned this illness, or rather this change of conduct? Has anything unpleasant happened since I saw you?"

"No, massa, dey aint bin noffin onpleasant *since* den—it 'twas *fore* den I'm feared—'twas de berry day you was dare."

"How? what do you mean?"

"Why, massa, I mean de bug—dare now."

"The what?"

"De bug—I'm berry sartin dat Massa Will bin bit somewhere bout de head by dat goole-bug."

"And what cause have you, Jupiter, for such a supposition?"

"Claws enuff, massa, and mouff too. I nebber did see sich a d——d bug—he kick and he bite ebery ting what cum near him. Massa Will cotch him fuss, but had for to let him go gin mighty quick, I tell you—den was de time he must ha got de bite. I didn't like de look ob de bug mouff, myself, no how, so I wouldn't take hold ob him wid my finger, but I cotch him wid a piece ob paper dat I found. I rap him up in de paper and stuff piece of it in he mouff—dat was de way."

"And you think, then, that your master was really bitten by the beetle, and that the bite made him sick?"

"I don't tink noffin about it—I nose it. What make him dream bout de goole so much, if taint cause he bit by de goole-bug? Ise heerd bout dem goole-bugs fore dis."

"But how do you know he dreams about gold?"

"How I know? why, cause he talk about it in he sleep—dat's how I nose."

"Well, Jup, perhaps you are right; but to what fortunate circumstance am I to attribute the honor of a visit from you to-day?"

"What de matter, massa?"

"Did you bring any message from Mr. Legrand?"

"No, massa, I bring dis here pissel;" and here Jupiter handed me a note which ran thus:

> My Dear ——,
>
> Why have I not seen you for so long a time? I hope you have not been so foolish as to take offence at any little *brusquerie* of mine; but no, that is improbable.
>
> "Since I saw you I have had great cause for anxiety. I have something to tell you, yet scarcely know how to tell it, or whether I should tell it at all.
>
> "I have not been quite well for some days past, and poor old Jup annoys me, almost beyond endurance, by his well-meant attentions. Would you believe it?—he had prepared a huge stick, the other day, with which to chastise me for giving him the slip, and spending the day, *solus*, among the hills on the mainland. I verily believe that my ill looks alone saved me a flogging.
>
> "I have made no addition to my cabinet since we met.
>
> "If you can, in any way, make it convenient, come over with Jupiter. *Do* come. I wish to see you *to-night*, upon

business of importance. I assure you that it is of the *highest* importance.

Ever yours,
William Legrand

There was something in the tone of this note which gave me great uneasiness. Its whole style differed materially from that of Legrand. What could he be dreaming of? What new crotchet possessed his excitable brain? What "business of the highest importance" could *he* possibly have to transact? Jupiter's account of him boded no good. I dreaded lest the continued pressure of misfortune had, at length, fairly unsettled the reason of my friend. Without a moment's hesitation, therefore, I prepared to accompany the negro.

Upon reaching the wharf, I noticed a scythe and three spades, all apparently new, lying in the bottom of the boat in which we were to embark.

"What is the meaning of all this, Jup?" I inquired.

"Him syfe, massa, and spade."

"Very true; but what are they doing here?

"Him de syfe and de spade what Massa Will sis pon my buying for him in de town, and de debbil's own lot of money I had to gib for em."

"But what, in the name of all that is mysterious, is your 'Massa Will' going to do with scythes and spades?"

"Dat's more dan *I* know, and debbil take me if I don't blieve 'tis more dan he know, too. But it's all cum ob de bug."

Finding that no satisfaction was to be obtained of Jupiter, whose whole intellect seemed to be absorbed by "de bug," I now stepped into the boat and made sail. With a fair and strong breeze we soon ran into the little cove to the northward of Fort Moultrie, and a walk of some two miles brought us to the hut. It was about three in the afternoon when we arrived. Legrand had been awaiting us in eager expectation. He grasped my hand with a nervous *empressement*, which alarmed me and strengthened the suspicions already entertained. His countenance was pale even to ghastliness, and his deep-set eyes glared with unnatural lustre. After some inquiries respecting his health, I asked him, not knowing what better to say, if he had yet obtained the *scarabæus* from Lieutenant G——.

"Oh, yes," he replied, coloring violently, "I got it from him the next morning. Nothing should tempt me to part with that *scarabæus*. Do you know that Jupiter is quite right about it?"

"In what way?" I asked, with a sad foreboding at heart.

"In supposing it to be a bug of *real gold*." He said this with an air of profound seriousness, and I felt inexpressibly shocked.

"This bug is to make my fortune," he continued, with a triumphant smile, "to reinstate me in my family possessions. Is it any wonder, then, that I prize it? Since Fortune has thought fit to bestow it upon me, I have only to use it properly and I shall arrive at the gold of which it is the index. Jupiter, bring me that *scarabæus*!"

"What! de bug, massa? I'd rudder not go fer trubble dat bug—you mus git him for your own self." Hereupon Legrand arose, with a grave and stately air, and brought me the beetle from a glass case in which it was enclosed. It was a beautiful *scarabæus*, and, at that time, unknown to naturalists—of course a great prize in a scientific point of view. There were two round, black spots near one extremity of the back, and a long one near the other. The scales were exceedingly hard and glossy, with all the appearance of burnished gold. The weight of the insect was very remarkable, and, taking all things into consideration, I could hardly blame Jupiter for his opinion respecting it; but what to make of Legrand's agreement with that opinion, I could not, for the life of me, tell.

"I sent for you," said he, in a grandiloquent tone, when I had completed my examination of the beetle, "I sent for you that I might have your counsel and assistance in furthering the views of Fate and of the bug—"

"My dear Legrand," I cried, interrupting him, "you are certainly unwell, and had better use some little precautions. You shall go to bed, and I will remain with you a few days, until you get over this. You are feverish and—"

"Feel my pulse," said he.

I felt it, and, to say the truth, found not the slightest indication of fever.

"But you may be ill, and yet have no fever. Allow me this once to prescribe for you. In the first place, go to bed. In the next—"

"You are mistaken," he interposed, "I am as well as I can expect to be under the excitement which I suffer. If you really wish me well, you will relieve this excitement."

"And how is this to be done?"

"Very easily. Jupiter and myself are going upon an expedition into the hills, upon the mainland, and, in this expedition, we shall need the aid of some person in whom we can confide. You are the only one we can trust. Whether we succeed or fail, the excitement which you now perceive in me will be equally allayed."

"I am anxious to oblige you in any way," I replied; "but do you mean to say that this infernal beetle has any connection with your expedition into the hills?"

"It has."

"Then, Legrand, I can become a party to no such absurd proceeding."

"I am sorry—very sorry—for we shall have to try it by ourselves."

"Try it by yourselves! The man is surely mad!—but stay—how long do you propose to be absent?"

"Probably all night. We shall start immediately, and be back, at all events, by sunrise."

"And will you promise me, upon your honor, that when this freak of yours is over, and the bug business (good God!) settled to your satisfaction, you will then return home and follow my advice implicitly, as that of your physician?"

"Yes; I promise; and now let us be off, for we have no time to lose."

With a heavy heart I accompanied my friend. We started about four o'clock—Legrand, Jupiter, the dog, and myself. Jupiter had with him the scythe and spades—the whole of which he insisted upon carrying, more through fear, it seemed to me, of trusting either of the implements within reach of his master, than from any excess of industry or complaisance His demeanor was dogged in the extreme, and "dat d——d bug" were the sole words which escaped his lips during the journey. For my own part, I had charge of a couple of dark lanterns, while Legrand contented himself with the *scarabæus,* which he carried attached to the end of a bit of whip-cord; twirling it to and fro, with the air of a conjurer, as he went. When I observed this last, plain evidence of my friend's aberation of mind, I could scarcely refrain from tears. I thought it best, however, to humor his fancy, at least for the present, or until I could adopt some more energetic measures with a chance of success. In the meantime I endeavored, but all in vain, to sound him in regard to the object of the expedition. Having succeeded in inducing me to accompany him, he seemed unwilling to hold conversation upon any topic of minor importance, and to all my questions vouchsafed no other reply than "we shall see!"

We crossed the creek at the head of the island by means of a skiff, and, ascending the high grounds on the shore of the mainland, proceeded in a northwesterly direction, through a tract of country excessively wild and desolate, where no trace of a human footstep was to be seen. Legrand led the way with decision; pausing only for an instant, here and there, to consult what appeared to be certain landmarks of his own contrivance upon a former occasion.

In this manner we journeyed for about two hours, and the sun was just setting when we entered a region infinitely more dreary than any yet seen. It was a species of tableland, near the summit of an almost inaccessible hill, densely wooded from base to pinnacle, and interspersed with huge crags that appeared to lie loosely upon the soil, and in many cases were prevented from precipitating themselves into the valleys below merely by the support of the trees against which they reclined. Deep ravines, in various directions, gave an air of still sterner solemnity to the scene.

The natural platform to which we had clambered was thickly overgrown with brambles, through which we soon discovered that it would have been impossible to force our way but for the scythe; and Jupiter, by direction of his master, proceeded to clear for us a path to the foot of an enormously tall tulip tree, which stood, with some eight or ten oaks, upon the level, and far surpassed them all, and all other trees which I had then ever seen, in the beauty of its foliage and form, in the wide spread of its branches, and in the general majesty of its appearance. When we reached this tree, Legrand turned to Jupiter, and asked him if he thought he could climb it. The old man seemed a little staggered by the question, and for some moments made no reply. At length he approached the huge trunk, walked slowly around it, and examined it with minute attention. When he had completed his scrutiny, he merely said:

"Yes, massa, Jup climb any tree he ebber see in he life."

"Then up with you as soon as possible, for it will soon be too dark to see what we are about."

"How far mus go up, massa?" inquired Jupiter.

"Get up the main trunk first, and then I will tell you which way to go—and here—stop! take this beetle with you."

"De bug, Massa Will!—de goole-bug!" cried the negro, drawing back in dismay—"what for mus tote de bug way up de tree?—d—n if I do!"

"If you are afraid, Jup, a great big negro like you, to take hold of a harmless little dead beetle, why, you can carry it up by this string—but, if you do not take it up with you in some way, I shall be under the necessity of breaking your head with this shovel."

"What de matter now, massa?" said Jup, evidently shamed into compliance; "always want fur to raise fuss wid old nigger. Was only funnin anyhow. *Me* feered de bug! what I keer for de bug?" Here he took cautiously hold of the extreme end of the string, and, maintaining the insect as far from his person as circumstances would permit, prepared to ascend the tree.

In youth, the tulip tree, or *Liriodendron Tulipifera*, the most magnificent of American foresters, has a trunk peculiarly smooth, and often rises to a great height without lateral branches; but, in its riper age, the bark becomes gnarled and uneven, while many short limbs make their appearance on the stem. Thus the difficulty of ascension, in the present case, lay more in semblance than in reality. Embracing the huge cylinder, as closely as possible, with his arms and knees, seizing with his hands some projections, and resting his naked toes upon others, Jupiter, after one or two narrow escapes from falling, at length wriggled himself into the first great fork, and seemed to consider the whole business as virtually accomplished. The *risk* of the achievement was, in fact, now over, although the climber was some sixty or seventy feet from the ground.

"Which way mus go now, Massa Will?" he asked.

"Keep up the largest branch,—the one on this side," said Legrand. The negro obeyed him promptly, and apparently with but little trouble, ascending higher and higher, until no glimpse of his squat figure could be obtained through the dense foliage which enveloped it. Presently his voice was heard in a sort of halloo.

"How much fudder is got for go?"

"How high up are you?" asked Legrand.

"Ebber so fur," replied the negro; "can see de sky fru de top ob de tree."

"Never mind the sky, but attend to what I say. Look down the trunk and count the limbs below you on this side. How many limbs have you passed?"

"One, two, tree, four, fibe—I done pass fibe big limb, massa, pon dis side."

"Then go one limb higher."

In a few minutes the voice was heard again, announcing that the seventh limb was attained.

"Now, Jup," cried Legrand, evidently much excited, "I want you to work your way out upon that limb as far as you can. If you see anything strange, let me know."

By this time what little doubt I might have entertained of my poor friend's insanity was put finally at rest. I had no alternative but to conclude him stricken with lunacy, and I became seriously anxious about getting him home. While I was pondering upon what was best to be done, Jupiter's voice was again heard.

"Mos feerd for to ventur pon dis limb berry far—'tis dead limb putty much all de way."

"Did you say it was a *dead* limb, Jupiter?" cried Legrand in a quavering voice.

"Yes, massa, him dead as de door-nail—done up for sartain—done departed dis here life."

"What in the name of heaven shall I do?" asked Legrand, seemingly in the greatest distress.

"Do!" said I, glad of an opportunity to interpose a word, "why come home and go to bed. Come now!—that's a fine fellow. It's getting late, and, besides, you remember your promise."

"Jupiter," cried he, without heeding me in the least, "do you hear me?"

"Yes, Massa Will, hear you ebber so plain."

"Try the wood well, then, with your knife, and see if you think it *very* rotten."

"Him rotten, massa, sure nuff," replied the negro in a few moments, "but not so berry rotten as mought be. Mought ventur out leetle way pon de limb by myself, dat's true."

"By yourself?—what do you mean?"

"Why, I mean de bug. 'Tis *berry* hebby bug. Spose I drop him down fuss, and den de limb won't break wid just de weight ob one nigger."

"You infernal scoundrel!" cried Legrand, apparently much relieved, "what do you mean by telling me such nonsense as that? As sure as you let that beetle fall, I'll break your neck. Look here, Jupiter! do you hear me?"

"Yes, massa, needn't hollo at poor nigger dat style."

"Well! now listen!—if you will venture out on the limb as far as you think safe, and not let go the beetle, I'll make you a present of a silver dollar as soon as you get down."

"I'm gwine, Massa Will—deed I is," replied the negro very promptly—"mos out to the eend now."

"*Out to the end!*" here fairly screamed Legrand, "do you say you are out to the end of that limb?"

"Soon be to de eend, massa,—o-o-o-o-oh! Lor-gol-a-marcy! what *is* dis here pon de tree?"

"Well!" cried Legrand, highly delighted, "what is it?"

"Why taint noffin but a skull—somebody bin lef him head up de tree, and de crows done gobble ebery bit ob de meat off."

"A skull, you say!—very well!—how is it fastened to the limb?—what holds it on?"

"Sure nuff, massa; mus look. Why, dis berry curous sarcumstance, pon my word—dare's a great big nail in de skull, what fastens ob it on to de tree."

"Well now, Jupiter, do exactly as I tell you—do you hear?"

"Yes, massa."

"Pay attention, then!—find the left eye of the skull."

"Hum! hoo! dat 's good! why, dar ain't no eye lef at all."

"Curse your stupidity! do you know your right hand from your left?"

Yes, I nose dat—nose all bout dat—'tis my lef hand what I chops de wood wid."

"To be sure! you are left-handed; and your left eye is on the same side as your left hand. Now, I suppose, you can find the left eye of the skull, or the place where the left eye has been. Have you found it?"

Here was a long pause. At length the negro asked, "Is de lef eye of de skull pon de same side as de lef hand of de skull, too?—cause de skull ain't got not a bit ob a hand at all—nebber mind! I got de lef eye now—here de lef eye! what mus do wid it?"

"Let the beetle drop through it, as far as the string will reach—but be careful and not let go your hold of the string."

"All dat done, Massa Will; mighty easy ting for to put de bug fru de hole—look out for him dar below!"

During this colloquy no portion of Jupiter's person could be seen; but the beetle, which he had suffered to descend, was now visible at the end of the string, and glistened like a globe of burnished gold in the last rays of the setting sun, some of which still faintly illumined the eminence upon which we stood. The *scarabæus* hung quite clear of any branches, and, if allowed to fall, would have fallen at our feet. Legrand immediately took the scythe, and cleared with it a circular space, three or four yards in diameter, just beneath the insect, and, having accomplished this, ordered Jupiter to let go the string and come down from the tree.

Driving a peg, with great nicety, into the ground at the precise spot where the beetle fell, my friend now produced from his pocket a tape-measure. Fastening one end of this at that point of the trunk of the tree which was nearest the peg, he unrolled it till it reached the peg, and thence farther unrolled it, in the direction already established by the two points of the tree and the peg, for the distance of fifty feet—Jupiter clearing away the brambles with the scythe. At the spot thus attained a second peg was driven, and about this, as a centre, a rude circle, about four feet in diameter, described. Taking now a spade himself, and giving one to Jupiter and one to me, Legrand begged us to set about digging as quickly as possible.

To speak the truth, I had no especial relish for such amusement at any time, and, at that particular moment, would most willingly have declined it; for the night was coming on, and I felt much fatigued with the exercise already taken; but I saw no mode of escape, and was fearful of disturbing my poor friend's equanimity by a refusal. Could I have depended, indeed, upon Jupiter's aid, I would have had no hesitation in attempting to get the lunatic home by force; but I was too well assured of the old negro's disposition to hope that he would assist me, under any circumstances, in a personal contest with his master. I made no doubt that the latter had been infected with some of the innumerable Southern superstitions about money buried, and that his fantasy had received confirmation by the finding of the *scarabæus*, or, perhaps, by Jupiter's obstinacy in maintaining it to be "a bug of real gold." A mind disposed to lunacy would readily be led away by such suggestions, especially if chiming in with favorite preconceived ideas; and then I called to mind the poor fellow's speech about the beetle's being "the index of his fortune." Upon the whole, I was sadly vexed and puzzled, but at length I concluded to make a virtue of necessity—to dig with a good will, and thus the sooner to convince the visionary, by ocular demonstration, of the fallacy of the opinions he entertained.

The lanterns having been lit, we all fell to work with a zeal worthy a more rational cause; and, as the glare fell upon our persons and implements, I could not help thinking how picturesque a group we composed, and how strange and suspicious our labors must have appeared to any interloper who, by chance, might have stumbled upon our whereabouts.

We dug very steadily for two hours. Little was said; and our chief embarrassment lay in the yelpings of the dog, who took exceeding interest in our proceedings. He, at length, became so obstreperous that we grew fearful of his giving the alarm to some stragglers in the vicinity; or, rather, this was the apprehension of Legrand; for myself, I should have rejoiced at any interruption which might have enabled me to get the wanderer home. The noise was, at length, very effectually silenced by Jupiter, who, getting out of the hole with a dogged air of deliberation, tied the brute's mouth up with one of his suspenders, and then returned, with a grave chuckle, to his task.

When the time mentioned had expired, we had reached a depth of five feet, and yet no signs of any treasure became manifest. A general pause ensued, and I began to hope that the farce was at an end. Legrand, however, although evidently much disconcerted, wiped his brow thoughtfully and recommenced. We had excavated the entire circle of four feet diameter, and now we slightly enlarged the limit, and went to the farther depth of two feet. Still nothing appeared. The gold-seeker, whom I sincerely pitied, at length clambered from the pit, with the bitterest disappointment imprinted upon every feature, and proceeded, slowly and reluctantly, to put on his coat, which he had thrown off at the beginning of his labor. In the meantime I made no remark. Jupiter, at a signal from his master, began to gather up his tools. This done, and the dog having been unmuzzled, we turned in profound silence towards home.

We had taken, perhaps, a dozen steps in this direction, when, with a loud oath, Legrand strode up to Jupiter, and seized him by the collar. The astonished negro opened his eyes and mouth to the fullest extent, let fall the spades, and fell upon his knees.

"You scoundrel," said Legrand, hissing out the syllables from between his clenched teeth—"you infernal black villain!—speak, I tell you!—answer me this instant, without prevarication!—which—which is your left eye?"

"Oh, my golly, Massa Will! aint dis here my lef eye for sartain?" roared the terrified Jupiter, placing his hand upon his *right* organ of vision, and holding it there with a desperate pertinacity, as if in immediate dread of his master's attempt at a gouge.

"I thought so! I knew it! Hurrah!" vociferated Legrand, letting the negro go, and executing a series of curvets and caracoles, much to the astonishment of his valet, who, arising from his knees, looked mutely from his master to myself, and then from myself to his master.

"Come! we must go back," said the latter, "the game's not up yet;" and he again led the way to the tulip tree.

"Jupiter," said he, when we reached its foot, "come here! Was the skull nailed to the limb with the face outward, or with the face to the limb?"

"De face was out, massa, so dat de crows could get at de eyes good, widout any trouble."

"Well, then, was it this eye or that through which you dropped the beetle?" here Legrand touched each of Jupiter's eyes.

"'Twas dis eye, massa—de lef eye—jis as you tell me," and here it was his right eye that the negro indicated.

"That will do—we must try it again."

Here my friend, about whose madness I now saw, or fancied that I saw, certain indications of method, removed the peg which marked the spot where the beetle fell, to a spot about three inches to the westward of its former position. Taking, now, the tape-measure from the nearest point of the trunk to the peg, as before, and continuing the extension in a straight line to the distance of fifty feet, a spot was indicated, removed, by several yards, from the point at which we had been digging.

Around the new position a circle, somewhat larger than in the former instance, was now described, and we again set to work with the spades. I was dreadfully weary, but, scarcely understanding what had occasioned the change in my thoughts, I felt no longer any great aversion from the labor imposed. I had become most unaccountably interested—nay, even excited. Perhaps there was something, amid all the extravagant demeanor of Legrand—some air of forethought, or of deliberation—which impressed me. I dug eagerly, and now and then caught myself actually looking, with something that very much resembled expectation, for the fancied treasure, the vision of which had demented my unfortunate companion. At a period when such vagaries of thought most fully possessed me, and when we had been at work perhaps an hour and a half, we were again interrupted by the violent howlings of the dog. His uneasiness, in the first instance, had been evidently but the result of playfulness or caprice, but he now assumed a bitter and serious tone. Upon Jupiter's again attempting to muzzle him, he made furious resistance, and, leaping into the hole, tore up the mould frantically with his claws. In a few seconds he had uncovered a mass of human bones, forming two complete skeletons, intermingled with several buttons of metal, and what appeared to be the dust of decayed woollen. One or two strokes of a spade upturned the blade of a large Spanish knife, and, as he dug farther, three or four loose pieces of gold and silver coin came to light.

At sight of these the joy of Jupiter could scarcely be restrained, but the countenance of his master wore an air of extreme disappointment.

He urged us, however, to continue our exertions, and the words were hardly uttered when I stumbled and fell forward, having caught the toe of my boot in a large ring of iron that lay half buried in the loose earth.

We now worked in earnest, and never did I pass ten minutes of more intense excitement. During this interval we had fairly unearthed an oblong chest of wood, which, from its perfect preservation and wonderful hardness, had plainly been subjected to some mineralizing process—perhaps that of the bichloride of mercury. This box was three feet and a half long, three feet broad, and two and a half feet deep. It was firmly secured by bands of wrought iron, riveted, and forming a kind of trellis-work over the whole. On each side of the chest, near the top, were three rings of iron—six in all—by means of which a firm hold could be obtained by six persons. Our utmost united endeavors served only to disturb the coffer very slightly in its bed. We at once saw the impossibility of removing so great a weight. Luckily, the sole fastenings of the lid consisted of two sliding bolts. These we drew back—trembling and panting with anxiety. In an instant, a treasure of incalculable value lay gleaming before us. As the rays of the lanterns fell within the pit, there flashed upwards, from a confused heap of gold and of jewels, a glow and a glare that absolutely dazzled our eyes.

I shall not pretend to describe the feelings with which I gazed. Amazement was, of course, predominant. Legrand appeared exhausted with excitement, and spoke very few words. Jupiter's countenance wore, for some minutes, as deadly a pallor as it is possible, in the nature of things, for any negro's visage to assume. He seemed stupified—thunder-stricken. Presently he fell upon his knees in the pit, and, burying his naked arms up to the elbows in gold, let them there remain, as if enjoying the luxury of a bath. At length, with a deep sigh, he exclaimed, as if in a soliloquy:

"And dis all cum ob de goole-bug! de putty goole-bug! de poor little goole-bug, what I boosed in dat sabage kind ob style! Aint you shamed ob yourself, nigger?—answer me dat!"

It became necessary, at last, that I should arouse both master and valet to the expediency of removing the treasure. It was growing late, and it behooved us to make exertion, that we might get everything housed before daylight. It was difficult to say what should be done, and much time was spent in deliberation—so confused were the ideas of all. We finally lightened the box by removing two-thirds of its contents, when we were enabled, with some trouble, to raise it from the hole. The articles taken out were deposited among the brambles, and the dog left to guard them, with strict orders from Jupiter neither, upon any pretence, to stir from the spot, nor to open his mouth until our return. We then hurriedly made for home with the chest; reaching the hut in safety, but after excessive toil, at one o'clock in the morning. Worn out as we were, it was not in human nature to do more just now. We rested until two, and had supper; starting for the hills immediately afterwards, armed with three stout sacks, which by good luck were upon the premises. A little before four we arrived at the pit, divided the remainder of the booty, as equally as might be, among us, and, leaving the holes unfilled, again set out for the hut, at which, for the second time, we deposited our golden burdens, just as the first streaks of the dawn gleamed from over the tree-tops in the East.

We were now thoroughly broken down; but the intense excitement of the time denied us repose. After an unquiet slumber of some three or four hours' duration, we arose, as if by preconcert, to make examination of our treasure.

The chest had been full to the brim, and we spent the whole day, and the greater part of the next night, in a scrutiny of its contents. There had been nothing like order or arrangement. Everything had been heaped in promiscuously. Having assorted all with care, we found ourselves possessed of even vaster wealth than we had at first supposed. In coin there was rather more than four hundred and fifty thousand dollars: estimating the value of the pieces, as accurately as we could, by the tables of the period. There was not a particle of silver. All was gold of antique date and of great variety: French, Spanish, and German money, with a few English guineas, and some counters, of which we had never seen specimens before. There were several very large and heavy coins, so worn that we could make nothing of their inscriptions. There was no American money. The value of the jewels we found more difficulty in estimating. There were diamonds—some of them exceedingly large and fine—a hundred and ten in all, and not one of them small; eighteen rubies of remarkable brilliancy; three hundred and ten emeralds, all very beautiful; and twenty-one sapphires, with an opal. These stones had all been broken from their settings and thrown loose in the chest. The settings themselves, which we picked out from among the other gold, appeared to have been beaten up with hammers, as if to prevent identification. Besides all this, there was a vast quantity of solid gold ornaments: nearly two hundred massive finger and ear-rings; rich chains—thirty of these, if I remember; eighty-three very large and heavy crucifixes; five gold censers of great value; a prodigious golden punch-bowl, ornamented with richly chased vine-leaves and Bacchanalian figures; with two sword-handles exquisitely embossed, and many other smaller articles which I cannot recollect. The weight of these valuables exceeded three hundred and fifty pounds avoirdupois; and in this estimate I have not included one hundred and ninety-seven superb gold watches; three of the number being worth each five hundred dollars, if one. Many of them were very old, and as time-keepers valueless, the works having suffered more or less from corrosion; but all were richly jewelled and in cases of great worth. We estimated the entire contents of the chest, that night, at a million and a half of dollars; and, upon the subsequent disposal of the trinkets and jewels (a few being retained for our own use), it was found that we had greatly undervalued the treasure.

When, at length, we had concluded our examination, and the intense excitement of the time had in some measure subsided, Legrand, who saw that I was dying with impatience for a solution of this most extraordinary riddle, entered into a full detail of all the circumstances connected with it.

"You remember," said he, "the night when I handed you the rough sketch I had made of the *scarabæus*. You recollect, also, that I became quite vexed at you for insisting that my drawing resembled a death's-head. When you first made this assertion I thought you were jesting; but afterwards I called to mind the peculiar spots on the back of the insect, and admitted to myself that your remark had some little foundation in fact. Still, the sneer at my graphic powers irritated me—for I am considered a good artist—and, therefore, when you handed me the scrap of parchment, I was about to crumple it up and throw it angrily into the fire."

"The scrap of paper, you mean," said I.

"No: it had much of the appearance of paper, and at first I supposed it to be such, but when I came to draw upon it, I discovered it, at once, to be a piece of very thin parchment. It was quite dirty, you remember. Well, as I was in the very act of crumpling it up, my glance fell upon the sketch at which you had been looking, and you may imagine my astonishment when I perceived, in, fact, the figure of a death's-head just where, it seemed to me, I had made the drawing of the beetle. For a moment I was too much amazed to think with accuracy. I knew that my design was very different in detail from this—although there was a certain similarity in general outline. Presently I took a candle and, seating myself at the other end of the room, proceeded to scrutinize the parchment more closely. Upon turning it over, I saw my own sketch upon the reverse, just as I had made it. My first idea, now, was mere surprise at the really remarkable similarity of outline—at the singular coincidence involved in the fact that, unknown to me, there should have been a skull upon the other side of the parchment, immediately beneath my figure of the *scarabæus*, and that this skull, not only in outline, but in size, should so closely resemble my drawing. I say the singularity of this coincidence absolutely stupified me for a time. This is the usual effect of such coincidences. The mind struggles to establish a connection—a sequence of cause and effect—and, being unable to do so, suffers a species of temporary paralysis. But, when I recovered from this stupor, there dawned upon me gradually a conviction which startled me even far more than the coincidence. I began distinctly, positively, to remember that there had been *no* drawing on the parchment when I made my sketch of the *scarabæus*. I became perfectly certain of this; for I recollected turning up first one side and then the other, in search of the cleanest spot. Had the skull been then there, of course I could not have failed to notice it. Here was indeed a mystery which I felt it impossible to explain; but, even at that early moment, there seemed to glimmer, faintly, within the most remote and secret chambers of my intellect, a glow-worm-like conception of that truth which last night's adventure brought to so magnificent a demonstration. I arose at once, and, putting the parchment securely away, dismissed all farther reflection until I should be alone.

"When you had gone, and when Jupiter was fast asleep, I betook myself to a more methodical investigation of the affair. In the first place I considered the manner in which the parchment had come into my possession. The spot where we discovered the *scarabæus* was on the coast of the mainland, about a mile eastward of the island, and but a short distance above high-water mark. Upon my taking hold of it, it gave me a sharp bite, which caused me to let it drop. Jupiter, with his accustomed caution, before seizing the insect, which had flown towards him, looked about him for a leaf, or something of that nature, by which to take hold of it. It was at this moment that his eyes, and mine also, fell upon the scrap of parchment, which I then supposed to be paper. It was lying half-buried in the sand, a corner sticking up. Near the spot where we found it, I observed the remnants of the hull of what appeared to have been a ship's long boat. The wreck seemed to have been there for a very great while; for the resemblance to boat timbers could scarcely be traced.

"Well, Jupiter picked up the parchment, wrapped the beetle in it, and gave it to me. Soon afterwards we turned to go home, and on the way met Lieutenant G——. I showed him the insect, and he begged me to let him take it to the fort. On my consenting, he thrust it forthwith into his waistcoat pocket, without the parchment in which it had been wrapped, and which I had continued to hold in my hand during his inspection. Perhaps he dreaded my changing my mind, and thought it best to make sure of the prize at once—you know how enthusiastic he is on all subjects connected with Natural History. At the same time, without being conscious of it, I must have deposited the parchment in my own pocket.

"You remember that when I went to the table, for the purpose of making a sketch of the beetle, I found no paper where it was usually kept. I looked in the drawer, and found none there. I searched my pockets, hoping to find an old letter, and then my hand fell upon the parchment. I thus detail the precise mode in which it came into my possession; for the circumstances impressed me with peculiar force.

"No doubt you will think me fanciful—but I had already established a kind of *connection*. I had put together two links of a great chain. There was a boat lying on a seacoast, and not far from the boat was a parchment—*not a paper*—with a skull depicted on it. You will, of course, ask 'where is the connection?' I reply that the skull, or death's-head, is the well-known emblem of the pirate. The flag of the death's-head is hoisted in all engagements.

"I have said that the scrap was parchment, and not paper. Parchment is durable—almost imperishable. Matters of little moment are rarely consigned to parchment; since, for the mere ordinary purposes of drawing or writing, it is not nearly so well adapted as paper. This reflection suggested some meaning—some relevancy—in the deaths-head. I did not fail to observe, also, the *form* of the parchment. Although one of its corners had been, by some accident, destroyed, it could be seen that the original form was oblong. It was just such a slip, indeed, as might have been chosen for a memorandum—for a record of something to be long remembered and carefully preserved."

"But," I interposed, "you say that the skull, was *not* upon the parchment when you made the drawing of the beetle. How then do you trace any connection between the boat and the skull—since this latter, according to your own admission, must have been designed (God only knows how or by whom) at some period subsequent to your sketching the *scarabæus*?"

"Ah, hereupon turns the whole mystery; although the secret, at this point, I had comparatively little difficulty in solving. My steps were sure, and could afford but a single result. I reasoned, for example, thus: When I drew the *scarabæus,* there was no skull apparent on the parchment. When I had completed the drawing I gave it to you, and observed you narrowly until you returned it. *You*, therefore, did not design the skull, and no one else was present to do it. Then it was not done by human agency. And nevertheless it was done.

"At this stage of my reflections I endeavored to remember, and *did* remember, with entire distinctness, every incident which occurred about the period in question. The weather was chilly (O rare and happy accident!), and a fire was blazing on the hearth. I was heated with exercise and sat near the table. You, however, had drawn a chair close to the chimney. Just as I placed the parchment in your hand, and as you were in the act of inspecting it, Wolf, the Newfoundland, entered, and leaped upon your shoulders. With your left hand you caressed him and kept him off, while your right, holding the parchment, was permitted, to fall listlessly between your knees, and in close proximity to the fire. At one moment I thought the blaze had caught it, and was about to caution you, but, before I could speak, you had withdrawn it, and were engaged in its examination. When I considered all these particulars, I doubted not for a moment that *heat* had been the agent in bringing to light, on the parchment, the skull which I saw designed on it. You are well aware that chemical preparations exist, and have existed time out of mind, by means of which it is possible to write on either paper or vellum, so that the characters shall become visible only when subjected to the action of fire. Zaffre, digested in *aqua regia*, and diluted with four times its weight of water, is sometimes employed; a green tint results. The regulus of cobalt, dissolved in spirit of nitre, gives a red. These colors disappear at longer or shorter intervals after the material written upon cools, but again become apparent upon the re-application of heat.

"I now scrutinized the death's-head with care. Its outer edges—the edges of the drawing nearest the edge of the vellum—were far more *distinct* than the others. It was clear that the action of the caloric had been imperfect or unequal. I immediately kindled a fire, and subjected every portion of the parchment to a glowing heat. At first, the only effect was the strengthening of the faint lines in the skull; but, on persevering in the experiment, there became visible at the corner of the slip, diagonally opposite to the spot in which the death's-head was delineated, the figure of what I at first supposed to be a goat. A closer scrutiny, however, satisfied me that it was intended for a kid."

"Ha! ha!" said I, "to be sure I have no right to laugh at you—a million and a half of money is too serious a matter for mirth—but you are not about to establish a third link in your chain: you will not find any especial connection between your pirates and a goat; pirates, you know, have nothing to do with goats; they appertain to the farming interest."

"But I have just said that the figure was *not* that of a goat."

"Well, a kid, then—pretty much the same thing."

"Pretty much, but not altogether," said Legrand. "You may have heard of one *Captain* Kidd. I at once looked on the figure of the animal as a kind of punning or hieroglyphical signature. I say signature, because its position on the vellum suggested this idea. The death's-head at the corner diagonally opposite had, in the same manner, the air of a stamp, or seal. But I was sorely put out by the absence of all else—of the body to my imagined instrument—of the text for my context."

"I presume you expected to find a letter between the stamp and the signature."

"Something of that kind. The fact is, I felt irresistibly impressed with a presentiment of some vast good fortune impending. I can scarcely say why. Perhaps, after all, it was rather a desire than an actual belief;—but do you know that Jupiter's silly words, about the bug being of solid gold, had a remarkable effect on my fancy? And then the series of accidents and coincidences—these were so *very* extraordinary. Do you observe how mere an accident it was that these events should have occurred on the *sole* day of all the year in which it has been, or may be, sufficiently cool for fire, and that without the fire, or without the intervention of the dog at the precise moment in which he appeared, I should never have become aware of the death's-head, and so never the possessor of the treasure?"

"But proceed—I am all impatience."

"Well; you have heard, of course, the many stories current—the thousand vague rumors afloat about money buried, somewhere on the Atlantic coast, by Kidd and his associates. These rumors must have had some foundation in fact. And that the rumors have existed so long and so continuously, could have resulted, it appeared to me, only from the circumstance of the buried treasure still *remaining* entombed. Had Kidd concealed his plunder for a time, and afterwards reclaimed it, the rumors would scarcely have reached us in their present unvarying form. You will observe that the stories told are all about money-seekers, not about money-finders. Had the pirate recovered his money, there the affair would have dropped. It seemed to me that some accident—say the loss of a memorandum indicating its locality—had deprived him of the means of recovering it, and that this accident had become known to his followers, who otherwise might never have heard that treasure had been concealed at all, and who, busying themselves in vain, because unguided, attempts to regain it, had given first birth, and then universal currency, to the reports which are now so common. Have you ever heard of any important treasure being unearthed along the coast?"

"Never."

"But that Kidd's accumulations were immense is well known. I took it for granted, therefore, that the earth still held them; and you will scarcely be surprised when I tell you that I felt a hope, nearly amounting to certainty, that the parchment so strangely found involved a lost record of the place of deposit."

"But how did you proceed?"

"I held the vellum again to the fire, after increasing the heat, but nothing appeared. I now thought it possible that the coating of dirt might have something to do with the failure; so I carefully rinsed the parchment by pouring warm water over it, and, having done this, I placed it in a tin pan, with the skull downwards, and put the pan upon a furnace of lighted charcoal. In a few minutes, the pan having become thoroughly heated, I removed the slip, and, to my inexpressible joy, found it spotted, in several places, with what appeared to be figures arranged in lines. Again I placed it in the pan, and suffered it to remain another minute. Upon taking it off, the whole was just as you see it now."

Here Legrand, having reheated the parchment, submitted it to my inspection. The following characters were rudely traced, in a red tint, between the death's-head and the goat:—

53‡‡†305))6*;4826)4‡.)4‡);806*;48†8¶60))85;;]8*;:‡*8†83(8
8)5*†;46(;88*96*?;8)*‡(;485);5*†2:*‡(;4956*2(5*—4)8¶8*;4069
285);)6†8)4‡‡;1(‡9;48081;8:8‡1;48†85;4)485†528806*81(‡9;4
8;(8 8;4(‡?34;48)4‡;161;:188;‡?;

"But," said I, returning him the slip, "I am as much in the dark as ever. Were all the jewels of Golconda awaiting me on my solution of this enigma, I am quite sure, that I should be unable to earn them."

"And yet," said Legrand, "the solution is by no means so difficult as you might be led to imagine from the first hasty inspection of the characters. These characters, as any one might readily guess, form a cipher—that is to say, they convey a meaning; but then, from what is known of Kidd, I could not suppose, him capable of constructing any of the more abstruse cryptographs. I made up my mind, at once, that this was of a simple species—such, however, as would appear, to the crude intellect of the sailor, absolutely insoluble without the key."

"And you really solved it?"

"Readily; I have solved others of an abstruseness ten thousand times greater. Circumstances, and a certain bias of mind, have led me to take interest in such riddles, and it may well be doubted whether human ingenuity can construct an enigma of the kind which human ingenuity may not, by proper application, resolve. In fact, having once established connected and legible characters, I scarcely gave a thought to the mere difficulty of developing their import.

"In the present case—indeed in all cases of secret writing—the first question regards the *language* of the cipher; for the principles of solution, so far, especially, as the more simple ciphers are concerned, depend on, and are varied by, the genius of the particular idiom. In general, there is no alternative but experiment (directed by probabilities) of every tongue known to him who attempts the solution, until the true one be attained. But, with the cipher now before us, all difficulty is removed by the signature. The pun upon the word 'Kidd' is appreciable in no other language than the English. But for this consideration I should have begun my attempts with the Spanish and French, as the tongues in which a secret of this kind would most naturally have been written by a pirate of the Spanish main. As it was, I assumed the cryptograph to be English.

"You observe there are no divisions between the words. Had there been divisions, the task would have been comparatively easy. In such case I should have commenced with a collation and analysis of the shorter words, and, had a word of a single letter occurred, as is most likely (*a* or *I*, for example), I should have considered the solution as assured. But, there being no division, my first step was to ascertain the predominant letters, as well as the least frequent. Counting all, I constructed a table, thus:

Of the character	8	there are	33
	;	"	26
	4	"	19
	‡)	"	16
	*	"	13
	5	"	12
	6	"	11
	†1	"	8
	0	"	6
	92	"	5
	:3	"	4
	?	"	3
	¶	"	2
	]	"	1

"Now, in English, the letter which most frequently occurs is *e*. Afterwards the succession runs thus: *a o i d h n r s t u y c f g l m w b k p q x z*. *E* predominates, however, so remarkably that an individual sentence of any length is rarely seen, in which it is not the prevailing character.

"Here, then, we have, in the very beginning, the groundwork for something more than a mere guess. The general use which may be made of the table is obvious—but, in this particular cipher, we shall only very partially require its aid. As our predominant character is 8, we will commence by assuming it as the *e* of the natural alphabet. To verify the supposition, let us observe if the 8 be seen often in couples—for *e* is doubled with great frequency in English—in such words, for example, as 'meet,' 'fleet,' 'speed,' 'seen,' 'been,' 'agree,' etc. In the present instance we see it doubled no less than five times, although the cryptograph is brief.

"Let us assume 8, then, as *e*. Now, of all *words* in the language, 'the' is most usual; let us see, therefore, whether there are not repetitions of any three characters, in the same order of collocation, the last of them being 8. If we discover repetitions of such letters, so arranged, they will most probably represent the word 'the.' On inspection, we find no less than seven such arrangements, the characters being ;48. We may, therefore, assume that the semicolon represents *t*, that 4 represents *h*, and that 8 represents *e*—the last being now well confirmed. Thus a great step has been taken.

"But, having established a single word, we are enabled to establish a vastly important point; that is to say, several commencements and terminations of other words. Let us refer, for example, to the last instance but one, in which combination ;48 occurs—not far from the end of the cipher. We know that the semicolon immediately ensuing is the commencement of a word, and, of the six characters succeeding this 'the,' we are cognizant of no less than five. Let us set these characters down, thus, by the letters we know them to represent, leaving a space for the unknown—

t eeth

"Here we are enabled, at once, to discard the '*th*,' as forming no portion of the word commencing with the first *t*; since, by experiment of the entire alphabet for a letter adapted to the vacancy, we perceive that no word can be formed of which this *th* can be a part. We are thus narrowed into

t ee,

and, going through the alphabet, if necessary, as before, we arrive at the word 'tree' as the sole possible reading. We thus gain another letter *r*, represented by (, with the words 'the tree' in juxtaposition.

"Looking beyond these words, for a short distance, we again see the combination ;48, and employ it by way of *termination* to what immediately precedes. We have thus this arrangement:

the tree ;4(‡?34 the,

or, substituting the natural letters, where known, it reads thus:

the tree thr‡?3h the.

"Now, if, in place of the unknown characters, we leave blank spaces, or substitute dots, we read thus:

the tree thr. . . h the,

when the word '*through*' makes itself evident at once. But this discovery gives us three new letters, *o*, *u*, and *g*, represented by ‡ ? and 3.

"Looking now, narrowly, through the cipher for combinations of known characters, we find, not very far from the beginning, this arrangement,

83(88, or egree,

which, plainly, is the conclusion of the word 'degree,' and gives us another letter, *d*, represented by †.

"Four letters beyond the word 'degree,' we perceive the combination

;46(;88*

"Translating the known characters, and representing the unknown by dots, as before, we read thus:

th . rtee,

an arrangement immediately suggestive of the word 'thirteen,' and again furnishing us with two new characters, *i* and *n*, represented by 6 and *.

"Referring, now, to the beginning of the cryptograph, we find the combination,

53‡‡†,

"Translating as before, we obtain

good,

which assures us that the first letter is *A*, and that the first two words are 'A good.'

"To avoid confusion, it is now time that we arrange our key, as far as discovered, in a tabular form. It will stand thus:

5	represents	a
†	"	d
8	"	e
3	"	g
4	"	h
6	"	i
*	"	n
‡	"	o
(	"	r
;	"	t

"We have, therefore, no less than ten of the most important letters represented, and it will be unnecessary to proceed with the details of the solution. I have said enough to convince you that ciphers of this nature are readily soluble, and to give you some insight into the rationale of their development. But be assured that the specimen before us appertains to the very simplest species of cryptograph. It now only remains to give you the full translation of the characters upon the parchment, 5 as unriddled. Here it is:

"'*A good glass in the bishop's hostel in the devil's seat twenty-one degrees and thirteen minutes northeast and by north main branch seventh limb east side shoot from the left eye of the death's-head a bee line from the tree through the shot fifty feet out.*'"

"But," said I, "the enigma seems still in as bad a condition as ever. How is it possible to extort a meaning from all this jargon about 'devil's seats,' 'death's-heads,' and 'bishop's hotels'?"

"I confess," replied Legrand, "that the matter still wears a serious aspect, when regarded with a casual glance. My first endeavor was to divide the sentence into the natural division intended by the cryptographist."

"You mean, to punctuate it?"

"Something of that kind."

"But how was it possible to effect this?"

"I reflected that it had been a *point* with the writer to run his words together without division, so as to increase the difficulty of solution. Now, a not over-acute man, in pursuing such an object, would be nearly certain to overdo the matter. When, in the course of his composition, he arrived at a break in his subject which would naturally require a pause, or a point, he would be exceedingly apt to run his characters, at this place, more than usually close together. If you will observe the MS., in the present instance, you will easily detect five such cases of unusual crowding. Acting on this hint, I made the division thus:

"'*A good glass in the bishop's hostel in the devil's seat—twenty-one degrees and thirteen minutes—northeast and by north—main branch seventh limb east side—shoot from the left eye of the deaths-head—a bee line from the tree through the shot fifty feet out.*'"

"Even this division," said I, "leaves me still in the dark."

"It left me also in the dark," replied Legrand, "for a few days; during which I made diligent inquiry, in the neighborhood of Sullivan's Island, for any building which went by the name of the 'Bishop's Hotel'; for, of course, I dropped the obsolete word 'hostel.' Gaining no information on the subject, I was on the point of extending my sphere of search, and proceeding in a more systematic manner, when one morning it entered into my head, quite suddenly, that this 'Bishop's Hostel' might have some reference to an old family, of the name of Bessop, which, time out of mind, had held possession of an ancient manor-house, about four miles to the northward of the island. I accordingly went over to the plantation, and reinstituted my inquiries among the older negroes of the place. At length one of the most aged of the women said that she had heard of such a place as *Bessop's Castle*, and thought that she could guide me to it, but that it was not a castle, nor a tavern, but a high rock.

"I offered to pay her well for her trouble, and, after some demur, she consented to accompany me to the spot. We found it without much difficulty, when, dismissing her, I proceeded to examine the place. The 'castle' consisted of an irregular assemblage of cliffs and rocks—one of the latter being quite remarkable for its height as well as for its insulated and artificial appearance. I clambered to its apex, and then felt much at a loss as to what should be next done.

"While I was busied in reflection, my eyes fell on a narrow ledge in the eastern face of the rock, perhaps a yard below the summit upon which I stood. This ledge projected about eighteen inches, and was not more than a foot wide, while a niche in the cliff just above it gave it a rude resemblance to one of the hollow-backed chairs used by our ancestors. I made no doubt that here was the 'devil's seat' alluded to in the MS., and now I seemed to grasp the full secret of the riddle.

"The 'good glass,' I knew, could have reference to nothing but a telescope; for the word 'glass' is rarely employed in any other sense by seamen. Now here, I at once saw, was a telescope to be used, and a definite point of view, *admitting no variation*, from which to use it. Nor did I hesitate to believe that the phrases, 'twenty-one degrees and thirteen minutes,' and 'northeast and by north,' were intended as directions for the levelling of the glass. Greatly excited by these discoveries, I hurried home, procured a telescope, and returned to the rock.

"I let myself down to the ledge, and found that it was impossible to retain a seat on it unless in one particular position. This fact confirmed my preconceived idea. I proceeded to use the glass. Of course, the 'twenty-one degrees and thirteen minutes' could allude to nothing but elevation above the visible horizon, since the horizontal direction was clearly indicated by the words, 'northeast and by north.' This latter direction I at once established by means of a pocket-compass; then, pointing the glass as nearly at an angle of twenty-one degrees of elevation as I could do it by guess, I moved it cautiously up or down, until my attention was arrested by a circular rift or opening in the foliage of a large tree that over-topped its fellows in the distance. In the centre of this rift I perceived a white spot, but could not, at first, distinguish what it was. Adjusting the focus of the telescope, I again looked, and now made it out to be a human skull.

"On this discovery I was so sanguine as to consider the enigma solved; for the phrase 'main branch, seventh limb, east side,' could refer only to the position of the skull on the tree, while 'shoot from the left eye of the death's-head' admitted, also, of but one interpretation, in regard to a search for buried treasure. I perceived that the design was to drop a bullet from the left eye of the skull, and that a bee-line, or, in other words, a straight line, drawn from the nearest point of the trunk through 'the shot' (or the spot where the bullet fell), and thence extended to a distance of fifty feet, would indicate a definite point—and beneath this point I thought it at least *possible* that a deposit of value lay concealed."

"All this," I said, "is exceedingly clear, and, although ingenious, still simple and explicit. When you left the Bishop's Hotel, what then?"

"Why, having carefully taken the bearings of the tree, I turned homewards. The instant that I left 'the devil's seat,' however, the circular rift vanished; nor could I get a glimpse of it afterwards, turn as I would. What seems to me the chief ingenuity in this whole business, is the fact (for repeated experiment has convinced me it *is* a fact) that the circular opening in question is visible from no other attainable point of view than that afforded by the narrow ledge on the face of the rock.

"In this expedition to the 'Bishop's Hotel' I had been attended by Jupiter, who had no doubt observed, for some weeks past, the abstraction of my demeanor, and took especial care not to leave me alone. But on the next day, getting up very early, I contrived to give him the slip, and went into the hills in search of the tree. After much toil I found it. When I came home at night my valet proposed to give me a flogging. With the rest of the adventure I believe you are as well acquainted as myself."

"I suppose," said I, "you missed the spot, in the first attempt at digging, through Jupiter's stupidity in letting the bug fall through the right instead of through the left eye of the skull."

"Precisely. This mistake made a difference of about two inches and a half in the 'shot'—that is to say, in the position of the peg nearest the tree; and had the treasure been *beneath* the 'shot,' the error would have been of little moment; but 'the shot,' together with the nearest point of the tree, were merely two points for the establishment of a line of direction; of course the error, however trivial in the beginning, increased as we proceeded with the line, and, by the time we had gone fifty feet, threw us quite off the scent. But for my deep-seated convictions that treasure was here somewhere actually buried, we might have had all our labor in vain."

"I presume the fancy of *the skull*—of letting fall a bullet through the skull's eye—was suggested to Kidd by the piratical flag. No doubt he felt a kind of poetical consistency in recovering his money through this ominous insignium."

"Perhaps so; still, I cannot help thinking that common sense had quite as much to do with the matter as poetical consistency. To be visible from the devil's seat, it was necessary that the object, if small, should be *white*; and there is nothing like your human skull for retaining and even increasing its whiteness under exposure to all vicissitudes of weather."

"But your grandiloquence, and your conduct in swinging the beetle—how excessively odd! I was sure you were mad. And why did you insist on letting fall the bug, instead of a bullet, from the skull?"

"Why, to be frank, I felt somewhat annoyed by your evident suspicions touching my sanity, and so resolved to punish you quietly, in my own way, by a little bit of sober mystification. For this reason I swung the beetle, and for this reason I let it fall from the tree. An observation of yours about its great weight suggested the latter idea."

"Yes, I perceive; and now there is only one point which puzzles me. What are we to make of the skeletons found in the hole?"

"That is a question I am no more able to answer than yourself. There seems, however, only one plausible way of accounting for them—and yet it is dreadful to believe in such atrocity as my suggestion would imply. It is clear that Kidd—if Kidd indeed secreted this treasure, which I doubt not—it is clear 30 that he must have had assistance in the labor. But, the worst of this labor concluded, he may have thought it expedient to remove all participants in his secret. Perhaps a couple of blows with a mattock were sufficient, while his coadjutors were busy in the pit; perhaps it required a dozen—who shall tell?"

The Masque of the Red Death

The "Red Death" had long devastated the country. No pestilence had ever been so fatal, or so hideous. Blood was its Avatar and its seal—the redness and the horror of blood. There were sharp pains, and sudden dizziness, and then profuse bleeding at the pores, with dissolution. The scarlet stains upon the body and especially upon the face of the victim, were the pest ban which shut him out from the aid and from the sympathy of his fellow-men. And the whole seizure, progress and termination of the disease, were the incidents of half an hour.

But the Prince Prospero was happy and dauntless and sagacious. When his dominions were half depopulated, he summoned to his presence a thousand hale and light-hearted friends from among the knights and dames of his court, and with these retired to the deep seclusion of one of his castellated abbeys. This was an extensive and magnificent structure, the creation of the prince's own eccentric yet august taste. A strong and lofty wall girdled it in. This wall had gates of iron. The courtiers, having entered, brought furnaces and massy hammers and welded the bolts. They resolved to leave means neither of ingress nor egress to the sudden impulses of despair or of frenzy from within. The abbey was amply provisioned. With such precautions the courtiers might bid defiance to contagion. The external world could take care of itself. In the meantime it was folly to grieve, or to think. The prince had provided all the appliances of pleasure. There were buffoons, there were improvisatori, there were ballet-dancers, there were musicians, there was Beauty, there was wine. All these and security were within. Without was the "Red Death".

It was towards the close of the fifth or sixth month of his seclusion, and while the pestilence raged most furiously abroad, that the Prince Prospero entertained his thousand friends at a masked ball of the most unusual magnificence.

It was a voluptuous scene, that masquerade. But first let me tell of the rooms in which it was held. These were seven—an imperial suite. In many palaces, however, such suites form a long and straight vista, while the folding doors slide back nearly to the walls on either hand, so that the view of the whole extent is scarcely impeded. Here the case was very different, as might have been expected from the duke's love of the *bizarre*. The apartments were so irregularly disposed that the vision embraced but little more than one at a time. There was a sharp turn at every twenty or thirty yards, and at each turn a novel effect. To the right and left, in the middle of each wall, a tall and narrow Gothic window looked out upon a closed corridor which pursued the windings of the suite. These windows were of stained glass whose colour varied in accordance with the prevailing hue of the decorations of the chamber into which it opened. That at the eastern extremity was hung, for example in blue—and vividly blue were its windows. The second chamber was purple in its ornaments and tapestries, and here the panes were purple. The third was green throughout, and so were the casements. The fourth was furnished and lighted with orange—the fifth with white—the sixth with violet. The seventh apartment was closely shrouded in black velvet tapestries that hung all over the ceiling and down the walls, falling in heavy folds upon a carpet of the same material and hue. But in this chamber only, the colour of the windows failed to correspond with the decorations. The panes here were scarlet—a deep blood colour. Now in no one of the seven apartments was there any lamp or candelabrum, amid the profusion of golden ornaments that lay scattered to and fro or depended from the roof. There was no light of any kind emanating from lamp or candle within the suite of chambers. But in the corridors that followed the suite, there stood, opposite to each window, a heavy tripod, bearing a brazier of fire, that projected its rays through the tinted glass and so glaringly illumined the room. And thus were produced a multitude of gaudy and fantastic appearances. But in the western or black chamber the effect of the fire-light that streamed upon the dark hangings through the blood-tinted panes, was ghastly in the extreme, and produced so wild a look upon the countenances of those who entered, that there were few of the company bold enough to set foot within its precincts at all.

It was in this apartment, also, that there stood against the western wall, a gigantic clock of ebony. Its pendulum swung to and fro with a dull, heavy, monotonous clang; and when the minute-hand made the circuit of the face, and the hour was to be stricken, there came from the brazen lungs of the clock a sound which was clear and loud and deep and exceedingly musical, but of so peculiar a note and emphasis that, at each lapse of an hour, the musicians of the orchestra were constrained to pause, momentarily, in their performance, to harken to the sound; and thus the waltzers perforce ceased their evolutions; and there was a brief disconcert of the whole gay company; and, while the chimes of the clock yet rang, it was observed that the giddiest grew pale, and the more aged and sedate passed their hands over their brows as if in confused reverie or meditation. But when the echoes had fully ceased, a light laughter at once pervaded the assembly; the musicians looked at each other and smiled as if at their own nervousness and folly, and made whispering vows, each to the other, that the next chiming of the clock should produce in them no similar emotion; and then, after the lapse of sixty minutes, (which embrace three thousand and six hundred seconds of the Time that flies,) there came yet another chiming of the clock, and then were the same disconcert and tremulousness and meditation as before.

But, in spite of these things, it was a gay and magnificent revel. The tastes of the duke were peculiar. He had a fine eye for colours and effects. He disregarded the *decora* of mere fashion. His plans were bold and fiery, and his conceptions glowed with barbaric lustre. There are some who would have thought him mad. His followers felt that he was not. It was necessary to hear and see and touch him to be *sure* that he was not.

He had directed, in great part, the movable embellishments of the seven chambers, upon occasion of this great *fête*; and it was his own guiding taste which had given character to the masqueraders. Be sure they were grotesque. There were much glare and glitter and piquancy and phantasm—much of what has been since seen in "Hernani". There were arabesque figures with unsuited limbs and appointments. There were delirious fancies such as the madman fashions. There were much of the beautiful, much of the wanton, much of the *bizarre*, something of the terrible, and not a little of that which might have excited disgust. To and fro in the seven chambers there stalked, in fact, a multitude of dreams. And these—the dreams—writhed in and about taking hue from the rooms, and causing the wild music of the orchestra to seem as the echo of their steps. And, anon, there strikes the ebony clock which stands in the hall of the velvet. And then, for a moment, all is still, and all is silent save the voice of the clock. The dreams are stiff-frozen as they stand. But the echoes of the chime die away—they have endured but an instant—and a light, half-subdued laughter floats after them as they depart. And now again the music swells, and the dreams live, and writhe to and fro more merrily than ever, taking hue from the many tinted windows through which stream the rays from the tripods. But to the chamber which lies most westwardly of the seven, there are now none of the maskers who venture; for the night is waning away; and there flows a ruddier light through the blood-coloured panes; and the blackness of the sable drapery appals; and to him whose foot falls upon the sable carpet, there comes from the near clock of ebony a muffled peal more solemnly emphatic than any which reaches *their* ears who indulged in the more remote gaieties of the other apartments.

But these other apartments were densely crowded, and in them beat feverishly the heart of life. And the revel went whirlingly on, until at length there commenced the sounding of midnight upon the clock. And then the music ceased, as I have told; and the evolutions of the waltzers were quieted; and there was an uneasy cessation of all things as before. But now there were twelve strokes to be sounded by the bell of the clock; and thus it happened, perhaps, that more of thought crept, with more of time, into the meditations of the thoughtful among those who revelled. And thus too, it happened, perhaps, that before the last echoes of the last chime had utterly sunk into silence, there were many individuals in the crowd who had found leisure to become aware of the presence of a masked figure which had arrested the attention of no single individual before. And the rumour of this new presence having spread itself whisperingly around, there arose at length from the whole company a buzz, or murmur, expressive of disapprobation and surprise—then, finally, of terror, of horror, and of disgust.

In an assembly of phantasms such as I have painted, it may well be supposed that no ordinary appearance could have excited such sensation. In truth the masquerade licence of the night was nearly unlimited; but the figure in question had out-Heroded Herod, and gone beyond the bounds of even the prince's indefinite decorum. There are chords in the hearts of the most reckless which cannot be touched without emotion. Even with the utterly lost, to whom life and death are equally jests, there are matters of which no jest can be made. The whole company, indeed, seemed now deeply to feel that in the costume and bearing of the stranger neither wit nor propriety existed. The figure was tall and gaunt, and shrouded from head to foot in the habiliments of the grave. The mask which concealed the visage was made so nearly to resemble the countenance of a stiffened corpse that the closest scrutiny must have had difficulty in detecting the cheat. And yet all this might have been endured, if not approved, by the mad revellers around. But the mummer had gone so far as to assume the type of the Red Death. His vesture was dabbled in *blood*—

and his broad brow, with all the features of the face, was besprinkled with the scarlet horror.

When the eyes of the Prince Prospero fell upon this spectral image (which, with a slow and solemn movement, as if more fully to sustain its role, stalked to and fro among the waltzers) he was seen to be convulsed, in the first moment with a strong shudder either of terror or distaste; but, in the next, his brow reddened with rage.

"Who dares,"—he demanded hoarsely of the courtiers who stood near him—"who dares insult us with this blasphemous mockery? Seize him and unmask him—that we may know whom we have to hang, at sunrise, from the battlements!"

It was in the eastern or blue chamber in which stood the Prince Prospero as he uttered these words. They rang throughout the seven rooms loudly and clearly, for the prince was a bold and robust man, and the music had become hushed at the waving of his hand.

It was in the blue room where stood the prince, with a group of pale courtiers by his side. At first, as he spoke, there was a slight rushing movement of this group in the direction of the intruder, who at the moment was also near at hand, and now, with deliberate and stately step, made closer approach to the speaker. But from a certain nameless awe with which the mad assumptions of the mummer had inspired the whole party, there were found none who put forth hand to seize him; so that, unimpeded, he passed within a yard of the prince's person; and, while the vast assembly, as if with one impulse, shrank from the centres of the rooms to the walls, he made his way uninterruptedly, but with the same solemn and measured step which had distinguished him from the first, through the blue chamber to the purple—through the purple to the green—through the green to the orange—through this again to the white—and even thence to the violet, ere a decided movement had been made to arrest him. It was then, however, that the Prince Prospero, maddening with rage and the shame of his own momentary cowardice, rushed hurriedly through the six chambers, while none followed him on account of a deadly terror that had seized upon all. He bore aloft a drawn dagger, and had approached, in rapid impetuosity, to within three or four feet of the retreating figure, when the latter, having attained the extremity of the velvet apartment, turned suddenly and confronted his pursuer. There was a sharp cry—and the dagger dropped gleaming upon the sable carpet, upon which, instantly afterwards, fell prostrate in death the Prince Prospero. Then, summoning the wild courage of despair, a throng of the revellers at once threw themselves into the black apartment, and, seizing the mummer, whose tall figure stood erect and motionless within the shadow of the ebony clock, gasped in unutterable horror at finding the grave cerements and corpse-like mask, which they handled with so violent a rudeness, untenanted by any tangible form.

And now was acknowledged the presence of the Red Death. He had come like a thief in the night. And one by one dropped the revellers in the blood-bedewed halls of their revel, and died each in the despairing posture of his fall. And the life of the ebony clock went out with that of the last of the gay. And the flames of the tripods expired. And Darkness and Decay and the Red Death held illimitable dominion over all.

The Murders in the Rue Morgue

What song the Syrens sang, or what name Achilles assumed when he hid himself among women, although puzzling questions, are not beyond all *conjecture.*

—*Sir Thomas Browne*

The mental features discoursed of as the analytical, are, in themselves, but little susceptible of analysis. We appreciate them only in their effects. We know of them, among other things, that they are always to their possessor, when inordinately possessed, a source of the liveliest enjoyment. As the strong man exults in his physical ability, delighting in such exercises as call his muscles into action, so glories the analyst in that moral activity which *disentangles.* He derives pleasure from even the most trivial occupations bringing his talent into play. He is fond of enigmas, of conundrums, of hieroglyphics; exhibiting in his solutions of each a degree of *acumen* which appears to the ordinary apprehension præternatural. His results, brought about by the very soul and essence of method, have, in truth, the whole air of intuition.

The faculty of re-solution is possibly much invigorated by mathematical study, and especially by that highest branch of it which, unjustly, and merely on account of its retrograde operations, has been called, as if *par excellence*, analysis. Yet to calculate is not in itself to analyse. A chess-player, for example, does the one without effort at the other. It follows that the game of chess, in its effects upon mental character, is greatly misunderstood. I am not now writing a treatise, but simply prefacing a somewhat peculiar narrative by observations very much at random; I will, therefore, take occasion to assert that the higher powers of the reflective intellect are more decidedly and more usefully tasked by the unostentatious game of draughts than by all the elaborate frivolity of chess. In this latter, where the pieces have different and *bizarre* motions, with various and variable values, what is only complex is mistaken (a not unusual error) for what is profound. The *attention* is here called powerfully into play. If it flag for an instant, an oversight is committed resulting in injury or defeat. The possible moves being not only manifold but involute, the chances of such oversights are multiplied; and in nine cases out of ten it is the more concentrative rather than the more acute player who conquers.

In draughts, on the contrary, where the moves are *unique* and have but little variation, the probabilities of inadvertence are diminished, and the mere attention being left comparatively unemployed, what advantages are obtained by either party are obtained by superior *acumen*. To be less abstract—Let us suppose a game of draughts where the pieces are reduced to four kings, and where, of course, no oversight is to be expected. It is obvious that here the victory can be decided (the players being at all equal) only by some *recherché* movement, the result of some strong exertion of the intellect. Deprived of ordinary resources, the analyst throws himself into the spirit of his opponent, identifies himself therewith, and not unfrequently sees thus, at a glance, the sole methods (sometime indeed absurdly simple ones) by which he may seduce into error or hurry into miscalculation.

Whist has long been noted for its influence upon what is termed the calculating power; and men of the highest order of intellect have been known to take an apparently unaccountable delight in it, while eschewing chess as frivolous. Beyond doubt there is nothing of a similar nature so greatly tasking the faculty of analysis. The best chess-player in Christendom *may* be little more than the best player of chess; but proficiency in whist implies capacity for success in all those more important undertakings where mind struggles with mind. When I say proficiency, I mean that perfection in the game which includes a comprehension of *all* the sources whence legitimate advantage may be derived. These are not only manifold but multiform, and lie frequently among recesses of thought altogether inaccessible to the ordinary understanding. To observe attentively is to remember distinctly; and, so far, the concentrative chess-player will do very well at whist; while the rules of Hoyle (themselves based upon the mere mechanism of the game) are sufficiently and generally comprehensible. Thus to have a retentive memory, and to proceed by "the book," are points commonly regarded as the sum total of good playing. But it is in matters beyond the limits of mere rule that the skill of the analyst is evinced. He makes, in silence, a host of observations and inferences. So, perhaps, do his companions; and the difference in the extent of the information obtained, lies not so much in the validity of the inference as in the quality of the observation. The necessary knowledge is that of *what* to observe. Our player confines himself not at all; nor, because the game is the object, does he reject deductions from things external to the game. He examines the countenance of his partner, comparing it carefully with that of each of his opponents. He considers the mode of assorting the cards in each hand; often counting trump by trump, and honor by honor, through the glances bestowed by their holders upon each. He notes every variation of face as the play progresses, gathering a fund of thought from the differences in the expression of certainty, of surprise, of triumph, or of chagrin. From the manner of gathering up a trick he judges whether the person taking it can make another in the suit. He recognises what is played through feint, by the air with which it is thrown upon the table. A casual or inadvertent word; the accidental dropping or turning of a card, with the accompanying anxiety or carelessness in regard to its concealment; the counting of the tricks, with the order of their arrangement; embarrassment, hesitation, eagerness or trepidation—all afford, to his apparently intuitive perception, indications of the true state of affairs. The first two or three rounds having been played, he is in full possession of the contents of each hand, and thenceforward puts down his cards with as absolute a precision of purpose as if the rest of the party had turned outward the faces of their own.

The analytical power should not be confounded with ample ingenuity; for while the analyst is necessarily ingenious, the ingenious man is often remarkably incapable of analysis. The constructive or combining power, by which ingenuity is usually manifested, and to which the phrenologists (I believe erroneously) have assigned a separate organ, supposing it a primitive faculty, has been so frequently seen in those whose intellect bordered otherwise upon idiocy, as to have attracted general observation among writers on morals. Between ingenuity and the analytic ability there exists a difference far greater, indeed, than that between the fancy and the imagination, but of a character very strictly analogous. It will be found, in fact, that the ingenious are always fanciful, and the *truly* imaginative never otherwise than analytic.

The narrative which follows will appear to the reader somewhat in the light of a commentary upon the propositions just advanced.

Residing in Paris during the spring and part of the summer of 18—, I there became acquainted with a Monsieur C. Auguste Dupin. This young gentleman was of an excellent—indeed of an illustrious family, but, by a variety of untoward events, had been reduced to such poverty that the energy of his character succumbed beneath it, and he ceased to bestir himself in the world, or to care for the retrieval of his fortunes. By courtesy of his creditors, there still remained in his possession a small remnant of his patrimony; and, upon the income arising from this, he managed, by means of a rigorous economy, to procure the necessaries of life, without troubling himself about its superfluities. Books, indeed, were his sole luxuries, and in Paris these are easily obtained.

Our first meeting was at an obscure library in the Rue Montmartre, where the accident of our both being in search of the same very rare and very remarkable volume, brought us into closer communion. We saw each other again and again. I was deeply interested in the little family history which he detailed to me with all that candor which a Frenchman indulges whenever mere self is his theme. I was astonished, too, at the vast extent of his reading; and, above all, I felt my soul enkindled within me by the wild fervor, and the vivid freshness of his imagination. Seeking in Paris the objects I then sought, I felt that the society of such a man would be to me a treasure beyond price; and this feeling I frankly confided to him. It was at length arranged that we should live together during my stay in the city; and as my worldly circumstances were somewhat less embarrassed than his own, I was permitted to be at the expense of renting, and furnishing in a style which suited the rather fantastic gloom of our common temper, a time-eaten and grotesque mansion, long deserted through superstitions into which we did not inquire, and tottering to its fall in a retired and desolate portion of the Faubourg St. Germain.

Had the routine of our life at this place been known to the world, we should have been regarded as madmen—although, perhaps, as madmen of a harmless nature. Our seclusion was perfect. We admitted no visitors. Indeed the locality of our retirement had been carefully kept a secret from my own former associates; and it had been many years since Dupin had ceased to know or be known in Paris. We existed within ourselves alone.

It was a freak of fancy in my friend (for what else shall I call it?) to be enamored of the Night for her own sake; and into this *bizarrerie*, as into all his others, I quietly fell; giving myself up to his wild whims with a perfect *abandon*. The sable divinity would not herself dwell with us always; but we could counterfeit her presence. At the first dawn of the morning we closed all the messy shutters of our old building; lighting a couple of tapers which, strongly perfumed, threw out only the ghastliest and feeblest of rays. By the aid of these we then busied our souls in dreams—reading, writing, or conversing, until warned by the clock of the advent of the true Darkness. Then we sallied forth into the streets arm in arm, continuing the topics of the day, or roaming far and wide until a late hour, seeking, amid the wild lights and shadows of the populous city, that infinity of mental excitement which quiet observation can afford.

At such times I could not help remarking and admiring (although from his rich ideality I had been prepared to expect it) a peculiar analytic ability in Dupin. He seemed, too, to take an eager delight in its exercise—if not exactly in its display—and did not hesitate to confess the pleasure thus derived. He boasted to me, with a low chuckling laugh, that most men, in respect to himself, wore windows in their bosoms, and was wont to follow up such assertions by direct and very startling proofs of his intimate knowledge of my own. His manner at these moments was frigid and abstract; his eyes were vacant in expression; while his voice, usually a rich tenor, rose into a treble which would have sounded petulantly but for the deliberateness and entire distinctness of the enunciation. Observing him in these moods, I often dwelt meditatively upon the old philosophy of the Bi-Part Soul, and amused myself with the fancy of a double Dupin—the creative and the resolvent.

Let it not be supposed, from what I have just said, that I am detailing any mystery, or penning any romance. What I have described in the Frenchman, was merely the result of an excited, or perhaps of a diseased intelligence. But of the character of his remarks at the periods in question an example will best convey the idea.

We were strolling one night down a long dirty street in the vicinity of the Palais Royal. Being both, apparently, occupied with thought, neither of us had spoken a syllable for fifteen minutes at least. All at once Dupin broke forth with these words:

"He is a very little fellow, that's true, and would do better for the *Théâtre des Variétés*."

"There can be no doubt of that," I replied unwittingly, and not at first observing (so much had I been absorbed in reflection) the extraordinary manner in which the speaker had chimed in with my meditations. In an instant afterward I recollected myself, and my astonishment was profound.

"Dupin," said I, gravely, "this is beyond my comprehension. I do not hesitate to say that I am amazed, and can scarcely credit my senses. How was it possible you should know I was thinking of—?" Here I paused, to ascertain beyond a doubt whether he really knew of whom I thought.

—"of Chantilly," said he, "why do you pause? You were remarking to yourself that his diminutive figure unfitted him for tragedy."

This was precisely what had formed the subject of my reflections. Chantilly was a *quondam* cobbler of the Rue St. Denis, who, becoming stage-mad, had attempted the *rôle* of Xerxes, in Crébillon's tragedy so called, and been notoriously Pasquinaded for his pains.

"Tell me, for Heaven's sake," I exclaimed, "the method—if method there is—by which you have been enabled to fathom my soul in this matter." In fact I was even more startled than I would have been willing to express.

"It was the fruiterer," replied my friend, "who brought you to the conclusion that the mender of soles was not of sufficient height for Xerxes *et id genus omne*."

"The fruiterer!—you astonish me—I know no fruiterer whomsoever."

"The man who ran up against you as we entered the street—it may have been fifteen minutes ago."

I now remembered that, in fact, a fruiterer, carrying upon his head a large basket of apples, had nearly thrown me down, by accident, as we passed from the Rue C—into the thoroughfare where we stood; but what this had to do with Chantilly I could not possibly understand.

There was not a particle of *charlatanerie* about Dupin. "I will explain," he said, "and that you may comprehend all clearly, we will first retrace the course of your meditations, from the moment in which I spoke to you until that of the *rencontre* with the fruiterer in question. The larger links of the chain run thus—Chantilly, Orion, Dr. Nichols, Epicurus, Stereotomy, the street stones, the fruiterer."

There are few persons who have not, at some period of their lives, amused themselves in retracing the steps by which particular conclusions of their own minds have been attained. The occupation is often full of interest and he who attempts it for the first time is astonished by the apparently illimitable distance and incoherence between the starting-point and the goal. What, then, must have been my amazement when I heard the Frenchman speak what he had just spoken, and when I could not help acknowledging that he had spoken the truth. He continued:

"We had been talking of horses, if I remember aright, just before leaving the Rue C—. This was the last subject we discussed. As we crossed into this street, a fruiterer, with a large basket upon his head, brushing quickly past us, thrust you upon a pile of paving stones collected at a spot where the causeway is undergoing repair. You stepped upon one of the loose fragments, slipped, slightly strained your ankle, appeared vexed or sulky, muttered a few words, turned to look at the pile, and then proceeded in silence. I was not particularly attentive to what you did; but observation has become with me, of late, a species of necessity.

"You kept your eyes upon the ground—glancing, with a petulant expression, at the holes and ruts in the pavement, (so that I saw you were still thinking of the stones,) until we reached the little alley called Lamartine, which has been paved, by way of experiment, with the overlapping and riveted blocks. Here your countenance brightened up, and, perceiving your lips move, I could not doubt that you murmured the word 'stereotomy,' a term very affectedly applied to this species of pavement. I knew that you could not say to yourself 'stereotomy' without being brought to think of atomies, and thus of the theories of Epicurus; and since, when we discussed this subject not very long ago, I mentioned to you how singularly, yet with how little notice, the vague guesses of that noble Greek had met with confirmation in the late nebular cosmogony, I felt that you could not avoid casting your eyes upward to the great *nebula* in Orion, and I certainly expected that you would do so. You did look up; and I was now assured that I had correctly followed your steps. But in that bitter *tirade* upon Chantilly, which appeared in yesterday's '*Musée*,' the satirist, making some disgraceful allusions to the cobbler's change of name upon assuming the buskin, quoted a Latin line about which we have often conversed. I mean the line

Perdidit antiquum litera sonum.

"I had told you that this was in reference to Orion, formerly written Urion; and, from certain pungencies connected with this explanation, I was aware that you could not have forgotten it. It was clear, therefore, that you would not fail to combine the two ideas of Orion and Chantilly. That you did combine them I saw by the character of the smile which passed over your lips. You thought of the poor cobbler's immolation. So far, you had been stooping in your gait; but now I saw you draw yourself up to your full height. I was then sure that you reflected upon the diminutive figure of Chantilly. At this point I interrupted your meditations to remark that as, in fact, he was a very little fellow—that Chantilly—he would do better at the *Théâtre des Variétés*."

Not long after this, we were looking over an evening edition of the "Gazette des Tribunaux," when the following paragraphs arrested our attention.

"Extraordinary Murders.—This morning, about three o'clock, the inhabitants of the Quartier St. Roch were aroused from sleep by a succession of terrific shrieks, issuing, apparently, from the fourth story of a house in the Rue Morgue, known to be in the sole occupancy of one Madame L'Espanaye, and her daughter Mademoiselle Camille L'Espanaye. After some delay, occasioned by a fruitless attempt to procure admission in the usual manner, the gateway was broken in with a crowbar, and eight or ten of the neighbors entered accompanied by two *gendarmes*. By this time the cries had ceased; but, as the party rushed up the first flight of stairs, two or more rough voices in angry contention were distinguished and seemed to proceed from the upper part of the house. As the second landing was reached, these sounds, also, had ceased and everything remained perfectly quiet. The party spread themselves and hurried from room to room. Upon arriving at a large back chamber in the fourth story, (the door of which, being found locked, with the key inside, was forced open,) a spectacle presented itself which struck every one present not less with horror than with astonishment.

"The apartment was in the wildest disorder—the furniture broken and thrown about in all directions. There was only one bedstead; and from this the bed had been removed, and thrown into the middle of the floor. On a chair lay a razor, besmeared with blood. On the hearth were two or three long and thick tresses of grey human hair, also dabbled in blood, and seeming to have been pulled out by the roots. Upon the floor were found four Napoleons, an ear-ring of topaz, three large silver spoons, three smaller of *métal d'Alger*, and two bags, containing nearly four thousand francs in gold. The drawers of a *bureau*, which stood in one corner were open, and had been, apparently, rifled, although many articles still remained in them. A small iron safe was discovered under the *bed* (not under the bedstead). It was open, with the key still in the door. It had no contents beyond a few old letters, and other papers of little consequence.

"Of Madame L'Espanaye no traces were here seen; but an unusual quantity of soot being observed in the fire-place, a search was made in the chimney, and (horrible to relate!) the corpse of the daughter, head downward, was dragged therefrom; it having been thus forced up the narrow aperture for a considerable distance. The body was quite warm. Upon examining it, many excoriations were perceived, no doubt occasioned by the violence with which it had been thrust up and disengaged. Upon the face were many severe scratches, and, upon the throat, dark bruises, and deep indentations of finger nails, as if the deceased had been throttled to death.

"After a thorough investigation of every portion of the house, without farther discovery, the party made its way into a small paved yard in the rear of the building, where lay the corpse of the old lady, with her throat so entirely cut that, upon an attempt to raise her, the head fell off. The body, as well as the head, was fearfully mutilated—the former so much so as scarcely to retain any semblance of humanity.

"To this horrible mystery there is not as yet, we believe, the slightest clew."

The next day's paper had these additional particulars.

"*The Tragedy in the Rue Morgue.* Many individuals have been examined in relation to this most extraordinary and frightful affair. (The word 'affaire' has not yet, in France, that levity of import which it conveys with us,) "but nothing whatever has transpired to throw light upon it. We give below all the material testimony elicited.

"*Pauline Dubourg*, laundress, deposes that she has known both the deceased for three years, having washed for them during that period. The old lady and her daughter seemed on good terms—very affectionate towards each other. They were excellent pay. Could not speak in regard to their mode or means of living. Believed that Madame L. told fortunes for a living. Was reputed to have money put by. Never met any persons in the house when she called for the clothes or took them home. Was sure that they had no servant in employ. There appeared to be no furniture in any part of the building except in the fourth story.

"*Pierre Moreau*, tobacconist, deposes that he has been in the habit of selling small quantities of tobacco and snuff to Madame L'Espanaye for nearly four years. Was born in the neighborhood, and has always resided there. The deceased and her daughter had occupied the house in which the corpses were found, for more than six years. It was formerly occupied by a jeweller, who under-let the upper rooms to various persons. The house was the property of Madame L. She became dissatisfied with the abuse of the premises by her tenant, and moved into them herself, refusing to let any portion. The old lady was childish. Witness had seen the daughter some five or six times during the six years. The two lived an exceedingly retired life—were reputed to have money. Had heard it said among the neighbors that Madame L. told fortunes—did not believe it. Had never seen any person enter the door except the old lady and her daughter, a porter once or twice, and a physician some eight or ten times.

"Many other persons, neighbors, gave evidence to the same effect. No one was spoken of as frequenting the house. It was not known whether there were any living connexions of Madame L. and her daughter. The shutters of the front windows were seldom opened. Those in the rear were always closed, with the exception of the large back room, fourth story. The house was a good house—not very old.

"*Isidore Muset*, *gendarme*, deposes that he was called to the house about three o'clock in the morning, and found some twenty or thirty persons at the gateway, endeavoring to gain admittance. Forced it open, at length, with a bayonet—not with a crowbar. Had but little difficulty in getting it open, on account of its being a double or folding gate, and bolted neither at bottom not top. The shrieks were continued until the gate was forced—and then suddenly ceased. They seemed to be screams of some person (or persons) in great agony—were loud and drawn out, not short and quick. Witness led the way up stairs. Upon reaching the first landing, heard two voices in loud and angry contention—the one a gruff voice, the other much shriller—a very strange voice. Could distinguish some words of the former, which was that of a Frenchman. Was positive that it was not a woman's voice. Could distinguish the words '*sacré*' and '*diable*.' The shrill voice was that of a foreigner. Could not be sure whether it was the voice of a man or of a woman. Could not make out what was said, but believed the language to be Spanish. The state of the room and of the bodies was described by this witness as we described them yesterday.

"*Henri Duval*, a neighbor, and by trade a silver-smith, deposes that he was one of the party who first entered the house. Corroborates the testimony of Muset in general. As soon as they forced an entrance, they reclosed the door, to keep out the crowd, which collected very fast, notwithstanding the lateness of the hour. The shrill voice, this witness thinks, was that of an Italian. Was certain it was not French. Could not be sure that it was a man's voice. It might have been a woman's. Was not acquainted with the Italian language. Could not distinguish the words, but was convinced by the intonation that the speaker was an Italian. Knew Madame L. and her daughter. Had conversed with both frequently. Was sure that the shrill voice was not that of either of the deceased.

"—*Odenheimer, restaurateur.* This witness volunteered his testimony. Not speaking French, was examined through an interpreter. Is a native of Amsterdam. Was passing the house at the time of the shrieks. They lasted for several minutes—probably ten. They were long and loud—very awful and distressing. Was one of those who entered the building. Corroborated the previous evidence in every respect but one. Was sure that the shrill voice was that of a man—of a Frenchman. Could not distinguish the words uttered. They were loud and quick—unequal—spoken apparently in fear as well as in anger. The voice was harsh—not so much shrill as harsh. Could not call it a shrill voice. The gruff voice said repeatedly '*sacré*,' '*diable*,' and once '*mon Dieu.*'

"*Jules Mignaud*, banker, of the firm of Mignaud et Fils, Rue Deloraine. Is the elder Mignaud. Madame L'Espanaye had some property. Had opened an account with his banking house in the spring of the year—(eight years previously). Made frequent deposits in small sums. Had checked for nothing until the third day before her death, when she took out in person the sum of 4000 francs. This sum was paid in gold, and a clerk went home with the money.

"*Adolphe Le Bon*, clerk to Mignaud et Fils, deposes that on the day in question, about noon, he accompanied Madame L'Espanaye to her residence with the 4000 francs, put up in two bags. Upon the door being opened, Mademoiselle L. appeared and took from his hands one of the bags, while the old lady relieved him of the other. He then bowed and departed. Did not see any person in the street at the time. It is a bye-street—very lonely.

"*William Bird*, tailor deposes that he was one of the party who entered the house. Is an Englishman. Has lived in Paris two years. Was one of the first to ascend the stairs. Heard the voices in contention. The gruff voice was that of a Frenchman. Could make out several words, but cannot now remember all. Heard distinctly '*sacré*' and '*mon Dieu.*' There was a sound at the moment as if of several persons struggling—a scraping and scuffling sound. The shrill voice was very loud—louder than the gruff one. Is sure that it was not the voice of an Englishman. Appeared to be that of a German. Might have been a woman's voice. Does not understand German.

"Four of the above-named witnesses, being recalled, deposed that the door of the chamber in which was found the body of Mademoiselle L. was locked on the inside when the party reached it. Every thing was perfectly silent—no groans or noises of any kind. Upon forcing the door no person was seen. The windows, both of the back and front room, were down and firmly fastened from within. A door between the two rooms was closed, but not locked. The door leading from the front room into the passage was locked, with the key on the inside. A small room in the front of the house, on the fourth story, at the head of the passage was open, the door being ajar. This room was crowded with old beds, boxes, and so forth. These were carefully removed and searched. There was not an inch of any portion of the house which was not carefully searched. Sweeps were sent up and down the chimneys. The house was a four story one, with garrets (*mansardes.*) A trap-door on the roof was nailed down very securely—did not appear to have been opened for years. The time elapsing between the hearing of the voices in contention and the breaking open of the room door, was variously stated by the witnesses. Some made it as short as three minutes—some as long as five. The door was opened with difficulty.

"*Alfonzo Garcio*, undertaker, deposes that he resides in the Rue Morgue. Is a native of Spain. Was one of the party who entered the house. Did not proceed up stairs. Is nervous, and was apprehensive of the consequences of agitation. Heard the voices in contention. The gruff voice was that of a Frenchman. Could not distinguish what was said. The shrill voice was that of an Englishman—is sure of this. Does not understand the English language, but judges by the intonation.

"*Alberto Montani*, confectioner, deposes that he was among the first to ascend the stairs. Heard the voices in question. The gruff voice was that of a Frenchman. Distinguished several words. The speaker appeared to be expostulating. Could not make out the words of the shrill voice. Spoke quick and unevenly. Thinks it the voice of a Russian. Corroborates the general testimony. Is an Italian. Never conversed with a native of Russia.

"Several witnesses, recalled, here testified that the chimneys of all the rooms on the fourth story were too narrow to admit the passage of a human being. By 'sweeps' were meant cylindrical sweeping brushes, such as are employed by those who clean chimneys. These brushes were passed up and down every flue in the house. There is no back passage by which any one could have descended while the party proceeded up stairs. The body of Mademoiselle L'Espanaye was so firmly wedged in the chimney that it could not be got down until four or five of the party united their strength.

"*Paul Dumas*, physician, deposes that he was called to view the bodies about day-break. They were both then lying on the sacking of the bedstead in the chamber where Mademoiselle L. was found. The corpse of the young lady was much bruised and excoriated. The fact that it had been thrust up the chimney would sufficiently account for these appearances. The throat was greatly chafed. There were several deep scratches just below the chin, together with a series of livid spots which were evidently the impression of fingers. The face was fearfully discolored, and the eye-balls protruded. The tongue had been partially bitten through. A large bruise was discovered upon the pit of the stomach, produced, apparently, by the pressure of a knee. In the opinion of M. Dumas, Mademoiselle L'Espanaye had been throttled to death by some person or persons unknown. The corpse of the mother was horribly mutilated. All the bones of the right leg and arm were more or less shattered. The left *tibia* much splintered, as well as all the ribs of the left side. Whole body dreadfully bruised and discolored. It was not possible to say how the injuries had been inflicted. A heavy club of wood, or a broad bar of iron—a chair—any large, heavy, and obtuse weapon would have produced such results, if wielded by the hands of a very powerful man. No woman could have inflicted the blows with any weapon. The head of the deceased, when seen by witness, was entirely separated from the body, and was also greatly shattered. The throat had evidently been cut with some very sharp instrument—probably with a razor.

"*Alexandre Etienne*, surgeon, was called with M. Dumas to view the bodies. Corroborated the testimony, and the opinions of M. Dumas.

"Nothing farther of importance was elicited, although several other persons were examined. A murder so mysterious, and so perplexing in all its particulars, was never before committed in Paris—if indeed a murder has been committed at all. The police are entirely at fault—an unusual occurrence in affairs of this nature. There is not, however, the shadow of a clew apparent."

The evening edition of the paper stated that the greatest excitement still continued in the Quartier St. Roch—that the premises in question had been carefully re-searched, and fresh examinations of witnesses instituted, but all to no purpose. A postscript, however, mentioned that Adolphe Le Bon had been arrested and imprisoned—although nothing appeared to criminate him, beyond the facts already detailed.

Dupin seemed singularly interested in the progress of this affair—at least so I judged from his manner, for he made no comments. It was only after the announcement that Le Bon had been imprisoned, that he asked me my opinion respecting the murders.

I could merely agree with all Paris in considering them an insoluble mystery. I saw no means by which it would be possible to trace the murderer.

"We must not judge of the means," said Dupin, "by this shell of an examination. The Parisian police, so much extolled for *acumen*, are cunning, but no more. There is no method in their proceedings, beyond the method of the moment. They make a vast parade of measures; but, not unfrequently, these are so ill adapted to the objects proposed, as to put us in mind of Monsieur Jourdain's calling for his *robe-de-chambre—pour mieux entendre la musique.* The results attained by them are not unfrequently surprising, but, for the most part, are brought about by simple diligence and activity. When these qualities are unavailing, their schemes fail. Vidocq, for example, was a good guesser and a persevering man. But, without educated thought, he erred continually by the very intensity of his investigations. He impaired his vision by holding the object too close. He might see, perhaps, one or two points with unusual clearness, but in so doing he, necessarily, lost sight of the matter as a whole. Thus there is such a thing as being too profound. Truth is not always in a well. In fact, as regards the more important knowledge, I do believe that she is invariably superficial. The depth lies in the valleys where we seek her, and not upon the mountain-tops where she is found. The modes and sources of this kind of error are well typified in the contemplation of the heavenly bodies. To look at a star by glances—to view it in a side-long way, by turning toward it the exterior portions of the *retina* (more susceptible of feeble impressions of light than the interior), is to behold the star distinctly—is to have the best appreciation of its lustre—a lustre which grows dim just in proportion as we turn our vision *fully* upon it. A greater number of rays actually fall upon the eye in the latter case, but, in the former, there is the more refined capacity for comprehension. By undue profundity we perplex and enfeeble thought; and it is possible to make even Venus herself vanish from the firmament by a scrutiny too sustained, too concentrated, or too direct.

"As for these murders, let us enter into some examinations for ourselves, before we make up an opinion respecting them. An inquiry will afford us amusement," (I thought this an odd term, so applied, but said nothing) "and, besides, Le Bon once rendered me a service for which I am not ungrateful. We will go and see the premises with our own eyes. I know G——, the Prefect of Police, and shall have no difficulty in obtaining the necessary permission."

The permission was obtained, and we proceeded at once to the Rue Morgue. This is one of those miserable thoroughfares which intervene between the Rue Richelieu and the Rue St. Roch. It was late in the afternoon when we reached it; as this quarter is at a great distance from that in which we resided. The house was readily found; for there were still many persons gazing up at the closed shutters, with an objectless curiosity, from the opposite side of the way. It was an ordinary Parisian house, with a gateway, on one side of which was a glazed watch-box, with a sliding panel in the window, indicating a *loge de concierge.* Before going in we walked up the street, turned down an alley, and then, again turning, passed in the rear of the building—Dupin, meanwhile examining the whole neighborhood, as well as the house, with a minuteness of attention for which I could see no possible object.

Retracing our steps, we came again to the front of the dwelling, rang, and, having shown our credentials, were admitted by the agents in charge. We went up stairs—into the chamber where the body of Mademoiselle L'Espanaye had been found, and where both the deceased still lay. The disorders of the room had, as usual, been suffered to exist. I saw nothing beyond what had been stated in the "Gazette des Tribunaux." Dupin scrutinized every thing—not excepting the bodies of the victims. We then went into the other rooms, and into the yard; a *gendarme* accompanying us throughout. The examination occupied us until dark, when we took our departure. On our way home my companion stepped in for a moment at the office of one of the daily papers.

I have said that the whims of my friend were manifold, and that *Je les ménageais*:—for this phrase there is no English equivalent. It was his humor, now, to decline all conversation on the subject of the murder, until about noon the next day. He then asked me, suddenly, if I had observed any thing *peculiar* at the scene of the atrocity.

There was something in his manner of emphasizing the word "peculiar," which caused me to shudder, without knowing why.

"No, nothing *peculiar*," I said; "nothing more, at least, than we both saw stated in the paper."

"The 'Gazette,'" he replied, "has not entered, I fear, into the unusual horror of the thing. But dismiss the idle opinions of this print. It appears to me that this mystery is considered insoluble, for the very reason which should cause it to be regarded as easy of solution—I mean for the *outré* character of its features. The police are confounded by the seeming absence of motive—not for the murder itself—but for the atrocity of the murder. They are puzzled, too, by the seeming impossibility of reconciling the voices heard in contention, with the facts that no one was discovered up stairs but the assassinated Mademoiselle L'Espanaye, and that there were no means of egress without the notice of the party ascending. The wild disorder of the room; the corpse thrust, with the head downward, up the chimney; the frightful mutilation of the body of the old lady; these considerations, with those just mentioned, and others which I need not mention, have sufficed to paralyze the powers, by putting completely at fault the boasted *acumen*, of the government agents. They have fallen into the gross but common error of confounding the unusual with the abstruse. But it is by these deviations from the plane of the ordinary, that reason feels its way, if at all, in its search for the true. In investigations such as we are now pursuing, it should not be so much asked 'what has occurred,' as 'what has occurred that has never occurred before.' In fact, the facility with which I shall arrive, or have arrived, at the solution of this mystery, is in the direct ratio of its apparent insolubility in the eyes of the police."

I stared at the speaker in mute astonishment.

"I am now awaiting," continued he, looking toward the door of our apartment—"I am now awaiting a person who, although perhaps not the perpetrator of these butcheries, must have been in some measure implicated in their perpetration. Of the worst portion of the crimes committed, it is probable that he is innocent. I hope that I am right in this supposition; for upon it I build my expectation of reading the entire riddle. I look for the man here—in this room—every moment. It is true that he may not arrive; but the probability is that he will. Should he come, it will be necessary to detain him. Here are pistols; and we both know how to use them when occasion demands their use."

I took the pistols, scarcely knowing what I did, or believing what I heard, while Dupin went on, very much as if in a soliloquy. I have already spoken of his abstract manner at such times. His discourse was addressed to myself; but his voice, although by no means loud, had that intonation which is commonly employed in speaking to some one at a great distance. His eyes, vacant in expression, regarded only the wall.

"That the voices heard in contention," he said, "by the party upon the stairs, were not the voices of the women themselves, was fully proved by the evidence. This relieves us of all doubt upon the question whether the old lady could have first destroyed the daughter and afterward have committed suicide. I speak of this point chiefly for the sake of method; for the strength of Madame L'Espanaye would have been utterly unequal to the task of thrusting her daughter's corpse up the chimney as it was found; and the nature of the wounds upon her own person entirely preclude the idea of self-destruction. Murder, then, has been committed by some third party; and the voices of this third party were those heard in contention. Let me now advert—not to the whole testimony respecting these voices—but to what was *peculiar* in that testimony. Did you observe any thing peculiar about it?"

I remarked that, while all the witnesses agreed in supposing the gruff voice to be that of a Frenchman, there was much disagreement in regard to the shrill, or, as one individual termed it, the harsh voice.

"That was the evidence itself," said Dupin, "but it was not the peculiarity of the evidence. You have observed nothing distinctive. Yet there *was* something to be observed. The witnesses, as you remark, agreed about the gruff voice; they were here unanimous. But in regard to the shrill voice, the peculiarity is—not that they disagreed—but that, while an Italian, an Englishman, a Spaniard, a Hollander, and a Frenchman attempted to describe it, each one spoke of it as that *of a foreigner*. Each is sure that it was not the voice of one of his own countrymen. Each likens it—not to the voice of an individual of any nation with whose language he is conversant—but the converse. The Frenchman supposes it the voice of a Spaniard, and 'might have distinguished some words *had he been acquainted with the Spanish.*' The Dutchman maintains it to have been that of a Frenchman; but we find it stated that '*not understanding French this witness was examined through an interpreter.*' The Englishman thinks it the voice of a German, and '*does not understand German.*' The Spaniard 'is sure' that it was that of an Englishman, but 'judges by the intonation' altogether, '*as he has no knowledge of the English.*' The Italian believes it the voice of a Russian, but '*has never conversed with a native of Russia.*' A second Frenchman differs, moreover, with the first, and is positive that the voice was that of an Italian; but, *not being cognizant of that tongue*, is, like the Spaniard, 'convinced by the intonation.' Now, how strangely unusual must that voice have really been, about which such testimony as this *could* have been elicited!—in whose *tones*, even, denizens of the five great divisions of Europe could recognise nothing familiar! You will say that it might have been the voice of an Asiatic—of an African. Neither Asiatics nor Africans abound in Paris; but, without denying the inference, I will now merely call your attention to three points. The voice is termed by one witness 'harsh rather than shrill.' It is represented by two others to have been 'quick and *unequal.*' No words—no sounds resembling words—were by any witness mentioned as distinguishable.

"I know not," continued Dupin, "what impression I may have made, so far, upon your own understanding; but I do not hesitate to say that legitimate deductions even from this portion of the testimony—the portion respecting the gruff and shrill voices—are in themselves sufficient to engender a suspicion which should give direction to all farther progress in the investigation of the mystery. I said 'legitimate deductions;' but my meaning is not thus fully expressed. I designed to imply that the deductions are the *sole* proper ones, and that the suspicion arises *inevitably* from them as the single result. What the suspicion is, however, I will not say just yet. I merely wish you to bear in mind that, with myself, it was sufficiently forcible to give a definite form—a certain tendency—to my inquiries in the chamber.

"Let us now transport ourselves, in fancy, to this chamber. What shall we first seek here? The means of egress employed by the murderers. It is not too much to say that neither of us believe in præternatural events. Madame and Mademoiselle L'Espanaye were not destroyed by spirits. The doers of the deed were material, and escaped materially. Then how? Fortunately, there is but one mode of reasoning upon the point, and that mode *must* lead us to a definite decision.—Let us examine, each by each, the possible means of egress. It is clear that the assassins were in the room where Mademoiselle L'Espanaye was found, or at least in the room adjoining, when the party ascended the stairs. It is then only from these two apartments that we have to seek issues. The police have laid bare the floors, the ceilings, and the masonry of the walls, in every direction. No *secret* issues could have escaped their vigilance. But, not trusting to *their* eyes, I examined with my own. There were, then, no secret issues. Both doors leading from the rooms into the passage were securely locked, with the keys inside. Let us turn to the chimneys. These, although of ordinary width for some eight or ten feet above the hearths, will not admit, throughout their extent, the body of a large cat. The impossibility of egress, by means already stated, being thus absolute, we are reduced to the windows. Through those of the front room no one could have escaped without notice from the crowd in the street. The murderers *must* have passed, then, through those of the back room. Now, brought to this conclusion in so unequivocal a manner as we are, it is not our part, as reasoners, to reject it on account of apparent impossibilities. It is only left for us to prove that these apparent 'impossibilities' are, in reality, not such.

"There are two windows in the chamber. One of them is unobstructed by furniture, and is wholly visible. The lower portion of the other is hidden from view by the head of the unwieldy bedstead which is thrust close up against it. The former was found securely fastened from within. It resisted the utmost force of those who endeavored to raise it. A large gimlet-hole had been pierced in its frame to the left, and a very stout nail was found fitted therein, nearly to the head. Upon examining the other window, a similar nail was seen similarly fitted in it; and a vigorous attempt to raise this sash, failed also. The police were now entirely satisfied that egress had not been in these directions. And, *therefore*, it was thought a matter of supererogation to withdraw the nails and open the windows.

"My own examination was somewhat more particular, and was so for the reason I have just given—because here it was, I knew, that all apparent impossibilities *must* be proved to be not such in reality.

"I proceeded to think thus—*a posteriori*. The murderers did escape from one of these windows. This being so, they could not have refastened the sashes from the inside, as they were found fastened;—the consideration which put a stop, through its obviousness, to the scrutiny of the police in this quarter. Yet the sashes *were* fastened. They *must*, then, have the power of fastening themselves. There was no escape from this conclusion. I stepped to the unobstructed casement, withdrew the nail with some difficulty and attempted to raise the sash. It resisted all my efforts, as I had anticipated. A concealed spring must, I now know, exist; and this corroboration of my idea convinced me that my premises at least, were correct, however mysterious still appeared the circumstances attending the nails. A careful search soon brought to light the hidden spring. I pressed it, and, satisfied with the discovery, forbore to upraise the sash.

"I now replaced the nail and regarded it attentively. A person passing out through this window might have reclosed it, and the spring would have caught—but the nail could not have been replaced. The conclusion was plain, and again narrowed in the field of my investigations. The assassins *must* have escaped through the other window. Supposing, then, the springs upon each sash to be the same, as was probable, there *must* be found a difference between the nails, or at least between the modes of their fixture. Getting upon the sacking of the bedstead, I looked over the head-board minutely at the second casement. Passing my hand down behind the board, I readily discovered and pressed the spring, which was, as I had supposed, identical in character with its neighbor. I now looked at the nail. It was as stout as the other, and apparently fitted in the same manner—driven in nearly up to the head.

"You will say that I was puzzled; but, if you think so, you must have misunderstood the nature of the inductions. To use a sporting phrase, I had not been once 'at fault.' The scent had never for an instant been lost. There was no flaw in any link of the chain. I had traced the secret to its ultimate result,—and that result was *the nail.* It had, I say, in every respect, the appearance of its fellow in the other window; but this fact was an absolute nullity (conclusive us it might seem to be) when compared with the consideration that here, at this point, terminated the clew. 'There *must* be something wrong,' I said, 'about the nail.' I touched it; and the head, with about a quarter of an inch of the shank, came off in my fingers. The rest of the shank was in the gimlet-hole where it had been broken off. The fracture was an old one (for its edges were incrusted with rust), and had apparently been accomplished by the blow of a hammer, which had partially imbedded, in the top of the bottom sash, the head portion of the nail. I now carefully replaced this head portion in the indentation whence I had taken it, and the resemblance to a perfect nail was complete—the fissure was invisible. Pressing the spring, I gently raised the sash for a few inches; the head went up with it, remaining firm in its bed. I closed the window, and the semblance of the whole nail was again perfect.

"The riddle, so far, was now unriddled. The assassin had escaped through the window which looked upon the bed. Dropping of its own accord upon his exit (or perhaps purposely closed), it had become fastened by the spring; and it was the retention of this spring which had been mistaken by the police for that of the nail,—farther inquiry being thus considered unnecessary.

"The next question is that of the mode of descent. Upon this point I had been satisfied in my walk with you around the building. About five feet and a half from the casement in question there runs a lightning-rod. From this rod it would have been impossible for any one to reach the window itself, to say nothing of entering it. I observed, however, that the shutters of the fourth story were of the peculiar kind called by

Parisian carpenters *ferrades*—a kind rarely employed at the present day, but frequently seen upon very old mansions at Lyons and Bordeaux. They are in the form of an ordinary door, (a single, not a folding door) except that the lower half is latticed or worked in open trellis—thus affording an excellent hold for the hands. In the present instance these shutters are fully three feet and a half broad. When we saw them from the rear of the house, they were both about half open—that is to say, they stood off at right angles from the wall. It is probable that the police, as well as myself, examined the back of the tenement; but, if so, in looking at these *ferrades* in the line of their breadth (as they must have done), they did not perceive this great breadth itself, or, at all events, failed to take it into due consideration. In fact, having once satisfied themselves that no egress could have been made in this quarter, they would naturally bestow here a very cursory examination. It was clear to me, however, that the shutter belonging to the window at the head of the bed, would, if swung fully back to the wall, reach to within two feet of the lightning-rod. It was also evident that, by exertion of a very unusual degree of activity and courage, an entrance into the window, from the rod, might have been thus effected.—By reaching to the distance of two feet and a half (we now suppose the shutter open to its whole extent) a robber might have taken a firm grasp upon the trellis-work. Letting go, then, his hold upon the rod, placing his feet securely against the wall, and springing boldly from it, he might have swung the shutter so as to close it, and, if we imagine the window open at the time, might even have swung himself into the room.

"I wish you to bear especially in mind that I have spoken of a *very* unusual degree of activity as requisite to success in so hazardous and so difficult a feat. It is my design to show you, first, that the thing might possibly have been accomplished:—but, secondly and *chiefly*, I wish to impress upon your understanding the *very extraordinary*—the almost præternatural character of that agility which could have accomplished it.

"You will say, no doubt, using the language of the law, that 'to make out my case,' I should rather undervalue, than insist upon a full estimation of the activity required in this matter. This may be the practice in law, but it is not the usage of reason. My ultimate object is only the truth. My immediate purpose is to lead you to place in juxtaposition, that *very unusual* activity of which I have just spoken with that *very peculiar* shrill (or harsh) and *unequal* voice, about whose nationality no two persons could be found to agree, and in whose utterance no syllabification could be detected."

At these words a vague and half-formed conception of the meaning of Dupin flitted over my mind. I seemed to be upon the verge of comprehension without power to comprehend—men, at times, find themselves upon the brink of remembrance without being able, in the end, to remember. My friend went on with his discourse.

"You will see," he said, "that I have shifted the question from the mode of egress to that of ingress. It was my design to convey the idea that both were effected in the same manner, at the same point. Let us now revert to the interior of the room. Let us survey the appearances here. The drawers of the bureau, it is said, had been rifled, although many articles of apparel still remained within them. The conclusion here is absurd. It is a mere guess—a very silly one—and no more. How are we to know that the articles found in the drawers were not all these drawers had originally contained? Madame L'Espanaye and her daughter lived an exceedingly retired life—saw no company—seldom went out—had little use for numerous changes of habiliment. Those found were at least of as good quality as any likely to be possessed by these ladies. If a thief had taken any, why did he not take the best—why did he not take all? In a word, why did he abandon four thousand francs in gold to encumber himself with a bundle of linen? The gold *was* abandoned. Nearly the whole sum mentioned by Monsieur Mignaud, the banker, was discovered, in bags, upon the floor. I wish you, therefore, to discard from your thoughts the blundering idea of *motive*, engendered in the brains of the police by that portion of the evidence which speaks of money delivered at the door of the house. Coincidences ten times as remarkable as this (the delivery of the money, and murder committed within three days upon the party receiving it), happen to all of us every hour of our lives, without attracting even momentary notice. Coincidences, in general, are great stumbling-blocks in the way of that class of thinkers who have been educated to know nothing of the theory of probabilities—that theory to which the most glorious objects of human research are indebted for the most glorious of illustration. In the present instance, had the gold been gone, the fact of its delivery three days before would have formed something more than a coincidence. It would have been corroborative of this idea of motive. But, under the real circumstances of the case, if we are to suppose gold the motive of this outrage, we must also imagine the perpetrator so vacillating an idiot as to have abandoned his gold and his motive together.

"Keeping now steadily in mind the points to which I have drawn your attention—that peculiar voice, that unusual agility, and that startling absence of motive in a murder so singularly atrocious as this—let us glance at the butchery itself. Here is a woman strangled to death by manual strength, and thrust up a chimney, head downward. Ordinary assassins employ no such modes of murder as this. Least of all, do they thus dispose of the murdered. In the manner of thrusting the corpse up the chimney, you will admit that there was something *excessively outré*—something altogether irreconcilable with our common notions of human action, even when we suppose the actors the most depraved of men. Think, too, how great must have been that strength which could have thrust the body *up* such an aperture so forcibly that the united vigor of several persons was found barely sufficient to drag it *down!*

"Turn, now, to other indications of the employment of a vigor most marvellous. On the hearth were thick tresses—very thick tresses—of grey human hair. These had been torn out by the roots. You are aware of the great force necessary in tearing thus from the head even twenty or thirty hairs together. You saw the locks in question as well as myself. Their roots (a hideous sight!) were clotted with fragments of the flesh of the scalp—sure token of the prodigious power which had been exerted in uprooting perhaps half a million of hairs at a time. The throat of the old lady was not merely cut, but the head absolutely severed from the body: the instrument was a mere razor. I wish you also to look at the *brutal* ferocity of these deeds. Of the bruises upon the body of Madame L'Espanaye I do not speak. Monsieur Dumas, and his worthy coadjutor Monsieur Etienne, have pronounced that they were inflicted by some obtuse instrument; and so far these gentlemen are very correct. The obtuse instrument was clearly the stone pavement in the yard, upon which the victim had fallen from the window which looked in upon the bed. This idea, however simple it may now seem, escaped the police for the same reason that the breadth of the shutters escaped them—because, by the affair of the nails, their perceptions had been hermetically sealed against the possibility of the windows having ever been opened at all.

"If now, in addition to all these things, you have properly reflected upon the odd disorder of the chamber, we have gone so far as to combine the ideas of an agility astounding, a strength superhuman, a ferocity brutal, a butchery without motive, a *grotesquerie* in horror absolutely alien from humanity, and a voice foreign in tone to the ears of men of many nations, and devoid of all distinct or intelligible syllabification. What result, then, has ensued? What impression have I made upon your fancy?"

I felt a creeping of the flesh as Dupin asked me the question. "A madman," I said, "has done this deed—some raving maniac, escaped from a neighboring *Maison de Santé*."

"In some respects," he replied, "your idea is not irrelevant. But the voices of madmen, even in their wildest paroxysms, are never found to tally with that peculiar voice heard upon the stairs. Madmen are of some nation, and their language, however incoherent in its words, has always the coherence of syllabification. Besides, the hair of a madman is not such as I now hold in my hand. I disentangled this little tuft from the rigidly clutched fingers of Madame L'Espanaye. Tell me what you can make of it."

"Dupin!" I said, completely unnerved; "this hair is most unusual—this is no *human* hair."

"I have not asserted that it is," said he; "but, before we decide this point, I wish you to glance at the little sketch I have here traced upon this paper. It is a *fac-simile* drawing of what has been described in one portion of the testimony as 'dark bruises, and deep indentations of finger nails,' upon the throat of Mademoiselle L'Espanaye, and in another, (by Messrs. Dumas and Etienne,) as a 'series of livid spots, evidently the impression of fingers.'

"You will perceive," continued my friend, spreading out the paper upon the table before us, "that this drawing gives the idea of a firm and fixed hold. There is no *slipping* apparent. Each finger has retained—possibly until the death of the victim—the fearful grasp by which it originally imbedded itself. Attempt, now, to place all your fingers, at the same time, in the respective impressions as you see them."

I made the attempt in vain.

"We are possibly not giving this matter a fair trial," he said. "The paper is spread out upon a plane surface; but the human throat is cylindrical. Here is a billet of wood, the circumference of which is about that of the throat. Wrap the drawing around it, and try the experiment again."

I did so; but the difficulty was even more obvious than before. "This," I said, "is the mark of no human hand."

"Read now," replied Dupin, "this passage from Cuvier."

It was a minute anatomical and generally descriptive account of the large fulvous Ourang-Outang of the East Indian Islands. The gigantic stature, the prodigious strength and activity, the wild ferocity, and the imitative propensities of these mammalia are sufficiently well known to all. I understood the full horrors of the murder at once.

"The description of the digits," said I, as I made an end of reading, "is in exact accordance with this drawing. I see that no animal but an Ourang-Outang, of the species here mentioned, could have impressed the indentations as you have traced them. This tuft of tawny hair, too, is identical in character with that of the beast of Cuvier. But I cannot possibly comprehend the particulars of this frightful mystery. Besides, there were *two* voices heard in contention, and one of them was unquestionably the voice of a Frenchman."

"True; and you will remember an expression attributed almost unanimously, by the evidence, to this voice,—the expression, '*mon Dieu!*' This, under the circumstances, has been justly characterized by one of the witnesses (Montani, the confectioner,) as an expression of remonstrance or expostulation. Upon these two words, therefore, I have mainly built my hopes of a full solution of the riddle. A Frenchman was cognizant of the murder. It is possible—indeed it is far more than probable—that he was innocent of all participation in the bloody transactions which took place. The Ourang-Outang may have escaped from him. He may have traced it to the chamber; but, under the agitating circumstances which ensued, he could never have re-captured it. It is still at large. I will not pursue these guesses—for I have no right to call them more—since the shades of reflection upon which they are based are scarcely of sufficient depth to be appreciable by my own intellect, and since I could not pretend to make them intelligible to the understanding of another. We will call them guesses then, and speak of them as such. If the Frenchman in question is indeed, as I suppose, innocent of this atrocity, this advertisement which I left last night, upon our return home, at the office of 'Le Monde,' (a paper devoted to the shipping interest, and much sought by sailors,) will bring him to our residence."

He handed me a paper, and I read thus:

CAUGHT—*In the Bois de Boulogne, early in the morning of the—inst.,* (the morning of the murder,) *a very large, tawny Ourang-Outang of the Bornese species. The owner, (who is ascertained to be a sailor, belonging to a Maltese vessel,) may have the animal again, upon identifying it satisfactorily, and paying a few charges arising from its capture and keeping. Call at No.—, Rue—, Faubourg St. Germain—au troisième.*

"How was it possible," I asked, "that you should know the man to be a sailor, and belonging to a Maltese vessel?"

"I do *not* know it," said Dupin. "I am not *sure* of it. Here, however, is a small piece of ribbon, which from its form, and from its greasy appearance, has evidently been used in tying the hair in one of those long *queues* of which sailors are so fond. Moreover, this knot is one which few besides sailors can tie, and is peculiar to the Maltese. I picked the ribbon up at the foot of the lightning-rod. It could not have belonged to either of the deceased. Now if, after all, I am wrong in my induction from this ribbon, that the Frenchman was a sailor belonging to a Maltese vessel, still I can have done no harm in saying what I did in the advertisement. If I am in error, he will merely suppose that I have been misled by some circumstance into which he will not take the trouble to inquire. But if I am right, a great point is gained. Cognizant although innocent of the murder, the Frenchman will naturally hesitate about replying to the advertisement—about demanding the Ourang-Outang. He will reason thus:—'I am innocent; I am poor; my Ourang-Outang is of great value—to one in my circumstances a fortune of itself—why should I lose it through idle apprehensions of danger? Here it is, within my grasp. It was found in the Bois de Boulogne—at a vast distance from the scene of that butchery. How can it ever be suspected that a brute beast should have done the deed? The police are at fault—they have failed to procure the slightest clew. Should they even trace the animal, it would be impossible to prove me cognizant of the murder, or to implicate me in guilt on account of that cognizance. Above all, *I am known*. The advertiser designates me as the possessor of the beast. I am not sure to what limit his knowledge may extend. Should I avoid claiming a property of so great value, which it is known that I possess, I will render the animal at least, liable to suspicion. It is not my policy to attract attention either to myself or to the beast. I will answer the advertisement, get the Ourang-Outang, and keep it close until this matter has blown over.'"

At this moment we heard a step upon the stairs.

"Be ready," said Dupin, "with your pistols, but neither use them nor show them until at a signal from myself."

The front door of the house had been left open, and the visitor had entered, without ringing, and advanced several steps upon the staircase. Now, however, he seemed to hesitate. Presently we heard him descending. Dupin was moving quickly to the door, when we again heard him coming up. He did not turn back a second time, but stepped up with decision, and rapped at the door of our chamber.

"Come in," said Dupin, in a cheerful and hearty tone.

A man entered. He was a sailor, evidently,—a tall, stout, and muscular-looking person, with a certain dare-devil expression of countenance, not altogether unprepossessing. His face, greatly sunburnt, was more than half hidden by whisker and *mustachio.* He had with him a huge oaken cudgel, but appeared to be otherwise unarmed. He bowed awkwardly, and bade us "good evening," in French accents, which, although somewhat Neufchatelish, were still sufficiently indicative of a Parisian origin.

"Sit down, my friend," said Dupin. "I suppose you have called about the Ourang-Outang. Upon my word, I almost envy you the possession of him; a remarkably fine, and no doubt a very valuable animal. How old do you suppose him to be?"

The sailor drew a long breath, with the air of a man relieved of some intolerable burden, and then replied, in an assured tone:

"I have no way of telling—but he can't be more than four or five years old. Have you got him here?"

"Oh no, we had no conveniences for keeping him here. He is at a livery stable in the Rue Dubourg, just by. You can get him in the morning. Of course you are prepared to identify the property?"

"To be sure I am, sir."

"I shall be sorry to part with him," said Dupin.

"I don't mean that you should be at all this trouble for nothing, sir," said the man. "Couldn't expect it. Am very willing to pay a reward for the finding of the animal—that is to say, any thing in reason."

"Well," replied my friend, "that is all very fair, to be sure. Let me think!—what should I have? Oh! I will tell you. My reward shall be this. You shall give me all the information in your power about these murders in the Rue Morgue."

Dupin said the last words in a very low tone, and very quietly. Just as quietly, too, he walked toward the door, locked it and put the key in his pocket. He then drew a pistol from his bosom and placed it, without the least flurry, upon the table.

The sailor's face flushed up as if he were struggling with suffocation. He started to his feet and grasped his cudgel, but the next moment he fell back into his seat, trembling violently, and with the countenance of death itself. He spoke not a word. I pitied him from the bottom of my heart.

"My friend," said Dupin, in a kind tone, "you are alarming yourself unnecessarily—you are indeed. We mean you no harm whatever. I pledge you the honor of a gentleman, and of a Frenchman, that we intend you no injury. I perfectly well know that you are innocent of the atrocities in the Rue Morgue. It will not do, however, to deny that you are in some measure implicated in them. From what I have already said, you must know that I have had means of information about this matter—means of which you could never have dreamed. Now the thing stands thus. You have done nothing which you could have avoided—nothing, certainly, which renders you culpable. You were not even guilty of robbery, when you might have robbed with impunity. You have nothing to conceal. You have no reason for concealment. On the other hand, you are bound by every principle of honor to confess all you know. An innocent man is now imprisoned, charged with that crime of which you can point out the perpetrator."

The sailor had recovered his presence of mind, in a great measure, while Dupin uttered these words; but his original boldness of bearing was all gone.

"So help me God," said he, after a brief pause, "I will tell you all I know about this affair;—but I do not expect you to believe one half I say—I would be a fool indeed if I did. Still, I am innocent, and I will make a clean breast if I die for it."

What he stated was, in substance, this. He had lately made a voyage to the Indian Archipelago. A party, of which he formed one, landed at Borneo, and passed into the interior on an excursion of pleasure. Himself and a companion had captured the Ourang-Outang. This companion dying, the animal fell into his own exclusive possession. After great trouble, occasioned by the intractable ferocity of his captive during the home voyage, he at length succeeded in lodging it safely at his own residence in Paris, where, not to attract toward himself the unpleasant curiosity of his neighbors, he kept it carefully secluded, until such time as it should recover from a wound in the foot, received from a splinter on board ship. His ultimate design was to sell it.

Returning home from some sailors' frolic the night, or rather in the morning of the murder, he found the beast occupying his own bed-room, into which it had broken from a closet adjoining, where it had been, as was thought, securely confined. Razor in hand, and fully lathered, it was sitting before a looking-glass, attempting the operation of shaving, in which it had no doubt previously watched its master through the key-hole of the closet. Terrified at the sight of so dangerous a weapon in the possession of an animal so ferocious, and so well able to use it, the man, for some moments, was at a loss what to do. He had been accustomed, however, to quiet the creature, even in its fiercest moods, by the use of a whip, and to this he now resorted. Upon sight of it, the Ourang-Outang sprang at once through the door of the chamber, down the stairs, and thence, through a window, unfortunately open, into the street.

The Frenchman followed in despair; the ape, razor still in hand, occasionally stopping to look back and gesticulate at its pursuer, until the latter had nearly come up with it. It then again made off. In this manner the chase continued for a long time. The streets were profoundly quiet, as it was nearly three o'clock in the morning. In passing down an alley in the rear of the Rue Morgue, the fugitive's attention was arrested by a light gleaming from the open window of Madame L'Espanaye's chamber, in the fourth story of her house. Rushing to the building, it perceived the lightning rod, clambered up with inconceivable agility, grasped the shutter, which was thrown fully back against the wall, and, by its means, swung itself directly upon the headboard of the bed. The whole feat did not occupy a minute. The shutter was kicked open again by the Ourang-Outang as it entered the room.

The sailor, in the meantime, was both rejoiced and perplexed. He had strong hopes of now recapturing the brute, as it could scarcely escape from the trap into which it had ventured, except by the rod, where it might be intercepted as it came down. On the other hand, there was much cause for anxiety as to what it might do in the house. This latter reflection urged the man still to follow the fugitive. A lightning rod is ascended without difficulty, especially by a sailor; but, when he had arrived as high as the window, which lay far to his left, his career was stopped; the most that he could accomplish was to reach over so as to obtain a glimpse of the interior of the room. At this glimpse he nearly fell from his hold through excess of horror. Now it was that those hideous shrieks arose upon the night, which had startled from slumber the inmates of the Rue Morgue. Madame L'Espanaye and her daughter, habited in their night clothes, had apparently been occupied in arranging some papers in the iron chest already mentioned, which had been wheeled into the middle of the room. It was open, and its contents lay beside it on the floor. The victims must have been sitting with their backs toward the window; and, from the time elapsing between the ingress of the beast and the screams, it seems probable that it was not immediately perceived. The flapping-to of the shutter would naturally have been attributed to the wind.

As the sailor looked in, the gigantic animal had seized Madame L'Espanaye by the hair, (which was loose, as she had been combing it,) and was flourishing the razor about her face, in imitation of the motions of a barber. The daughter lay prostrate and motionless; she had swooned. The screams and struggles of the old lady (during which the hair was torn from her head) had the effect of changing the probably pacific purposes of the Ourang-Outang into those of wrath. With one determined sweep of its muscular arm it nearly severed her head from her body. The sight of blood inflamed its anger into phrenzy. Gnashing its teeth, and flashing fire from its eyes, it flew upon the body of the girl, and imbedded its fearful talons in her throat, retaining its grasp until she expired. Its wandering and wild glances fell at this moment upon the head of the bed, over which the face of its master, rigid with horror, was just discernible. The fury of the beast, who no doubt bore still in mind the dreaded whip, was instantly converted into fear. Conscious of having deserved punishment, it seemed desirous of concealing its bloody deeds, and skipped about the chamber in an agony of nervous agitation; throwing down and breaking the furniture as it moved, and dragging the bed from the bedstead. In conclusion, it seized first the corpse of the daughter, and thrust it up the chimney, as it was found; then that of the old lady, which it immediately hurled through the window headlong.

As the ape approached the casement with its mutilated burden, the sailor shrank aghast to the rod, and, rather gliding than clambering down it, hurried at once home—dreading the consequences of the butchery, and gladly abandoning, in his terror, all solicitude about the fate of the Ourang-Outang. The words heard by the party upon the staircase were the Frenchman's exclamations of horror and affright, commingled with the fiendish jabberings of the brute.

I have scarcely anything to add. The Ourang-Outang must have escaped from the chamber, by the rod, just before the break of the door. It must have closed the window as it passed through it. It was subsequently caught by the owner himself, who obtained for it a very large sum at the *Jardin des Plantes.* Le Don was instantly released, upon our narration of the circumstances (with some comments from Dupin) at the bureau of the Prefect of Police. This functionary, however well disposed to my friend, could not altogether conceal his chagrin at the turn which affairs had taken, and was fain to indulge in a sarcasm or two, about the propriety of every person minding his own business.

"Let him talk," said Dupin, who had not thought it necessary to reply. "Let him discourse; it will ease his conscience, I am satisfied with having defeated him in his own castle. Nevertheless, that he failed in the solution of this mystery, is by no means that matter for wonder which he supposes it; for, in truth, our friend the Prefect is somewhat too cunning to be profound. In his wisdom is no *stamen.* It is all head and no body, like the pictures of the Goddess Laverna,—or, at best, all head and shoulders, like a codfish. But he is a good creature after all. I like him especially for one master stroke of cant, by which he has attained his reputation for ingenuity. I mean the way he has '*de nier ce qui est, et d'expliquer ce qui n'est pas.*'"

The Mystery of Marie Roget

A Sequel to "The Murders in the Rue Morgue"

Es giebt eine Reihe idealischer Begebenheiten, die der Wirklichkeit parallel lauft. Selten fallen sie zusammen. Menschen und zufalle modificiren gewohulich die idealische Begebenheit, so dass sie unvollkommen erscheint, und ihre Folgen gleichfalls unvollkommen sind. So bei der Reformation; statt des Protestantismus kam das Lutherthum hervor.

There are ideal series of events which run parallel with the real ones. They rarely coincide. Men and circumstances generally modify the ideal train of events, so that it seems imperfect, and its consequences are equally imperfect. Thus with the Reformation; instead of Protestantism came Lutheranism.

—Novalis

There are few persons, even among the calmest thinkers, who have not occasionally been startled into a vague yet thrilling half-credence in the supernatural, by coincidences of so seemingly marvellous a character that, as mere coincidences, the intellect has been unable to receive them. Such sentiments—for the half-credences of which I speak have never the full force of thought—such sentiments are seldom thoroughly stifled unless by reference to the doctrine of chance, or, as it is technically termed, the Calculus of Probabilities. Now this Calculus is, in its essence, purely mathematical; and thus we have the anomaly of the most rigidly exact in science applied to the shadow and spirituality of the most intangible in speculation.

The extraordinary details which I am now called upon to make public, will be found to form, as regards sequence of time, the primary branch of a series of scarcely intelligible coincidences, whose secondary or concluding branch will be recognized by all readers in the late murder of Mary Cecila Rogers, at New York.

When, in an article entitled "The Murders in the Rue Morgue," I endeavored, about a year ago, to depict some very remarkable features in the mental character of my friend, the Chevalier C. Auguste Dupin, it did not occur to me that I should ever resume the subject. This depicting of character constituted my design; and this design was thoroughly fulfilled in the wild train of circumstances brought to instance Dupin's idiosyncrasy. I might have adduced other examples, but I should have proven no more. Late events, however, in their surprising development, have startled me into some farther details, which will carry with them the air of extorted confession. Hearing what I have lately heard, it would be indeed strange should I remain silent in regard to what I both heard and saw so long ago.

Upon the winding up of the tragedy involved in the deaths of Madame L'Espanaye and her daughter, the Chevalier dismissed the affair at once from his attention, and relapsed into his old habits of moody reverie. Prone, at all times, to abstraction, I readily fell in with his humor; and, continuing to occupy our chambers in the Faubourg Saint Germain, we gave the Future to the winds, and slumbered tranquilly in the Present, weaving the dull world around us into dreams.

But these dreams were not altogether uninterrupted. It may readily be supposed that the part played by my friend, in the drama at the Rue Morgue, had not failed of its impression upon the fancies of the Parisian police. With its emissaries, the name of Dupin had grown into a household word. The simple character of those inductions by which he had disentangled the mystery never having been explained even to the Prefect, or to any other individual than myself, of course it is not surprising that the affair was regarded as little less than miraculous, or that the Chevalier's analytical abilities acquired for him the credit of intuition. His frankness would have led him to disabuse every inquirer of such prejudice; but his indolent humor forbade all farther agitation of a topic whose interest to himself had long ceased. It thus happened that he found himself the cynosure of the political eyes; and the cases were not few in which attempt was made to engage his services at the Prefecture. One of the most remarkable instances was that of the murder of a young girl named Marie Rogêt.

This event occurred about two years after the atrocity in the Rue Morgue. Marie, whose Christian and family name will at once arrest attention from their resemblance to those of the unfortunate "cigargirl," was the only daughter of the widow Estelle Rogêt. The father had died during the child's infancy, and from the period of his death, until within eighteen months before the assassination which forms the subject of our narrative, the mother and daughter had dwelt together in the Rue

Pavée Saint Andrée; Madame there keeping a pension, assisted by Marie. Affairs went on thus until the latter had attained her twenty-second year, when her great beauty attracted the notice of a perfumer, who occupied one of the shops in the basement of the Palais Royal, and whose custom lay chiefly among the desperate adventurers infesting that neighborhood. Monsieur Le Blanc was not unaware of the advantages to be derived from the attendance of the fair Marie in his perfumery; and his liberal proposals were accepted eagerly by the girl, although with somewhat more of hesitation by Madame.

The anticipations of the shopkeeper were realized, and his rooms soon became notorious through the charms of the sprightly grisette. She had been in his employ about a year, when her admirers were thrown info confusion by her sudden disappearance from the shop. Monsieur Le Blanc was unable to account for her absence, and Madame Rogêt was distracted with anxiety and terror. The public papers immediately took up the theme, and the police were upon the point of making serious investigations, when, one fine morning, after the lapse of a week, Marie, in good health, but with a somewhat saddened air, made her re-appearance at her usual counter in the perfumery. All inquiry, except that of a private character, was of course immediately hushed. Monsieur Le Blanc professed total ignorance, as before. Marie, with Madame, replied to all questions, that the last week had been spent at the house of a relation in the country. Thus the affair died away, and was generally forgotten; for the girl, ostensibly to relieve herself from the impertinence of curiosity, soon bade a final adieu to the perfumer, and sought the shelter of her mother's residence in the Rue Pavée Saint Andrée.

It was about five months after this return home, that her friends were alarmed by her sudden disappearance for the second time. Three days elapsed, and nothing was heard of her. On the fourth her corpse was found floating in the Seine, * near the shore which is opposite the Quartier of the Rue Saint Andree, and at a point not very far distant from the secluded neighborhood of the Barrière du Roule.

The atrocity of this murder, (for it was at once evident that murder had been committed,) the youth and beauty of the victim, and, above all, her previous notoriety, conspired to produce intense excitement in the minds of the sensitive Parisians. I can call to mind no similar occurrence producing so general and so intense an effect. For several weeks, in the discussion of this one absorbing theme, even the momentous political topics of the day were forgotten. The Prefect made unusual exertions; and the powers of the whole Parisian police were, of course, tasked to the utmost extent.

Upon the first discovery of the corpse, it was not supposed that the murderer would be able to elude, for more than a very brief period, the inquisition which was immediately set on foot. It was not until the expiration of a week that it was deemed necessary to offer a reward; and even then this reward was limited to a thousand francs. In the mean time the investigation proceeded with vigor, if not always with judgment, and numerous individuals were examined to no purpose; while, owing to the continual absence of all clue to the mystery, the popular excitement greatly increased. At the end of the tenth day it was thought advisable to double the sum originally proposed; and, at length, the second week having elapsed without leading to any discoveries, and the prejudice which always exists in Paris against the Police having given vent to itself in several serious émeutes, the Prefect took it upon himself to offer the sum of twenty thousand francs "for the conviction of the assassin," or, if more than one should prove to have been implicated, "for the conviction of any one of the assassins." In the proclamation setting forth this reward, a full pardon was promised to any accomplice who should come forward in evidence against his fellow; and to the whole was appended, wherever it appeared, the private placard of a committee of citizens, offering ten thousand francs, in addition to the amount proposed by the Prefecture. The entire reward thus stood at no less than thirty thousand francs, which will be regarded as an extraordinary sum when we consider the humble condition of the girl, and the great frequency, in large cities, of such atrocities as the one described.

No one doubted now that the mystery of this murder would be immediately brought to light. But although, in one or two instances, arrests were made which promised elucidation, yet nothing was elicited which could implicate the parties suspected; and they were discharged forthwith. Strange as it may appear, the third week from the discovery of the body had passed, and passed without any light being thrown upon the subject, before even a rumor of the events which had so agitated the public mind, reached the ears of Dupin and myself. Engaged in researches which absorbed our whole attention, it had been nearly a month since either of us had gone abroad, or received a visitor, or more than glanced at the leading political articles in one of the daily papers.

The first intelligence of the murder was brought us by G——, in person. He called upon us early in the afternoon of the thirteenth of July, 18—, and remained with us until late in the night. He had been piqued by the failure of all his endeavors to ferret out the assassins. His reputation—so he said with a peculiarly Parisian air—was at stake. Even his honor was concerned. The eyes of the public were upon him; and there was really no sacrifice which he would not be willing to make for the development of the mystery. He concluded a somewhat droll speech with a compliment upon what he was pleased to term the tact of Dupin, and made him a direct, and certainly a liberal proposition, the precise nature of which I do not feel myself at liberty to disclose, but which has no bearing upon the proper subject of my narrative.

The compliment my friend rebutted as best he could, but the proposition he accepted at once, although its advantages were altogether provisional. This point being settled, the Prefect broke forth at once into explanations of his own views, interspersing them with long comments upon the evidence; of which latter we were not yet in possession. He discoursed much, and beyond doubt, learnedly; while I hazarded an occasional suggestion as the night wore drowsily away. Dupin, sitting steadily in his accustomed arm-chair, was the embodiment of respectful attention. He wore spectacles, during the whole interview; and an occasional signal glance beneath their green glasses, sufficed to convince me that he slept not the less soundly, because silently, throughout the seven or eight leaden-footed hours which immediately preceded the departure of the Prefect.

In the morning, I procured, at the Prefecture, a full report of all the evidence elicited, and, at the various newspaper offices, a copy of every paper in which, from first to last, had been published any decisive information in regard to this sad affair. Freed from all that was positively disproved, this mass of information stood thus:

Marie Rogêt left the residence of her mother, in the Rue Pavée St. Andrée, about nine o'clock in the morning of Sunday June the twenty-second, 18—. In going out, she gave notice to a Monsieur Jacques St. Eustache, and to him only, of her intent intention to spend the day with an aunt who resided in the Rue des Drâmes. The Rue des Drâmes is a short and narrow but populous thoroughfare, not far from the banks of the river, and at a distance of some two miles, in the most direct course possible, from the pension of Madame Rogêt. St. Eustache was the accepted suitor of Marie, and lodged, as well as took his meals, at the pension. He was to have gone for his betrothed at dusk, and to have escorted her home. In the afternoon, however, it came on to rain heavily; and, supposing that she would remain all night at her aunt's, (as she had done under similar circumstances before,) he did not think it necessary to keep his promise. As night drew on, Madame Rogêt (who was an infirm old lady, seventy years of age,) was heard to express a fear "that she should never see Marie again;" but this observation attracted little attention at the time.

On Monday, it was ascertained that the girl had not been to the Rue des Drâmes; and when the day elapsed without tidings of her, a tardy search was instituted at several points in the city, and its environs. It was not, however until the fourth day from the period of disappearance that any thing satisfactory was ascertained respecting her. On this day, (Wednesday, the twenty-fifth of June,) a Monsieur Beauvais, who, with a friend, had been making inquiries for Marie near the Barrière du Roule, on the shore of the Seine which is opposite the Rue Pavée St. Andrée, was informed that a corpse had just been towed ashore by some fishermen, who had found it floating in the river. Upon seeing the body, Beauvais, after some hesitation, identified it as that of the perfumery-girl. His friend recognized it more promptly.

The face was suffused with dark blood, some of which issued from the mouth. No foam was seen, as in the case of the merely drowned. There was no discoloration in the cellular tissue. About the throat were bruises and impressions of fingers. The arms were bent over on the chest and were rigid. The right hand was clenched; the left partially open. On the left wrist were two circular excoriations, apparently the effect of ropes, or of a rope in more than one volution. A part of the right wrist, also, was much chafed, as well as the back throughout its extent, but more especially at the shoulder-blades. In bringing the body to the shore the fishermen had attached to it a rope; but none of the excoriations had been effected by this. The flesh of the neck was much swollen. There were no cuts apparent, or bruises which appeared the effect of blows. A piece of lace was found tied so tightly around the neck as to be hidden from sight; it was completely buried in the flesh, and was fasted by a knot which lay just under the left ear. This alone would have sufficed to produce death. The medical testimony spoke confidently of the virtuous character of the deceased. She had been subjected, it said, to brutal violence. The corpse was in such condition when found, that there could have been no difficulty in its recognition by friends.

The dress was much torn and otherwise disordered. In the outer garment, a slip, about a foot wide, had been torn upward from the bottom hem to the waist, but not torn off. It was wound three times around the waist, and secured by a sort of hitch in the back. The dress immediately beneath the frock was of fine muslin; and from this a slip eighteen inches wide had been torn entirely out—torn very evenly and with great care. It was found around her neck, fitting loosely, and secured with a hard knot. Over this muslin slip and the slip of lace, the strings of a bonnet were attached; the bonnet being appended. The knot by which the strings of the bonnet were fastened, was not a lady's, but a slip or sailor's knot.

After the recognition of the corpse, it was not, as usual, taken to the Morgue, (this formality being superfluous,) but hastily interred not far from the spot at which it was brought ashore. Through the exertions of Beauvais, the matter was industriously hushed up, as far as possible; and several days had elapsed before any public emotion resulted. A weekly paper, however, at length took up the theme; the corpse was disinterred, and a re-examination instituted; but nothing was elicited beyond what has been already noted. The clothes, however, were now submitted to the mother and friends of the deceased, and fully identified as those worn by the girl upon leaving home.

Meantime, the excitement increased hourly. Several individuals were arrested and discharged. St. Eustache fell especially under suspicion; and he failed, at first, to give an intelligible account of his whereabouts during the Sunday on which Marie left home. Subsequently, however, he submitted to Monsieur G——, affidavits, accounting satisfactorily for every hour of the day in question. As time passed and no discovery ensued, a thousand contradictory rumors were circulated, and journalists busied themselves in suggestions. Among these, the one which attracted the most notice, was the idea that Marie Rogêt still lived—that the corpse found in the Seine was that of some other unfortunate. It will be proper that I submit to the reader some passages which embody the suggestion alluded to. These passages are literal translations from L'Etoile, a paper conducted, in general, with much ability.

"Mademoiselle Rogêt left her mother's house on Sunday morning, June the twenty-second, 18—, with the ostensible purpose of going to see her aunt, or some other connexion, in the Rue des Drâmes. From that hour, nobody is proved to have seen her. There is no trace or tidings of her at all. . . There has no person, whatever, come forward, so far, who saw her at all, on that day, after she left her mother's door. . . Now, though we have no evidence that Marie Rogêt was in the land of the living after nine o'clock on Sunday, June the twenty-second, we have proof that, up to that hour, she was alive. On Wednesday noon, at twelve, a female body was discovered afloat on the shore of the Barrière de Roule. This was, even if we presume that Marie Rogêt was thrown into the river within three hours after she left her mother's house, only three days from the time she left her home—three days to an hour. But it is folly to suppose that the murder, if murder was committed on her body, could have been consummated soon enough to have enabled her murderers to throw the body into the river before midnight. Those who are guilty of such horrid crimes, choose darkness rather the light. . . Thus we see that if the body found in the river was that of Marie Rogêt, it could only have been in the water two and a half days, or three at the outside. All experience has shown that drowned bodies, or bodies thrown into the water immediately after death by violence, require from six to ten days for decomposition to take place to bring them to the top of the water. Even where a cannon is fired over a corpse, and it rises before at least five or six days' immersion, it sinks again, if let alone. Now, we ask, what was there in this case to cause a departure from the ordinary course of nature? . . . If the body had been kept in its mangled state on shore until Tuesday night, some trace would be found on shore of the murderers. It is a doubtful point, also, whether the body would be so soon afloat, even were it thrown in after having been dead two days. And, furthermore, it is exceedingly improbable that any villains who had committed such a murder as is here supposed, would have thrown the body in without weight to sink it, when such a precaution could have so easily been taken."

The editor here proceeds to argue that the body must have been in the water "not three days merely, but, at least, five times three days," because it was so far decomposed that Beauvais had great difficulty in recognizing it. This latter point, however, was fully disproved. I continue the translation:

"What, then, are the facts on which M. Beauvais says that he has no doubt the body was that of Marie Rogêt? He ripped up the gown sleeve, and says he found marks which satisfied him of the identity. The public generally supposed those marks to have consisted of some description of scars. He rubbed the arm and found hair upon it—

something as indefinite, we think, as can readily be imagined—as little conclusive as finding an arm in the sleeve. M. Beauvais did not return that night, but sent word to Madame Rogêt, at seven o'clock, on Wednesday evening, that an investigation was still in progress respecting her daughter. If we allow that Madame Rogêt, from her age and grief, could not go over, (which is allowing a great deal,) there certainly must have been some one who would have thought it worth while to go over and attend the investigation, if they thought the body was that of Marie. Nobody went over. There was nothing said or heard about the matter in the Rue Pavée St. Andrée, that reached even the occupants of the same building. M. St. Eustache, the lover and intended husband of Marie, who boarded in her mother's house, deposes that he did not hear of the discovery of the body of his intended until the next morning, when M. Beauvais came into his chamber and told him of it. For an item of news like this, it strikes us it was very coolly received."

In this way the journal endeavored to create the impression of an apathy on the part of the relatives of Marie, inconsistent with the supposition that these relatives believed the corpse to be hers. Its insinuations amount to this:—that Marie, with the connivance of her friends, had absented herself from the city for reasons involving a charge against her chastity; and that these friends, upon the discovery of a corpse in the Seine, somewhat resembling that of the girl, had availed themselves of the opportunity to impress the public with the belief of her death. But L'Etoile was again over-hasty. It was distinctly proved that no apathy, such as was imagined, existed; that the old lady was exceedingly feeble, and so agitated as to be unable to attend to any duty, that St. Eustache, so far from receiving the news coolly, was distracted with grief, and bore himself so frantically, that M. Beauvais prevailed upon a friend and relative to take charge of him, and prevent his attending the examination at the disinterment. Moreover, although it was stated by L'Etoile, that the corpse was re-interred at the public expense—that an advantageous offer of private sculpture was absolutely declined by the family—and that no member of the family attended the ceremonial:—although, I say, all this was asserted by L'Etoile in furtherance of the impression it designed to convey—yet all this was satisfactorily disproved. In a subsequent number of the paper, an attempt was made to throw suspicion upon Beauvais himself. The editor says:

"Now, then, a change comes over the matter. We are told that on one occasion, while a Madame B—— was at Madame Rogêt's house, M. Beauvais, who was going out, told her that a gendarme was expected there, and she, Madame B., must not say anything to the gendarme until he returned, but let the matter be for him. . . In the present posture of affairs, M. Beauvais appears to have the whole matter locked up in his head. A single step cannot be taken without M. Beauvais; for, go which way you will, you run against him. . . For some reason, he determined that nobody shall have any thing to do with the proceedings but himself, and he has elbowed the male relatives out of the way, according to their representations, in a very singular manner. He seems to have been very much averse to permitting the relatives to see the body."

By the following fact, some color was given to the suspicion thus thrown upon Beauvais. A visitor at his office, a few days prior to the girl's disappearance, and during the absence of its occupant, had observed a rose in the key-hole of the door, and the name "Marie" inscribed upon a slate which hung near at hand.

The general impression, so far as we were enabled to glean it from the newspapers, seemed to be, that Marie had been the victim of a gang of desperadoes—that by these she had been borne across the river, maltreated and murdered. Le Commerciel, however, a print of extensive influence, was earnest in combating this popular idea. I quote a passage or two from its columns:

"We are persuaded that pursuit has hitherto been on a false scent, so far as it has been directed to the Barrière du Roule. It is impossible that a person so well known to thousands as this young woman was, should have passed three blocks without some one having seen her; and any one who saw her would have remembered it, for she interested all who knew her. It was when the streets were full of people, when she went out. . . It is impossible that she could have gone to the Barrière du Roule, or to the Rue des Drâmes, without being recognized by a dozen persons; yet no one has come forward who saw her outside of her mother's door, and there is no evidence, except the testimony concerning her expressed intentions, that she did go out at all. Her gown was torn, bound round her, and tied; and by that the body was carried as a bundle. If the murder had been committed at the Barrière du Roule, there would have been no necessity for any such arrangement. The fact that the body was found floating near the Barrière, is no proof as to where it was thrown into the water. . . A piece of one of the unfortunate girl's petticoats, two feet long and one foot wide, was torn out and tied under her chin around the back of her head, probably to prevent screams. This was done by fellows who had no pocket-handkerchief."

A day or two before the Prefect called upon us, however, some important information reached the police, which seemed to overthrow, at least, the chief portion of Le Commerciel's argument. Two small boys, sons of a Madame Deluc, while roaming among the woods near the Barrière du Roule, chanced to penetrate a close thicket, within which were three or four large stones, forming a kind of seat, with a back and footstool. On the upper stone lay a white petticoat; on the second a silk scarf. A parasol, gloves, and a pocket-handkerchief were also here found. The handkerchief bore the name "Marie Rogêt." Fragments of dress were discovered on the brambles around. The earth was trampled, the bushes were broken, and there was every evidence of a struggle. Between the thicket and the river, the fences were found taken down, and the ground bore evidence of some heavy burthen having been dragged along it.

A weekly paper, Le Soleil, had the following comments upon this discovery—comments which merely echoed the sentiment of the whole Parisian press:

"The things had all evidently been there at least three or four weeks; they were all mildewed down hard with the action of the rain and stuck together from mildew. The grass had grown around and over some of them. The silk on the parasol was strong, but the threads of it were run together within. The upper part, where it had been doubled and folded, was all mildewed and rotten, and tore on its being opened. . . The pieces of her frock torn out by the bushes were about three inches wide and six inches long. One part was the hem of the frock, and it had been mended; the other piece was part of the skirt, not the hem. They looked like strips torn off, and were on the thorn bush, about a foot from the ground. . . There can be no doubt, therefore, that the spot of this appalling outrage has been discovered."

Consequent upon this discovery, new evidence appeared. Madame Deluc testified that she keeps a roadside inn not far from the bank of the river, opposite the Barrière du Roule. The neighborhood is secluded—particularly so. It is the usual Sunday resort of blackguards from the city, who cross the river in boats. About three o'clock, in the afternoon of the Sunday in question, a young girl arrived at the inn, accompanied by a young man of dark complexion. The two remained here for some time. On their departure, they took the road to some thick woods in the vicinity. Madame Deluc's attention was called to the dress worn by the girl, on account of its resemblance to one worn by a deceased relative. A scarf was particularly noticed. Soon after the departure of the couple, a gang of miscreants made their appearance, behaved boisterously, ate and drank without making payment, followed in the route of the young man and girl, returned to the inn about dusk, and re-crossed the river as if in great haste.

It was soon after dark, upon this same evening, that Madame Deluc, as well as her eldest son, heard the screams of a female in the vicinity of the inn. The screams were violent but brief. Madame D. recognized not only the scarf which was found in the thicket, but the dress which was discovered upon the corpse. An omnibus driver, Valence, now also testified that he saw Marie Rogêt cross a ferry on the Seine, on the Sunday in question, in company with a young man of dark complexion. He, Valence, knew Marie, and could not be mistaken in her identity. The articles found in the thicket were fully identified by the relatives of Marie.

The items of evidence and information thus collected by myself, from the newspapers, at the suggestion of Dupin, embraced only one more point—but this was a point of seemingly vast consequence. It appears that, immediately after the discovery of the clothes as above described, the lifeless, or nearly lifeless body of St. Eustache, Marie's betrothed, was found in the vicinity of what all now supposed the scene of the outrage. A phial labelled "laudanum," and emptied, was found near him. His breath gave evidence of the poison. He died without speaking. Upon his person was found a letter, briefly stating his love for Marie, with his design of self-destruction.

"I need scarcely tell you," said Dupin, as he finished the perusal of my notes, "that this is a far more intricate case than that of the Rue Morgue; from which it differs in one important respect. This is an ordinary, although an atrocious instance of crime. There is nothing peculiarly outré about it. You will observe that, for this reason, the mystery has been considered easy, when, for this reason, it should have been considered difficult, of solution. Thus; at first, it was thought unnecessary to offer a reward. The myrmidons of G—— were able at once to comprehend how and why such an atrocity might have been committed. They could picture to their imaginations a mode—many modes—and a motive—many motives; and because it was not impossible that either of these numerous modes and motives could have been the actual one, they have taken it for granted that one of them must. But the case with which these variable fancies were entertained, and the very plausibility which each assumed, should have been understood as indicative rather of the difficulties than of the facilities which must attend elucidation. I have before observed that it is by prominences above the plane of the ordinary, that reason feels her way, if at all, in her search for the true, and that the proper question in cases such as this, is not so much 'what has occurred?' as 'what has occurred that has never occurred before?' In the investigations at the house of Madame L'Espanaye, the agents of G—— were discouraged and confounded by that very unusualness which, to a properly regulated intellect, would have afforded the surest omen of success; while this same intellect might have been plunged in despair at the ordinary character of all that met the eye in the case of the perfumery-girl, and yet told of nothing but easy triumph to the functionaries of the Prefecture.

"In the case of Madame L'Espanaye and her daughter there was, even at the beginning of our investigation, no doubt that murder had been committed. The idea of suicide was excluded at once. Here, too, we are freed, at the commencement, from all supposition of self-murder. The body found at the Barrière du Roule, was found under such circumstances as to leave us no room for embarrassment upon this important point. But it has been suggested that the corpse discovered, is not that of the Marie Rogêt for the conviction of whose assassin, or assassins, the reward is offered, and respecting whom, solely, our agreement has been arranged with the Prefect. We both know this gentleman well. It will not do to trust him too far. If, dating our inquiries from the body found, and thence tracing a murderer, we yet discover this body to be that of some other individual than Marie; or, if starting from the living Marie, we find her, yet find her unassassinated—in either case we lose our labor; since it is Monsieur G—— with whom we have to deal. For our own purpose, therefore, if not for the purpose of justice, it is indispensable that our first step should be the determination of the identity of the corpse with the Marie Rogêt who is missing.

"With the public the arguments of L'Etoile have had weight; and that the journal itself is convinced of their importance would appear from the manner in which it commences one of its essays upon the subject—'Several of the morning papers of the day,' it says, 'speak of the *conclusive* article in Monday's Etoile.' To me, this article appears conclusive of little beyond the zeal of its inditer. We should bear in mind that, in general, it is the object of our newspapers rather to create a sensation—to make a point—than to further the cause of truth. The latter end is only pursued when it seems coincident with the former. The print which merely falls in with ordinary opinion (however well founded this opinion may be) earns for itself no credit with the mob. The mass of the people regard as profound only him who suggests *pungent contradictions* of the general idea. In ratiocination, not less than in literature, it is the epigram which is the most immediately and the most universally appreciated. In both, it is of the lowest order of merit.

"What I mean to say is, that it is the mingled epigram and melodrame of the idea, that Marie Rogêt still lives, rather than any true plausibility in this idea, which have suggested it to L'Etoile, and secured it a favorable reception with the public. Let us examine the heads of this journal's argument; endeavoring to avoid the incoherence with which it is originally set forth.

"The first aim of the writer is to show, from the brevity of the interval between Marie's disappearance and the finding of the floating corpse, that this corpse cannot be that of Marie. The reduction of this interval to its smallest possible dimension, becomes thus, at once, an object with the reasoner. In the rash pursuit of this object, he rushes into mere assumption at the outset. 'It is folly to suppose,' he says, 'that the murder, if murder was committed on her body, could have been consummated soon enough to have enabled her murderers to throw the body into the river before midnight.' We demand at once, and very naturally, why? Why is it folly to suppose that the murder was committed *within five minutes* after the girl's quitting her mother's house? Why is it folly to suppose that the murder was committed at any given period of the day? There have been assassinations at all hours. But, had the murder taken place at any moment between nine o'clock in the morning of Sunday, and a quarter before midnight, there would still have been time enough 'to throw the body into the river before midnight.' This assumption, then, amounts precisely to this—that the murder was not committed on Sunday at all—and, if we allow L'Etoile to assume this, we may permit it any liberties whatever. The paragraph beginning 'It is folly to suppose that the murder, etc.,' however it appears as printed in L'Etoile, may be imagined to have existed actually thus in the brain of its inditer—'It is folly to suppose that the murder, if murder was committed on the body, could have been committed soon enough to have enabled her murderers to throw the body into the river before midnight; it is folly, we say, to suppose all this, and to suppose at the same time, (as we are resolved to suppose,) that the body was not thrown in until after midnight'—a sentence sufficiently inconsequential in itself, but not so utterly preposterous as the one printed.

"Were it my purpose," continued Dupin, "merely to *make out a case* against this passage of L'Etoile's argument, I might safely leave it where it is. It is not, however, with L'Etoile that we have to do, but with the truth. The sentence in question has but one meaning, as it stands; and this meaning I have fairly stated: but it is material that we go behind the mere words, for an idea which these words have obviously intended, and failed to convey. It was the design of the journalist to say that, at whatever period of the day or night of Sunday this murder was committed, it was improbable that the assassins would have ventured to bear the corpse to the river before midnight. And herein lies, really, the assumption of which I complain. It is assumed that the murder was committed at such a position, and under such circumstances, that the bearing it to the river became necessary. Now, the assassination might have taken place upon the river's brink, or on the river itself; and, thus, the throwing the corpse in the water might have been resorted to, at any period of the day or night, as the most obvious and most immediate mode of disposal. You will understand that I suggest nothing here as probable, or as cöincident with my own opinion. My design, so far, has no reference to the facts of the case. I wish merely to caution you against the whole tone of L'Etoile's suggestion, by calling your attention to its ex parte character at the outset.

"Having prescribed thus a limit to suit its own preconceived notions; having assumed that, if this were the body of Marie, it could have been in the water but a very brief time; the journal goes on to say:

'All experience has shown that drowned bodies, or bodies thrown into the water immediately after death by violence, require from six to ten days for sufficient decomposition to take place to bring them to the top of the water. Even when a cannon is fired over a corpse, and it rises before at least five or six days' immersion, it sinks again if let alone.'

"These assertions have been tacitly received by every paper in Paris, with the exception of Le Moniteur. This latter print endeavors to combat that portion of the paragraph which has reference to 'drowned bodies' only, by citing some five or six instances in which the bodies of individuals known to be drowned were found floating after the lapse of less time than is insisted upon by L'Etoile. But there is something excessively unphilosophical in the attempt on the part of Le Moniteur, to rebut the general assertion of L'Etoile, by a citation of particular instances militating against that assertion. Had it been possible to adduce fifty instead of five examples of bodies found floating at the end of two or three days, these fifty examples could still have been properly regarded only as exceptions to L'Etoile's rule, until such time as the rule itself should be confuted. Admitting the rule, (and this Le Moniteur does not deny, insisting merely upon its exceptions,) the argument of L'Etoile is suffered to remain in full force; for this argument does not pretend to involve more than a question of the probability of the body having risen to the surface in less than three days; and this probability will be in favor of L'Etoile's position until the instances so childishly adduced shall be sufficient in number to establish an antagonistical rule.

"You will see at once that all argument upon this head should be urged, if at all, against the rule itself; and for this end we must examine the rationale of the rule. Now the human body, in general, is neither much lighter nor much heavier than the water of the Seine; that is to say, the specific gravity of the human body, in its natural condition, is about equal to the bulk of fresh water which it displaces. The bodies of fat and fleshy persons, with small bones, and of women generally, are lighter than those of the lean and large-boned, and of men; and the specific gravity of the water of a river is somewhat influenced by the presence of the tide from sea. But, leaving this tide out of question, it may be said that very few human bodies will sink at all, even in fresh water, of their own accord. Almost any one, falling into a river, will be enabled to float, if he suffer the specific gravity of the water fairly to be adduced in comparison with his own—that is to say, if he suffer his whole person to be immersed, with as little exception as possible. The proper position for one who cannot swim, is the upright position of the walker on land, with the head thrown fully back, and immersed; the mouth and nostrils alone remaining above the surface. Thus circumstanced, we shall find that we float without difficulty and without exertion. It is evident, however, that the gravities of the body, and of the bulk of water displaced, are very nicely balanced, and that a trifle will cause either to preponderate. An arm, for instance, uplifted from the water, and thus deprived of its support, is an additional weight sufficient to immerse the whole head, while the accidental aid of the smallest piece of timber will enable us to elevate the head so as to look about. Now, in the struggles of one unused to swimming, the arms are invariably thrown upwards, while an attempt is made to keep the head in its usual perpendicular position. The result is the immersion of the mouth and nostrils, and the inception, during efforts to breathe while beneath the surface, of water into the lungs. Much is also received into the stomach, and the whole body becomes heavier by the difference between the weight of the air originally distending these cavities, and that of the fluid which now fills them. This difference is sufficient to cause the body to sink, as a general rule; but is insufficient in the cases of individuals with small bones and an abnormal quantity of flaccid or fatty matter. Such individuals float even after drowning.

"The corpse, being supposed at the bottom of the river, will there remain until, by some means, its specific gravity again becomes less than that of the bulk of water which it displaces. This effect is brought about by decomposition, or otherwise. The result of decomposition is the generation of gas, distending the cellular tissues and all the cavities, and giving the puffed appearance which is so horrible. When this distension has so far progressed that the bulk of the corpse is materially increased without a corresponding increase of mass or weight, its specific gravity becomes less than that of the water displaced, and it forthwith makes its appearance at the surface. But decomposition is modified by innumerable circumstances—is hastened or retarded by innumerable agencies; for example, by the heat or cold of the season, by the mineral impregnation or purity of the water, by its depth or shallowness, by its currency or stagnation, by the temperament of the body, by its infection or freedom from disease before death. Thus it is evident that we can assign no period, with any thing like accuracy, at which the corpse shall rise through decomposition. Under certain conditions this result would be brought about within an hour; under others, it might not take place at all. There are chemical infusions by which the animal frame can be preserved forever from corruption; the Bi-chloride of Mercury is one. But, apart from decomposition, there may be, and very usually is, a generation of gas within the stomach, from the acetous fermentation of vegetable matter (or within other cavities from other causes) sufficient to induce a distension which will bring the body to the surface. The effect produced by the firing of a cannon is that of simple vibration. This may either loosen the corpse from the soft mud or ooze in which it is imbedded, thus permitting it to rise when other agencies have already prepared it for so doing; or it may overcome the tenacity of some putrescent portions of the cellular tissue; allowing the cavities to distend under the influence of the gas.

"Having thus before us the whole philosophy of this subject, we can easily test by it the assertions of L'Etoile. 'All experience shows,' says this paper, 'that drowned bodies, or bodies thrown into the water immediately after death by violence, require from six to ten days for sufficient decomposition to take place to bring them to the top of the water. Even when a cannon is fired over a corpse, and it rises before at least five or six days' immersion, it sinks again if let alone.'

"The whole of this paragraph must now appear a tissue of inconsequence and incoherence. All experience does not show that 'drowned bodies' require from six to ten days for sufficient decomposition to take place to bring them to the surface. Both science and experience show that the period of their rising is, and necessarily must be, indeterminate. If, moreover, a body has risen to the surface through firing of cannon, it will not 'sink again if let alone,' until decomposition has so far progressed as to permit the escape of the generated gas. But I wish to call your attention to the distinction which is made between 'drowned bodies,' and 'bodies thrown into the water immediately after death by violence.' Although the writer admits the distinction, he yet includes them all in the same category. I have shown how it is that the body of a drowning man becomes specifically heavier than its bulk of water, and that he would not sink at all, except for the struggles by which he elevates his arms above the surface, and his gasps for breath while beneath the surface—gasps which supply by water the place of the original air in the lungs. But these struggles and these gasps would not occur in the body 'thrown into the water immediately after death by violence.' Thus, in the latter instance, the body, as a general rule, would not sink at all—a fact of which L'Etoile is evidently ignorant. When decomposition had proceeded to a very great extent—when the flesh had in a great measure left the bones—then, indeed, but not till then, should we lose sight of the corpse.

"And now what are we to make of the argument, that the body found could not be that of Marie Rogêt, because, three days only having elapsed, this body was found floating? If drowned, being a woman, she might never have sunk; or having sunk, might have reappeared in twenty-four hours, or less. But no one supposes her to have been drowned; and, dying before being thrown into the river, she might have been found floating at any period afterwards whatever.

"'But,' says L'Etoile, 'if the body had been kept in its mangled state on shore until Tuesday night, some trace would be found on shore of the murderers.' Here it is at first difficult to perceive the intention of the reasoner. He means to anticipate what he imagines would be an objection to his theory—viz: that the body was kept on shore two days, suffering rapid decomposition—more rapid than if immersed in water. He supposes that, had this been the case, it might have appeared at the surface on the Wednesday, and thinks that only under such circumstances it could so have appeared. He is accordingly in haste to show that it was not kept on shore; for, if so, 'some trace would be found on shore of the murderers.' I presume you smile at the sequitur. You cannot be made to see how the mere duration of the corpse on the shore could operate to multiply traces of the assassins. Nor can I.

"'And furthermore it is exceedingly improbable,' continues our journal, 'that any villains who had committed such a murder as is here supposed, would have thrown the body in without weight to sink it, when such a precaution could have so easily been taken.' Observe, here, the laughable confusion of thought! No one—not even L'Etoile—disputes the murder committed *on the body found*. The marks of violence are too obvious. It is our reasoner's object merely to show that this body is not Marie's. He wishes to prove that Marie is not assassinated—not that the corpse was not. Yet his observation proves only the latter point. Here is a corpse without weight attached. Murderers, casting it in, would not have failed to attach a weight. Therefore it was not thrown in by murderers. This is all which is proved, if any thing is. The question of identity is not even approached, and L'Etoile has been at great pains merely to gainsay now what it has admitted only a moment before. 'We are perfectly convinced,' it says, 'that the body found was that of a murdered female.'

"Nor is this the sole instance, even in this division of his subject, where our reasoner unwittingly reasons against himself. His evident object, I have already said, is to reduce, as much as possible, the interval between Marie's disappearance and the finding of the corpse. Yet we find him urging the point that no person saw the girl from the moment of her leaving her mother's house. 'We have no evidence,' he says, 'that Marie Rogêt was in the land of the living after nine o'clock on Sunday, June the twenty-second.' As his argument is obviously an ex parte one, he should, at least, have left this matter out of sight; for had any one been known to see Marie, say on Monday, or on Tuesday, the interval in question would have been much reduced, and, by his own ratiocination, the probability much diminished of the corpse being that of the grisette. It is, nevertheless, amusing to observe that L'Etoile insists upon its point in the full belief of its furthering its general argument.

"Reperuse now that portion of this argument which has reference to the identification of the corpse by Beauvais. In regard to the hair upon the arm, L'Etoile has been obviously disingenuous. M. Beauvais, not being an idiot, could never have urged, in identification of the corpse, simply hair upon its arm. No arm is without hair. The generality of the expression of L'Etoile is a mere perversion of the witness' phraseology. He must have spoken of some peculiarity in this hair. It must have been a peculiarity of color, of quantity, of length, or of situation.

"'Her foot,' says the journal, 'was small—so are thousands of feet. Her garter is no proof whatever—nor is her shoe—for shoes and garters are sold in packages. The same may be said of the flowers in her hat. One thing upon which M. Beauvais strongly insists is, that the clasp on the garter found, had been set back to take it in. This amounts to nothing; for most women find it proper to take a pair of garters home and fit them to the size of the limbs they are to encircle, rather than to try them in the store where they purchase.' Here it is difficult to suppose the reasoner in earnest. Had M. Beauvais, in his search for the body of Marie, discovered a corpse corresponding in general size and appearance to the missing girl, he would have been warranted (without reference to the question of habiliment at all) in forming an opinion that his search had been successful. If, in addition to the point of general size and contour, he had found upon the arm a peculiar hairy appearance which he had observed upon the living Marie, his opinion might have been justly strengthened; and the increase of positiveness might well have been in the ratio of the peculiarity, or unusualness, of the hairy mark. If, the feet of Marie being small, those of the corpse were also small, the increase of probability that the body was that of Marie would not be an increase in a ratio merely arithmetical, but in one highly geometrical, or accumulative. Add to all this shoes such as she had been known to wear upon the day of her disappearance, and, although these shoes may be 'sold in packages,' you so far augment the probability as to verge upon the certain. What, of itself, would be no evidence of identity, becomes through its corroborative position, proof most sure. Give us, then, flowers in the hat corresponding to those worn by the missing girl, and we seek for nothing farther. If only one flower, we seek for nothing farther—what then if two or three, or more? Each successive one is multiple evidence—proof not *added* to proof, but multiplied by hundreds or thousands. Let us now discover, upon the deceased, garters such as the living used, and it is almost folly to proceed. But these garters are found to be tightened, by the setting back of a clasp, in just such a manner as her own had been tightened by Marie, shortly previous to her leaving home. It is now madness or hypocrisy to doubt. What L'Etoile says in respect to this abbreviation of the garter's being an usual occurrence, shows nothing beyond its own pertinacity in error. The elastic nature of the clasp-garter is self-demonstration of the unusualness of the abbreviation. What is made to adjust itself, must of necessity require foreign adjustment but rarely. It must have been by an accident, in its strictest sense, that these garters of Marie needed the tightening described. They alone would have amply established her identity. But it is not that the corpse was found to have the garters of the missing girl, or found to have her shoes, or her bonnet, or the flowers of her bonnet, or her feet, or a peculiar mark upon the arm, or her general size and appearance—it is that the corpse had each, and *all collectively*. Could it be proved that the editor of L'Etoile *really* entertained a doubt, under the circumstances, there would be no need, in his case, of a commission de lunatico inquirendo. He has thought it sagacious to echo the small talk of the lawyers, who, for the most part, content themselves with echoing the rectangular precepts of the courts. I would here observe that very much of what is rejected as evidence by a court, is the best of evidence to the intellect. For the court, guiding itself by the general principles of evidence—the recognized and *booked* principles—is averse from swerving at particular instances. And this steadfast adherence to principle, with rigorous disregard of the conflicting exception, is a sure mode of attaining the maximum of attainable truth, in any long sequence of time. The practice, in mass, is therefore philosophical; but it is not the less certain that it engenders vast individual error.

"In respect to the insinuations levelled at Beauvais, you will be willing to dismiss them in a breath. You have already fathomed the true character of this good gentleman. He is a busy-body, with much of romance and little of wit. Any one so constituted will readily so conduct himself, upon occasion of real excitement, as to render himself liable to suspicion on the part of the over acute, or the ill-disposed. M. Beauvais (as it appears from your notes) had some personal interviews with the editor of L'Etoile, and offended him by venturing an opinion that the corpse, notwithstanding the theory of the editor, was, in sober fact, that of Marie. 'He persists,' says the paper, 'in asserting the corpse to be that of Marie, but cannot give a circumstance, in addition to those which we have commented upon, to make others believe.' Now, without re-adverting to the fact that stronger evidence 'to make others believe,' could never have been adduced, it may be remarked that a man may very well be understood to believe, in a case of this kind, without the ability to advance a single reason for the belief of a second party. Nothing is more vague than impressions of individual identity. Each man recognizes his neighbor, yet there are few instances in which any one is prepared to give a reason for his recognition. The editor of L'Etoile had no right to be offended at M. Beauvais' unreasoning belief.

"The suspicious circumstances which invest him, will be found to tally much better with my hypothesis of romantic busy-bodyism, than with the reasoner's suggestion of guilt. Once adopting the more charitable interpretation, we shall find no difficulty in comprehending the rose in the key-hole; the 'Marie' upon the slate; the 'elbowing the male relatives out of the way;' the 'aversion to permitting them to see the body;' the caution given to Madame B——, that she must hold no conversation with the gendarme until his return (Beauvais'); and, lastly, his apparent determination 'that nobody should have anything to do with the proceedings except himself.' It seems to me unquestionable that Beauvais was a suitor of Marie's; that she coquetted with him; and that he was ambitious of being thought to enjoy her fullest intimacy and confidence. I shall say nothing more upon this point; and, as the evidence fully rebuts the assertion of L'Etoile, touching the matter of apathy on the part of the mother and other relatives—an apathy inconsistent with the supposition of their believing the corpse to be that of the perfumery-girl—we shall now proceed as if the question of identity were settled to our perfect satisfaction."

"And what," I here demanded, "do you think of the opinions of Le Commerciel?"

"That, in spirit, they are far more worthy of attention than any which have been promulgated upon the subject. The deductions from the premises are philosophical and acute; but the premises, in two instances, at least, are founded in imperfect observation. Le Commerciel wishes to intimate that Marie was seized by some gang of low ruffians not far from her mother's door. 'It is impossible,' it urges, 'that a person so well known to thousands as this young woman was, should have passed three blocks without some one having seen her.' This is the idea of a man long resident in Paris—a public man—and one whose walks to and fro in the city, have been mostly limited to the vicinity of the public offices. He is aware that he seldom passes so far as a dozen blocks from his own bureau, without being recognized and accosted. And, knowing the extent of his personal acquaintance with others, and of others with him, he compares his notoriety with that of the perfumery-girl, finds no great difference between them, and reaches at once the conclusion that she, in her walks, would be equally liable to recognition with himself in his. This could only be the case were her walks of the same unvarying, methodical character, and within the same species of limited region as are his own. He passes to and fro, at regular intervals, within a confined periphery, abounding in individuals who are led to observation of his person through interest in the kindred nature of his occupation with their own. But the walks of Marie may, in general, be supposed discursive. In this particular instance, it will be understood as most probable, that she proceeded upon a route of more than average diversity from her accustomed ones. The parallel which we imagine to have existed in the mind of Le Commerciel would only be sustained in the event of the two individuals' traversing the whole city. In this case, granting the personal acquaintances to be equal, the chances would be also equal that an equal number of personal rencounters would be made. For my own part, I should hold it not only as possible, but as very far more than probable, that Marie might have proceeded, at any given period, by any one of the many routes between her own residence and that of her aunt, without meeting a single individual whom she knew, or by whom she was known. In viewing this question in its full and proper light, we must hold steadily in mind the great disproportion between the personal acquaintances of even the most noted individual in Paris, and the entire population of Paris itself.

"But whatever force there may still appear to be in the suggestion of Le Commerciel, will be much diminished when we take into consideration the hour at which the girl went abroad. 'It was when the streets were full of people,' says Le Commerciel, 'that she went out.' But not so. It was at nine o'clock in the morning. Now at nine o'clock of every morning in the week, *with the exception of Sunday*, the streets of the city are, it is true, thronged with people. At nine on Sunday, the populace are chiefly within doors *preparing for church*. No observing person can have failed to notice the peculiarly deserted air of the town, from about eight until ten on the morning of every Sabbath. Between ten and eleven the streets are thronged, but not at so early a period as that designated.

"There is another point at which there seems a deficiency of observation on the part of Le Commerciel. 'A piece,' it says, 'of one of the unfortunate girl's petticoats, two feet long, and one foot wide, was torn out and tied under her chin, and around the back of her head, probably to prevent screams. This was done, by fellows who had no pocket-handkerchiefs.' Whether this idea is, or is not well founded, we will endeavor to see hereafter; but by 'fellows who have no pocket-handkerchiefs' the editor intends the lowest class of ruffians. These, however, are the very description of people who will always be found to have handkerchiefs even when destitute of shirts. You must have had occasion to observe how absolutely indispensable, of late years, to the thorough blackguard, has become the pocket-handkerchief."

"And what are we to think," I asked, "of the article in Le Soleil?"

"That it is a vast pity its inditer was not born a parrot—in which case he would have been the most illustrious parrot of his race. He has merely repeated the individual items of the already published opinion; collecting them, with a laudable industry, from this paper and from that. 'The things had all evidently been there,' he says, 'at least, three or four weeks, and there can be *no doubt* that the spot of this appalling outrage has been discovered.' The facts here re-stated by Le Soleil, are very far indeed from removing my own doubts upon this subject, and we will examine them more particularly hereafter in connexion with another division of the theme.

"At present we must occupy ourselves with other investigations. You cannot fail to have remarked the extreme laxity of the examination of the corpse. To be sure, the question of identity was readily determined, or should have been; but there were other points to be ascertained. Had the body been in any respect despoiled? Had the deceased any articles of jewelry about her person upon leaving home? if so, had she any when found? These are important questions utterly untouched by the evidence; and there are others of equal moment, which have met with no attention. We must endeavor to satisfy ourselves by personal inquiry. The case of St. Eustache must be re-examined. I have no suspicion of this person; but let us proceed methodically. We will ascertain beyond a doubt the validity of the affidavits in regard to his whereabouts on the Sunday. Affidavits of this character are readily made matter of mystification. Should there be nothing wrong here, however, we will dismiss St. Eustache from our investigations. His suicide, however corroborative of suspicion, were there found to be deceit in the affidavits, is, without such deceit, in no respect an unaccountable circumstance, or one which need cause us to deflect from the line of ordinary analysis.

"In that which I now propose, we will discard the interior points of this tragedy, and concentrate our attention upon its outskirts. Not the least usual error, in investigations such as this, is the limiting of inquiry to the immediate, with total disregard of the collateral or circumstantial events. It is the mal-practice of the courts to confine evidence and discussion to the bounds of apparent relevancy. Yet experience has shown, and a true philosophy will always show, that a vast, perhaps the larger portion of truth, arises from the seemingly irrelevant. It is through the spirit of this principle, if not precisely through its letter, that modern science has resolved to calculate upon the unforeseen. But perhaps you do not comprehend me. The history of human knowledge has so uninterruptedly shown that to collateral, or incidental, or accidental events we are indebted for the most numerous and most valuable discoveries, that it has at length become necessary, in any prospective view of improvement, to make not only large, but the largest allowances for inventions that shall arise by chance, and quite out of the range of ordinary expectation. It is no longer philosophical to base, upon what has been, a vision of what is to be. Accident is admitted as a portion of the substructure. We make chance a matter of absolute calculation. We subject the unlooked for and unimagined, to the mathematical *formulae* of the schools.

"I repeat that it is no more than fact, that the larger portion of all truth has sprung from the collateral; and it is but in accordance with the spirit of the principle involved in this fact, that I would divert inquiry, in the present case, from the trodden and hitherto unfruitful ground of the event itself, to the contemporary circumstances which surround it. While you ascertain the validity of the affidavits, I will examine the newspapers more generally than you have as yet done. So far, we have only reconnoitred the field of investigation; but it will be strange indeed if a comprehensive survey, such as I propose, of the public prints, will not afford us some minute points which shall establish a direction for inquiry."

In pursuance of Dupin's suggestion, I made scrupulous examination of the affair of the affidavits. The result was a firm conviction of their validity, and of the consequent innocence of St. Eustache. In the mean time my friend occupied himself, with what seemed to me a minuteness altogether objectless, in a scrutiny of the various newspaper files. At the end of a week he placed before me the following extracts:

"About three years and a half ago, a disturbance very similar to the present, was caused by the disappearance of this same Marie Rogêt, from the parfumerie of Monsieur Le Blanc, in the Palais Royal. At the end of a week, however, she re-appeared at her customary comptoir, as well as ever, with the exception of a slight paleness not altogether usual. It was given out by Monsieur Le Blanc and her mother, that she had merely been on a visit to some friend in the country; and the affair was speedily hushed up. We presume that the present absence is a freak of the same nature, and that, at the expiration of a week, or perhaps of a month, we shall have her among us again."—Evening Paper—Monday June 23.

"An evening journal of yesterday, refers to a former mysterious disappearance of Mademoiselle Rogêt. It is well known that, during the week of her absence from Le Blanc's parfumerie, she was in the company of a young naval officer, much noted for his debaucheries. A quarrel, it is supposed, providentially led to her return home. We have the name of the Lothario in question, who is, at present, stationed in Paris, but, for obvious reasons, forbear to make it public."—Le Mercurie—Tuesday Morning, June 24.

"An outrage of the most atrocious character was perpetrated near this city the day before yesterday. A gentleman, with his wife and daughter, engaged, about dusk, the services of six young men, who were idly rowing a boat to and fro near the banks of the Seine, to convey him across the river. Upon reaching the opposite shore, the three passengers stepped out, and had proceeded so far as to be beyond the view of the boat, when the daughter discovered that she had left in it her parasol. She returned for it, was seized by the gang, carried out into the stream, gagged, brutally treated, and finally taken to the shore at a point not far from that at which she had originally entered the boat with her parents. The villains have escaped for the time, but the police are upon their trail, and some of them will soon be taken."—Morning Paper—June 25.

"We have received one or two communications, the object of which is to fasten the crime of the late atrocity upon Mennais; but as this gentleman has been fully exonerated by a loyal inquiry, and as the arguments of our several correspondents appear to be more zealous than profound, we do not think it advisable to make them public."—Morning Paper—June 28.

"We have received several forcibly written communications, apparently from various sources, and which go far to render it a matter of certainty that the unfortunate Marie Rogêt has become a victim of one of the numerous bands of blackguards which infest the vicinity of the city upon Sunday. Our own opinion is decidedly in favor of this supposition. We shall endeavor to make room for some of these arguments hereafter."—Evening Paper—Tuesday, June 31.

"On Monday, one of the bargemen connected with the revenue service, saw a empty boat floating down the Seine. Sails were lying in the bottom of the boat. The bargeman towed it under the barge office. The next morning it was taken from thence, without the knowledge of any of the officers. The rudder is now at the barge office."—Le Diligence—Thursday, June 26.

Upon reading these various extracts, they not only seemed to me irrelevant, but I could perceive no mode in which any one of them could be brought to bear upon the matter in hand. I waited for some explanation from Dupin.

"It is not my present design," he said, "to dwell upon the first and second of those extracts. I have copied them chiefly to show you the extreme remissness of the police, who, as far as I can understand from the Prefect, have not troubled themselves, in any respect, with an examination of the naval officer alluded to. Yet it is mere folly to say that between the first and second disappearance of Marie, there is no *supposable* connection. Let us admit the first elopement to have resulted in a quarrel between the lovers, and the return home of the betrayed. We are now prepared to view a second elopement (if we know that an elopement has again taken place) as indicating a renewal of the betrayer's advances, rather than as the result of new proposals by a second individual—we are prepared to regard it as a 'making up' of the old amour, rather than as the commencement of a new one. The chances are ten to one, that he who had once eloped with Marie, would again propose an elopement, rather than that she to whom proposals of elopement had been made by one individual, should have them made to her by another. And here let me call your attention to the fact, that the time elapsing between the first ascertained, and the second supposed elopement, is a few months more than the general period of the cruises of our men-of-war. Had the lover been interrupted in his first villany by the necessity of departure to sea, and had he seized the first moment of his return to renew the base designs not yet altogether accomplished—or not yet altogether accomplished by *him?* Of all these things we know nothing.

"You will say, however, that, in the second instance, there was no elopement as imagined. Certainly not—but are we prepared to say that there was not the frustrated design? Beyond St. Eustache, and perhaps Beauvais, we find no recognized, no open, no honorable suitors of Marie. Of none other is there any thing said. Who, then, is the secret lover, of whom the relatives (at least most of them) know nothing, but whom Marie meets upon the morning of Sunday, and who is so deeply in her confidence, that she hesitates not to remain with him until the shades of the evening descend, amid the solitary groves of the Barrière du Roule? Who is that secret lover, I ask, of whom, at least, most of the relatives know nothing? And what means the singular prophecy of Madame Rogêt on the morning of Marie's departure?—'I fear that I shall never see Marie again.'

"But if we cannot imagine Madame Rogêt privy to the design of elopement, may we not at least suppose this design entertained by the girl? Upon quitting home, she gave it to be understood that she was about to visit her aunt in the Rue des Drâmes and St. Eustache was requested to call for her at dark. Now, at first glance, this fact strongly militates against my suggestion;—but let us reflect. That she did meet some companion, and proceed with him across the river, reaching the Barrière du Roule at so late an hour as three o'clock in the afternoon, is known. But in consenting so to accompany this individual, (*for whatever purpose—to her mother known or unknown,*) she must have thought of her expressed intention when leaving home, and of the surprise and suspicion aroused in the bosom of her affianced suitor, St. Eustache, when, calling for her, at the hour appointed, in the Rue des Drâmes, he should find that she had not been there, and when, moreover, upon returning to the pension with this alarming intelligence, he should become aware of her continued absence from home. She must have thought of these things, I say. She must have foreseen the chagrin of St. Eustache, the suspicion of all. She could not have thought of returning to brave this suspicion; but the suspicion becomes a point of trivial importance to her, if we suppose her not intending to return.

"We may imagine her thinking thus—'I am to meet a certain person for the purpose of elopement, or for certain other purposes known only to myself. It is necessary that there be no chance of interruption—there must be sufficient time given us to elude pursuit—I will give it to be understood that I shall visit and spend the day with my aunt at the Rue des Drâmes—I well tell St. Eustache not to call for me until dark—in this way, my absence from home for the longest possible period, without causing suspicion or anxiety, will be accounted for, and I shall gain more time than in any other manner. If I bid St. Eustache call for me at dark, he will be sure not to call before; but, if I wholly neglect to bid him call, my time for escape will be diminished, since it will be expected that I return the earlier, and my absence will the sooner excite anxiety. Now, if it were my design to return at all—if I had in contemplation merely a stroll with the individual in question—it would not be my policy to bid St. Eustache call; for, calling, he will be sure to ascertain that I have played him false—a fact of which I might keep him for ever in ignorance, by leaving home without notifying him of my intention, by returning before dark, and by then stating that I had been to visit my aunt in the Rue des Drâmes. But, as it is my design never to return—or not for some weeks—or not until certain concealments are effected—the gaining of time is the only point about which I need give myself any concern.'

"You have observed, in your notes, that the most general opinion in relation to this sad affair is, and was from the first, that the girl had been the victim of a gang of blackguards. Now, the popular opinion, under certain conditions, is not to be disregarded. When arising of itself—when manifesting itself in a strictly spontaneous manner—we should look upon it as analogous with that *intuition* which is the idiosyncrasy of the individual man of genius. In ninety-nine cases from the hundred I would abide by its decision. But it is important that we find no palpable traces of *suggestion*. The opinion must be rigorously *the public's own*; and the distinction is often exceedingly difficult to perceive and to maintain. In the present instance, it appears to me that this 'public opinion' in respect to a gang, has been superinduced by the collateral event which is detailed in the third of my extracts. All Paris is excited by the discovered corpse of Marie, a girl young, beautiful and notorious. This corpse is found, bearing marks of violence, and floating in the river. But it is now made known that, at the very period, or about the very period, in which it is supposed that the girl was assassinated, an outrage similar in nature to that endured by the deceased, although less in extent, was perpetuated, by a gang of young ruffians, upon the person of a second young female. Is it wonderful that the one known atrocity should influence the popular judgment in regard to the other unknown? This judgment awaited direction, and the known outrage seemed so opportunely to afford it! Marie, too, was found in the river; and upon this very river was this known outrage committed. The connexion of the two events had about it so much of the palpable, that the true wonder would have been a failure of the populace to appreciate and to seize it. But, in fact, the one atrocity, known to be so committed, is, if any thing, evidence that the other, committed at a time nearly coincident, was not so committed. It would have been a miracle indeed, if, while a gang of ruffians were perpetrating, at a given locality, a most unheard-of wrong, there should have been another similar gang, in a similar locality, in the same city, under the same circumstances, with the same means and appliances, engaged in a wrong of precisely the same aspect, at precisely the same period of time! Yet in what, if not in this marvellous train of coincidence, does the accidentally suggested opinion of the populace call upon us to believe?

"Before proceeding farther, let us consider the supposed scene of the assassination, in the thicket at the Barrière du Roule. This thicket, although dense, was in the close vicinity of a public road. Within were three or four large stones, forming a kind of seat with a back and footstool. On the upper stone was discovered a white petticoat; on the second, a silk scarf. A parasol, gloves, and a pocket-handkerchief, were also here found. The handkerchief bore the name, 'Marie Rogêt.' Fragments of dress were seen on the branches around. The earth was trampled, the bushes were broken, and there was every evidence of a violent struggle.

"Notwithstanding the acclamation with which the discovery of this thicket was received by the press, and the unanimity with which it was supposed to indicate the precise scene of the outrage, it must be admitted that there was some very good reason for doubt. That it was the scene, I may or I may not believe—but there was excellent reason for doubt. Had the true scene been, as Le Commerciel suggested, in the neighborhood of the Rue Pavée St. Andrée, the perpetrators of the crime, supposing them still resident in Paris, would naturally have been stricken with terror at the public attention thus acutely directed into the proper channel; and, in certain classes of minds, there would have arisen, at once, a sense of the necessity of some exertion to redivert this attention. And thus, the thicket of the Barrière du Roule having been already suspected, the idea of placing the articles where they were found, might have been naturally entertained. There is no real evidence, although Le Soleil so supposes, that the articles discovered had been more than a very few days in the thicket; while there is much circumstantial proof that they could not have remained there, without attracting attention, during the twenty days elapsing between the fatal Sunday and the afternoon upon which they were found by the boys. 'They were all *mildewed* down hard,' says Le Soleil, adopting the opinions of its predecessors, 'with the action of the rain, and stuck together from *mildew*. The grass had grown around and over some of them. The silk of the parasol was strong, but the threads of it were run together within. The upper part, where it had been doubled and folded, was all *mildewed* and rotten, and tore on being opened.' In respect to the grass having 'grown around and over some of them,' it is obvious that the fact could only have been ascertained from the words, and thus from the recollections, of two small boys; for these boys removed the articles and took them home before they had been seen by a third party. But grass will grow, especially in warm and damp weather, (such as was that of the period of the murder,) as much as two or three inches in a single day. A parasol lying upon a newly turfed ground, might, in a single week, be entirely concealed from sight by the upspringing grass. And touching that mildew upon which the editor of Le Soleil so pertinaciously insists, that he employs the word no less than three times in the brief paragraph just quoted, is he really unaware of the nature of this mildew? Is he to be told that it is one of the many classes of fungus, of which the most ordinary feature is its upspringing and decadence within twenty-four hours?

"Thus we see, at a glance, that what has been most triumphantly adduced in support of the idea that the articles had been 'for at least three or four weeks' in the thicket, is most absurdly null as regards any evidence of that fact. On the other hand, it is exceedingly difficult to believe that these articles could have remained in the thicket specified, for a longer period than a single week—for a longer period than from one Sunday to the next. Those who know any thing of the vicinity of Paris, know the extreme difficulty of finding seclusion unless at a great distance from its suburbs. Such a thing as an unexplored, or even an unfrequently visited recess, amid its woods or groves, is not for a moment to be imagined. Let any one who, being at heart a lover of nature, is yet chained by duty to the dust and heat of this great metropolis—let any such one attempt, even during the weekdays, to slake his thirst for solitude amid the scenes of natural loveliness which immediately surround us. At every second step, he will find the growing charm dispelled by the voice and personal intrusion of some ruffian or party of carousing blackguards. He will seek privacy amid the densest foliage, all in vain. Here are the very nooks where the unwashed most abound—here are the temples most desecrate. With sickness of the heart the wanderer will flee back to the polluted Paris as to a less odious because less incongruous sink of pollution. But if the vicinity of the city is so beset during the working days of the week, how much more so on the Sabbath! It is now especially that, released from the claims of labor, or deprived of the customary opportunities of crime, the town blackguard seeks the precincts of the town, not through love of the rural, which in his heart he despises, but by way of escape from the restraints and conventionalities of society. He desires less the fresh air and the green trees, than the utter license of the country. Here, at the road-side inn, or beneath the foliage of the woods, he indulges, unchecked by any eye except those of his boon companions, in all the mad excess of a counterfeit hilarity—the joint offspring of liberty and of rum. I say nothing more than what must be obvious to every dispassionate observer, when I repeat that the circumstance of the articles in question having remained undiscovered, for a longer period—than from one Sunday to another, in any thicket in the immediate neighborhood of Paris, is to be looked upon as little less than miraculous.

"But there are not wanting other grounds for the suspicion that the articles were placed in the thicket with the view of diverting attention from the real scene of the outrage. And, first, let me direct your notice to the date of the discovery of the articles. Collate this with the date of the fifth extract made by myself from the newspapers. You will find that the discovery followed, almost immediately, the urgent communications sent to the evening paper. These communications, although various and apparently from various sources, tended all to the same point—viz., the directing of attention to a gang as the perpetrators of the outrage, and to the neighborhood of the Barrière du Roule as its scene. Now here, of course, the suspicion is not that, in consequence of these communications, or of the public attention by them directed, the articles were found by the boys; but the suspicion might and may well have been, that the articles were not before found by the boys, for the reason that the articles had not before been in the thicket; having been deposited there only at so late a period as at the date, or shortly prior to the date of the communications by the guilty authors of these communications themselves.

"This thicket was a singular—an exceedingly singular one. It was unusually dense. Within its naturally walled enclosure were three extraordinary stones, forming a seat with a back and footstool. And this thicket, so full of a natural art, was in the immediate vicinity, within a few rods, of the dwelling of Madame Deluc, whose boys were in the habit of closely examining the shrubberies about them in search of the bark of the sassafras. Would it be a rash wager—a wager of one thousand to one—that a day never passed over the heads of these boys without finding at least one of them ensconced in the umbrageous hall, and enthroned upon its natural throne? Those who would hesitate at such a wager, have either never been boys themselves, or have forgotten the boyish nature. I repeat—it is exceedingly hard to comprehend how the articles could have remained in this thicket undiscovered, for a longer period than one or two days; and that thus there is good ground for suspicion, in spite of the dogmatic ignorance of Le Soleil, that they were, at a comparatively late date, deposited where found.

"But there are still other and stronger reasons for believing them so deposited, than any which I have as yet urged. And, now, let me beg your notice to the highly artificial arrangement of the articles. On the upper stone lay a white petticoat; on the second a silk scarf; scattered around, were a parasol, gloves, and a pocket-handkerchief bearing the name, 'Marie Rogêt.' Here is just such an arrangement as would naturally be made by a not over-acute person wishing to dispose the articles naturally. But it is by no means a really natural arrangement. I should rather have looked to see the things all lying on the ground and trampled under foot. In the narrow limits of that bower, it would have been scarcely possible that the petticoat and scarf should have retained a position upon the stones, when subjected to the brushing to and fro of many struggling persons. 'There was evidence,' it is said, 'of a struggle; and the earth was trampled, the bushes were broken,'—but the petticoat and the scarf are found deposited as if upon shelves. 'The pieces of the frock torn out by the bushes were about three inches wide and six inches long. One part was the hem of the frock and it had been mended. They looked like strips torn off.' Here, inadvertently, Le Soleil has employed an exceedingly suspicious phrase. The pieces, as described, do indeed 'look like strips torn off;' but purposely and by hand. It is one of the rarest of accidents that a piece is 'torn off,' from any garment such as is now in question, by the agency of a thorn. From the very nature of such fabrics, a thorn or nail becoming entangled in them, tears them rectangularly—divides them into two longitudinal rents, at right angles with each other, and meeting at an apex where the thorn enters—but it is scarcely possible to conceive the piece 'torn off.' I never so knew it, nor did you. To tear a piece off from such fabric, two distinct forces, in different directions, will be, in almost every case, required. If there be two edges to the fabric—if, for example, it be a pocket-handkerchief, and it is desired to tear from it a slip, then, and then only, will the one force serve the purpose. But in the present case the question is of a dress, presenting but one edge. To tear a piece from the interior, where no edge is presented, could only be effected by a miracle through the agency of thorns, and no one thorn could accomplish it. But, even where an edge is presented, two thorns will be necessary, operating, the one in two distinct directions, and the other in one. And this in the supposition that the edge is unhemmed. If hemmed, the matter is nearly out of the question. We thus see the numerous and great obstacles in the way of pieces being 'torn off' through the simple agency of 'thorns;' yet we are required to believe not only that one piece but that many have been so torn. 'And one part,' too, 'was the hem of the frock!' Another piece was 'part of the skirt, not the hem,'—that is to say, was torn completely out through the agency of thorns, from the uncaged interior of the dress! These, I say, are things which one may well be pardoned for disbelieving; yet, taken collectedly, they form, perhaps, less of reasonable ground for suspicion, than the one startling circumstance of the articles' having been left in this thicket at all, by any murderers who had enough precaution to think of removing the corpse. You will not have apprehended me rightly, however, if you suppose it my design to deny this thicket as the scene of the outrage. There might have been a wrong here, or, more possibly, an accident at Madame Deluc's. But, in fact, this is a point of minor importance. We are not engaged in an attempt to discover the scene, but to produce the perpetrators of the murder. What I have adduced, notwithstanding the minuteness with which I have adduced it, has been with the view, first, to show the folly of the positive and headlong assertions of Le Soleil, but secondly and chiefly, to bring you, by the most natural route, to a further contemplation of the doubt whether this assassination has, or has not been, the work of a gang.

"We will resume this question by mere allusion to the revolting details of the surgeon examined at the inquest. It is only necessary to say that his published inferences, in regard to the number of ruffians, have been properly ridiculed as unjust and totally baseless, by all the reputable anatomists of Paris. Not that the matter might not have been as inferred, but that there was no ground for the inference:—was there not much for another?

"Let us reflect now upon 'the traces of a struggle;' and let me ask what these traces have been supposed to demonstrate. A gang. But do they not rather demonstrate the absence of a gang? What struggle could have taken place—what struggle so violent and so enduring as to have left its 'traces' in all directions—between a weak and defenceless girl and the gang of ruffians imagined? The silent grasp of a few rough arms and all would have been over. The victim must have been absolutely passive at their will. You will here bear in mind that the arguments urged against the thicket as the scene, are applicable in chief part, only against it as the scene of an outrage committed by more than a single individual. If we imagine but one violator, we can conceive, and thus only conceive, the struggle of so violent and so obstinate a nature as to have left the 'traces' apparent.

"And again. I have already mentioned the suspicion to be excited by the fact that the articles in question were suffered to remain at all in the thicket where discovered. It seems almost impossible that these evidences of guilt should have been accidentally left where found. There was sufficient presence of mind (it is supposed) to remove the corpse; and yet a more positive evidence than the corpse itself (whose features might have been quickly obliterated by decay,) is allowed to lie conspicuously in the scene of the outrage—I allude to the handkerchief with the name of the deceased. If this was accident, it was not the accident of a gang. We can imagine it only the accident of an individual. Let us see. An individual has committed the murder. He is alone with the ghost of the departed. He is appalled by what lies motionless before him. The fury of his passion is over, and there is abundant room in his heart for the natural awe of the deed. His is none of that confidence which the presence of numbers inevitably inspires. He is alone with the dead. He trembles and is bewildered. Yet there is a necessity for disposing of the corpse. He bears it to the river, but leaves behind him the other evidences of guilt; for it is difficult, if not impossible to carry all the burthen at once, and it will be easy to return for what is left. But in his toilsome journey to the water his fears redouble within him. The sounds of life encompass his path. A dozen times he hears or fancies the step of an observer. Even the very lights from the city bewilder him. Yet, in time and by long and frequent pauses of deep agony, he reaches the river's brink, and disposes of his ghastly charge—perhaps through the medium of a boat. But now what treasure does the world hold—what threat of vengeance could it hold out—which would have power to urge the return of that lonely murderer over that toilsome and perilous path, to the thicket and its blood chilling recollections? He returns not, let the consequences be what they may. He could not return if he would. His sole thought is immediate escape. He turns his back forever upon those dreadful shrubberies and flees as from the wrath to come.

"But how with a gang? Their number would have inspired them with confidence; if, indeed confidence is ever wanting in the breast of the arrant blackguard; and of arrant blackguards alone are the supposed gangs ever constituted. Their number, I say, would have prevented the bewildering and unreasoning terror which I have imagined to paralyze the single man. Could we suppose an oversight in one, or two, or three, this oversight would have been remedied by a fourth. They would have left nothing behind them; for their number would have enabled them to carry all at once. There would have been no need of return.

"Consider now the circumstance that in the outer garment of the corpse when found, 'a slip, about a foot wide had been torn upward from the bottom hem to the waist wound three times round the waist, and secured by a sort of hitch in the back.' This was done with the obvious design of affording a handle by which to carry the body. But would any number of men have dreamed of resorting to such an expedient? To three or four, the limbs of the corpse would have afforded not only a sufficient, but the best possible hold. The device is that of a single individual; and this brings us to the fact that 'between the thicket and the river, the rails of the fences were found taken down, and the ground bore evident traces of some heavy burden having been dragged along it!' But would a number of men have put themselves to the superfluous trouble of taking down a fence, for the purpose of dragging through it a corpse which they might have lifted over any fence in an instant? Would a number of men have so dragged a corpse at all as to have left evident traces of the dragging?

"And here we must refer to an observation of Le Commerciel; an observation upon which I have already, in some measure, commented.

'A piece,' says this journal, 'of one of the unfortunate girl's petticoats was torn out and tied under her chin, and around the back of her head, probably to prevent screams. This was done by fellows who had no pocket-handkerchiefs.'

"I have before suggested that a genuine blackguard is never without a pocket-handkerchief. But it is not to this fact that I now especially advert. That it was not through want of a handkerchief for the purpose imagined by Le Commerciel, that this bandage was employed, is rendered apparent by the handkerchief left in the thicket; and that the object was not 'to prevent screams' appears, also, from the bandage having been employed in preference to what would so much better have answered the purpose. But the language of the evidence speaks of the strip in question as 'found around the neck, fitting loosely, and secured with a hard knot.' These words are sufficiently vague, but differ materially from those of Le Commerciel. The slip was eighteen inches wide, and therefore, although of muslin, would form a strong band when folded or rumpled longitudinally. And thus rumpled it was discovered. My inference is this. The solitary murderer, having borne the corpse, for some distance, (whether from the thicket or elsewhere) by means of the bandage hitched around its middle, found the weight, in this mode of procedure, too much for his strength. He resolved to drag the burthen—the evidence goes to show that it was dragged. With this object in view, it became necessary to attach something like a rope to one of the extremities. It could be best attached about the neck, where the head would prevent its slipping off. And, now, the murderer bethought him, unquestionably, of the bandage about the loins. He would have used this, but for its volution about the corpse, the hitch which embarrassed it, and the reflection that it had not been 'torn off' from the garment. It was easier to tear a new slip from the petticoat. He tore it, made it fast about the neck, and so dragged his victim to the brink of the river. That this 'bandage,' only attainable with trouble and delay, and but imperfectly answering its purpose—that this bandage was employed at all, demonstrates that the necessity for its employment sprang from circumstances arising at a period when the handkerchief was no longer attainable—that is to say, arising, as we have imagined, after quitting the thicket, (if the thicket it was), and on the road between the thicket and the river.

"But the evidence, you will say, of Madame Deluc, (!) points especially to the presence of a gang, in the vicinity of the thicket, at or about the epoch of the murder. This I grant. I doubt if there were not a dozen gangs, such as described by Madame Deluc, in and about the vicinity of the Barrière du Roule at or about the period of this tragedy. But the gang which has drawn upon itself the pointed animadversion, although the somewhat tardy and very suspicious evidence of Madame Deluc, is the only gang which is represented by that honest and scrupulous old lady as having eaten her cakes and swallowed her brandy, without putting themselves to the trouble of making her payment. *Et hinc illæ iræ?*

"But what is the precise evidence of Madame Deluc? 'A gang of miscreants made their appearance, behaved boisterously, ate and drank without making payment, followed in the route of the young man and girl, returned to the inn about dusk, and recrossed the river as if in great haste.'

"Now this 'great haste' very possibly seemed greater haste in the eyes of Madame Deluc, since she dwelt lingeringly and lamentingly upon her violated cakes and ale—cakes and ale for which she might still have entertained a faint hope of compensation. Why, otherwise, since it was about dusk, should she make a point of the haste? It is no cause for wonder, surely, that even a gang of blackguards should make haste to get home, when a wide river is to be crossed in small boats, when storm impends, and when night approaches.

"I say approaches; for the night had not yet arrived. It was only about dusk that the indecent haste of these 'miscreants' offended the sober eyes of Madame Deluc. But we are told that it was upon this very evening that Madame Deluc, as well as her eldest son, 'heard the screams of a female in the vicinity of the inn.' And in what words does Madame Deluc designate the period of the evening at which these screams were heard? 'It was soon after dark,' she says. But 'soon after dark,' is, at least, dark; and 'about dusk' is as certainly daylight. Thus it is abundantly clear that the gang quitted the Barrière du Roule prior to the screams overheard (?) by Madame Deluc. And although, in all the many reports of the evidence, the relative expressions in question are distinctly and invariably employed just as I have employed them in this conversation with yourself, no notice whatever of the gross discrepancy has, as yet, been taken by any of the public journals, or by any of the Myrmidons of police.

"I shall add but one to the arguments against a gang; but this one has, to my own understanding at least, a weight altogether irresistible. Under the circumstances of large reward offered, and full pardon to any King's evidence, it is not to be imagined, for a moment, that some member of a gang of low ruffians, or of any body of men, would not long ago have betrayed his accomplices. Each one of a gang so placed, is not so much greedy of reward, or anxious for escape, as fearful of betrayal. He betrays eagerly and early that he may not himself be betrayed. That the secret has not been divulged, is the very best of proof that it is, in fact, a secret. The horrors of this dark deed are known only to one, or two, living human beings, and to God.

"Let us sum up now the meagre yet certain fruits of our long analysis. We have attained the idea either of a fatal accident under the roof of Madame Deluc, or of a murder perpetrated, in the thicket at the Barrière du Roule, by a lover, or at least by an intimate and secret associate of the deceased. This associate is of swarthy complexion. This complexion, the 'hitch' in the bandage, and the 'sailor's knot,' with which the bonnet-ribbon is tied, point to a seaman. His companionship with the deceased, a gay, but not an abject young girl, designates him as above the grade of the common sailor. Here the well written and urgent communications to the journals are much in the way of corroboration. The circumstance of the first elopement, as mentioned by Le Mercurie, tends to blend the idea of this seaman with that of the 'naval officer' who is first known to have led the unfortunate into crime.

"And here, most fitly, comes the consideration of the continued absence of him of the dark complexion. Let me pause to observe that the complexion of this man is dark and swarthy; it was no common swarthiness which constituted the sole point of remembrance, both as regards Valence and Madame Deluc. But why is this man absent? Was he murdered by the gang? If so, why are there only traces of the assassinated girl? The scene of the two outrages will naturally be supposed identical. And where is his corpse? The assassins would most probably have disposed of both in the same way. But it may be said that this man lives, and is deterred from making himself known, through dread of being charged with the murder. This consideration might be supposed to operate upon him now—at this late period—since it has been given in evidence that he was seen with Marie—but it would have had no force at the period of the deed. The first impulse of an innocent man would have been to announce the outrage, and to aid in identifying the ruffians. This policy would have suggested. He had been seen with the girl. He had crossed the river with her in an open ferry-boat. The denouncing of the assassins would have appeared, even to an idiot, the surest and sole means of relieving himself from suspicion. We cannot suppose him, on the night of the fatal Sunday, both innocent himself and incognizant of an outrage committed. Yet only under such circumstances is it possible to imagine that he would have failed, if alive, in the denouncement of the assassins.

"And what means are ours, of attaining the truth? We shall find these means multiplying and gathering distinctness as we proceed. Let us sift to the bottom this affair of the first elopement. Let us know the full history of 'the officer,' with his present circumstances, and his whereabouts at the precise period of the murder. Let us carefully compare with each other the various communications sent to the evening paper, in which the object was to inculpate a gang. This done, let us compare these communications, both as regards style and MS., with those sent to the morning paper, at a previous period, and insisting so vehemently upon the guilt of Mennais. And, all this done, let us again compare these various communications with the known MSS. of the officer. Let us endeavor to ascertain, by repeated questionings of Madame Deluc and her boys, as well as of the omnibus driver, Valence, something more of the personal appearance and bearing of the 'man of dark complexion.' Queries, skilfully directed, will not fail to elicit, from some of these parties, information on this particular point (or upon others)—information which the parties themselves may not even be aware of possessing. And let us now trace the boat picked up by the bargeman on the morning of Monday the twenty-third of June, and which was removed from the barge-office, without the cognizance of the officer in attendance, and without the rudder, at some period prior to the discovery of the corpse. With a proper caution and perseverance we shall infallibly trace this boat; for not only can the bargeman who picked it up identify it, but the rudder is at hand. The rudder of a sail-boat would not have been abandoned, without inquiry, by one altogether at ease in heart. And here let me pause to insinuate a question. There was no advertisement of the picking up of this boat. It was silently taken to the barge-office, and as silently removed. But its owner or employer—how happened he, at so early a period as Tuesday morning, to be informed, without the agency of advertisement, of the locality of the boat taken up on Monday, unless we imagine some connexion with the navy—some personal permanent connexion leading to cognizance of its minute in interests—its petty local news?

"In speaking of the lonely assassin dragging his burden to the shore, I have already suggested the probability of his availing himself of a boat.

Now we are to understand that Marie Rogêt was precipitated from a boat. This would naturally have been the case. The corpse could not have been trusted to the shallow waters of the shore. The peculiar marks on the back and shoulders of the victim tell of the bottom ribs of a boat. That the body was found without weight is also corroborative of the idea. If thrown from the shore a weight would have been attached. We can only account for its absence by supposing the murderer to have neglected the precaution of supplying himself with it before pushing off. In the act of consigning the corpse to the water, he would unquestionably have noticed his oversight; but then no remedy would have been at hand. Any risk would have been preferred to a return to that accursed shore. Having rid himself of his ghastly charge, the murderer would have hastened to the city. There, at some obscure wharf, he would have leaped on land. But the boat—would he have secured it? He would have been in too great haste for such things as securing a boat. Moreover, in fastening it to the wharf, he would have felt as if securing evidence against himself. His natural thought would have been to cast from him, as far as possible, all that had held connection with his crime. He would not only have fled from the wharf, but he would not have permitted the boat to remain. Assuredly he would have cast it adrift. Let us pursue our fancies.—In the morning, the wretch is stricken with unutterable horror at finding that the boat has been picked up and detained at a locality which he is in the daily habit of frequenting—at a locality, perhaps, which his duty compels him to frequent. The next night, without daring to ask for the rudder, he removes it. Now where is that rudderless boat? Let it be one of our first purposes to discover. With the first glimpse we obtain of it, the dawn of our success shall begin. This boat shall guide us, with a rapidity which will surprise even ourselves, to him who employed it in the midnight of the fatal Sabbath. Corroboration will rise upon corroboration, and the murderer will be traced."

(For reasons which we shall not specify, but which to many readers will appear obvious, we have taken the liberty of here omitting, from the MSS. placed in our hands, such portion as details the following up of the apparently slight clew obtained by Dupin. We feel it advisable only to state, in brief, that the result desired was brought to pass; and that the Prefect fulfilled punctually, although with reluctance, the terms of his compact with the Chevalier. Mr. Poe's article concludes with the following words.—Eds.)

It will be understood that I speak of coincidences and no more. What I have said above upon this topic must suffice. In my own heart there dwells no faith in præter-nature. That Nature and its God are two, no man who thinks, will deny. That the latter, creating the former, can, at will, control or modify it, is also unquestionable. I say "at will;" for the question is of will, and not, as the insanity of logic has assumed, of power. It is not that the Deity cannot modify his laws, but that we insult him in imagining a possible necessity for modification. In their origin these laws were fashioned to embrace all contingencies which could lie in the Future. With God all is Now.

I repeat, then, that I speak of these things only as of coincidences. And farther: in what I relate it will be seen that between the fate of the unhappy Mary Cecilia Rogers, so far as that fate is known, and the fate of one Marie Rogêt up to a certain epoch in her history, there has existed a parallel in the contemplation of whose wonderful exactitude the reason becomes embarrassed. I say all this will be seen. But let it not for a moment be supposed that, in proceeding with the sad narrative of Marie from the epoch just mentioned, and in tracing to its dénouement the mystery which enshrouded her, it is my covert design to hint at an extension of the parallel, or even to suggest that the measures adopted in Paris for the discovery of the assassin of a grisette, or measures founded in any similar ratiocination, would produce any similar result.

For, in respect to the latter branch of the supposition, it should be considered that the most trifling variation in the facts of the two cases might give rise to the most important miscalculations, by diverting thoroughly the two courses of events; very much as, in arithmetic, an error which, in its own individuality, may be inappreciable, produces, at length, by dint of multiplication at all points of the process, a result enormously at variance with truth. And, in regard to the former branch, we must not fail to hold in view that the very Calculus of Probabilities to which I have referred, forbids all idea of the extension of the parallel:—forbids it with a positiveness strong and decided just in proportion as this parallel has already been long-drawn and exact. This is one of those anomalous propositions which, seemingly appealing to thought altogether apart from the mathematical, is yet one which only the mathematician can fully entertain. Nothing, for example, is more difficult than to convince the merely general reader that the fact of sixes having been thrown twice in succession by a player at dice, is sufficient cause for betting the largest odds that sixes will not be thrown in the third attempt. A suggestion to this effect is usually rejected by the intellect at once. It does not appear that the two throws which have been completed, and which lie now absolutely in the Past, can have influence upon the throw which exists only in the Future. The chance for throwing sixes seems to be precisely as it was at any ordinary time—that is to say, subject only to the influence of the various other throws which may be made by the dice. And this is a reflection which appears so exceedingly obvious that attempts to controvert it are received more frequently with a derisive smile than with anything like respectful attention. The error here involved—a gross error redolent of mischief—I cannot pretend to expose within the limits assigned me at present; and with the philosophical it needs no exposure. It may be sufficient here to say that it forms one of an infinite series of mistakes which arise in the path of Reason through her propensity for seeking truth in detail.

The Purloined Letter

Nil sapientiæ odiosius acumine nimio.

—Seneca

At Paris, just after dark one gusty evening in the autumn of 18—, I was enjoying the twofold luxury of meditation and a meerschaum, in company with my friend C. Auguste Dupin, in his little back library, or book closet, *au troisième*, No. 33, Rue Dunôt, Faubourg St. Germain. For one hour at least we had maintained a profound silence; while each, to any casual observer, might have seemed intently and exclusively occupied with the curling eddies of smoke that oppressed the atmosphere of the chamber. For myself, however, I was mentally discussing certain topics which had formed matter for conversation between us at an earlier period of the evening; I mean the affair of the Rue Morgue, and the mystery attending the murder of Marie Rogêt. I looked upon it, therefore, as something of a coincidence, when the door of our apartment was thrown open and admitted our old acquaintance, Monsieur G——, the Prefect of the Parisian police.

We gave him a hearty welcome; for there was nearly half as much of the entertaining as of the contemptible about the man, and we had not seen him for several years. We had been sitting in the dark, and Dupin now arose for the purpose of lighting a lamp, but sat down again, without doing so, upon G——'s saying that he had called to consult us, or rather to ask the opinion of my friend, about some official business which had occasioned a great deal of trouble.

"If it is any point requiring reflection," observed Dupin, as he forebore to enkindle the wick, "we shall examine it to better purpose in the dark."

"That is another of your odd notions," said the Prefect, who had a fashion of calling everything "odd" that was beyond his comprehension, and thus lived amid an absolute legion of "oddities."

"Very true," said Dupin, as he supplied his visitor with a pipe, and rolled towards him a comfortable chair.

"And what is the difficulty now?" I asked. "Nothing more in the assassination way, I hope?"

"Oh, no; nothing of that nature. The fact is, the business is *very* simple indeed, and I make no doubt that we can manage it sufficiently well ourselves; but then I thought Dupin would like to hear the details of it, because it is so excessively *odd*."

"Simple and odd," said Dupin.

"Why, yes; and not exactly that, either. The fact is, we have all been a good deal puzzled because the affair *is* so simple, and yet baffles us altogether."

"Perhaps it is the very simplicity of the thing which puts you at fault," said my friend.

"What nonsense you *do* talk!" replied the Prefect, laughing heartily.

"Perhaps the mystery is a little *too* plain," said Dupin.

"Oh, good Heavens! who ever heard of such an idea?"

"A little *too* self-evident."

"Ha! ha! ha!—ha! ha! ha!—ho! ho! ho!" roared our visitor, profoundly amused. "O Dupin, you will be the death of me yet!"

"And what, after all, *is* the matter on hand?" I asked.

"Why, I will tell you," replied the Prefect, as he gave a long, steady, and contemplative puff, and settle'd himself in his chair. "I will tell you in a few words; but, before I begin, let me caution you that this is an affair demanding the greatest secrecy, and that I should most probably lose the position I now hold were it known that I confided it to any one."

"Proceed," said I.

"Or not," said Dupin.

"Well, then; I have received personal information, from a very high quarter, that a certain document of the last importance has been purloined from the royal apartments. The individual who purloined it is known; this beyond a doubt; he was seen to take it. It is known, also, that it still remains in his possession."

"How is this known?" asked Dupin.

"It is clearly inferred," replied the Prefect, "from the nature of the document, and from the non-appearance of certain results which would at once arise from its passing *out* of the robber's possession; that is to say, from his employing it as he must design in the end to employ it."

"Be a little more explicit," I said.

"Well, I may venture so far as to say that the paper gives its holder a certain power in a certain quarter where such power is immensely valuable." The Prefect was fond of the cant of diplomacy.

"Still I do not quite understand," said Dupin.

"No? well; the disclosure of the document to a third person, who shall be nameless, would bring in question the honor of a personage of most exalted station; and this fact gives the holder of the document an ascendency over the illustrious personage whose honor and peace are so jeopardized."

"But this ascendency," I interposed, "would depend upon the robber's knowledge of the loser's knowledge of the robber. Who would dare—"

"The thief," said G——, "is the Minister D——, who dares all things, those unbecoming as well as those becoming a man. The method of the theft was not less ingenious than bold. The document in question—a letter, to be frank—had been received by the personage robbed while alone in the royal boudoir. During its perusal she was suddenly interrupted by the entrance of the other exalted personage, from whom especially it was her wish to conceal it. After a hurried and vain endeavor to thrust it in a drawer, she was forced to place it, open as it was, upon a table. The address, however, was uppermost, and, the contents thus unexposed, the letter escaped notice. At this juncture enters the Minister D——. His lynx eye immediately perceives the paper, recognizes the handwriting of the address, observes the confusion of the personage addressed, and fathoms her secret. After some business transactions, hurried through in his ordinary manner, he produces a letter somewhat similar to the one in question, opens it, pretends to read it, and then places it in close juxtaposition to the other. Again he converses for some fifteen minutes upon the public affairs. At length, in taking leave, he takes also from the table the letter to which he had no claim. Its rightful owner saw, but, of course, dared not call attention to the act, in the presence of the third personage, who stood at her elbow. The Minister decamped, leaving his own letter—one of no importance—upon the table."

"Here, then," said Dupin to me, "you have precisely what you demand to make the ascendancy complete—the robber's knowledge of the loser's knowledge of the robber."

"Yes," replied the Prefect; "and the power thus attained has, for some months past, been wielded, for political purposes, to a very dangerous extent. The personage robbed is more thoroughly convinced, every day, of the necessity of reclaiming her letter. But this, of course, cannot be done openly. In fine, driven to despair, she has committed the matter to me."

"Than whom," said Dupin, amid a perfect whirlwind of smoke, "no more sagacious agent could, I suppose, be desired, or even imagined."

"You flatter me," replied the Prefect; "but it is possible that some such opinion may have been entertained."

"It is clear," said I, "as you observe, that the letter is still in possession of the Minister; since it is this possession, and not any employment of the letter, which bestows the power. With the employment the power departs."

"True," said G——; "and upon this conviction I proceeded. My first care was to make thorough search of the Minister's Hotel; and here my chief embarrassment lay in the necessity of searching without his knowledge. Beyond all things, I have been warned of the danger which would result from giving him reason to suspect our design."

"But," said I, "you are quite *au fait* in these investigations. The Parisian police have done this thing often before."

"Oh, yes; and for this reason I did not despair. The habits of the Minister gave me, too, a great advantage. He is frequently absent from home all night. His servants are by no means numerous. They sleep at a distance from their master's apartment, and, being chiefly Neapolitans, are readily made drunk. I have keys, as you know, with which I can open any chamber or cabinet in Paris. For three months a night has not passed, during the greater part of which I have not been engaged, personally, in ransacking the D—— Hotel. My honor is interested, and, to mention a great secret, the reward is enormous. So I did not abandon the search until I had become fully satisfied the thief is a more astute man than myself. I fancy that I have investigated every nook and corner of the premises in which it is possible that the paper can be concealed."

"But is it not possible," I suggested, "that although the letter may be in possession of the Minister, as it unquestionably is, he may have concealed it elsewhere than upon his own premises?"

"This is barely possible," said Dupin. "The present peculiar condition of affairs at court, and especially of those intrigues in which D—— is known to be involved, would render the instant availability of the document—its susceptibility of being produced at a moment's notice—a point of nearly equal importance with its possession."

"Its susceptibility of being produced?" said I.

"That is to say, of being *destroyed*," said Dupin.

"True," I observed; "the paper is clearly then upon the premises. As for its being upon the person of the Minister, we may consider that as out of the question."

"Entirely," said the Prefect. "He has been twice waylaid, as if by footpads, and his person rigorously searched under my own inspection."

"You might have spared yourself this trouble," said Dupin. "D——, I presume, is not altogether a fool, and, if not, must have anticipated these waylayings, as a matter of course."

"Not *altogether* a fool," said G——, "but then he's a poet, which I take to be only one remove from a fool."

"True," said Dupin, after a long and thoughtful whiff from his meerschaum, "although I have been guilty of certain doggerel myself."

"Suppose you detail," said I, "the particulars of your search."

"Why, the fact is, we took our time, and we searched *everywhere*. I have had long experience in these affairs. I took the entire building, room by room, devoting the nights of a whole week to each. We examined, first, the furniture of each apartment. We opened every possible drawer; and I presume you know that, to a properly trained police agent, such a thing as a *secret* drawer is impossible. Any man is a dolt who permits a 'secret' drawer to escape him in a search of this kind. The thing is *so* plain. There is a certain amount of bulk—of space—to be accounted for in every cabinet. Then we have accurate rules. The fiftieth part of a line could not escape us. After the cabinets we took the chairs. The cushions we probed with the fine long needles you have seen me employ. From the tables we removed the tops."

"Why so?"

"Sometimes the top of a table, or other similarly arranged piece of furniture, is removed by the person wishing to conceal an article; then the leg is excavated, the article deposited within the cavity, and the top replaced. The bottoms and tops of bedposts are employed in the same way."

"But could not the cavity be detected by sounding?" I asked.

"By no means, if, when the article is deposited, a sufficient wadding of cotton be placed around it. Besides, in our case we were obliged to proceed without noise."

"But you could not have removed—you could not have taken to pieces *all* articles of furniture in which it would have been possible to make a deposit in the manner you mention. A letter may be compressed into a thin spiral roll, not differing much in shape or bulk from a large knitting-needle, and in this form it might be inserted into the rung of a chair, for example. You did not take to pieces all the chairs?"

"Certainly not; but we did better—we examined the rungs of every chair in the Hotel, and indeed, the jointings of every description of furniture, by the aid of a most powerful microscope. Had there been any traces of recent disturbance we should not have failed to detect it instantly. A single grain of gimlet-dust, for example, would have been as obvious as an apple. Any disorder in the gluing—any unusual gaping in the joints—would have sufficed to insure detection."

"I presume you looked to the mirrors, between the boards and the plates, and you probed the beds and the bedclothes, as well as the curtains and carpets?"

"That, of course; and when we had absolutely completed every particle of the furniture in this way, then we examined the house itself. We divided its entire surface into compartments, which we numbered, so that none might be missed; then we scrutinized each individual square inch throughout the premises, including the two houses immediately adjoining, with the microscope, as before."

"The two houses adjoining!" I exclaimed; "you must have had a great deal of trouble."

"We had; but the reward offered is prodigious."

"You include the *grounds* about the houses?"

"All the grounds are paved with bricks. They gave us comparatively little trouble. We examined the moss between the bricks, and found it undisturbed."

"You looked among D——'s papers, of course, and into the books of the library?"

"Certainly; we opened every package and parcel; we not only opened every book, but we turned over every leaf in each volume, not contenting ourselves with a mere shake, according to the fashion of some of our police officers. We also measured the thickness of every book-*cover*, with the most accurate admeasurement, and applied to each the most jealous scrutiny of the microscope. Had any of the bindings been recently meddled with, it would have been utterly impossible that the fact should have escaped observation. Some five or six volumes, just from the hands of the binder, we carefully probed, longitudinally, with the needles."

"You explored the floors beneath the carpets?"

"Beyond doubt. We removed every carpet, and examined the boards with the microscope."

"And the paper on the walls?"

"Yes."

"You looked into the cellars?"

"We did."

"Then," I said, "you have been making a miscalculation, and the letter is *not* upon the premises, as you suppose."

"I fear you are right there," said the Prefect. "And now, Dupin, what would you advise me to do?"

"To make a thorough re-search of the premises."

"That is absolutely needless," replied G——. "I am not more sure that I breathe than I am that the letter is not at the Hotel."

"I have no better advice to give you," said Dupin.

"You have, of course, an accurate description of the letter?"

"Oh, yes!"—And here the Prefect, producing a memorandum-book, proceeded to read aloud a minute account of the internal, and especially of the external appearance of the missing document. Soon after finishing the perusal of this description, he took his departure, more entirely depressed in spirits than I had ever known the good gentleman before.

In about a month afterwards he paid us another visit, and found us occupied very nearly as before. He took a pipe and a chair and entered into some ordinary conversation. At length I said,—

"Well, but, G——, what of the purloined letter? I presume you have at last made up your mind that there is no such thing as overreaching the Minister?"

"Confound him, say I—yes; I made the re-examination, however, as Dupin suggested—but it was all labor lost, as I knew it would be."

"How much was the reward offered, did you say?" asked Dupin.

"Why, a very great deal—a *very* liberal reward—I don't like to say how much, precisely; but one thing I *will* say, that I wouldn't mind giving my individual check for fifty thousand francs to any one who could obtain me that letter. The fact is, it is becoming of more and more importance every day; and the reward has been lately doubled. If it were trebled, however, I could do no more than I have done."

"Why, yes," said Dupin, drawlingly, between the whiffs of his meerschaum, "I really—think, G——, you have not exerted yourself—to the utmost in this matter. You might—do a little more, I think, eh?"

"How?—in what way?"

"Why—puff, puff—you might—puff, puff—employ counsel in the matter, eh?—puff, puff, puff. Do you remember the story they tell of Abernethy?"

"No; hang Abernethy!"

"To be sure! hang him and welcome. But, once upon a time, a certain rich miser conceived the design of sponging upon this Abernethy for a medical opinion. Getting up, for this purpose, an ordinary conversation in a private company, he insinuated his case to the physician, as that of an imaginary individual.

"'We will suppose,' said the miser, 'that his symptoms are such and such; now, doctor, what would *you* have directed him to take?'

"'Take!' said Abernethy, 'why, take *advice*, to be sure.'"

"But," said the Prefect, a little discomposed, "I am *perfectly* willing to take advice, and to pay for it. I would *really* give fifty thousand francs to any one who would aid me in the matter."

"In that case," replied Dupin, opening a drawer, and producing a check-book, "you may as well fill me up a check for the amount mentioned. When you have signed it, I will hand you the letter."

I was astounded. The Prefect appeared absolutely thunder-stricken. For some minutes he remained speechless and motionless, looking incredulously at my friend with open mouth, and eyes that seemed starting from their sockets; then, apparently recovering himself in some measure, he seized a pen, and after several pauses and vacant stares, finally filled up and signed a check for fifty thousand francs, and handed it across the table to Dupin. The latter examined it carefully and deposited it in his pocketbook; then, unlocking an *escritoire*, took thence a letter and gave it to the Prefect. This functionary grasped it in a perfect agony of joy, opened it with a trembling hand, cast a rapid glance at its contents, and then, scrambling and struggling to the door, rushed at length unceremoniously from the room and from the house, without having uttered a syllable since Dupin had requested him to fill up the check.

When he had gone, my friend entered into some explanations.

"The Parisian police," he said, "are exceedingly able in their way. They are persevering, ingenious, cunning, and thoroughly versed in the knowledge which their duties seem chiefly to demand. Thus, when G—— detailed to us his mode of searching the premises at the Hotel D——, I felt entire confidence in his having made a satisfactory investigation—so far as his labors extended."

"So far as his labors extended?" said I.

"Yes," said Dupin. "The measures adopted were not only the best of their kind, but carried out to absolute perfection. Had the letter been deposited within the range of their search, these fellows would, beyond a question, have found it."

I merely laughed—but he seemed quite serious in all that he said.

"The measures, then," he continued, "were good in their kind, and well executed; their defect lay in their being inapplicable to the case, and to the man. A certain set of highly ingenious resources are, with the Prefect, a sort of Procrustean bed to which he forcibly adapts his designs. But he perpetually errs by being too deep or too shallow, for the matter in hand; and many a schoolboy is a better reasoner than he. I knew one about eight years of age, whose success at guessing in the game of 'even and odd' attracted universal admiration. This game *is* simple, and is played with marbles. One player holds in his hand a number of these toys, and demands of another whether that number is even or odd. If the guess is right, the guesser wins one; if wrong, he loses one. The boy to whom I allude won all the marbles of the school. Of course he had some principle of guessing; and this lay in mere observation and admeasurement of the astuteness of his opponents. For example, an arrant simpleton is his opponent, and, holding up his closed hand asks, 'Are they even or odd?' Our schoolboy replies, 'Odd' and loses; but upon the second trial he wins, for he then says to himself, 'the simpleton had them even upon the first trial, and his amount of cunning is just sufficient to make him have them odd upon the second; I will therefore guess odd;' he guesses odd, and wins. Now, with a simpleton a degree above the first he would have reasoned thus: 'This fellow finds that in the first instance I guessed odd, and, in the second, he will propose to himself, upon the first impulse, a simple variation from even to odd, as did the first simpleton; but then a second thought will suggest that this is too simple a variation, and finally he will decide upon putting it even as before. I will therefore guess even;' he guesses even, and wins. Now this mode of reasoning in the schoolboy, whom his fellows term 'lucky,'—what, in its last analysis, is it?"

"It is merely," I said, "an identification of the reasoner's intellect with that of his opponent."

"It is," said Dupin; "and, upon inquiring of the boy by what means he effected the *thorough* identification in which his success consisted, I received answer as follows: 'When I wish to find out how wise, or how stupid, or how good, or how wicked is any one, or what are his thoughts at the moment, I fashion the expression of my face, as accurately as possible, in accordance with the expression of his, and then wait to see what thoughts or sentiments arise in my mind or heart, as if to match or correspond with the expression.' This response of the schoolboy lies at the bottom of all the spurious profundity which has been attributed to Rochefoucauld, to La Bruyère, to Machiavelli, and to Campanella."

"And the identification," I said, "of the reasoner's intellect with that of his opponent, depends, if I understand you aright, upon the accuracy with which the opponent's intellect is admeasured."

"For its practical value it depends upon this," replied Dupin, "and the Prefect and his cohort fail so frequently, first, by default of this identification, and, secondly, by ill-admeasurement, or rather through non-admeasurement, of the intellect with which they are engaged. They consider only their *own* ideas of ingenuity; and, in searching for anything hidden, advert only to the modes in which *they* would have hidden it. They are right in this much—that their own ingenuity is a faithful representative of that of *the mass*: but when the cunning of the individual felon is diverse in character from their own, the felon foils them, of course. This always happens when it is above their own, and very usually when it is below. They have no variation of principle in their investigations; at best, when urged by some unusual emergency—by some extraordinary reward—they extend or exaggerate their old modes of *practice*, without touching their principles. What, for example, in this case of D——, has been done to vary the principle of action? What is all this boring, and probing, and sounding, and scrutinizing with the microscope, and dividing the surface of the building into registered square inches—what is it all but an exaggeration *of the application* of the one principle or set of principles of search, which are based upon the one set of notions regarding human ingenuity, to which the Prefect, in the long routine of his duty, has been accustomed? Do you not see he has taken it for granted that *all* men proceed to conceal a letter,—not exactly in a gimlet-hole bored in a chair leg—but, at least, in *some* out-of-the-way hole or corner suggested by the same tenor of thought which would urge a man to secrete a letter in a gimlet-hole bored in a chair-leg? And do you not see, also, that such *recherchés* nooks for concealment are adapted only for ordinary occasions and would be adopted only by ordinary intellects; for, in all cases of concealment, a disposal of the article concealed—a disposal of it in this *recherché* manner—is, in the very first instance, presumable and presumed; and thus its discovery depends, not at all upon the acumen, but altogether upon the mere care, patience, and determination of the seekers; and where the case is of importance—or, what amounts to the same thing in policial eyes, when the reward is of magnitude—the qualities in question have *never* been known to fail. You will now understand what I meant in suggesting that, had the purloined letter been hidden anywhere within the limits of the Prefect's examination—in other words, had the principle of its concealment been comprehended within the principles of the Prefect—its discovery would have been a matter altogether beyond question. This functionary, however, has been thoroughly mystified; and the remote source of his defeat lies in the supposition that the Minister is a fool, because he has acquired renown as a poet. All fools are poets; this the Prefect *feels*; and he is merely guilty of a *non distributio medii* in thence inferring that all poets are fools."

"But is this really the poet?" I asked. "There are two brothers, I know; and both have attained reputation in letters. The Minister, I believe, has written learnedly on the Differential Calculus. He is a mathematician, and no poet"

"You are mistaken; I know him well; he is both. As poet *and* mathematician, he would reason well; as mere mathematician, he could not have reasoned at all, and thus would have been at the mercy of the Prefect."

"You surprise me," I said, "by these opinions, which have been contradicted by the voice of the world. You do not mean to set at naught the well-digested idea of centuries. The mathematical reason has long been regarded as *the* reason *par excellence*."

"'*Il-y-a à parier*,'" replied Dupin, quoting from Chamfort, "'*que toute idée publique, toute convention reçue, est une sottise, car elle a convenue au plus grand nombre*.' The mathematicians, I grant you, have done their best to promulgate the popular error to which you allude, and which is none the less an error for its promulgation as truth. With an art worthy a better cause, for example, they have insinuated the term 'analysis' into application to algebra. The French are the originators of this particular deception ; but if a term is of any importance—if words derive any value from applicability—then 'analysis' conveys 'algebra,' about as much as, in Latin, '*ambitus*' implies 'ambition,' '*religio*,' 'religion,' or '*homines honesti*,'a set of honorable men."

"You have a quarrel on hand, I see," said I, "with some of the algebraists of Paris; but proceed."

"I dispute the availability, and thus the value, of that reason which is cultivated in any especial form other than the abstractly logical. I dispute, in particular, the reason educed by mathematical study. The mathematics are the science of form and quantity; mathematical reasoning is merely logic applied to observation upon form and quantity. The great error lies in supposing that even the truths of what is called *pure* algebra are abstract or general truths. And this error is so egregious that I am confounded at the universality with which it has been received. Mathematical axioms are *not* axioms of general truth. What is true of *relation*—of form and quantity—is often grossly false in regard to morals, for example. In this latter science it is very usually *un*true that the aggregated parts are equal to the whole. In chemistry also the axiom fails. In the consideration of motive it fails; for two motives, each of a given value, have not, necessarily, a value when united, equal to the sum of their values apart. There are numerous other mathematical truths which are only truths within the limits of *relation*. But the mathematician argues, from his *finite truths*, through habit, as if they were of an absolutely general applicability—as the world indeed imagines them to be. Bryant, in his very learned 'Mythology,' mentions an analogous source of error, when he says that 'although the Pagan fables are not believed, yet we forget ourselves continually, and make inferences from them as existing realities.' With the algebraists, however, who are Pagans themselves, the 'Pagan fables' *are* believed, and the inferences are made, not so much through lapse of memory, as through an unaccountable addling of the brains. In short, I neyer yet encountered the mere mathematician who could be trusted out of equal roots, or one who did not clandestinely hold it as a point of his faith that x^2+px was absolutely and unconditionally equal to q. Say to one of these gentlemen, by way of experiment, if you please, that you believe occasions may occur where x^2+px is *not* altogether equal to q, and, having made him understand what you mean, get out of his reach as speedily as convenient, for, beyond doubt, he will endeavor to knock you down.

"I mean to say," continued Dupin, while I merely laughed at his last observations, "that if the Minister had been no more than a mathematician, the Prefect would have been under no necessity of giving me this check. I knew him, however, as both mathematician and poet, and my measures were adapted to his capacity, with reference to the circumstances by which he was surrounded. I knew him as courtier, too, and as a bold *intriguant*. Such a man, I considered, could not fail to be aware of the ordinary policial modes of action. He could not have failed to anticipate—and events have proved that he did not fail to anticipate—the waylayings to which he was subjected. He must have foreseen, I reflected, the secret investigations of his premises. His frequent absences from home at night, which were hailed by the Prefect as certain aids to his success, I regarded only as ruses, to afford opportunity for thorough search to the police, and thus the sooner to impress them with the conviction to which G——, in fact, did finally arrive—the conviction that the letter was not upon the premises. I felt, also, that the whole train of thought, which I was at some pains in detailing to you just now, concerning the invariable principle of policial action in searches for articles concealed—I felt that this whole train of thought would necessarily pass through the mind of the Minister. It would imperatively lead him to despise all the ordinary *nooks* of concealment. *He* could not, I reflected, be so weak as not to see that the most intricate and remote recess of his Hotel would be as open as his commonest closets to the eyes, to the probes, to the gimlets, and to the microscopes of the Prefect. I saw, in fine, that he would be driven, as a matter of course, to *simplicity*, if not deliberately induced to it as a matter of choice. You will remember, perhaps, how desperately the Prefect laughed when I suggested, upon our first interview, that it was just possible this mystery troubled him so much on account of its being so *very* self-evident."

"Yes," said I, "I remember his merriment well. I really thought he would have fallen into convulsions."

"The material world," continued Dupin, "abounds with very strict analogies to the immaterial; and thus some color of truth has been given to the rhetorical dogma, that metaphor, or simile, may be made to strengthen an argument, as well as to embellish a description. The principle of the *vis inertiæ*, for example, seems to be identical in physics and metaphysics. It is not more true in the former, that a large body is with more difficulty set in motion than a smaller one, and that its subsequent momentum is commensurate with this difficulty, than it is, in the latter, that intellects of the vaster capacity, while more forcible, more constant, and more eventful in their movements than those of inferior grade, are yet the less readily moved, and more embarrassed and full of hesitation in the first few steps of their progress. Again: have you ever noticed which of the street signs, over the shop-doors, are the most attractive of attention?"

"I have never given the matter a thought," I said.

"There is a game of puzzles," he resumed, "which is played upon a map. One party playing requires another to find a given word—the name of town, river, state, or empire—any word, in short, upon the motley and perplexed surface of the chart. A novice in the game generally seeks to embarrass his opponents by giving them the most minutely lettered names; but the adept selects such words as stretch, in large characters, from one end of the chart to the other. These, like the over-largely lettered signs and placards of the street, escape observation by dint of being excessively obvious; and here the physical oversight is precisely analogous with the moral inapprehension by which the intellect suffers to pass unnoticed those considerations which are too obtrusively and too palpably self-evident. But this is a point, it appears, somewhat above or beneath the understanding of the Prefect. He never once thought it probable, or possible, that the Minister had deposited the letter immediately beneath the nose of the whole world, by way of best preventing any portion of that world from perceiving it.

"But the more I reflected upon the daring, dashing, and discriminating ingenuity of D——; upon the fact that the document must always have been *at hand*, if he intended to use it to good purpose; and upon the decisive evidence, obtained by the Prefect, that it was not hidden within the limits of that dignitary's ordinary search—the more satisfied I became that, to conceal this letter, the Minister had resorted to the comprehensive and sagacious expedient of not attempting to conceal it at all.

"Full of these ideas, I prepared myself with a pair of green spectacles, and called one fine morning, quite by accident, at the Ministerial Hotel. I found D—— at home, yawning, lounging, and dawdling, as usual, and pretending to be in the last extremity of ennui. He is, perhaps, the most really energetic human being now alive—but that is only when nobody sees him.

"To be even with him, I complained of my weak eyes, and lamented the necessity of the spectacles, under cover of which I cautiously and thoroughly surveyed the apartment, while seemingly intent only upon the conversation of my host.

"I paid especial attention to a large writing-table near which he sat, and upon which lay confusedly some miscellaneous letters and other papers, with one or two musical instruments and a few books. Here, however, after a long and very deliberate scrutiny, I saw nothing to excite particular suspicion.

"At length my eyes, in going the circuit of the room, fell upon a trumpery filigree card-rack of pasteboard, that hung dangling by a dirty blue ribbon from a little brass knob just beneath the middle of the mantelpiece. In this rack, which had three or four compartments, were five or six visiting cards and a solitary letter. This last was much soiled and crumpled. It was torn nearly in two, across the middle—as if a design, in the first instance, to tear it entirely up as worthless, had been altered, or stayed, in the second. It had a large black seal, bearing the D—— cipher *very* conspicuously, and was addressed, in a diminutive female hand, to D——, the Minister himself. It was thrust carelessly, and even, as it seemed, contemptuously, into one of the upper divisions of the rack.

"No sooner had I glanced at this letter, than I concluded it to be that of which I was in search. To be sure, it was, to all appearance, radically different from the one of which the Prefect had read us so minute a description. Here the seal was large and black, with the D—— cipher; there it was small and red, with the ducal arms of the S—— family. Here, the address, to the Minister, was diminutive and feminine; there the superscription, to a certain royal personage, was markedly bold and decided; the size alone formed a point of correspondence. But then, the *radicalness* of these differences, which was excessive; the dirt; the soiled and torn condition of the paper, so inconsistent with the *true* methodical habits of D——, and so suggestive of a design to delude the beholder into an idea of the worthlessness of the document; these things, together with the hyperobtrusive situation of this document, full in the view of every visitor, and thus exactly in accordance with the conclusions to which I had previously arrived; these things, I say, were strongly corroborative of suspicion, in one who came with the intention to suspect.

"I protracted my visit as long as possible, and, while I maintained a most animated discussion with the Minister, upon a topic which I knew well had never failed to interest and excite him, I kept my attention really riveted upon the letter. In this examination, I committed to memory its external appearance and arrangement in the rack; and also fell, at length, upon a discovery which set at rest whatever trivial doubt I might have entertained. In scrutinizing the edges of the paper, I observed them to be more *chafed* than seemed necessary. They presented the *broken* appearance which is manifested when a stiff paper, having been once folded and pressed with a folder, is refolded in a reversed direction, in the same creases or edges which had formed the original fold. This discovery was sufficient. It was clear to me that the letter had been turned, as a glove, inside out, re-directed, and re-sealed. I bade the Minister good-morning, and took my departure at once, leaving a gold snuff-box upon the table.

"The next morning I called for the snuff-box, when we resumed, quite eagerly, the conversation of the preceding day. While thus engaged, however, a loud report, as if of a pistol, was heard immediately beneath the windows of the Hotel, and was succeeded by a series of fearful screams, and the shoutings of a mob. D—— rushed to a casement, threw it open, and looked out. In the meantime, I stepped to the card-rack, took the letter, put it in my pocket, and replaced it by a facsimile (so far as regards externals), which I had carefully prepared at my lodgings—imitating the D—— cipher, very readily, by means of a seal formed of bread.

"The disturbance in the street had been occasioned by the frantic behavior of a man with a musket. He had fired it among a crowd of women and children. It proved, however, to have been without ball, and the fellow was suffered to go his way as a lunatic or a drunkard. When he had gone, D—— came from the window, whither I had followed him immediately upon securing the object in view. Soon afterwards I bade him farewell. The pretended lunatic was a man in my own pay."

"But what purpose had you," I asked, "in replacing the letter by a facsimile? Would it not have been better, at the first visit, to have seized it openly, and departed?"

"D——," replied Dupin, "is a desperate man, and a man of nerve. His Hotel, too, is not without attendants devoted to his interests. Had I made the wild attempt you suggest, I might never have left the Ministerial presence alive. The good 30 people of Paris might have heard of me no more. But I had an object apart from these considerations. You know my political prepossessions. In this matter, I act as a partisan of the lady concerned. For eighteen months the Minister has had her in his power. She has now him in hers—since, being unaware that the letter is not in his possession, he will proceed with his exactions as if it was. Thus will he inevitably commit himself, at once, to his political destruction. His downfall, too, will not be more precipitate than awkward. It is all very well to talk about the *facilis descensus Averni*; but in all kinds of climbing, as Catalani said of singing, it is far more easy to get up than to come down. In the present instance I have no sympathy—at least no pity—for him who descends. He is that *monstrum horrendum*, an unprincipled man of genius. I confess, however, that I should like very well to know the precise character of his thoughts, when, being defied by her whom the Prefect terms 'a certain personage,' he is reduced to opening the letter which I left for him in the card-rack."

"How? Did you put anything particular in it?"

"Why—it did not seem altogether right to leave the interior blank—that would have been insulting. D——, at Vienna once, did me an evil turn, which I told him, quite good-humoredly, that I should remember. So, as I knew he would feel some curiosity in regard to the identity of the person who had outwitted him, I thought it a pity not to give him a clew. He is well acquainted with my MS., and I just copied into the middle of the blank sheet the words—

'—Un dessein si funeste,
S'il n'est digne d'Atrée, est digne de Thyeste.'

They are to be found in Crébillon's *Atrée*."

The Tell-Tale Heart

True!—nervous—very, very dreadfully nervous I had been and am; but why will you say that I am mad? The disease had sharpened my senses—not destroyed—not dulled them. Above all was the sense of hearing acute. I heard all things in the heaven and in the earth. I heard many things in hell. How, then, am I mad? Hearken! and observe how healthily—how calmly I can tell you the whole story.

It is impossible to say how first the idea entered my brain; but once conceived, it haunted me day and night. Object there was none. Passion there was none. I loved the old man. He had never wronged me. He had never given me insult. For his gold I had no desire. I think it was his eye! yes, it was this! He had the eye of a vulture—a pale blue eye, with a film over it. Whenever it fell upon me, my blood ran cold; and so by degrees—very gradually—I made up my mind to take the life of the old man, and thus rid myself of the eye forever.

Now this is the point. You fancy me mad. Madmen know nothing. But you should have seen me. You should have seen how wisely I proceeded—with what caution—with what foresight—with what dissimulation I went to work! I was never kinder to the old man than during the whole week before I killed him. And every night, about midnight, I turned the latch of his door and opened it—oh so gently! And then, when I had made an opening sufficient for my head, I put in a dark lantern, all closed, closed, that no light shone out, and then I thrust in my head. Oh, you would have laughed to see how cunningly I thrust it in! I moved it slowly—very, very slowly, so that I might not disturb the old man's sleep. It took me an hour to place my whole head within the opening so far that I could see him as he lay upon his bed. Ha! would a madman have been so wise as this? And then, when my head was well in the room, I undid the lantern cautiously—oh, so cautiously—cautiously (for the hinges creaked)—I undid it just so much that a single thin ray fell upon the vulture eye. And this I did for seven long nights—every night just at midnight—but I found the eye always closed; and so it was impossible to do the work; for it was not the old man who vexed me, but his Evil Eye. And every morning, when the day broke, I went boldly into the chamber, and spoke courageously to him, calling him by name in a hearty tone, and inquiring how he has passed the night. So you see he would have been a very profound old man, indeed, to suspect that every night, just at twelve, I looked in upon him while he slept.

Upon the eighth night I was more than usually cautious in opening the door. A watch's minute hand moves more quickly than did mine. Never before that night had I felt the extent of my own powers—of my sagacity. I could scarcely contain my feelings of triumph. To think that there I was, opening the door, little by little, and he not even to dream of my secret deeds or thoughts. I fairly chuckled at the idea; and perhaps he heard me; for he moved on the bed suddenly, as if startled. Now you may think that I drew back—but no. His room was as black as pitch with the thick darkness, (for the shutters were close fastened, through fear of robbers,) and so I knew that he could not see the opening of the door, and I kept pushing it on steadily, steadily.

I had my head in, and was about to open the lantern, when my thumb slipped upon the tin fastening, and the old man sprang up in bed, crying out—"Who's there?"

I kept quite still and said nothing. For a whole hour I did not move a muscle, and in the meantime I did not hear him lie down. He was still sitting up in the bed listening;—just as I have done, night after night, hearkening to the death watches in the wall.

Presently I heard a slight groan, and I knew it was the groan of mortal terror. It was not a groan of pain or of grief—oh, no!—it was the low stifled sound that arises from the bottom of the soul when overcharged with awe. I knew the sound well. Many a night, just at midnight, when all the world slept, it has welled up from my own bosom, deepening, with its dreadful echo, the terrors that distracted me. I say I knew it well. I knew what the old man felt, and pitied him, although I chuckled at heart. I knew that he had been lying awake ever since the first slight noise, when he had turned in the bed. His fears had been ever since growing upon him. He had been trying to fancy them causeless, but could not. He had been saying to himself—"It is nothing but the wind in the chimney—it is only a mouse crossing the floor," or "It is merely a cricket which has made a single chirp." Yes, he had been trying to comfort himself with these suppositions: but he had found all in vain. All in vain; because Death, in approaching him had stalked with his black shadow before him, and enveloped the victim. And it was the mournful influence of the unperceived shadow that caused him to feel—although he neither saw nor heard—to feel the presence of my head within the room.

When I had waited a long time, very patiently, without hearing him lie down, I resolved to open a little—a very, very little crevice in the lantern. So I opened it—you cannot imagine how stealthily, stealthily—until, at length a simple dim ray, like the thread of the spider, shot from out the crevice and fell full upon the vulture eye.

It was open—wide, wide open—and I grew furious as I gazed upon it. I saw it with perfect distinctness—all a dull blue, with a hideous veil over it that chilled the very marrow in my bones; but I could see nothing else of the old man's face or person: for I had directed the ray as if by instinct, precisely upon the damned spot.

And have I not told you that what you mistake for madness is but over-acuteness of the sense?—now, I say, there came to my ears a low, dull, quick sound, such as a watch makes when enveloped in cotton. I knew that sound well, too. It was the beating of the old man's heart. It increased my fury, as the beating of a drum stimulates the soldier into courage.

But even yet I refrained and kept still. I scarcely breathed. I held the lantern motionless. I tried how steadily I could maintain the ray upon the eve. Meantime the hellish tattoo of the heart increased. It grew quicker and quicker, and louder and louder every instant. The old man's terror must have been extreme! It grew louder, I say, louder every moment!—do you mark me well I have told you that I am nervous: so I am. And now at the dead hour of the night, amid the dreadful silence of that old house, so strange a noise as this excited me to uncontrollable terror. Yet, for some minutes longer I refrained and stood still. But the beating grew louder, louder! I thought the heart must burst. And now a new anxiety seized me—the sound would be heard by a neighbour! The old man's hour had come! With a loud yell, I threw open the lantern and leaped into the room. He shrieked once—once only. In an instant I dragged him to the floor, and pulled the heavy bed over him. I then smiled gaily, to find the deed so far done. But, for many minutes, the heart beat on with a muffled sound. This, however, did not vex me; it would not be heard through the wall. At length it ceased. The old man was dead. I removed the bed and examined the corpse. Yes, he was stone, stone dead. I placed my hand upon the heart and held it there many minutes. There was no pulsation. He was stone dead. His eye would trouble me no more.

If still you think me mad, you will think so no longer when I describe the wise precautions I took for the concealment of the body. The night waned, and I worked hastily, but in silence. First of all I dismembered the corpse. I cut off the head and the arms and the legs.

I then took up three planks from the flooring of the chamber, and deposited all between the scantlings. I then replaced the boards so cleverly, so cunningly, that no human eye—not even his—could have detected any thing wrong. There was nothing to wash out—no stain of any kind—no blood-spot whatever. I had been too wary for that. A tub had caught all—ha! ha!

When I had made an end of these labors, it was four o'clock—still dark as midnight. As the bell sounded the hour, there came a knocking at the street door. I went down to open it with a light heart,—for what had I now to fear? There entered three men, who introduced themselves, with perfect suavity, as officers of the police. A shriek had been heard by a neighbour during the night; suspicion of foul play had been aroused; information had been lodged at the police office, and they (the officers) had been deputed to search the premises.

I smiled,—for what had I to fear? I bade the gentlemen welcome. The shriek, I said, was my own in a dream. The old man, I mentioned, was absent in the country. I took my visitors all over the house. I bade them search—search well. I led them, at length, to his chamber. I showed them his treasures, secure, undisturbed. In the enthusiasm of my confidence, I brought chairs into the room, and desired them here to rest from their fatigues, while I myself, in the wild audacity of my perfect triumph, placed my own seat upon the very spot beneath which reposed the corpse of the victim.

The officers were satisfied. My manner had convinced them. I was singularly at ease. They sat, and while I answered cheerily, they chatted of familiar things. But, ere long, I felt myself getting pale and wished them gone. My head ached, and I fancied a ringing in my ears: but still they sat and still chatted. The ringing became more distinct:—It continued and became more distinct: I talked more freely to get rid of the feeling: but it continued and gained definiteness—until, at length, I found that the noise was not within my ears.

No doubt I now grew *very* pale;—but I talked more fluently, and with a heightened voice. Yet the sound increased—and what could I do? It was a low, dull, quick sound—much such a sound as a watch makes when enveloped in cotton. I gasped for breath—and yet the officers heard it not. I talked more quickly—more vehemently; but the noise steadily increased. I arose and argued about trifles, in a high key and with violent gesticulations; but the noise steadily increased. Why would they not be gone? I paced the floor to and fro with heavy strides, as if excited to fury by the observations of the men—but the noise steadily increased. Oh God! what could I do? I foamed—I raved—I swore! I swung the chair upon which I had been sitting, and grated it upon the boards, but the noise arose over all and continually increased. It grew louder—louder—louder! And still the men chatted pleasantly, and smiled. Was it possible they heard not? Almighty God!—no, no! They heard!—they suspected!—they knew!—they were making a mockery of my horror!-this I thought, and this I think. But anything was better than this agony! Anything was more tolerable than this derision! I could bear those hypocritical smiles no longer! I felt that I must scream or die! and now—again!—hark! louder! louder! louder! louder!

"Villains!" I shrieked, "dissemble no more! I admit the deed!—tear up the planks! here, here!—It is the beating of his hideous heart!"

POEMS

The Bells

I

The bells!—ah the bells!
The little silver bells!
How fairy-like a melody there floats
From their throats—
From their merry little throats—
From the silver, tinkling throats
Of the bells, bells, bells—
Of the bells!

II

The bells!—ah, the bells!
The heavy iron bells!
How horrible a monody there floats
From their throats—
From their deep-toned throats—
From their melancholy throats
How I shudder at the notes
Of the bells, bells, bells—
Of the bells!

The City in the Sea

Lo! Death has reared himself a throne
In a strange city lying alone
Far down within the dim West,
Where the good and the bad and the worst and the best
Have gone to their eternal rest.
There shrines and palaces and towers
(Time-eaten towers and tremble not!)
Resemble nothing that is ours.
Around, by lifting winds forgot,
Resignedly beneath the sky
The melancholy waters lie.

No rays from the holy Heaven come down
On the long night-time of that town;
But light from out the lurid sea
Streams up the turrets silently—
Gleams up the pinnacles far and free—
Up domes—up spires—up kingly halls—
Up fanes—up Babylon-like walls—
Up shadowy long-forgotten bowers
Of sculptured ivy and stone flowers—
Up many and many a marvellous shrine
Whose wreathed friezes intertwine
The viol, the violet, and the vine.

Resignedly beneath the sky
The melancholy waters lie.
So blend the turrets and shadows there
That all seem pendulous in air,
While from a proud tower in the town
Death looks gigantically down.

There open fanes and gaping graves
Yawn level with the luminous waves;
But not the riches there that lie
In each idol's diamond eye—

Not the gaily-jewelled dead
Tempt the waters from their bed;
For no ripples curl, alas!
Along that wilderness of glass—
No swellings tell that winds may be
Upon some far-off happier sea—
No heavings hint that winds have been
On seas less hideously serene.

But lo, a stir is in the air!
The wave—there is a movement there!
As if the towers had thrust aside,
In slightly sinking, the dull tide—
As if their tops had feebly given
A void within the filmy Heaven.
The waves have now a redder glow—
The hours are breathing faint and low—
And when, amid no earthly moans,
Down, down that town shall settle hence,
Hell, rising from a thousand thrones,
Shall do it reverence.

The Conqueror Worm

Lo! 'tis a gala night
  Within the lonesome latter years!
An angel throng, bewinged, bedight
  In veils, and drowned in tears,
Sit in a theatre, to see
  A play of hopes and fears,
While the orchestra breathes fitfully
  The music of the spheres.

Mimes, in the form of God on high,
  Mutter and mumble low,
And hither and thither fly—
  Mere puppets they, who come and go
At bidding of vast formless things
  That shift the scenery to and fro,
Flapping from out their Condor wings
  Invisible Wo!

That motley drama—oh, be sure
  It shall not be forgot!
With its Phantom chased for evermore,
  By a crowd that seize it not,
Through a circle that ever returneth in
  To the self-same spot,
And much of Madness, and more of Sin,
  And Horror the soul of the plot.

But see, amid the mimic rout
  A crawling shape intrude!
A blood-red thing that writhes from out
  The scenic solitude!
It writhes!—it writhes!—with mortal pangs
  The mimes become its food,
And the angels sob at vermin fangs
  In human gore imbued.

Out—out are the lights—out all!
    And, over each quivering form,
The curtain, a funeral pall,
    Comes down with the rush of a storm,
And the angels, all pallid and wan,
    Uprising, unveiling, affirm
That the play is the tragedy, "Man,"
    And its hero the Conqueror Worm.

A Dream Within a Dream

Take this kiss upon the brow!
And, in parting from you now,
Thus much let me avow—
You are not wrong, who deem
That my days have been a dream:
Yet if hope has flown away
In a night, or in a day,
In a vision or in none,
Is it therefore the less *gone*?
All that we see or seem
Is but a dream within a dream.

I stand amid the roar
Of a surf-tormented shore,
And I hold within my hand
Grains of the golden sand—
How few! yet how they creep
Through my fingers to the deep
While I weep—while I weep!
O God! can I not grasp
Them with a tighter clasp?
O God! can I not save
One from the pitiless wave?
Is *all* that we see or seem
But a dream within a dream?

Dreamland

By a route obscure and lonely,
Haunted by ill angels only,
Where an Eidolon, named Night,
On a black throne reigns upright,
I have reached these lands but newly
From an ultimate dim Thule—
From a wild weird clime that lieth, sublime,
    Out of Space—out of Time.

Bottomless vales and boundless floods,
And chasms, and caves, and Titan woods,
With forms that no man can discover
For the dews that drip all over;
Mountains toppling evermore
Into seas without a shore;
Seas that restlessly aspire,
Surging, unto skies of fire;
Lakes that endlessly outspread
Their lone waters—lone and dead,
Their still waters—still and chilly
With the snows of the lolling lily.

By the lakes that thus outspread
Their lone waters, lone and dead,—
Their sad waters, sad and chilly
With the snows of the lolling lily,—

By the mountains—near the river
Murmuring lowly, murmuring ever,—
By the gray woods,—by the swamp
Where the toad and the newt encamp,—
By the dismal tarns and pools
    Where dwell the Ghouls,—
By each spot the most unholy—
In each nook most melancholy,—

There the traveller meets aghast
Sheeted Memories of the past—
Shrouded forms that start and sigh
As they pass the wanderer by—
White-robed forms of friends long given,
In agony, to the Earth—and Heaven.

For the heart whose woes are legion
'Tis a peaceful, soothing region—
For the spirit that walks in shadow
'Tis—oh, 'tis an Eldorado!
But the traveller, travelling through it,
May not—dare not openly view it;
Never its mysteries are exposed
To the weak human eye unclosed;
So wills its King, who hath forbid
The uplifting of the fringed lid;
And thus the sad Soul that here passes
Beholds it but through darkened glasses.

By a route obscure and lonely,
Haunted by ill angels only.

Where an Eidolon, named NIGHT,
On a black throne reigns upright,
I have wandered home but newly
From this ultimate dim Thule.

Fairyland

Dim vales—and shadowy floods—
And cloudy-looking woods,
Whose forms we can't discover
For the tears that drip all over
Huge moons there wax and wane—
Again—again—again—
Every moment of the night—
Forever changing places—
And they put out the star-light
With the breath from their pale faces.
About twelve by the moon-dial
One more filmy than the rest
(A kind which, upon trial,
They have found to be the best)
Comes down—still down—and down
With its centre on the crown
Of a mountain's eminence,
While its wide circumference
In easy drapery falls
Over hamlets, over halls,
Wherever they may be—
O'er the strange woods—o'er the sea—
Over spirits on the wing—
Over every drowsy thing—
And buries them up quite
In a labyrinth of light—
And then, how deep!—O, deep!
Is the passion of their sleep.
In the morning they arise,
And their moony covering
Is soaring in the skies,
With the tempests as they toss,
Like—almost any thing—
Or a yellow Albatross.
They use that moon no more
For the same end as before—

Videlicet a tent—
Which I think extravagant:
Its atomies, however,
Into a shower dissever,
Of which those butterflies,
Of Earth, who seek the skies,
And so come down again
(Never-contented thing!)
Have brought a specimen
Upon their quivering wings.

The Haunted Palace

In the greenest of our valleys
By good angels tenanted,
Once a fair and stately palace—
Radiant palace—reared its head.
In the monarch Thought's dominion—
It stood there!
Never seraph spread a pinion
Over fabric half so fair!

Banners yellow, glorious, golden,
On its roof did float and flow,
(This—all this—was in the olden
Time long ago),
And every gentle air that dallied,
In that sweet day,
Along the ramparts plumed and pallid,
A winged odor went away.

Wanderers in that happy valley,
Through two luminous windows, saw
Spirits moving musically,
To a lute's well-tunëd law,
Bound about a throne where, sitting
(Porphyrogene!)
In state his glory well befitting,
The ruler of the realm was seen.

And all with pearl and ruby glowing
Was the fair palace door,
Through which came flowing, flowing, flowing,
And sparkling evermore,
A troop of Echoes, whose sweet duty
Was but to sing,
In voices of surpassing beauty,
The wit and wisdom of their king.

But evil things, in robes of sorrow,
    Assailed the monarch's high estate.
(Ah, let us mourn!—for never morrow
    Shall dawn upon him desolate!)
And round about his home the glory
    That blushed and bloomed,
Is but a dim-remembered story
    Of the old time entombed.

And travellers, now, within that valley,
    Through the red-litten windows see
Vast forms, that move fantastically
    To a discordant melody,
    While, like a ghastly rapid river,
    Through the pale door
A hideous throng rush out forever
    And laugh—but smile no more.

The Raven

Once upon a midnight dreary, while I pondered, weak and weary,
Over many a quaint and curious volume of forgotten lore,
While I nodded, nearly napping, suddenly there came a tapping,
As of some one gently rapping, rapping at my chamber door.
"'T is some visiter," I muttered, "tapping at my chamber door—
Only this, and nothing more."

Ah, distinctly I remember it was in the bleak December,
And each separate dying ember wrought its ghost upon the floor.
Eagerly I wished the morrow:—vainly I had sought to borrow
From my books surcease of sorrow—sorrow for the lost Lenore—
For the rare and radiant maiden whom the angels name Lenore—
Nameless here for evermore.

And the silken sad uncertain rustling of each purple curtain
Thrilled me—filled me with fantastic terrors never felt before;
So that now, to still the beating of my heart, I stood repeating
"'T is some visiter entreating entrance at my chamber door
Some late visiter entreating entrance at my chamber door;—
This it is, and nothing more."

Presently my soul grew stronger; hesitating then no longer,
"Sir," said I, "or Madam, truly your forgiveness I implore;
But the fact is I was napping, and so gently you came rapping,
And so faintly you came tapping, tapping at my chamber door,
That I scarce was sure I heard you"—here I opened wide the door;—
Darkness there, and nothing more.

Deep into that darkness peering, long I stood there wondering, fearing,
Doubting, dreaming dreams no mortal ever dared to dream before;
But the silence was unbroken, and the darkness gave no token,
And the only word there spoken was the whispered word, "Lenore!"
This I whispered, and an echo murmured back the word, "Lenore!"
Merely this and nothing more.

Back into the chamber turning, all my soul within me burning,
Soon again I heard a tapping, somewhat louder than before.
"Surely," said I, "surely that is something at my window lattice;
Let me see, then, what thereat is, and this mystery explore—
Let my heart be still a moment and this mystery explore;—
'T is the wind and nothing more!"

Open here I flung the shutter, when, with many a flirt and flutter,
In there stepped a stately Raven of the saintly days of yore.
Not the least obeisance made he; not a minute stopped or stayed he;
But, with mien of lord or lady, perched above my chamber door—
Perched upon a bust of Pallas just above my chamber door—
Perched, and sat, and nothing more.

Then this ebony bird beguiling my sad fancy into smiling,
By the grave and stern decorum of the countenance it wore,
"Though thy crest be shorn and shaven, thou," I said, "art sure no craven,
Ghastly grim and ancient Raven wandering from the Nightly shore,—
Tell me what thy lordly name is on the Night's Plutonian shore!"
Quoth the Raven, "Nevermore."

Much I marvelled this ungainly fowl to hear discourse so plainly,
Though its answer little meaning—little relevancy bore;
For we cannot help agreeing that no living human being
Ever yet was blessed with seeing bird above his chamber door—
Bird or beast upon the sculptured bust above his chamber door,
With such name as "Nevermore."

But the Raven, sitting lonely on the placid bust, spoke only
That one word, as if his soul in that one word he did outpour.
Nothing further then he uttered—not a feather then he fluttered—
Till I scarcely more than muttered, "Other friends have flown before—
On the morrow *he* will leave me, as my hopes have flown before."
Then the bird said, "Nevermore."

Startled at the stillness broken by reply so aptly spoken,
"Doubtless," said I, "what it utters is its only stock and store,
Caught from some unhappy master whom unmerciful Disaster

Followed fast and followed faster till his songs one burden bore—
Till the dirges of his Hope that melancholy burden bore
Of 'Never—nevermore.'"

But the Raven still beguiling all my sad soul into smiling,
Straight I wheeled a cushioned seat in front of bird and bust and door;
Then, upon the velvet sinking, I betook myself to linking
Fancy unto fancy, thinking what this ominous bird of yore—
What this grim, ungainly, ghastly, gaunt and ominous bird of yore
Meant in croaking "Nevermore."

This I sat engaged in guessing, but no syllable expressing
To the fowl whose fiery eyes now burned into my bosom's core;
This and more I sat divining, with my head at ease reclining
On the cushion's velvet lining that the lamplight gloated o'er,
But whose velvet violet lining with the lamplight gloating o'er
She shall press, ah, nevermore!

Then, methought, the air grew denser, perfumed from an unseen censer
Swung by seraphim whose foot-falls tinkled on the tufted floor.
"Wretch," I cried, "thy God hath lent thee—by these angels he hath sent thee
Respite—respite and nepenthe from thy memories of Lenore!
Quaff, oh quaff this kind nepenthe, and forget this lost Lenore!"
Quoth the Raven, "Nevermore."

"Prophet!" said I, "thing of evil!—prophet still, if bird or devil!—
Whether Tempter sent, or whether tempest tossed thee here ashore,
Desolate yet all undaunted, on this desert land enchanted—
On this home by Horror haunted—tell me truly, I implore—
Is there—*is* there balm in Gilead?—tell me—tell me, I implore!"
Quoth the Raven, "Nevermore."

"Prophet!" said I, "thing of evil—prophet still, if bird or devil!
By that Heaven that bends above, us—by that God we both adore—
Tell this soul with sorrow laden if, within the distant Aidenn,
It shall clasp a sainted maiden whom the angels name Lenore—
Clasp a rare and radiant maiden whom the angels name Lenore."
Quoth the Raven, "Nevermore."

"Be that word our sign of parting, bird or fiend!" I shrieked, upstarting—
"Get thee back into the tempest and the Night's Plutonian shore!
Leave no black plume as a token of that lie thy soul hath spoken!
Leave my loneliness unbroken!—quit the bust above my door!
Take thy beak from out my heart, and take thy form from off my door!"
Quoth the Raven, "Nevermore."

And the Raven, never flitting, still is sitting, still is sitting
On the pallid bust of Pallas just above my chamber door;
And his eyes have all the seeming of a demon's that is dreaming,
And the lamplight o'er him streaming throws his shadow on the floor;
And my soul from out that shadow that lies floating on the floor
Shall be lifted—nevermore!

Romance

Romance, who loves to nod and sing,
With drowsy head and folded wing,
Among the green leaves as they shake
Far down within some shadowy lake,
To me a painted paroquet
Hath been—a most familiar bird—
Taught me my alphabet to say—
To lisp my very earliest word
While in the wild wood I did lie,
A child—with a most knowing eye.

Of late, eternal Condor years
So shake the very Heaven on high
With tumult as they thunder by,
I have no time for idle cares
Though gazing on the unquiet sky.
And when an hour with calmer wings
Its down upon my spirit flings—
That little time with lyre and rhyme
To while away—forbidden things!
My heart would feel to be a crime
Unless it trembled with the strings.

Silence

There are some qualities—some incorporate things,
    That have a double life, which thus is made
A type of that twin entity which springs
    From matter and light, evinced in solid and shade.
There is a twofold *Silence*—sea and shore—
    Body and soul. One dwells in lonely places,
    Newly with grass o'ergrown; some solemn graces,
Some human memories and tearful lore,
Render him terrorless: his name's "No More."
He is the corporate Silence: dread him not!
    No power hath he of evil in himself;
But should some urgent fate (untimely lot!)
    Bring thee to meet his shadow (nameless elf,
That haunteth the lone regions where hath trod
No foot of man), commend thyself to God!

The Sleeper

At midnight, in the month of June,
I stand beneath the mystic moon.
An opiate vapor, dewy, dim,
Exhales from out her golden rim,
And, softly dripping, drop by drop,
Upon the quiet mountain top,
Steals drowsily and musically
Into the universal valley.
The rosemary nods upon the grave;
The lily lolls upon the wave;
Wrapping the fog about its breast,
The ruin moulders into rest;
Looking like Lethe, see! the lake
A conscious slumber seems to take,
And would not, for the world, awake.
All Beauty sleeps!—and lo! where lies
(Her casement open to the skies)
Irene, with her Destinies!

Oh, lady bright! can it be right—
This window open to the night!
The wanton airs, from the tree-top,
Laughingly through the lattice-drop—
The bodiless airs, a wizard rout,
Flit through thy chamber in and out,
And wave the curtain canopy
So fitfully—so fearfully—
Above the closed and fringed lid
'Neath which thy slumb'ring soul lies hid,
That, o'er the floor and down the wall,
Like ghosts the shadows rise and fall!
Oh, lady dear, hast thou no fear?
Why and what art thou dreaming here?
Sure thou art come o'er far-off seas,
A wonder to these garden trees!
Strange is thy pallor! strange thy dress!

Strange, above all, thy length of tress,
And this all-solemn silentness!

The lady sleeps! Oh, may her sleep
Which is enduring, so be deep!
Heaven have her in its sacred keep!
This chamber changed for one more holy,
This bed for one more melancholy,
I pray to God that she may lie
For ever with unopened eye,
While the dim sheeted ghosts go by!

My love, she sleeps! Oh, may her sleep,
As it is lasting, so be deep;
Soft may the worms about her creep!
Far in the forest, dim and old,
For her may some tall vault unfold—
Some vault that oft hath flung its black
And winged panels fluttering back,
Triumphant, o'er the crested palls,
Of her grand family funerals—
Some sepulchre, remote, alone,
Against whose portal she hath thrown,
In childhood many an idle stone—
Some tomb from out whose sounding door
She ne'er shall force an echo more,
Thrilling to think, poor child of sin!
It was the dead who groaned within.

Song

I saw thee on thy bridal day—
    When a burning blush came o'er thee,
Though happiness around thee lay,
    The world all love before thee:

And in thine eye a kindling light
    (Whatever it might be)
Was all on Earth my aching sight
    Of Loveliness could see.

That blush, perhaps, was maiden shame—
    As such it well may pass—
Though its glow hath raised a fiercer flame
    In the breast of him, alas!

Who saw thee on that bridal day,
    When that deep blush *would* come o'er thee,
Though happiness around thee lay,
    The world all love before thee.

Spirits of the Dead

Thy soul shall find itself alone
'Mid dark thoughts of the gray tombstone
Not one, of all the crowd, to pry
Into thine hour of secrecy.
Be silent in that solitude
    Which is not loneliness—for then
The spirits of the dead who stood
    In life before thee are again
In death around thee—and their will
Shall overshadow thee: be still.
The night—tho' clear—shall frown—
And the stars shall not look down
From their high thrones in the Heaven,
With light like Hope to mortals given—
But their red orbs, without beam,
To thy weariness shall seem
As a burning and a fever Which would cling to thee forever.
Now are thoughts thou shalt not banish—
Now are visions ne'er to vanish—
From thy spirit shall they pass
No more—like dew-drops from the grass.
The breeze—the breath of God—is still—
And the mist upon the hill
Shadowy—shadowy—yet unbroken,
    Is a symbol and a token—
    How it hangs upon the trees,
    A mystery of mysteries!

Ulalame

The skies they were ashen and sober;
    The leaves they were crisped and sere—
    The leaves they were withering and sere;
It was night in the lonesome October
    Of my most immemorial year;
It was hard by the dim lake of Auber,
    In the misty mid region of Weir—
It was down by the dank tarn of Auber,
    In the ghoul-haunted woodland of Weir.

Here once, through an alley Titanic.
    Of cypress, I roamed with my Soul—
    Of cypress, with Psyche, my Soul.
These were days when my heart was volcanic
    As the scoriac rivers that roll—
    As the lavas that restlessly roll
Their sulphurous currents down Yaanek
    In the ultimate climes of the pole—
That groan as they roll down Mount Yaanek
    In the realms of the boreal pole.

Our talk had been serious and sober,
    But our thoughts they were palsied and sere—
    Our memories were treacherous and sere—
For we knew not the month was October,
And we marked not the night of the year—
    (Ah, night of all nights in the year!)
We noted not the dim lake of Auber—
    (Though once we had journeyed down here)—
Remembered not the dank tarn of Auber,
    Nor the ghoul-haunted woodland of Weir.

And now as the night was senescent
    And star-dials pointed to morn—
    As the sun-dials hinted of morn—

At the end of our path a liquescent
    And nebulous lustre was born,
Out of which a miraculous crescent
    Arose with a duplicate horn—
Astarte's bediamonded crescent
    Distinct with its duplicate horn.

And I said—"She is warmer than Dian:
    She rolls through an ether of sighs—
    She revels in a region of sighs:
She has seen that the tears are not dry on
    These cheeks, where the worm never dies,
And has come past the stars of the Lion
    To point us the path to the skies—
    To the Lethean peace of the skies—
Come up, in despite of the Lion,
    To shine on us with her bright eyes—
Come up through the lair of the Lion,
    With love in her luminous eyes."

But Psyche, uplifting her finger,
    Said—"Sadly this star I mistrust—
    Her pallor I strangely mistrust:—
Oh, hasten!—oh, let us not linger!
    Oh, fly!—let us fly!—for we must."
In terror she spoke, letting sink her
    Wings till they trailed in the dust—
In agony sobbed, letting sink her
    Plumes till they trailed in the dust—
    Till they sorrowfully trailed in the dust.

I replied—"This is nothing but dreaming:
    Let us on by this tremulous light!
    Let us bathe in this crystalline light!
Its Sibyllic splendor is beaming
    With Hope and in Beauty to-night:—
    See!—it flickers up the sky through the night!
Ah, we safely may trust to its gleaming,
    And be sure it will lead us aright—

We safely may trust to a gleaming
  That cannot but guide us aright,
  Since it flickers up to Heaven through the night."

Thus I pacified Psyche and kissed her,
  And tempted her out of her gloom—
  And conquered her scruples and gloom;
And we passed to the end of a vista,
  But were stopped by the door of a tomb—
  By the door of a legended tomb;
And I said—"What is written, sweet sister,
  On the door of this legended tomb?"
  She replied—"Ulalume—Ulalume—
  'Tis the vault of thy lost Ulalume!"

Then my heart it grew ashen and sober
  As the leaves that were crisped and sere—
  As the leaves that were withering and sere;
And I cried—"It was surely October
  On *this* very night of last year
  That I journeyed—I journeyed down here—
  That I brought a dread burden down here!
  On this night of all nights in the year,
  Ah, what demon has tempted me here?
Well I know, now, this dim lake of Auber—
  This misty mid region of Weir—
Well I know, now, this dank tarn of Auber,—
  This ghoul-haunted woodland of Weir."

PROSE

Eureka: A Prose Poem

It is with humility really unassumed—it is with a sentiment even of awe—that I pen the opening sentence of this work: for of all conceivable subjects I approach the reader with the most solemn—the most comprehensive—the most difficult—the most august.

What terms shall I find sufficiently simple in their sublimity—sufficiently sublime in their simplicity—for the mere enunciation of my theme?

I design to speak of the *Physical, Metaphysical and Mathematical—of the Material and Spiritual Universe:—of its Essence, its Origin, its Creation, its Present Condition and its Destiny*. I shall be so rash, moreover, as to challenge the conclusions, and thus, in effect, to question the sagacity, of many of the greatest and most justly reverenced of men.

In the beginning, let me as distinctly as possible announce—not the theorem which I hope to demonstrate—for, whatever the mathematicians may assert, there is, in this world at least, *no such thing* as demonstration—but the ruling idea which, throughout this volume, I shall be continually endeavoring to suggest.

My general proposition, then, is this:—*In the Original Unity of the First Thing lies the Secondary Cause of All Things, with the Germ of their Inevitable Annihilation*.

In illustration of this idea, I propose to take such a survey of the Universe that the mind may be able really to receive and to perceive an individual impression.

He who from the top of Ætna casts his eyes leisurely around, is affected chiefly by the *extent* and *diversity* of the scene. Only by a rapid whirling on his heel could he hope to comprehend the panorama in the sublimity of its *oneness*. But as, on the summit of Ætna, *no* man has thought of whirling on his heel, so no man has ever taken into his brain the full uniqueness of the prospect; and so, again, whatever considerations lie involved in this uniqueness, have as yet no practical existence for mankind.

I do not know a treatise in which a survey of the *Universe*—using the word in its most comprehensive and only legitimate acceptation—is taken at all:—and it may be as well here to mention that by the term "Universe," wherever employed without qualification in this essay, I mean to designate *the utmost conceivable expanse of space, with all things, spiritual and material, that can be imagined to exist within the compass of that expanse*. In speaking of what is ordinarily implied by the expression, "Universe," I shall take a phrase of limitation—"the Universe of stars." Why this distinction is considered necessary, will be seen in the sequel.

But even of treatises on the really limited, although always assumed as the *un*limited, Universe of *stars*, I know none in which a survey, even of this limited Universe, is so taken as to warrant deductions from its *individuality*. The nearest approach to such a work is made in the "Cosmos" of Alexander Von Humboldt. He presents the subject, however, *not* in its individuality but in its generality. His theme, in its last result, is the law of *each* portion of the merely physical Universe, as this law is related to the laws of *every other* portion of this merely physical Universe. His design is simply syncœretical. In a word, he discusses the universality of material relation, and discloses to the eye of Philosophy whatever inferences have hitherto lain hidden *behind* this universality. But however admirable be the succinctness with which he has treated each particular point of his topic, the mere multiplicity of these points occasions, necessarily, an amount of detail, and thus an involution of idea, which precludes all *individuality* of impression.

It seems to me that, in aiming at this latter effect, and, through it, at the consequences—the conclusions—the suggestions—the speculations—or, if nothing better offer itself the mere guesses which may result from it—we require something like a mental gyration on the heel. We need so rapid a revolution of all things about the central point of sight that, while the minutiæ vanish altogether, even the more conspicuous objects become blended into one. Among the vanishing minutiæ, in a survey of this kind, would be all exclusively terrestrial matters. The Earth would be considered in its planetary relations alone. A man, in this view, becomes mankind; mankind a member of the cosmical family of Intelligences.

And now, before proceeding to our subject proper, let me beg the reader's attention to an extract or two from a somewhat remarkable letter, which appears to have been found corked in a bottle and floating on the *Mare Tenebrarum*—an ocean well described by the Nubian geographer, Ptolemy Hephestion, but little frequented in modern days unless by the Transcendentalists and some other divers for crotchets. The date of this letter, I confess, surprises me even more particularly than its contents; for it seems to have been written in the year *two* thousand eight hundred and forty-eight. As for the passages I am about to transcribe, they, I fancy, will speak for themselves.

"Do you know, my dear friend," says the writer, addressing, no doubt, a contemporary—"Do you know that it is scarcely more than eight or nine hundred years ago since the metaphysicians first consented to relieve the people of the singular fancy that there exist *but two practicable roads to Truth*? Believe it if you can! It appears, however, that long, long ago, in the night of Time, there lived a Turkish philosopher called Aries and surnamed Tottle." (Here, possibly, the letter-writer means Aristotle; the best names are wretchedly corrupted in two or three thousand years.) "The fame of this great man depended mainly upon his demonstration that sneezing is a natural provision, by means of which over-profound thinkers are enabled to expel superfluous ideas through the nose; but he obtained a scarcely less valuable celebrity as the founder, or at all events as the principal propagator, of what was termed the *de*ductive or *à priori* philosophy. He started with what he maintained to be axioms, or self-evident truths:—and the now well understood fact that *no* truths are *self*-evident, really does not make in the slightest degree against his speculations:—it was sufficient for his purpose that the truths in question were evident at all. From axioms he proceeded, logically, to results. His most illustrious disciples were one Tuclid, a geometrician," (meaning Euclid) "and one Kant, a Dutchman, the originator of that species of Transcendentalism which, with the change merely of a C for a K, now bears his peculiar name.

"Well, Aries Tottle flourished supreme, until the advent of one Hog, surnamed 'the Ettrick shepherd,' who preached an entirely different system, which he called the *à posteriori* or *in*ductive. His plan referred altogether to sensation. He proceeded by observing, analyzing, and classifying facts—*instantiæ Naturæ*, as they were somewhat affectedly called—and arranging them into general laws. In a word, while the mode of Aries rested on *noumena*, that of Hog depended on *phenomena*; and so great was the admiration excited by this latter system that, at its first introduction, Aries fell into general disrepute. Finally, however, he recovered ground, and was permitted to divide the empire of Philosophy with his more modern rival:—the savans contenting themselves with proscribing all *other* competitors, past, present, and to come; putting an end to all controversy on the topic by the promulgation of a Median law, to the effect that the Aristotelian and Baconian roads are, and of right ought to be, the solo possible avenues to knowledge:—'Baconian,' you must know, my dear friend," adds the letter-writer at this point, "was an adjective invented as equivalent to Hog-ian, and at the same time more dignified and euphonious.

"Now I do assure you most positively"—proceeds the epistle—"that I represent these matters fairly; and you can easily understand how restrictions so absurd on their very face must have operated, in those days, to retard the progress of true Science, which makes its most important advances—as all History will show—by seemingly intuitive *leaps*. These ancient ideas confined investigation to crawling; and I need not suggest to you that crawling, among varieties of locomotion, is a very capital thing of its kind;—but because the tortoise is sure of foot, for this reason must we clip the wings of the eagles? For many centuries, so great was the infatuation, about Hog especially, that a virtual stop was put to all thinking, properly so called. No man dared utter a truth for which he felt himself indebted to his soul alone. It mattered not whether the truth was even demonstrably such; for the dogmatizing philosophers of that epoch regarded only *the road* by which it professed to have been attained. The end, with them, was a point of no moment, whatever:—'the means!' they vociferated—'let us look at the means!'—and if, on scrutiny of the means, it was found to come neither under the category Hog, nor under the category Aries (which means ram), why then the savans went no farther, but, calling the thinker a fool and branding him a 'theorist,' would never, thenceforward, have any thing to do either with *him* or with his truths.

"Now, my dear friend," continues the letter-writer, "it cannot be maintained that by the crawling system, exclusively adopted, men would arrive at the maximum amount of truth, even in any long series of ages; for the repression of imagination was an evil not to be counterbalanced even by *absolute* certainty in the snail processes. But their certainty was very far from absolute. The error of our progenitors was quite analogous with that of the wiseacre who fancies he must necessarily see an object the more distinctly, the more closely he holds it to his eyes. They blinded themselves, too, with the impalpable, titillating Scotch snuff of *detail*; and thus the boasted facts of the Hog-ites were by no means always facts—a point of little importance but for the assumption that they always *were*. The vital taint, however, in Baconianism—its most lamentable fount of error—lay in its tendency to throw power and consideration into the hands of merely perceptive men—of those inter-Tritonic minnows, the microscopical savans—the diggers and pedlers of minute *facts*, for the most part in physical science—facts all of which they retailed at the same price upon the highway; their value depending, it was supposed, simply upon the *fact of their fact*, without reference to their applicability or inapplicability in the development of those ultimate and only legitimate facts, called Law.

"Than the persons"—the letter goes on to say—"Than the persons thus suddenly elevated by the Hog-ian philosophy into a station for which they were unfitted—thus transferred from the sculleries into the parlors of Science—from its pantries into its pulpits—than these individuals a more intolerant—a more intolerable set of bigots and tyrants never existed on the face of the earth. Their creed, their text and their sermon were, alike, the one word '*fact*'—but, for the most part, even of this one word, they knew not even the meaning. On those who ventured to *disturb* their facts with the view of putting them in order and to use, the disciples of Hog had no mercy whatever. All attempts at generalization were met at once by the words 'theoretical,' 'theory,' 'theorist'—all *thought*, to be brief, was very properly resented as a personal affront to themselves. Cultivating the natural sciences to the exclusion of Metaphysics, the Mathematics, and Logic, many of these Bacon-engendered philosophers—one-idead, one-sided and lame of a leg—were more wretchedly helpless—more miserably ignorant, in view of all the comprehensible objects of knowledge, than the veriest unlettered hind who proves that he knows something at least, in admitting that he knows absolutely nothing.

"Nor had our forefathers any better right to talk about *certainty*, when pursuing, in blind confidence, the *à priori* path of axioms, or of the Ram. At innumerable points this path was scarcely as straight as a ram's-horn. The simple truth is, that the Aristotelians erected their castles upon a basis far less reliable than air; *for no such things as axioms ever existed or can possibly exist at all*. This they must have been very blind, indeed, not to see, or at least to suspect; for, even in their own day, many of their long-admitted 'axioms' had been abandoned:—' *ex nihilo nihil fit*,' for example, and a 'thing cannot act where it is not,' and 'there cannot be antipodes,' and 'darkness cannot proceed from light.' These and numerous similar propositions formerly accepted, without hesitation, as axioms, or undeniable truths, were, even at the period of which I speak, seen to be altogether untenable:—how absurd in these people, then, to persist in relying upon a basis, as immutable, whose mutability had become so repeatedly manifest!

"But, even through evidence afforded by themselves against themselves, it is easy to convict these *à priori* reasoners of the grossest unreason—it is easy to show the futility—the impalpability of their axioms in general. I have now lying before me"—it will be observed that we still proceed with the letter—"I have now lying before me a book printed about a thousand years ago. Pundit assures me that it is decidedly the cleverest ancient work on its topic, which is 'Logic.' The author, who was much esteemed in his day, was one Miller, or Mill; and we find it recorded of him, as a point of some importance, that he rode a mill-horse whom he called Jeremy Bentham:—but let us glance at the volume itself!

"Ah!—'Ability or inability to conceive,' says Mr. Mill very properly, 'is *in no case* to be received as a criterion of axiomatic truth.' Now, that this is a palpable truism no one in his senses will deny. *Not* to admit the proposition, is to insinuate a charge of variability in Truth itself, whose very title is a synonym of the Steadfast. If ability to conceive be taken as a criterion of Truth, then a truth to *David* Hume would very seldom be a truth to *Joe*; and ninety-nine hundredths of what is undeniable in Heaven would be demonstrable falsity upon Earth. The proposition of Mr. Mill, then, is sustained. I will not grant it to be an *axiom*; and this merely because I am showing that *no* axioms exist; but, with a distinction which could not have been cavilled at even by Mr. Mill himself, I am ready to grant that, *if* an axiom *there be*, then the proposition of which we speak has the fullest right to be considered an axiom—that no *more* absolute axiom *is*—and, consequently, that any subsequent proposition which shall conflict with this one primarily advanced, must be either a falsity in itself—that is to say no axiom—or, if admitted axiomatic, must at once neutralize both itself and its predecessor.

"And now, by the logic of their own propounder, let us proceed to test any one of the axioms propounded. Let us give Mr. Mill the fairest of play. We will bring the point to no ordinary issue. We will select for investigation no common-place axiom—no axiom of what, not the less preposterously because only impliedly, he terms his secondary class—as if a positive truth by definition could be either more or less positively a truth:—we will select, I say, no axiom of an unquestionability so questionable as is to be found in Euclid. We will not talk, for example, about such propositions as that two straight lines cannot enclose a space, or that the whole is greater than any one of its parts. We will afford the logician *every* advantage. We will come at once to a proposition which he regards as the acme of the unquestionable—as the quintessence of axiomatic undeniability. Here it is:—'Contradictions cannot *both* be true—that is, cannot cöexist in nature.' Here Mr. Mill means, for instance,—and I give the most forcible instance conceivable—that a tree must be either a tree or *not* a tree—that it cannot be at the same time a tree *and* not a tree:—all which is quite reasonable of itself and will answer remarkably well as an axiom, until we bring it into collation with an axiom insisted upon a few pages before—in other words—words which I have previously employed—until we test it by the logic of its own propounder. 'A tree,' Mr. Mill asserts, 'must be either a tree or *not* a tree.' Very well:—and now let me ask him, *why*. To this little query there is but one response:—I defy any man living to invent a second. The sole answer is this:—'Because we find it *impossible to conceive* that a tree can be any thing else than a tree or not a tree.' This, I repeat, is Mr. Mill's sole answer:—he will not *pretend* to suggest another:—and yet, by his own showing, his answer is clearly no answer at all; for has he not already required us to admit, *as an axiom*, that ability or inability to conceive is *in no case* to be taken as a criterion of axiomatic truth? Thus all—absolutely *all* his argumentation is at sea without a rudder. Let it not be urged that an exception from the general rule is to be made, in cases where the 'impossibility to conceive' is so peculiarly great as when we are called upon to conceive a tree *both* a tree and *not* a tree. Let no attempt, I say, be made at urging this sotticism; for, in the first place, there are no *degrees* of 'impossibility,' and thus no one impossible conception can be *more* peculiarly impossible than another impossible conception:—in the second place, Mr. Mill himself, no doubt after thorough deliberation, has most distinctly, and most rationally, excluded all opportunity for exception, by the emphasis of his proposition, that, *in no case*, is ability or inability to conceive, to be taken as a criterion of axiomatic truth:—in the third place, even were exceptions admissible at all, it remains to be shown how any exception is admissible *here*. That a tree can be both a tree and not a tree, is an idea which the angels, or the devils, *may* entertain, and which no doubt many an earthly Bedlamite, or Transcendentalist, *does*.

"Now I do not quarrel with these ancients," continues the letter-writer, "*so much* on account of the transparent frivolity of their logic—which, to be plain, was baseless, worthless and fantastic altogether—as on account of their pompous and infatuate proscription of all *other* roads to Truth than the two narrow and crooked paths—the one of creeping and the other of crawling—to which, in their ignorant perversity, they have dared to confine the Soul—the Soul which loves nothing so well as to soar in those regions of illimitable intuition which are utterly incognizant of '*path*.'

"By the bye, my dear friend, is it not an evidence of the mental slavery entailed upon those bigoted people by their Hogs and Rams, that in spite of the eternal prating of their savans about *roads* to Truth, none of them fell, even by accident, into what we now so distinctly perceive to be the broadest, the straightest and most available of all mere roads—the great thoroughfare—the majestic highway of the *Consistent*? Is it not wonderful that they should have failed to deduce from the works of God the vitally momentous consideration that *a perfect consistency can be nothing but an absolute truth*? How plain—how rapid our progress since the late announcement of this proposition! By its means, investigation has been taken out of the hands of the ground-moles, and given as a duty, rather than as a task, to the true—to the *only* true thinkers—to the generally-educated men of ardent imagination. These latter—our Keplers—our Laplaces—'speculate'—'theorize'—these are the terms—can you not fancy the shout of scorn with which they would be received by our progenitors, were it possible for them to be looking over my shoulders as I write? The Keplers, I repeat, speculate—theorize—and their theories are merely corrected—reduced—sifted—cleared, little by little, of their chaff of inconsistency—until at length there stands apparent an unencumbered *Consistency*—a consistency which the most stolid admit—because it *is* a consistency—to be an absolute and an unquestionable *Truth*.

"I have often thought, my friend, that it must have puzzled these dogmaticians of a thousand years ago, to determine, even, by which of their two boasted roads it is that the cryptographist attains the solution of the more complicate cyphers—or by which of them Champollion guided mankind to those important and innumerable truths which, for so many centuries, have lain entombed amid the phonetical hieroglyphics of Egypt. In especial, would it not have given these bigots some trouble to determine by which of their two roads was reached the most momentous and sublime of *all* their truths—the truth—the fact of *gravitation*? Newton deduced it from the laws of Kepler. Kepler admitted that these laws he *guessed*—these laws whose investigation disclosed to the greatest of British astronomers that principle, the basis of all (existing) physical principle, in going behind which we enter at once the nebulous kingdom of Metaphysics. Yes!—these vital laws Kepler *guessed*—that is to say, he *imagined* them. Had he been asked to point out either the *de*ductive or *in*ductive route by which he attained them, his reply might have been—'I know nothing about *routes*—but I *do* know the machinery of the Universe. Here it is. I grasped it with *my soul*—I reached it through mere dint of *intuition*.' Alas, poor ignorant old man! Could not any metaphysician have told him that what he called 'intuition' was but the conviction resulting from *de*ductions or *in*ductions of which the processes were so shadowy as to have escaped his consciousness, eluded his reason, or bidden defiance to his capacity of expression? How great a pity it is that some 'moral philosopher' had not enlightened him about all this! How it would have comforted him on his death-bed to know that, instead of having gone intuitively and thus unbecomingly, he had, in fact, proceeded decorously and legitimately—that is to say Hog-ishly, or at least Ram-ishly—into the vast halls where lay gleaming, untended, and hitherto untouched by mortal hand—unseen by mortal eye—the imperishable and priceless secrets of the Universe!

"Yes, Kepler was essentially a *theorist*; but this title, *now* of so much sanctity, was, in those ancient days, a designation of supreme contempt. It is only *now* that men begin to appreciate that divine old man—to sympathize with the prophetical and poetical rhapsody of his ever-memorable words. For *my* part," continues the unknown correspondent, "I glow with a sacred fire when I even think of them, and feel that I shall never grow weary of their repetition:—in concluding this letter, let me have the real pleasure of transcribing them once again:—'*I care not whether my work be read now or by posterity. I can afford to wait a century for readers when God himself has waited six thousand years for an observer. I triumph. I have stolen the golden secret of the Egyptians. I will indulge my sacred fury.*'"

Here end my quotations from this very unaccountable and, perhaps, somewhat impertinent epistle; and perhaps it would be folly to comment, in any respect, upon the chimerical, not to say revolutionary, fancies of the writer—whoever he is—fancies so radically at war with the well-considered and well-settled opinions of this age. Let us proceed, then, to our legitimate thesis, *The Universe*.

This thesis admits a choice between two modes of discussion:—We may *as*cend or *de*scend. Beginning at our own point of view—at the Earth on which we stand—we may pass to the other planets of our system—thence to the Sun—thence to our system considered collectively—and thence, through other systems, indefinitely outwards; or, commencing on high at some point as definite as we can make it or conceive it, we may come down to the habitation of Man. Usually—that is to say, in ordinary essays on Astronomy—the first of these two modes is, with certain reservation, adopted:—this for the obvious reason that astronomical *facts*, merely, and principles, being the object, that object is best fulfilled in stepping from the known because proximate, gradually onward to the point where all certitude becomes lost in the remote. For my present purpose, however,—that of enabling the mind to take in, as if from afar and at one glance, a distinct conception of the *individual* Universe—it is clear that a descent to small from great—to the outskirts from the centre (if we could establish a centre)—to the end from the beginning (if we could fancy a beginning) would be the preferable course, but for the difficulty, if not impossibility, of presenting, in this course, to the unastronomical, a picture at all comprehensible in regard to such considerations as are involved in *quantity*—that is to say, in number, magnitude and distance.

Now, distinctness—intelligibility, at all points, is a primary feature in my general design. On important topics it is better to be a good deal prolix than even a very little obscure. But abstruseness is a quality appertaining to no subject *per se*. All are alike, in facility of comprehension, to him who approaches them by properly graduated steps. It is merely because a stepping-stone, here and there, is heedlessly left unsupplied in our road to the Differential Calculus, that this latter is not altogether as simple a thing as a sonnet by Mr. Solomon Seesaw.

By way of admitting, then, no *chance* for misapprehension, I think it advisable to proceed as if even the more obvious facts of Astronomy were unknown to the reader. In combining the two modes of discussion to which I have referred, I propose to avail myself of the advantages peculiar to each—and very especially of the *iteration in detail* which will be unavoidable as a consequence of the plan. Commencing with a descent, I shall reserve for the return upwards those indispensable considerations of *quantity* to which allusion has already been made.

Let us begin, then, at once, with that merest of words, "Infinity." This, like "God," "spirit," and some other expressions of which the equivalents exist in all languages, is by no means the expression of an idea—but of an effort at one. It stands for the possible attempt at an impossible conception. Man needed a term by which to point out the *direction* of this effort—the cloud behind which lay, forever invisible, the *object* of this attempt. A word, in fine, was demanded, by means of which one human being might put himself in relation at once with another human being and with a certain *tendency* of the human intellect. Out of this demand arose the word, "Infinity;" which is thus the representative but of the *thought of a thought*.

As regards *that* infinity now considered—the infinity of space—we often hear it said that "its idea is admitted by the mind—is acquiesced in—is entertained—on account of the greater difficulty which attends the conception of a limit." But this is merely one of those *phrases* by which even profound thinkers, time out of mind, have occasionally taken pleasure in deceiving *themselves*. The quibble lies concealed in the word "difficulty." "The mind," we are told, "entertains the idea of *limitless*, through the greater *difficulty* which it finds in entertaining that of *limited*, space." Now, were the proposition but fairly *put*, its absurdity would become transparent at once. Clearly, there is no mere *difficulty* in the case. The assertion intended, if presented *according* to its intention and without sophistry, would run thus:—"The mind admits the idea of limitless, through the greater *impossibility* of entertaining that of limited, space."

It must be immediately seen that this is not a question of two statements between whose respective credibilities—or of two arguments between whose respective validities—the *reason* is called upon to decide:—it is a matter of two conceptions, directly conflicting, and each avowedly impossible, one of which the *intellect* is supposed to be capable of entertaining, on account of the greater *impossibility* of entertaining the other. The choice is *not* made between two difficulties;—it is merely *fancied* to be made between two impossibilities. Now of the former, there *are* degrees—but of the latter, none:—just as our impertinent letter-writer has already suggested. A task *may* be more or less difficult; but it is either possible or not possible:—there are no gradations. It *might* be more *difficult* to overthrow the Andes than an ant-hill; but it *can* be no more *impossible* to annihilate the matter of the one than the matter of the other. A man may jump ten feet with less *difficulty* than he can jump twenty, but the *impossibility* of his leaping to the moon is not a whit less than that of his leaping to the dog-star.

Since all this is undeniable: since the choice of the mind is to be made between *impossibilities* of conception: since one impossibility cannot be greater than another: and since, thus, one cannot be preferred to another: the philosophers who not only maintain, on the grounds mentioned, man's *idea* of infinity but, on account of such supposititious idea, *infinity itself*—are plainly engaged in demonstrating one impossible thing to be possible by showing how it is that some one other thing—is impossible too. This, it will be said, is nonsense; and perhaps it is:—indeed I think it very capital nonsense—but forego all claim to it as nonsense of mine.

The readiest mode, however, of displaying the fallacy of the philosophical argument on this question, is by simply adverting to a *fact* respecting it which has been hitherto quite overlooked—the fact that the argument alluded to both proves and disproves its own proposition. "The mind is impelled," say the theologians and others, "to admit a *First Cause*, by the superior difficulty it experiences in conceiving cause beyond cause without end." The quibble, as before, lies in the word "difficulty"—but *here* what is it employed to sustain? A First Cause. And what is a First Cause? An ultimate termination of causes. And what is an ultimate termination of causes? Finity—the Finite. Thus the one quibble, in two processes, by God knows how many philosophers, is made to support now Finity and now Infinity—could it not be brought to support something besides? As for the quibblers—*they*, at least, are insupportable. But—to dismiss them:—what they prove in the one case is the identical nothing which they demonstrate in the other.

Of course, no one will suppose that I here contend for the absolute impossibility of *that* which we attempt to convey in the word "Infinity." My purpose is but to show the folly of endeavoring to prove Infinity itself or even our conception of it, by any such blundering ratiocination as that which is ordinarily employed.

Nevertheless, as an individual, I may be permitted to say that *I cannot* conceive Infinity, and am convinced that no human being can. A mind not thoroughly self-conscious—not accustomed to the introspective analysis of its own operations—will, it is true, often deceive itself by supposing that it *has* entertained the conception of which we speak. In the effort to entertain it, we proceed step beyond step—we fancy point still beyond point; and so long as we *continue* the effort, it may be said, in fact, that we are *tending* to the formation of the idea designed; while the strength of the impression that we actually form or have formed it, is in the ratio of the period during which we keep up the mental endeavor. But it is in the act of discontinuing the endeavor—of fulfilling (as we think) the idea—of putting the finishing stroke (as we suppose) to the conception—that we overthrow at once the whole fabric of our fancy by resting upon some one ultimate and therefore definite point. This fact, however, we fail to perceive, on account of the absolute coincidence, in time, between the settling down upon the ultimate point and the act of cessation in thinking.—In attempting, on the other hand, to frame the idea of a *limited* space, we merely converse the processes which involve the impossibility.

We *believe* in a God. We may or may not *believe* in finite or in infinite space; but our belief, in such cases, is more properly designated as *faith*, and is a matter quite distinct from that belief proper—from that *intellectual* belief—which presupposes the mental conception.

The fact is, that, upon the enunciation of any one of that class of terms to which "Infinity" belongs—the class representing *thoughts of thought*—he who has a right to say that he thinks *at all*, feels himself called upon, *not* to entertain a conception, but simply to direct his mental vision toward some given point, in the intellectual firmament, where lies a nebula never to be resolved. To solve it, indeed, he makes no effort; for with a rapid instinct he comprehends, not only the impossibility, but, as regards all human purposes, the *inessentiality*, of its solution. He perceives that the Deity has not *designed* it to be solved. He sees, at once, that it lies *out* of the brain of man, and even *how*, if not exactly *why*, it lies out of it. There *are* people, I am aware, who, busying themselves in attempts at the unattainable, acquire very easily, by dint of the jargon they emit, among those thinkers-that-they-think with whom darkness and depth are synonymous, a kind of cuttle-fish reputation for profundity; but the finest quality of Thought is its self-cognizance; and, with some little equivocation, it may be said that no fog of the mind can well be greater than that which, extending to the very boundaries of the mental domain, shuts out even these boundaries themselves from comprehension.

It will now be understood that, in using the phrase, "Infinity of Space," I make no call upon the reader to entertain the impossible conception of an *absolute* infinity. I refer simply to the "*utmost conceivable expanse*" of space—a shadowy and fluctuating domain, now shrinking, now swelling, in accordance with the vacillating energies of the imagination.

Hitherto, the Universe of stars has always been considered as coincident with the Universe proper, as I have defined it in the commencement of this Discourse. It has been always either directly or indirectly assumed—at least since the dawn of intelligible Astronomy—

that, were it possible for us to attain any given point in space, we should still find, on all sides of us, an interminable succession of stars. This was the untenable idea of Pascal when making perhaps the most successful attempt ever made, at periphrasing the conception for which we struggle in the word "Universe." "It is a sphere," he says, "of which the centre is everywhere, the circumference, nowhere." But although this intended definition is, in fact, *no* definition of the Universe of *stars*, we may accept it, with some mental reservation, as a definition (rigorous enough for all practical purposes) of the Universe *proper*—that is to say, of the Universe of *space*. This latter, then, let us regard as "*a sphere of which the centre is everywhere, the circumference nowhere*." In fact, while we find it impossible to fancy an *end* to space, we have no difficulty in picturing to ourselves any one of an infinity of *beginnings*.

As our starting-point, then, let us adopt the *Godhead*. Of this Godhead, *in itself*, he alone is not imbecile—he alone is not impious who propounds—nothing. "*Nous ne connaissons rien*," says the Baron de Bielfeld—"*Nous ne connaissons rien de la nature ou de l'essence de Dieu:—pour savoir ce qu'il est, il faut être Dieu même.*"—"We know absolutely *nothing* of the nature or essence of God:—in order to comprehend what he is, we should have to be God ourselves."

"*We should have to be God ourselves!*"—With a phrase so startling as this yet ringing in my ears, I nevertheless venture to demand if this our present ignorance of the Deity is an ignorance to which the soul is *everlastingly* condemned.

By *Him*, however—*now*, at least, the Incomprehensible—by Him—assuming him as *Spirit*—that is to say, as *not Matter*—a distinction which, for all intelligible purposes, will stand well instead of a definition—by Him, then, existing as Spirit, let us content ourselves, to-night, with supposing to have been *created*, or made out of Nothing, by dint of his Volition—at some point of Space which we will take as a centre—at some period into which we do not pretend to inquire, but at all events immensely remote—by Him, then again, let us suppose to have been created—*what*? This is a vitally momentous epoch in our considerations. *What* is it that we are justified—that alone we are justified in supposing to have been, primarily and solely, *created*?

We have attained a point where only *Intuition* can aid us:—but now let me recur to the idea which I have already suggested as that alone which we can properly entertain of intuition. It is but *the conviction arising from those inductions or deductions of which the processes are so shadowy as to escape our consciousness, elude our reason, or defy our capacity of expression*. With this understanding, I now assert—that an intuition altogether irresistible, although inexpressible, forces me to the conclusion that what God originally created—that that Matter which, by dint of his Volition, he first made from his Spirit, or from Nihility, *could* have been nothing but Matter in its utmost conceivable state of—what?—of *Simplicity*?

This will be found the sole absolute *assumption* of my Discourse. I use the word "assumption" in its ordinary sense; yet I maintain that even this my primary proposition, is very, very far indeed, from being really a mere assumption. Nothing was ever more certainly—no human conclusion was ever, in fact, more regularly—more rigorously *de*duced:—but, alas! the processes lie out of the human analysis—at all events are beyond the utterance of the human tongue.

Let us now endeavor to conceive what Matter must be, when, or if, in its absolute extreme of *Simplicity*. Here the Reason flies at once to Imparticularity—to a particle—to *one* particle—a particle of *one* kind—of *one* character—of *one* nature—of *one size*—of one form—a particle, therefore, "*without* form and void"—a particle positively a particle at all points—a particle absolutely unique, individual, undivided, and not indivisible only because He who *created* it, by dint of his Will, can by an infinitely less energetic exercise of the same Will, as a matter of course, divide it.

Oneness, then, is all that I predicate of the originally created Matter; but I propose to show that this *Oneness is a principle abundantly sufficient to account for the constitution, the existing phænomena and the plainly inevitable annihilation of at least the material Universe*.

The willing into being the primordial particle, has completed the act, or more properly the *conception*, of Creation. We now proceed to the ultimate purpose for which we are to suppose the Particle created—that is to say, the ultimate purpose so far as our considerations *yet* enable us to see it—the constitution of the Universe from it, the Particle.

This constitution has been effected by *forcing* the originally and therefore normally *One* into the abnormal condition of *Many*. An action of this character implies rëaction. A diffusion from Unity, under the conditions, involves a tendency to return into Unity—a tendency ineradicable until satisfied. But on these points I will speak more fully hereafter.

The assumption of absolute Unity in the primordial Particle includes that of infinite divisibility. Let us conceive the Particle, then, to be only not totally exhausted by diffusion into Space. From the one Particle, as a centre, let us suppose to be irradiated spherically—in all directions—to immeasurable but still to definite distances in the previously vacant space—a certain inexpressibly great yet limited number of unimaginably yet not infinitely minute atoms.

Now, of these atoms, thus diffused, or upon diffusion, what conditions are we permitted—not to assume, but to infer, from consideration as well of their source as of the character of the design apparent in their diffusion? *Unity* being their source, and *difference from Unity* the character of the design manifested in their diffusion, we are warranted in supposing this character to be at least *generally* preserved throughout the design, and to form a portion of the design itself:—that is to say, we shall be warranted in conceiving continual differences at all points from the uniquity and simplicity of the origin. But, for these reasons, shall we be justified in imagining the atoms heterogeneous, dissimilar, unequal, and inequidistant? More explicitly—are we to consider no two atoms as, at their diffusion, of the same nature, or of the same form, or of the same size?—and, after fulfilment of their diffusion into Space, is absolute inequidistance, each from each, to be understood of all of them? In such arrangement, under such conditions, we most easily and immediately comprehend the subsequent most feasible carrying out to completion of any such design as that which I have suggested—the design of variety out of unity—diversity out of sameness—heterogeneity out of homogeneity—complexity out of simplicity—in a word, the utmost possible multiplicity of *relation* out of the emphatically irrelative *One*. Undoubtedly, therefore, we *should* be warranted in assuming all that has been mentioned, but for the reflection, first, that supererogation is not presumable of any Divine Act; and, secondly, that the object supposed in view, appears as feasible when some of the conditions in question are dispensed with, in the beginning, as when all are understood immediately to exist. I mean to say that some are involved in the rest, or so instantaneous a consequence of them as to make the distinction inappreciable. Difference of *size*, for example, will at once be brought about through the tendency of one atom to a second, in preference to a third, on account of particular inequidistance; which is to be comprehended as *particular inequidistances between centres of quantity, in neighboring atoms of different form*—a matter not at all interfering with the generally-equable distribution of the atoms. Difference of *kind*, too, is easily conceived to be merely a result of differences in size and form, taken more or less conjointly:—in fact, since the *Unity* of the Particle Proper implies absolute homogeneity, we cannot imagine the atoms, at their diffusion, differing in kind, without imagining, at the same time, a special exercise of the Divine Will, at the emission of each atom, for the purpose of effecting, in each, a change of its essential nature:—so fantastic an idea is the less to be indulged, as the object proposed is seen to be thoroughly attainable without such minute and elaborate interposition. We perceive, therefore, upon the whole, that it would be supererogatory, and consequently unphilosophical, to predicate of the atoms, in view of their purposes, any thing more than *difference of form* at their dispersion, with particular inequidistance after it—all other differences arising at once out of these, in the very first processes of mass-constitution:—We thus establish the Universe on a purely *geometrical* basis. Of course, it is by no means necessary to assume absolute difference, even of form, among *all* the atoms irradiated—any more than absolute particular inequidistance of each from each. We are required to conceive merely that no *neighboring* atoms are of similar form—no atoms which can ever approximate, until their inevitable rëunition at the end.

Although the immediate and perpetual *tendency* of the disunited atoms to return into their normal Unity, is implied, as I have said, in their abnormal diffusion; still it is clear that this tendency will be without consequence—a tendency and no more—until the diffusive energy, in ceasing to be exerted, shall leave *it*, the tendency, free to seek its satisfaction. The Divine Act, however, being considered as determinate, and discontinued on fulfilment of the diffusion, we understand, at once, a *rëaction*—in other words, a *satisfiable* tendency of the disunited atoms to return into *One*.

But the diffusive energy being withdrawn, and the rëaction having commenced in furtherance of the ultimate design—*that of the utmost possible Relation*—this design is now in danger of being frustrated, in detail, by reason of that very tendency to return which is to effect its accomplishment in general. *Multiplicity* is the object; but there is nothing to prevent proximate atoms, from lapsing *at once*, through the now satisfiable tendency—*before* the fulfilment of any ends proposed in multiplicity—into absolute oneness among themselves:—there is nothing to impede the aggregation of various *unique* masses, at various points of space:—in other words, nothing to interfere with the accumulation of various masses, each absolutely One.

For the effectual and thorough completion of the general design, we thus see the necessity for a repulsion of limited capacity—a separative *something* which, on withdrawal of the diffusive Volition, shall at the same time allow the approach, and forbid the junction, of the atoms; suffering them infinitely to approximate, while denying them positive contact; in a word, having the power—*up to a certain epoch*—of preventing their *coalition*, but no ability to interfere with their *coalescence* in any respect *or degree*. The repulsion, already considered as so peculiarly limited in other regards, must be understood, let me repeat, as having power to prevent absolute coalition, *only up to a certain epoch*. Unless we are to conceive that the appetite for Unity among the atoms is doomed to be satisfied *never*;—unless we are to conceive that what had a beginning is to have no end—a conception which cannot *really* be entertained, however much we may talk or dream of entertaining it—we are forced to conclude that the repulsive influence imagined, will, finally—under pressure of the *Unitendency collectively* applied, but never and in no degree *until*, on fulfilment of the Divine purposes, such collective application shall be naturally made—yield to a force which, at that ultimate epoch, shall be the superior force precisely to the extent required, and thus permit the universal subsidence into the inevitable, because original and therefore normal, *One*.—The conditions here to be reconciled are difficult indeed:—we cannot even comprehend the possibility of their conciliation;—nevertheless, the apparent impossibility is brilliantly suggestive.

That the repulsive something actually exists, *we see*. Man neither employs, nor knows, a force sufficient to bring two atoms into contact. This is but the well-established proposition of the impenetrability of matter. All Experiment proves—all Philosophy admits it. The *design* of the repulsion—the necessity for its existence—I have endeavored to show; but from all attempt at investigating its nature have religiously abstained; this on account of an intuitive conviction that the principle at issue is strictly spiritual—lies in a recess impervious to our present understanding—lies involved in a consideration of what now—in our human state—is *not* to be considered—in a consideration of *Spirit in itself*. I feel, in a word, that here the God has interposed, and here only, because here and here only the knot demanded the interposition of the God.

In fact, while the tendency of the diffused atoms to return into Unity, will be recognized, at once, as the principle of the Newtonian Gravity, what I have spoken of as a repulsive influence prescribing limits to the (immediate) satisfaction of the tendency, will be understood as *that* which we have been in the practice of designating now as heat, now as magnetism, now as *electricity*; displaying our ignorance of its awful character in the vacillation of the phraseology with which we endeavor to circumscribe it.

Calling it, merely for the moment, electricity, we know that all experimental analysis of electricity has given, as an ultimate result, the principle, or seeming principle, *heterogeneity*. *Only* where things differ is electricity apparent; and it is presumable that they *never* differ where it is not developed at least, if not apparent. Now, this result is in the fullest keeping with that which I have reached unempirically. The design of the repulsive influence I have maintained to be that of preventing immediate Unity among the diffused atoms; and these atoms are represented as different each from each. *Difference* is their character—their essentiality—just as *no-difference* was the essentiality of their source. When we say, then, that an attempt to bring any two of these atoms together would induce an effort, on the part of the repulsive influence, to prevent the contact, we may as well use the strictly convertible sentence that an attempt to bring together any two differences will result in a development of electricity. All existing bodies, of course, are composed of these atoms in proximate contact, and are therefore to be considered as mere assemblages of more or fewer differences; and the resistance made by the repulsive spirit, on bringing together any two such assemblages, would be in the ratio of the two sums of the differences in each:—an expression which, when reduced, is equivalent to this:—*The amount of electricity developed on the approximation of two bodies, is proportional to the difference between the respective sums of the atoms of which the bodies are composed.* That *no* two bodies are absolutely alike, is a simple corollary from all that has been here said. Electricity, therefore, existing always, is *developed* whenever *any* bodies, but *manifested* only when bodies of appreciable difference, are brought into approximation.

To electricity—so, for the present, continuing to call it—we *may* not be wrong in referring the various physical appearances of light, heat and magnetism; but far less shall we be liable to err in attributing to this strictly spiritual principle the more important phænomena of vitality, consciousness and *Thought*. On this topic, however, I need pause *here* merely to suggest that these phænomena, whether observed generally or in detail, seem to proceed *at least in the ratio of the heterogeneous*.

Discarding now the two equivocal terms, "gravitation" and "electricity," let us adopt the more definite expressions, "*attraction*" and "*repulsion*." The former is the body; the latter the soul: the one is the material; the other the spiritual, principle of the Universe. *No other principles exist. All* phænomena are referable to one, or to the other, or to both combined. So rigorously is this the case—so thoroughly demonstrable is it that attraction and repulsion are the *sole* properties through which we perceive the Universe—in other words, by which Matter is manifested to Mind—that, for all merely argumentative purposes, we are fully justified in assuming that matter *exists* only as attraction and repulsion—that attraction and repulsion *are* matter:—there being no conceivable case in which we may not employ the term "matter" and the terms "attraction" and "repulsion," taken together, as equivalent, and therefore convertible, expressions in Logic.

I said, just now, that what I have described as the tendency of the diffused atoms to return into their original unity, would be understood as the principle of the Newtonian law of gravity: and, in fact, there can be little difficulty in such an understanding, if we look at the Newtonian gravity in a merely general view, as a force impelling matter to seek matter; that is to say, when we pay no attention to the known *modus operandi* of the Newtonian force. The general coincidence satisfies us; but, upon looking closely, we see, in detail, much that appears *in*coincident, and much in regard to which no coincidence, at least, is established. For example; the Newtonian gravity, when we think of it in certain moods, does *not* seem to be a tendency to *oneness* at all, but rather a tendency of all bodies in all directions—a phrase apparently expressive of a tendency to diffusion. Here, then, is an *in*coincidence. Again; when we reflect on the mathematical *law* governing the Newtonian tendency, we see clearly that no coincidence has been made good, in respect of the *modus operandi*, at least, between gravitation as known to exist and that seemingly simple and direct tendency which I have assumed.

In fact, I have attained a point at which it will be advisable to strengthen my position by reversing my processes. So far, we have gone on *à priori*, from an abstract consideration of *Simplicity*, as that quality most likely to have characterized the original action of God. Let us now see whether the established facts of the Newtonian Gravitation may not afford us, *à posteriori*, some legitimate inductions.

What does the Newtonian law declare?—That all bodies attract each other with forces proportional to their quantities of matter and inversely proportional to the squares of their distances. Purposely, I have here given, in the first place, the vulgar version of the law; and I confess that in this, as in most other vulgar versions of great truths, we find little of a suggestive character. Let us now adopt a more philosophical phraseology:—*Every atom, of every body, attracts every other atom, both of its own and of every other body, with a force which varies inversely as the squares of the distances between the attracting and attracted atom.*—Here, indeed, a flood of suggestion bursts upon the mind.

But let us see distinctly what it was that Newton *proved*—according to the grossly irrational definitions of *proof* prescribed by the metaphysical schools. He was forced to content himself with showing how thoroughly the motions of an imaginary Universe, composed of attracting and attracted atoms obedient to the law he announced, coincide with those of the actually existing Universe so far as it comes under our observation. This was the amount of his *demonstration*—that is to say, this was the amount of it, according to the conventional cant of the "philosophies." His successes added proof multiplied by proof—such proof as a sound intellect admits—but the *demonstration* of the law itself, persist the metaphysicians, had not been strengthened in any degree. "*Ocular*, *physical* proof," however, of attraction, here upon Earth, in accordance with the Newtonian theory, was, at length, much to the satisfaction of some intellectual grovellers, afforded. This proof arose collaterally and incidentally (as nearly all important truths have arisen) out of an attempt to ascertain the mean density of the Earth. In the famous Maskelyne, Cavendish and Bailly experiments for this purpose, the attraction of the mass of a mountain was seen, felt, measured, and found to be mathematically consistent with the immortal theory of the British astronomer.

But in spite of this confirmation of that which needed none—in spite of the so-called corroboration of the "theory" by the so-called "ocular and physical proof"—in spite of the *character* of this corroboration—the ideas which even really philosophical men cannot help imbibing of gravity—and, especially, the ideas of it which ordinary men get and contentedly maintain, are *seen* to have been derived, for the most part, from a consideration of the principle as they find it developed—*merely in the planet upon which they stand*.

Now, to what does so partial a consideration tend—to what species of error does it give rise? On the Earth we *see* and *feel*, only that gravity impels all bodies towards the *centre* of the Earth. No man in the common walks of life could be *made* to see or to feel anything else—could be made to perceive that anything, anywhere, has a perpetual, gravitating tendency in any *other* direction than to the centre of the Earth; yet (with an exception hereafter to be specified) it is a fact that every earthly thing (not to speak now of every heavenly thing) has a tendency not *only* to the Earth's centre but in every conceivable direction besides.

Now, although the philosophic cannot be said to *err with* the vulgar in this matter, they nevertheless permit themselves to be influenced, without knowing it, by the *sentiment* of the vulgar idea. "Although the Pagan fables are not believed," says Bryant, in his very erudite "Mythology," "yet we forget ourselves continually and make inferences from them as from existing realities." I mean to assert that the merely *sensitive perception* of gravity as we experience it on Earth, beguiles mankind into the fancy of *concentralization* or *especiality* respecting it—has been continually biasing towards this fancy even the mightiest intellects—perpetually, although imperceptibly, leading them away from the real characteristics of the principle; thus preventing them, up to this date, from ever getting a glimpse of that vital truth which lies in a diametrically opposite direction—behind the principle's *essential* characteristics—those, *not* of concentralization or especiality—but of *universality* and *diffusion*. This "vital truth" is *Unity* as the *source* of the phænomenon.

Let me now repeat the definition of gravity:—*Every atom, of every body, attracts every other atom, both of its own and of every other body*, with a force which varies inversely as the squares of the distances of the attracting and attracted atom.

Here let the reader pause with me, for a moment, in contemplation of the miraculous—of the ineffable—of the altogether unimaginable complexity of relation involved in the fact that *each atom attracts every other atom*—involved merely in this fact of the attraction, without reference to the law or mode in which the attraction is manifested—involved *merely* in the fact that each atom attracts every other atom *at all*, in a wilderness of atoms so numerous that those which go to the composition of a cannon-ball, exceed, probably, in mere point of number, all the stars which go to the constitution of the Universe.

Had we discovered, simply, that each atom tended to some one favorite point—to some especially attractive atom—we should still have fallen upon a discovery which, in itself, would have sufficed to overwhelm the mind:—but what is it that we are actually called upon to comprehend? That each atom attracts—sympathizes with the most delicate movements of every other atom, and with each and with all at the same time, and forever, and according to a determinate law of which the complexity, even considered by itself solely, is utterly beyond the grasp of the imagination of man. If I propose to ascertain the influence of one mote in a sunbeam upon its neighboring mote, I cannot accomplish my purpose without first counting and weighing all the atoms in the Universe and defining the precise positions of all at one particular moment. If I venture to displace, by even the billionth part of an inch, the microscopical speck of dust which lies now upon the point of my finger, what is the character of that act upon which I have adventured? I have done a deed which shakes the Moon in her path, which causes the Sun to be no longer the Sun, and which alters forever the destiny of the multitudinous myriads of stars that roll and glow in the majestic presence of their Creator.

These ideas—conceptions such as *these*—unthoughtlike thoughts—soul-reveries rather than conclusions or even considerations of the intellect:—ideas, I repeat, such as these, are such as we can alone hope profitably to entertain in any effort at grasping the great principle, *Attraction*.

But now,—*with* such ideas—with such a *vision* of the marvellous complexity of Attraction fairly in his mind—let any person competent of thought on such topics as these, set himself to the task of imagining a *principle* for the phænomena observed—a condition from which they sprang.

Does not so evident a brotherhood among the atoms point to a common parentage? Does not a sympathy so omniprevalent, so ineradicable, and so thoroughly irrespective, suggest a common paternity as its source? Does not one extreme impel the reason to the other? Does not the infinitude of division refer to the utterness of individuality? Does not the entireness of the complex hint at the perfection of the simple? It is *not* that the atoms, as we see them, are divided or that they are complex in their relations—but that they are inconceivably divided and unutterably complex:—it is the extremeness of the conditions to which I now allude, rather than to the conditions themselves. In a word, is it not because the atoms were, at some remote epoch of time, even *more than together*—is it not because originally, and therefore normally, they were *One*—that now, in all circumstances—at all points—in all directions—by all modes of approach—in all relations and through all conditions—they struggle *back* to this absolutely, this irrelatively, this unconditionally *one*?

Some person may here demand:—"Why—since it is to the *One* that the atoms struggle back—do we not find and define Attraction 'a merely general tendency to a centre?'—why, in especial, do not *your* atoms—the atoms which you describe as having been irradiated from a centre—proceed at once, rectilinearly, back to the central point of their origin?"

I reply that *they do*; as will be distinctly shown; but that the cause of their so doing is quite irrespective of the centre *as such*. They all tend rectilinearly towards a centre, because of the sphereicity with which they have been irradiated into space. Each atom, forming one of a generally uniform globe of atoms, finds more atoms in the direction of the centre, of course, than in any other, and in that direction, therefore, is impelled—but is *not* thus impelled because the centre is *the point of its origin*. It is not to any *point* that the atoms are allied. It is not any *locality*, either in the concrete or in the abstract, to which I suppose them bound. Nothing like *location* was conceived as their origin. Their source lies in the principle, *Unity*. *This* is their lost parent. *This* they seek always—immediately—in all directions—wherever it is even partially to be found; thus appeasing, in some measure, the ineradicable tendency, while on the way to its absolute satisfaction in the end. It follows from all this, that any principle which shall be adequate to account for the *law*, or *modus operandi*, of the attractive force in general, will account for this law in particular:—that is to say, any principle which will show why the atoms should tend to their *general centre of irradiation* with forces inversely proportional to the squares of the distances, will be admitted as satisfactorily accounting, at the same time, for the tendency, according to the same law, of these atoms each to each:—*for* the tendency to the centre *is* merely the tendency each to each, and not any tendency to a centre as such.—Thus it will be seen, also, that the establishment of my propositions would involve no *necessity* of modification in the terms of the Newtonian definition of Gravity, which declares that each atom attracts each other atom and so forth, and declares this merely; but (always under the supposition that what I propose be, in the end, admitted) it seems clear that some error might occasionally be avoided, in the future processes of Science, were a more ample phraseology adopted:—for instance:—"Each atom tends to every other atom &c. with a force &c.: *the general result being a tendency of all, with a similar force, to a general centre*."

The reversal of our processes has thus brought us to an identical result; but, while in the one process *intuition* was the starting-point, in the other it was the goal. In commencing the former journey I could only say that, with an irresistible intuition, I *felt* Simplicity to have been the characteristic of the original action of God:—in ending the latter I can only declare that, with an irresistible intuition, I perceive Unity to have been the source of the observed phænomena of the Newtonian gravitation. Thus, according to the schools, I *prove* nothing. So be it:—I design but to suggest—and to *convince* through the suggestion. I am proudly aware that there exist many of the most profound and cautiously discriminative human intellects which cannot *help* being abundantly content with my—suggestions. To these intellects—as to my own—there is no mathematical demonstration which *could* bring the least additional *true proof* of the great *Truth* which I have advanced—*the truth of Original Unity as the source—as the principle of the Universal Phænomena*. For my part, I am not so sure that I speak and see—I am not so sure that my heart beats and that my soul lives:—of the rising of to-morrow's sun—a probability that as yet lies in the Future—I do not pretend to be one thousandth part as sure—as I am of the irretrievably by-gone *Fact* that All Things and All Thoughts of Things, with all their ineffable Multiplicity of Relation, sprang at once into being from the primordial and irrelative *One*.

Referring to the Newtonian Gravity, Dr. Nichol, the eloquent author of "The Architecture of the Heavens," says:—"In truth we have no reason to suppose this great Law, as now revealed, to be the ultimate or simplest, and therefore the universal and all-comprehensive, form of a great Ordinance. The mode in which its intensity diminishes with the element of distance, has not the aspect of an ultimate *principle*; which always assumes the simplicity and self-evidence of those axioms which constitute the basis of Geometry."

Now, it is quite true that "ultimate principles," in the common understanding of the words, always assume the simplicity of geometrical axioms—(as for "self-evidence," there is no such thing)—but these principles are clearly *not* "ultimate;" in other terms what we are in the habit of calling principles are no principles, properly speaking—since there can be but one *principle*, the Volition of God. We have no right to assume, then, from what we observe in rules that we choose foolishly to name "principles," anything at all in respect to the characteristics of a principle proper. The "ultimate principles" of which Dr. Nichol speaks as having geometrical simplicity, may and do have this geometrical turn, as being part and parcel of a vast geometrical system, and thus a system of simplicity itself—in which, nevertheless, the *truly* ultimate principle is, *as we know*, the consummation of the complex—that is to say, of the unintelligible—for is it not the Spiritual Capacity of God?

I quoted Dr. Nichol's remark, however, not so much to question its philosophy, as by way of calling attention to the fact that, while all men have admitted *some* principle as existing behind the Law of Gravity, no attempt has been yet made to point out what this principle in particular *is*:—if we except, perhaps, occasional fantastic efforts at referring it to Magnetism, or Mesmerism, or Swedenborgianism, or Transcendentalism, or some other equally delicious *ism* of the same species, and invariably patronized by one and the same species of people. The great mind of Newton, while boldly grasping the Law itself, shrank from the principle of the Law. The more fluent and comprehensive at least, if not the more patient and profound, sagacity of Laplace, had not the courage to attack it. But hesitation on the part of these two astronomers it is, perhaps, not so very difficult to understand. They, as well as all the first class of mathematicians, were mathematicians *solely*:—their intellect, at least, had a firmly-pronounced mathematico-physical tone. What lay not distinctly within the domain of Physics, or of Mathematics, seemed to them either Non-Entity or Shadow. Nevertheless, we may well wonder that Leibnitz, who was a marked exception to the general rule in these respects, and whose mental temperament was a singular admixture of the mathematical with the physico-metaphysical, did not at once investigate and establish the point at issue. Either Newton or Laplace, seeking a principle and discovering none *physical*, would have rested contentedly in the conclusion that there was absolutely none; but it is almost impossible to fancy, of Leibnitz, that, having exhausted in his search the physical dominions, he would not have stepped at once, boldly and hopefully, amid his old familiar haunts in the kingdom of Metaphysics. Here, indeed, it is clear that he *must* have adventured in search of the treasure:—that he did not find it after all, was, perhaps, because his fairy guide, Imagination, was not sufficiently well-grown, or well-educated, to direct him aright.

I observed, just now, that, in fact, there had been certain vague attempts at referring Gravity to some very uncertain *isms*. These attempts, however, although considered bold and justly so considered, looked no farther than to the generality—the merest generality—of the Newtonian Law. Its *modus operandi* has never, to my knowledge, been approached in the way of an effort at explanation. It is, therefore, with no unwarranted fear of being taken for a madman at the outset, and before I can bring my propositions fairly to the eye of those who alone are competent to decide upon them, that I here declare the *modus operandi* of the Law of Gravity to be an exceedingly simple and perfectly explicable thing—that is to say, when we make our advances towards it in just gradations and in the true direction—when we regard it from the proper point of view.

Whether we reach the idea of absolute *Unity* as the source of All Things, from a consideration of Simplicity as the most probable characteristic of the original action of God;—whether we arrive at it from an inspection of the universality of relation in the gravitating phænomena;—or whether we attain it as a result of the mutual corroboration afforded by both processes;—still, the idea itself, if entertained at all, is entertained in inseparable connection with another idea—that of the condition of the Universe of stars as we *now* perceive it—that is to say, a condition of immeasurable *diffusion* through space. Now a connection between these two ideas—unity and diffusion—cannot be established unless through the entertainment of a third idea—that of *irradiation*. Absolute Unity being taken as a centre, then the existing Universe of stars is the result of *irradiation* from that centre.

Now, the laws of irradiation are *known*. They are part and parcel of the *sphere*. They belong to the class of *indisputable geometrical properties*. We say of them, "they are true—they are evident." To demand *why* they are true, would be to demand why the axioms are true upon which their demonstration is based. *Nothing* is demonstrable, strictly speaking; but *if* anything *be*, then the properties—the laws in question are demonstrated.

But these laws—what do they declare? Irradiation—how—by what steps does it proceed outwardly from a centre?

From a *luminous* centre, *Light* issues by irradiation; and the quantities of light received upon any given plane, supposed to be shifting its position so as to be now nearer the centre and now farther from it, will be diminished in the same proportion as the squares of the distances of the plane from the luminous body, are increased; and will be increased in the same proportion as these squares are diminished.

The expression of the law may be thus generalized:—the number of light-particles (or, if the phrase be preferred, the number of light-impressions) received upon the shifting plane, will be *inversely* proportional with the squares of the distances of the plane. Generalizing yet again, we may say that the diffusion—the scattering—the irradiation, in a word—is *directly* proportional with the squares of the distances.

For example: at the distance B, from the luminous centre A, a certain number of particles are so diffused as to occupy the surface B. Then at double the distance—that is to say at C—they will be so much farther diffused as to occupy four such surfaces:—at treble the distance, or at D, they will be so much farther separated as to occupy nine such surfaces:—while, at quadruple the distance, or at E, they will have become so scattered as to spread themselves over sixteen such surfaces—and so on forever.

In saying, generally, that the irradiation proceeds in direct proportion with the squares of the distances, we use the term irradiation to express *the degree of the diffusion* as we proceed outwardly from the centre. Conversing the idea, and employing the word "concentralization" to express *the degree of the drawing together* as we come back toward the centre from an outward position, we may say that concentralization proceeds *inversely* as the squares of the distances. In other words, we have reached the conclusion that, on the hypothesis that matter was originally irradiated from a centre and is now returning to it, the concentralization, in the return, proceeds *exactly as we know the force of gravitation to proceed*.

Now here, if we could be permitted to assume that concentralization exactly represented the *force of the tendency to the centre*—that the one was exactly proportional to the other, and that the two proceeded together—we should have shown all that is required. The sole difficulty existing, then, is to establish a direct proportion between "concentralization" and the *force* of concentralization; and this is done, of course, if we establish such proportion between "irradiation" and the *force* of irradiation.

A very slight inspection of the Heavens assures us that the stars have a certain general uniformity, equability, or equidistance, of distribution through that region of space in which, collectively, and in a roughly globular form, they are situated:—this species of very general, rather than absolute, equability, being in full keeping with my deduction of inequidistance, within certain limits, among the originally diffused atoms, as a corollary from the evident design of infinite complexity of relation out of irrelation. I started, it will be remembered, with the idea of a generally uniform but particularly *un*uniform distribution of the atoms;—an idea, I repeat, which an inspection of the stars, as they exist, confirms.

But even in the merely general equability of distribution, as regards the atoms, there appears a difficulty which, no doubt, has already suggested itself to those among my readers who have borne in mind that I suppose this equability of distribution effected through *irradiation from a centre*. The very first glance at the idea, irradiation, forces us to the entertainment of the hitherto unseparated and seemingly inseparable idea of agglomeration about a centre, with dispersion as we recede from it—the idea, in a word, of *in*equability of distribution in respect to the matter irradiated.

Now, I have elsewhere observed that it is by just such difficulties as the one now in question—such roughnesses—such peculiarities—such protuberances above the plane of the ordinary—that Reason feels her way, if at all, in her search for the True. By the difficulty—the "peculiarity"—now presented, I leap at once to *the* secret—a secret which I might never have attained *but* for the peculiarity and the inferences which, *in its mere character of peculiarity*, it affords me.

The process of thought, at this point, may be thus roughly sketched:—I say to myself—"Unity, as I have explained it, is a truth—I feel it. Diffusion is a truth—I see it. Irradiation, by which alone these two truths are reconciled, is a consequent truth—I perceive it. *Equability* of diffusion, first deduced *à priori* and then corroborated by the inspection of phænomena, is also a truth—I fully admit it. So far all is clear around me:—there are no clouds behind which *the* secret—the great secret of the gravitating *modus operandi*—can possibly lie hidden;—but this secret lies *hereabouts*, most assuredly; and *were* there but a cloud in view, I should be driven to suspicion of that cloud." And now, just as I say this, there actually comes a cloud into view. This cloud is the seeming impossibility of reconciling my truth, *irradiation*, with my truth, *equability of diffusion*. I say now:—"Behind this *seeming* impossibility is to be found what I desire." I do not say "*real* impossibility;" for invincible faith in my truths assures me that it is a mere difficulty after all—but I go on to say, with unflinching confidence, that, *when* this *difficulty* shall be solved, we shall find, *wrapped up in the process of solution*, the key to the secret at which we aim. Moreover—I *feel* that we shall discover *but one* possible solution of the difficulty; this for the reason that, were there two, one would be supererogatory—would be fruitless—would be empty—would contain no key—since no duplicate key can be needed to any secret of Nature.

And now, let us see:—Our usual notions of irradiation—in fact *all* our distinct notions of it—are caught merely from the process as we see it exemplified in *Light*. Here there is a *continuous* outpouring of *ray-streams*, and *with a force which we have at least no right to suppose varies at all*. Now, in any such irradiation *as this*—continuous and of unvarying force—the regions nearer the centre must *inevitably* be always more crowded with the irradiated matter than the regions more remote. But I have assumed *no* such irradiation *as this*. I assumed no *continuous* irradiation; and for the simple reason that such an assumption would have involved, first, the necessity of entertaining a conception which I have shown no man *can* entertain, and which (as I will more fully explain hereafter) all observation of the firmament refutes—the conception of the absolute infinity of the Universe of stars—and would have involved, secondly, the impossibility of understanding a rëaction—that is, gravitation—as existing now—since, while an act is continued, no rëaction, of course, can take place. My assumption, then, or rather my inevitable deduction from just premises—was that of a *determinate* irradiation—one finally *dis*continued.

Let me now describe the sole possible mode in which it is conceivable that matter could have been diffused through space, so as to fulfil the conditions at once of irradiation and of generally equable distribution.

For convenience of illustration, let us imagine, in the first place, a hollow sphere of glass, or of anything else, occupying the space throughout which the universal matter is to be thus equally diffused, by means of irradiation, from the absolute, irrelative, unconditional particle, placed in the centre of the sphere.

Now, a certain exertion of the diffusive power (presumed to be the Divine Volition)—in other words, a certain *force*—whose measure is the quantity of matter—that is to say, the number of atoms—emitted; emits, by irradiation, this certain number of atoms; forcing them in all directions outwardly from the centre—their proximity to each other diminishing as they proceed—until, finally, they are distributed, loosely, over the interior surface of the sphere.

When these atoms have attained this position, or while proceeding to attain it, a second and inferior exercise of the same force—or a second and inferior force of the same character—emits, in the same manner—that is to say, by irradiation as before—a second stratum of atoms which proceeds to deposit itself upon the first; the number of atoms, in this case as in the former, being of course the measure of the force which emitted them; in other words the force being precisely adapted to the purpose it effects—the force and the number of atoms sent out by the force, being *directly proportional*.

When this second stratum has reached its destined position—or while approaching it—a third still inferior exertion of the force, or a third inferior force of a similar character—the number of atoms emitted being in *all* cases the measure of the force—proceeds to deposit a third stratum upon the second:—and so on, until these concentric strata, growing gradually less and less, come down at length to the central point; and the diffusive matter, simultaneously with the diffusive force, is exhausted.

We have now the sphere filled, through means of irradiation, with atoms equably diffused. The two necessary conditions—those of irradiation and of equable diffusion—are satisfied; and by the *sole* process in which the possibility of their simultaneous satisfaction is conceivable. For this reason, I confidently expect to find, lurking in the present condition of the atoms as distributed throughout the sphere, the secret of which I am in search—the all-important principle of the *modus operandi* of the Newtonian law. Let us examine, then, the actual condition of the atoms.

They lie in a series of concentric strata. They are equably diffused throughout the sphere. They have been irradiated into these states.

The atoms being *equably* distributed, the greater the superficial extent of any of these concentric strata, or spheres, the more atoms will lie upon it. In other words, the number of atoms lying upon the surface of any one of the concentric spheres, is directly proportional with the extent of that surface.

But, in any series of concentric spheres, the surfaces are directly proportional with the squares of the distances from the centre.

Therefore the number of atoms in any stratum is directly proportional with the square of that stratum's distance from the centre.

But the number of atoms in any stratum is the measure of the force which emitted that stratum—that is to say, is *directly proportional* with the force.

Therefore the force which irradiated any stratum is directly proportional with the square of that stratum's distance from the centre:—or, generally,

The force of the irradiation has been directly proportional with the squares of the distances.

Now, Rëaction, as far as we know anything of it, is Action conversed. The *general* principle of Gravity being, in the first place, understood as the rëaction of an act—as the expression of a desire on the part of Matter, while existing in a state of diffusion, to return into the Unity whence it was diffused; and, in the second place, the mind being called upon to determine the *character* of the desire—the manner in which it would, naturally, be manifested; in other words, being called upon to conceive a probable law, or *modus operandi*, for the return; could not well help arriving at the conclusion that this law of return would be precisely the converse of the law of departure. That such would be the case, any one, at least, would be abundantly justified in taking for granted, until such time as some person should suggest something like a plausible reason why it should *not* be the case—until such period as a law of return shall be imagined which the intellect can consider as preferable.

Matter, then, irradiated into space with a force varying as the squares of the distances, might, *à priori*, be supposed to return towards its centre of irradiation with a force varying *inversely* as the squares of the distances: and I have already shown that any principle which will explain why the atoms should tend, according to any law, to the general centre, must be admitted as satisfactorily explaining, at the same time, why, according to the same law, they should tend each to each. For, in fact, the tendency to the general centre is not to a centre as such, but because of its being a point in tending towards which each atom tends most directly to its real and essential centre, *Unity*—the absolute and final Union of all.

The consideration here involved presents to my own mind no embarrassment whatever—but this fact does not blind me to the possibility of its being obscure to those who may have been less in the habit of dealing with abstractions:—and, upon the whole, it may be as well to look at the matter from one or two other points of view.

The absolute, irrelative particle primarily created by the Volition of God, must have been in a condition of positive *normality*, or rightfulness—for wrongfulness implies *relation*. Right is positive; wrong is negative—is merely the negation of right; as cold is the negation of heat—darkness of light. That a thing may be wrong, it is necessary that there be some other thing in *relation* to which it *is* wrong—some condition which it fails to satisfy; some law which it violates; some being whom it aggrieves. If there be no such being, law, or condition, in respect to which the thing is wrong—and, still more especially, if no beings, laws, or conditions exist at all—then the thing can*not* be wrong and consequently must be *right*. Any deviation from normality involves a tendency to return into it. A difference from the normal—from the right—from the just—can be understood as effected only by the overcoming a difficulty; and if the force which overcomes the difficulty be not infinitely continued, the ineradicable tendency to return will at length be permitted to act for its own satisfaction. Upon withdrawal of the force, the tendency acts. This is the principle of rëaction as the inevitable consequence of finite action. Employing a phraseology of which the seeming affectation will be pardoned for its expressiveness, we may say that Rëaction is the return from the condition of *as it is and ought not to be* into the condition of *as it was, originally, and therefore ought to be*:—and let me add here that the *absolute* force of Rëaction would no doubt be always found in direct proportion with the reality—the truth—the absoluteness—of the *originality*—if ever it were possible to measure this latter:—and, consequently, the greatest of all conceivable reactions must be that produced by the tendency which we now discuss—the tendency to return into the *absolutely original*—into the *supremely* primitive. Gravity, then, *must be the strongest of forces*—an idea reached *à priori* and abundantly confirmed by induction. What use I make of the idea, will be seen in the sequel.

The atoms, now, having been diffused from their normal condition of Unity, seek to return to—what? Not to any particular *point*, certainly; for it is clear that if, upon the diffusion, the whole Universe of matter had been projected, collectively, to a distance from the point of irradiation, the atomic tendency to the general centre of the sphere would not have been disturbed in the least:—the atoms would not have sought the point *in absolute space* from which they were originally impelled. It is merely the *condition*, and not the point or locality at which this condition took its rise, that these atoms seek to re-establish;—it is merely *that condition which is their normality*, that they desire. "But they seek a centre," it will be said, "and a centre is a point." True; but they seek this point not in its character of point—(for, were the whole sphere moved from its position, they would seek, equally, the centre; and the centre *then* would be a *new* point)—but because it so happens, on account of the form in which they collectively exist—(that of the sphere)—that only *through* the point in question—the sphere's centre—they can attain their true object, Unity. In the direction of the centre each atom perceives more atoms than in any other direction. Each atom is impelled towards the centre because along the straight line joining it and the centre and passing on to the circumference beyond, there lie a greater number of atoms than along any other straight line—a greater number of objects that seek it, the individual atom—a greater number of tendencies to Unity—a greater number of satisfactions for its own tendency to Unity—in a word, because in the direction of the centre lies the utmost possibility of satisfaction, generally, for its own individual appetite. To be brief, the *condition*, Unity, is all that is really sought; and if the atoms *seem* to seek the centre of the sphere, it is only impliedly, through implication—because such centre happens to imply, to include, or to involve, the only essential centre, Unity. But *on account of* this implication or involution, there is no possibility of practically separating the tendency to Unity in the abstract, from the tendency to the concrete centre. Thus the tendency of the atoms to the general centre *is*, to all practical intents and for all logical purposes, the tendency each to each; and the tendency each to each *is* the tendency to the centre; and the one tendency may be assumed *as* the other; whatever will apply to the one must be thoroughly applicable to the other; and, in conclusion, whatever principle will satisfactorily explain the one, cannot be questioned as an explanation of the other.

In looking carefully around me for rational objection to what I have advanced, I am able to discover *nothing*;—but of that class of objections usually urged by the doubters for Doubt's sake, I very readily perceive *three*; and proceed to dispose of them in order.

It may be said, first: "The proof that the force of irradiation (in the case described) is directly proportional to the squares of the distances, depends upon an unwarranted assumption—that of the number of atoms in each stratum being the measure of the force with which they are emitted."

I reply, not only that I am warranted in such assumption, but that I should be utterly *un*warranted in any other. What I assume is, simply, that an effect is the measure of its cause—that every exercise of the Divine Will will be proportional to that which demands the exertion—that the means of Omnipotence, or of Omniscience, will be exactly adapted to its purposes. Neither can a deficiency nor an excess of cause bring to pass any effect. Had the force which irradiated any stratum to its position, been either more or less than was needed for the purpose—that is to say, not *directly proportional* to the purpose—then to its position that stratum could not have been irradiated. Had the force which, with a view to general equability of distribution, emitted the proper number of atoms for each stratum, been not *directly proportional* to the number, then the number would *not* have been the number demanded for the equable distribution.

The second supposable objection is somewhat better entitled to an answer.

It is an admitted principle in Dynamics that every body, on receiving an impulse, or disposition to move, will move onward in a straight line, in the direction imparted by the impelling force, until deflected, or stopped, by some other force. How then, it may be asked, is my first or external stratum of atoms to be understood as discontinuing their movement at the circumference of the imaginary glass sphere, when no second force, of more than an imaginary character, appears, to account for the discontinuance?

I reply that the objection, in this case, actually does arise out of "an unwarranted assumption"—on the part of the objector—the assumption of a principle, in Dynamics, at an epoch when *no* "principles," in *anything*, exist:—I use the word "principle," of course, in the objector's understanding of the word.

"In the beginning" we can admit—indeed we can comprehend—but one *First Cause*—the truly ultimate *Principle*—the Volition of God. The primary *act*—that of Irradiation from Unity—must have been independent of all that which the world now calls "principle"—because all that we so designate is but a consequence of the rëaction of that primary act:—I say "*primary*" act; for the creation of the absolute material particle is more properly to be regarded as a *conception* than as an "*act*" in the ordinary meaning of the term. Thus, we must regard the primary act as an act for the establishment of what we now call "principles." But this primary act itself is to be considered as *continuous Volition*. The Thought of God is to be understood as originating the Diffusion—as proceeding with it—as regulating it—and, finally, as being withdrawn from it upon its completion. *Then* commences Rëaction, and through Rëaction, "Principle," as we employ the word. It will be advisable, however, to limit the application of this word to the two *immediate* results of the discontinuance of the Divine Volition—that is, to the two agents, *Attraction* and *Repulsion*. Every other Natural agent depends, either more or less immediately, upon these two, and therefore would be more conveniently designated as *sub*-principle.

It may be objected, thirdly, that, in general, the peculiar mode of distribution which I have suggested for the atoms, is "an hypothesis and nothing more."

Now, I am aware that the word hypothesis is a ponderous sledge-hammer, grasped immediately, if not lifted, by all very diminutive thinkers, upon the first appearance of any proposition wearing, in any particular, the garb of *a theory*. But "hypothesis" cannot be wielded *here* to any good purpose, even by those who succeed in lifting it—little men or great.

I maintain, first, that *only* in the mode described is it conceivable that Matter could have been diffused so as to fulfil at once the conditions of irradiation and of generally equable distribution. I maintain, secondly, that these conditions themselves have been imposed upon me, as necessities, in a train of ratiocination *as rigorously logical as that which establishes any demonstration in Euclid*; and I maintain, thirdly, that even if the charge of "hypothesis" were as fully sustained as it is, in fact, unsustained and untenable, still the validity and indisputability of my result would not, even in the slightest particular, be disturbed.

To explain:—The Newtonian Gravity—a law of Nature—a law whose existence as such no one out of Bedlam questions—a law whose admission as such enables us to account for nine-tenths of the Universal phænomena—a law which, merely because it does so enable us to account for these phænomena, we are perfectly willing, without reference to any other considerations, to admit, and cannot help admitting, as a law—a law, nevertheless, of which neither the principle nor the *modus operandi* of the principle, has ever yet been traced by the human analysis—a law, in short, which, neither in its detail nor in its generality, has been found susceptible of explanation *at all*—is at length seen to be at every point thoroughly explicable, provided only we yield our assent to—what? To an hypothesis? Why *if* an hypothesis—if the merest hypothesis—if an hypothesis for whose assumption—as in the case of that *pure* hypothesis the Newtonian law itself—no shadow of *à priori* reason could be assigned—if an hypothesis, even so absolute as all this implies, would enable us to perceive a principle for the Newtonian law—would enable us to understand as satisfied, conditions so miraculously—so ineffably complex and seemingly irreconcileable as those involved in the relations of which Gravity tells us,—what rational being *could* so expose his fatuity as to call even this absolute hypothesis an hypothesis any longer—unless, indeed, he were to persist in so calling it, with the understanding that he did so, simply for the sake of consistency *in words*?

But what is the true state of our present case? What is *the fact*? Not only that it is *not* an hypothesis which we are required *to adopt*, in order to admit the principle at issue explained, but that it *is* a logical conclusion which we are requested *not* to adopt if we can avoid it—which we are simply invited to *deny if we can*:—a conclusion of so accurate a logicality that to dispute it would be the effort—to doubt its validity beyond our power:—a conclusion from which we see no mode of escape, turn as we will; a result which confronts us either at the end of an *in*ductive journey from the phænomena of the very Law discussed, or at the close of a *de*ductive career from the most rigorously simple of all conceivable assumptions—*the assumption, in a word, of Simplicity itself.*

And if here, for the mere sake of cavilling, it be urged, that although my starting-point is, as I assert, the assumption of absolute Simplicity, yet Simplicity, considered merely in itself, is no axiom; and that only deductions from axioms are indisputable—it is thus that I reply:—

Every other science than Logic is the science of certain concrete relations. Arithmetic, for example, is the science of the relations of number—Geometry, of the relations of form—Mathematics in general, of the relations of quantity in general—of whatever can be increased or diminished. Logic, however, is the science of Relation in the abstract—of absolute Relation—of Relation considered solely in itself. An axiom in any particular science other than Logic is, thus, merely a proposition announcing certain concrete relations which seem to be too obvious for dispute—as when we say, for instance, that the whole is greater than its part:—and, thus again, the principle of the *Logical* axiom—in other words, of an axiom in the abstract—is, simply, *obviousness of relation*. Now, it is clear, not only that what is obvious to one mind may not be obvious to another, but that what is obvious to one mind at one epoch, may be anything but obvious, at another epoch, to the same mind. It is clear, moreover, that what, to-day, is obvious even to the majority of mankind, or to the majority of the best intellects of mankind, may to-morrow be, to either majority, more or less obvious, or in no respect obvious at all. It is seen, then, that the *axiomatic principle* itself is susceptible of variation, and of course that axioms are susceptible of similar change. Being mutable, the "truths" which grow out of them are necessarily mutable too; or, in other words, are never to be positively depended upon as truths at all—since Truth and Immutability are one.

It will now be readily understood that no axiomatic idea—no idea founded in the fluctuating principle, obviousness of relation—can possibly be so secure—so reliable a basis for any structure erected by the Reason, as *that* idea—(whatever it is, wherever we can find it, or *if* it be practicable to find it anywhere)—which is *ir*relative altogether—which not only presents to the understanding *no obviousness* of relation, either greater or less, to be considered, but subjects the intellect, not in the slightest degree, to the necessity of even looking at *any relation at all*. If such an idea be not what we too heedlessly term "an axiom," it is at least preferable, as a Logical basis, to any axiom ever propounded, or to all imaginable axioms combined:—and such, precisely, is the idea with which my deductive process, so thoroughly corroborated by induction, commences. My *particle proper* is but *absolute Irrelation*. To sum up what has been here advanced:—As a starting point I have taken it for granted, simply, that the Beginning had nothing behind it or before it—that it was a Beginning in fact—that it was a beginning and nothing different from a beginning—in short that this Beginning was—*that which it was*. If this be a "mere assumption" then a "mere assumption" let it be.

To conclude this branch of the subject:—I am fully warranted in announcing that *the Law which we have been in the habit of calling Gravity exists on account of Matter's having been irradiated, at its origin, atomically, into a limited sphere of Space, from one, individual, unconditional, irrelative, and absolute Particle Proper, by the sole process in which it was possible to satisfy, at the same time, the two conditions, irradiation, and generally-equable distribution throughout the sphere—that is to say, by a force varying in direct proportion with the squares of the distances between the irradiated atoms, respectively, and the Particular centre of Irradiation*.

I have already given my reasons for presuming Matter to have been diffused by a determinate rather than by a continuous or infinitely continued force. Supposing a continuous force, we should be unable, in the first place, to comprehend a rëaction at all; and we should be required, in the second place, to entertain the impossible conception of an infinite extension of Matter. Not to dwell upon the impossibility of the conception, the infinite extension of Matter is an idea which, if not positively disproved, is at least not in any respect warranted by telescopic observation of the stars—a point to be explained more fully hereafter; and this empirical reason for believing in the original finity of

Matter is unempirically confirmed. For example:—Admitting, for the moment, the possibility of understanding Space *filled* with the irradiated atoms—that is to say, admitting, as well as we can, for argument's sake, that the succession of the irradiated atoms had absolutely *no end*—then it is abundantly clear that, even when the Volition of God had been withdrawn from them, and thus the tendency to return into Unity permitted (abstractly) to be satisfied, this permission would have been nugatory and invalid—practically valueless and of no effect whatever. No Rëaction could have taken place; no movement toward Unity could have been made; no Law of Gravity could have obtained.

To explain:—Grant the *abstract* tendency of any one atom to any one other as the inevitable result of diffusion from the normal Unity:—or, what is the same thing, admit any given atom as *proposing* to move in any given direction—it is clear that, since there is an *infinity* of atoms on all sides of the atom proposing to move, it never can actually move toward the satisfaction of its tendency in the direction given, on account of a precisely equal and counterbalancing tendency in the direction diametrically opposite. In other words, exactly as many tendencies to Unity are behind the hesitating atom as before it; for it is a mere sotticism to say that one infinite line is longer or shorter than another infinite line, or that one infinite number is greater or less than another number that is infinite. Thus the atom in question must remain stationary forever. Under the impossible circumstances which we have been merely endeavoring to conceive for argument's sake, there could have been no aggregation of Matter—no stars—no worlds—nothing but a perpetually atomic and inconsequential Universe. In fact, view it as we will, the whole idea of unlimited Matter is not only untenable, but impossible and preposterous.

With the understanding of a *sphere* of atoms, however, we perceive, at once, a *satisfiable* tendency to union. The general result of the tendency each to each, being a tendency of all to the centre, the *general* process of condensation, or approximation, commences immediately, by a common and simultaneous movement, on withdrawal of the Divine Volition; the *individual* approximations, or coalescences—*not* cöalitions—of atom with atom, being subject to almost infinite variations of time, degree, and condition, on account of the excessive multiplicity of relation, arising from the differences of form assumed as characterizing the atoms at the moment of their quitting the Particle Proper; as well as from the subsequent particular inequidistance, each from each.

What I wish to impress upon the reader is the certainty of there arising, at once, (on withdrawal of the diffusive force, or Divine Volition,) out of the condition of the atoms as described, at innumerable points throughout the Universal sphere, innumerable agglomerations, characterized by innumerable specific differences of form, size, essential nature, and distance each from each. The development of Repulsion (Electricity) must have commenced, of course, with the very earliest particular efforts at Unity, and must have proceeded constantly in the ratio of Coalescence—that is to say, *in that of Condensation*, or, again, of Heterogeneity.

Thus the two Principles Proper, *Attraction* and *Repulsion*—the Material and the Spiritual—accompany each other, in the strictest fellowship, forever. Thus *The Body and The Soul walk hand in hand.*

If now, in fancy, we select *any one* of the agglomerations considered as in their primary stages throughout the Universal sphere, and suppose this incipient agglomeration to be taking place at that point where the centre of our Sun exists—or rather where it *did* exist originally; for the Sun is perpetually shifting his position—we shall find ourselves met, and borne onward for a time at least, by the most magnificent of theories—by the Nebular Cosmogony of Laplace:—although "Cosmogony" is far too comprehensive a term for what he really discusses—which is the constitution of our solar system alone—of one among the myriad of similar systems which make up the Universe Proper—that Universal sphere—that all-inclusive and absolute *Kosmos* which forms the subject of my present Discourse.

Confining himself to an *obviously limited* region—that of our solar system with its comparatively immediate vicinity—and *merely* assuming—that is to say, assuming without any basis whatever, either deductive or inductive—*much* of what I have been just endeavoring to place upon a more stable basis than assumption; assuming, for example, matter as diffused (without pretending to account for the diffusion) throughout, and somewhat beyond, the space occupied by our system—diffused in a state of heterogeneous nebulosity and obedient to that omniprevalent law of Gravity at whose principle he ventured to make no guess;—assuming all this (which is quite true, although he had no logical right to its assumption) Laplace has shown, dynamically and mathematically, that the results in such case necessarily ensuing, are those and those alone which we find manifested in the actually existing condition of the system itself.

To explain:—Let us conceive *that* particular agglomeration of which we have just spoken—the one at the point designated by our Sun's centre—to have so far proceeded that a vast quantity of nebulous matter has here assumed a roughly globular form; its centre being, of course, coincident with what is now, or rather was originally, the centre of our Sun; and its periphery extending out beyond the orbit of Neptune, the most remote of our planets:—in other words, let us suppose the diameter of this rough sphere to be some 6000 millions of miles. For ages, this mass of matter has been undergoing condensation, until at length it has become reduced into the bulk we imagine; having proceeded gradually, of course, from its atomic and imperceptible state, into what we understand of visible, palpable, or otherwise appreciable nebulosity.

Now, the condition of this mass implies a rotation about an imaginary axis—a rotation which, commencing with the absolute incipiency of the aggregation, has been ever since acquiring velocity. The very first two atoms which met, approaching each other from points not diametrically opposite, would, in rushing partially past each other, form a nucleus for the rotary movement described. How this would increase in velocity, is readily seen. The two atoms are joined by others:—an aggregation is formed. The mass continues to rotate while condensing. But any atom at the circumference has, of course, a more rapid motion than one nearer the centre. The outer atom, however, with its superior velocity, approaches the centre; carrying this superior velocity with it as it goes. Thus every atom, proceeding inwardly, and finally attaching itself to the condensed centre, adds something to the original velocity of that centre—that is to say, increases the rotary movement of the mass.

Let us now suppose this mass so far condensed that it occupies *precisely* the space circumscribed by the orbit of Neptune, and that the velocity with which the surface of the mass moves, in the general rotation, is precisely that velocity with which Neptune now revolves about the Sun. At this epoch, then, we are to understand that the constantly increasing centrifugal force, having gotten the better of the non-increasing centripetal, loosened and separated the exterior and least condensed stratum, or a few of the exterior and least condensed strata, at the equator of the sphere, where the tangential velocity predominated; so that these strata formed about the main body an independent ring encircling the equatorial regions:—just as the exterior portion thrown off, by excessive velocity of rotation, from a grindstone, would form a ring about the grindstone, but for the solidity of the superficial material: were this caoutchouc, or anything similar in consistency, precisely the phænomenon I describe would be presented.

The ring thus whirled from the nebulous mass, *revolved*, of course, *as* a separate ring, with just that velocity with which, while the surface of the mass, it *rotated*. In the meantime, condensation still proceeding, the interval between the discharged ring and the main body continued to increase, until the former was left at a vast distance from the latter.

Now, admitting the ring to have possessed, by some seemingly accidental arrangement of its heterogeneous materials, a constitution nearly uniform, then this ring, *as* such, would never have ceased revolving about its primary; but, as might have been anticipated, there appears to have been enough irregularity in the disposition of the materials, to make them cluster about centres of superior solidity; and thus the annular form was destroyed. No doubt, the band was soon broken up into several portions, and one of these portions, predominating in mass, absorbed the others into itself; the whole settling, spherically, into a planet. That this latter, *as* a planet, continued the revolutionary movement which characterized it while a ring, is sufficiently clear; and that it took upon itself also, an additional movement in its new condition of sphere, is readily explained. The ring being understood as yet unbroken, we see that its exterior, while the whole revolves about the parent body, moves more rapidly than its interior. When the rupture occurred, then, some portion in each fragment must have been moving with greater velocity than the others. The superior movement prevailing, must have whirled each fragment round—that is to say, have caused it to rotate; and the direction of the rotation must, of course, have been the direction of the revolution whence it arose. *All* the fragments having become subject to the rotation described, must, in coalescing, have imparted it to the one planet constituted by their coalescence.—This planet was Neptune. Its material continuing to undergo condensation, and the centrifugal force generated in its rotation getting, at length, the better of the centripetal, as before in the case of the parent orb, a ring was whirled also from the equatorial surface of this planet: this ring, having been ununiform in its constitution, was broken up, and its several fragments, being absorbed by the most massive, were collectively spherified into a moon. Subsequently, the operation was repeated, and a second moon was the result. We thus account for the planet Neptune, with the two satellites which accompany him.

In throwing off a ring from its equator, the Sun re-established that equilibrium between its centripetal and centrifugal forces which had been disturbed in the process of condensation; but, as this condensation still proceeded, the equilibrium was again immediately disturbed, through the increase of rotation. By the time the mass had so far shrunk that it occupied a spherical space just that circumscribed by the orbit of Uranus, we are to understand that the centrifugal force had so far obtained the ascendency that new relief was needed: a second equatorial band was, consequently, thrown off, which, proving ununiform, was broken up, as before in the case of Neptune; the fragments settling into the planet Uranus; the velocity of whose actual revolution about the Sun indicates, of course, the rotary speed of that Sun's equatorial surface at the moment of the separation. Uranus, adopting a rotation from the collective rotations of the fragments composing it, as previously explained, now threw off ring after ring; each of which, becoming broken up, settled into a moon:—three moons, at different epochs, having been formed, in this manner, by the rupture and general spherification of as many distinct ununiform rings.

By the time the Sun had shrunk until it occupied a space just that circumscribed by the orbit of Saturn, the balance, we are to suppose, between its centripetal and centrifugal forces had again become so far disturbed, through increase of rotary velocity, the result of condensation, that a third effort at equilibrium became necessary; and an annular band was therefore whirled off as twice before; which, on rupture through ununiformity, became consolidated into the planet Saturn. This latter threw off, in the first place, seven uniform bands, which, on rupture, were spherified respectively into as many moons; but, subsequently, it appears to have discharged, at three distinct but not very distant epochs, three rings whose equability of constitution was, by apparent accident, so considerable as to present no occasion for their rupture; thus they continue to revolve as rings. I use the phrase "*apparent* accident;" for of accident in the ordinary sense there was, of course, nothing:—the term is properly applied only to the result of indistinguishable or not immediately traceable *law*.

Shrinking still farther, until it occupied just the space circumscribed by the orbit of Jupiter, the Sun now found need of farther effort to restore the counterbalance of its two forces, continually disarranged in the still continued increase of rotation. Jupiter, accordingly, was now thrown off; passing from the annular to the planetary condition; and, on attaining this latter, threw off in its turn, at four different epochs, four rings, which finally resolved themselves into so many moons.

Still shrinking, until its sphere occupied just the space defined by the orbit of the Asteroids, the Sun now discarded a ring which appears to have had *eight* centres of superior solidity, and, on breaking up, to have separated into eight fragments no one of which so far predominated in mass as to absorb the others. All therefore, as distinct although comparatively small planets, proceeded to revolve in orbits whose distances, each from each, may be considered as in some degree the measure of the force which drove them asunder:—all the orbits, nevertheless, being so closely coincident as to admit of our calling them *one*, in view of the other planetary orbits.

Continuing to shrink, the Sun, on becoming so small as just to fill the orbit of Mars, now discharged this planet—of course by the process repeatedly described. Having no moon, however, Mars could have thrown off no ring. In fact, an epoch had now arrived in the career of the parent body, the centre of the system. The *de*crease of its nebulosity, which is the *in*crease of its density, and which again is the *de*crease of its condensation, out of which latter arose the constant disturbance of equilibrium—must, by this period, have attained a point at which the efforts for restoration would have been more and more ineffectual just in proportion as they were less frequently needed. Thus the processes of which we have been speaking would everywhere show signs of exhaustion—in the planets, first, and secondly, in the original mass. We must not fall into the error of supposing the decrease of interval observed among the planets as we approach the Sun, to be in any respect indicative of an increase of frequency in the periods at which they were discarded. Exactly the converse is to be understood. The longest interval of time must have occurred between the discharges of the two interior; the shortest, between those of the two exterior, planets. The decrease of the interval of space is, nevertheless, the measure of the density, and thus inversely of the condensation, of the Sun, throughout the processes detailed.

Having shrunk, however, so far as to fill only the orbit of our Earth, the parent sphere whirled from itself still one other body—the Earth—in a condition so nebulous as to admit of this body's discarding, in its turn, yet another, which is our Moon;—but here terminated the lunar formations.

Finally, subsiding to the orbits first of Venus and then of Mercury, the Sun discarded these two interior planets; neither of which has given birth to any moon.

Thus from his original bulk—or, to speak more accurately, from the condition in which we first considered him—from a partially spherified nebular mass, *certainly* much more than 5,600 millions of miles in diameter—the great central orb and origin of our solar-planetary-lunar system, has gradually descended, by condensation, in obedience to the law of Gravity, to a globe only 882,000 miles in diameter; but it by no means follows, either that its condensation is yet complete, or that it may not still possess the capacity of whirling from itself another planet.

I have here given—in outline of course, but still with all the detail necessary for distinctness—a view of the Nebular Theory as its author himself conceived it. From whatever point we regard it, we shall find it *beautifully true*. It is by far too beautiful, indeed, *not* to possess Truth as its essentiality—and here I am very profoundly serious in what I say. In the revolution of the satellites of Uranus, there does appear something seemingly inconsistent with the assumptions of Laplace; but that *one* inconsistency can invalidate a theory constructed from a million of intricate consistencies, is a fancy fit only for the fantastic. In prophecying, confidently, that the apparent anomaly to which I refer, will, sooner or later, be found one of the strongest possible corroborations of the general hypothesis, I pretend to no especial spirit of divination. It is a matter which the only difficulty seems *not* to foresee.

The bodies whirled off in the processes described, would exchange, it has been seen, the superficial *rotation* of the orbs whence they originated, for a *revolution* of equal velocity about these orbs as distant centres; and the revolution thus engendered must proceed, so long as the centripetal force, or that with which the discarded body gravitates toward its parent, is neither greater nor less than that by which it was discarded; that is, than the centrifugal, or, far more properly, than the tangential, velocity. From the unity, however, of the origin of these two forces, we might have expected to find them as they are found—the one accurately counterbalancing the other. It has been shown, indeed, that the act of whirling-off is, in every case, merely an act for the preservation of the counterbalance.

After referring, however, the centripetal force to the omniprevalent law of Gravity, it has been the fashion with astronomical treatises, to seek beyond the limits of mere Nature—that is to say, of *Secondary* Cause—a solution of the phænomenon of tangential velocity. This latter they attribute directly to a *First* Cause—to God. The force which carries a stellar body around its primary they assert to have originated in an impulse given immediately by the finger—this is the childish phraseology employed—by the finger of Deity itself. In this view, the planets, fully formed, are conceived to have been hurled from the Divine hand, to a position in the vicinity of the suns, with an impetus mathematically adapted to the masses, or attractive capacities, of the suns themselves. An idea so grossly unphilosophical, although so supinely adopted, could have arisen only from the difficulty of otherwise accounting for the absolutely accurate adaptation, each to each, of two forces so seemingly independent, one of the other, as are the gravitating and tangential. But it should be remembered that, for a long time, the coincidence between the moon's rotation and her sidereal revolution—two matters seemingly far more independent than those now considered—was looked upon as positively miraculous; and there was a strong disposition, even among astronomers, to attribute the marvel to the direct and continual agency of God—who, in this case, it was said, had found it necessary to interpose, specially, among his general laws, a set of subsidiary regulations, for the purpose of forever concealing from mortal eyes the glories, or perhaps the horrors, of the other side of the Moon—of that mysterious hemisphere which has always avoided, and must perpetually avoid, the telescopic scrutiny of mankind. The advance of Science, however, soon demonstrated—what to the philosophical instinct needed *no* demonstration—that the one movement is but a portion—something more, even, than a consequence—of the other.

For my part, I have no patience with fantasies at once so timorous, so idle, and so awkward. They belong to the veriest *cowardice* of thought. That Nature and the God of Nature are distinct, no thinking being can long doubt. By the former we imply merely the laws of the latter. But with the very idea of God, omnipotent, omniscient, we entertain, also, the idea of *the infallibility* of his laws. With Him there being neither Past nor Future—with Him all being *Now*—do we not insult him in supposing his laws so contrived as not to provide for every possible contingency?—or, rather, what idea *can* we have of *any* possible contingency, except that it is at once a result and a manifestation of his laws? He who, divesting himself of prejudice, shall have the rare courage to think absolutely for himself, cannot fail to arrive, in the end, at the condensation of *laws* into *Law*—cannot fail of reaching the conclusion that *each law of Nature is dependent at all points upon all other laws*, and that all are but consequences of one primary exercise of the Divine Volition. Such is the principle of the

Cosmogony which, with all necessary deference, I here venture to suggest and to maintain.

In this view, it will be seen that, dismissing as frivolous, and even impious, the fancy of the tangential force having been imparted to the planets immediately by "the finger of God," I consider this force as originating in the rotation of the stars:—this rotation as brought about by the in-rushing of the primary atoms, towards their respective centres of aggregation:—this in-rushing as the consequence of the law of Gravity:—this law as but the mode in which is necessarily manifested the tendency of the atoms to return into imparticularity:—this tendency to return as but the inevitable rëaction of the first and most sublime of Acts—that act by which a God, self-existing and alone existing, became all things at once, through dint of his volition, while all things were thus constituted a portion of God.

The radical assumptions of this Discourse suggest to me, and in fact imply, certain important *modifications* of the Nebular Theory as given by Laplace. The efforts of the repulsive power I have considered as made for the purpose of preventing contact among the atoms, and thus as made in the ratio of the approach to contact—that is to say, in the ratio of condensation. In other words, *Electricity*, with its involute phænomena, heat, light and magnetism, is to be understood as proceeding as condensation proceeds, and, of course, inversely as density proceeds, or the *cessation to condense*. Thus the Sun, in the process of its aggregation, must soon, in developing repulsion, have become excessively heated—perhaps incandescent: and we can perceive how the operation of discarding its rings must have been materially assisted by the slight incrustation of its surface consequent on cooling. Any common experiment shows us how readily a crust of the character suggested, is separated, through heterogeneity, from the interior mass. But, on every successive rejection of the crust, the new surface would appear incandescent as before; and the period at which it would again become so far encrusted as to be readily loosened and discharged, may well be imagined as exactly coincident with that at which a new effort would be needed, by the whole mass, to restore the equilibrium of its two forces, disarranged through condensation. In other words:—by the time the electric influence (Repulsion) has prepared the surface for rejection, we are to understand that the gravitating influence (Attraction) is precisely ready to reject it. Here, then, as everywhere, *the Body and the Soul walk hand in hand*.

These ideas are empirically confirmed at all points. Since condensation can never, in any body, be considered as absolutely at an end, we are warranted in anticipating that, whenever we have an opportunity of testing the matter, we shall find indications of resident luminosity in *all* the stellar bodies—moons and planets as well as suns. That our Moon is strongly self-luminous, we see at her every total eclipse, when, if not so, she would disappear. On the dark part of the satellite, too, during her phases, we often observe flashes like our own Auroras; and that these latter, with our various other so-called electrical phænomena, without reference to any more steady radiance, must give our Earth a certain appearance of luminosity to an inhabitant of the Moon, is quite evident. In fact, we should regard all the phænomena referred to, as mere manifestations, in different moods and degrees, of the Earth's feebly-continued condensation.

If my views are tenable, we should be prepared to find the newer planets—that is to say, those nearer the Sun—more luminous than those older and more remote:—and the extreme brilliancy of Venus (on whose dark portions, during her phases, the Auroras are frequently visible) does not seem to be altogether accounted for by her mere proximity to the central orb. She is no doubt vividly self-luminous, although less so than Mercury: while the luminosity of Neptune may be comparatively nothing.

Admitting what I have urged, it is clear that, from the moment of the Sun's discarding a ring, there must be a continuous diminution both of his heat and light, on account of the continuous encrustation of his surface; and that a period would arrive—the period immediately previous to a new discharge—when a *very material* decrease of both light and heat, must become apparent. Now, we know that tokens of such changes are distinctly recognizable. On the Melville islands—to adduce merely one out of a hundred examples—we find traces of *ultra-tropical* vegetation—of plants that never could have flourished without immensely more light and heat than are at present afforded by our Sun to any portion of the surface of the Earth. Is such vegetation referable to an epoch immediately subsequent to the whirling-off of Venus? At this epoch must have occurred to us our greatest access of solar influence; and, in fact, this influence must then have attained its maximum:—leaving out of view, of course, the period when the Earth itself was discarded—the period of its mere organization.

Again:—we know that there exist *non-luminous suns*—that is to say, suns whose existence we determine through the movements of others, but whose luminosity is not sufficient to impress us. Are these suns invisible merely on account of the length of time elapsed since their discharge of a planet? And yet again:—may we not—at least in certain cases—account for the sudden appearances of suns where none had been previously suspected, by the hypothesis that, having rolled with encrusted surfaces throughout the few thousand years of our astronomical history, each of these suns, in whirling off a new secondary, has at length been enabled to display the glories of its still incandescent interior?—To the well-ascertained fact of the proportional increase of heat as we descend into the Earth, I need of course, do nothing more than refer:—it comes in the strongest possible corroboration of all that I have said on the topic now at issue.

In speaking, not long ago, of the repulsive or electrical influence, I remarked that "the important phænomena of vitality, consciousness, and thought, whether we observe them generally or in detail, seem to proceed *at least in the ratio of the heterogeneous*." I mentioned, too, that I would recur to the suggestion:—and this is the proper point at which to do so. Looking at the matter, first, in detail, we perceive that not merely the *manifestation* of vitality, but its importance, consequence, and elevation of character, keep pace, very closely, with the heterogeneity, or complexity, of the animal structure. Looking at the question, now, in its generality, and referring to the first movements of the atoms towards mass-constitution, we find that heterogeneousness, brought about directly through condensation, is proportional with it forever. We thus reach the proposition that *the importance of the development of the terrestrial vitality proceeds equably with the terrestrial condensation*.

Now this is in precise accordance with what we know of the succession of animals on the Earth. As it has proceeded in its condensation, superior and still superior races have appeared. Is it impossible that the successive geological revolutions which have attended, at least, if not immediately caused, these successive elevations of vitalic character—is it improbable that these revolutions have themselves been produced by the successive planetary discharges from the Sun—in other words, by the successive variations in the solar influence on the Earth? Were this idea tenable, we should not be unwarranted in the fancy that the discharge of yet a new planet, interior to Mercury, may give rise to yet a new modification of the terrestrial surface—a modification from which may spring a race both materially and spiritually superior to Man. These thoughts impress me with all the force of truth—but I throw them out, of course, merely in their obvious character of suggestion.

The Nebular Theory of Laplace has lately received far more confirmation than it needed, at the hands of the philosopher, Compte. These two have thus together shown—*not*, to be sure, that Matter at any period actually existed as described, in a state of nebular diffusion, but that, admitting it so to have existed throughout the space and much beyond the space now occupied by our solar system, *and to have commenced a movement towards a centre*—it must gradually have assumed the various forms and motions which are now seen, in that system, to obtain. A demonstration such as this—a dynamical and mathematical demonstration, as far as demonstration can be—unquestionable and unquestioned—unless, indeed, by that unprofitable and disreputable tribe, the professional questioners—the mere madmen who deny the Newtonian law of Gravity on which the results of the French mathematicians are based—a demonstration, I say, such as this, would to most intellects be conclusive—and I confess that it is so to mine—of the validity of the nebular hypothesis upon which the demonstration depends.

That the demonstration does not *prove* the hypothesis, according to the common understanding of the word "proof," I admit, of course. To show that certain existing results—that certain established facts—may be, even mathematically, accounted for by the assumption of a certain hypothesis, is by no means to establish the hypothesis itself. In other words:—to show that, certain data being given, a certain existing result might, or even *must*, have ensued, will fail to prove that this result *did* ensue, *from the data*, until such time as it shall be also shown that there are, *and can be*, no other data from which the result in question might *equally* have ensued. But, in the case now discussed, although all must admit the deficiency of what we are in the habit of terming "proof," still there are many intellects, and those of the loftiest order, to which *no* proof could bring one iota of additional *conviction*. Without going into details which might impinge upon the Cloud-Land of Metaphysics, I may as well here observe that the force of conviction, in cases such as this, will always, with the right-thinking, be proportional to the amount of *complexity* intervening between the hypothesis and the result. To be less abstract:—The greatness of the complexity found existing among cosmical conditions, by rendering great in the same proportion the difficulty of accounting for all these conditions *at once*, strengthens, also in the same proportion, our faith in that hypothesis which does, in such manner, satisfactorily account for them:—and as *no* complexity can well be conceived greater than that of the astronomical conditions, so no conviction can be stronger—to *my* mind at least—than that with which I am impressed by an hypothesis that not only reconciles these conditions, with mathematical accuracy, and reduces them into a consistent and intelligible whole, but is, at the same time, the *sole* hypothesis by means of which the human intellect has been ever enabled to account for them *at all*.

A most unfounded opinion has become latterly current in gossiping and even in scientific circles—the opinion that the so-called Nebular Cosmogony has been overthrown. This fancy has arisen from the report of late observations made, among what hitherto have been termed the "nebulæ," through the large telescope of Cincinnati, and the world-renowned instrument of Lord Rosse. Certain spots in the firmament which presented, even to the most powerful of the old telescopes, the appearance of nebulosity, or haze, had been regarded for a long time as confirming the theory of Laplace. They were looked upon as stars in that very process of condensation which I have been attempting to describe. Thus it was supposed that we "had ocular evidence"—an evidence, by the way, which has always been found very questionable—of the truth of the hypothesis; and, although certain telescopic improvements, every now and then, enabled us to perceive that a spot, here and there, which we had been classing among the nebulæ, was, in fact, but a cluster of stars deriving its nebular character only from its immensity of distance—still it was thought that no doubt could exist as to the actual nebulosity of numerous other masses, the strong-holds of the nebulists, bidding defiance to every effort at segregation. Of these latter the most interesting was the great "nebulæ" in the constellation Orion:—but this, with innumerable other mis-called "nebulæ," when viewed through the magnificent modern telescopes, has become resolved into a simple collection of stars. Now this fact has been very generally understood as conclusive against the Nebular Hypothesis of Laplace; and, on announcement of the discoveries in question, the most enthusiastic defender and most eloquent popularizer of the theory, Dr. Nichol, went so far as to "admit the necessity of abandoning" an idea which had formed the material of his most praiseworthy book.

Many of my readers will no doubt be inclined to say that the result of these new investigations *has* at least a strong *tendency* to overthrow the hypothesis; while some of them, more thoughtful, will suggest that, although the theory is by no means disproved through the segregation of the particular "nebulæ," alluded to, still a *failure* to segregate them, with such telescopes, might well have been understood as a triumphant *corroboration* of the theory:—and this latter class will be surprised, perhaps, to hear me say that even with *them* I disagree. If the propositions of this Discourse have been comprehended, it will be seen that, in my view, a failure to segregate the "nebulæ" would have tended to the refutation, rather than to the confirmation, of the Nebular Hypothesis.

Let me explain:—The Newtonian Law of Gravity we may, of course, assume as demonstrated. This law, it will be remembered, I have referred to the rëaction of the first Divine Act—to the rëaction of an exercise of the Divine Volition temporarily overcoming a difficulty. This difficulty is that of forcing the normal into the abnormal—of impelling that whose originality, and therefore whose rightful condition, was *One*, to take upon itself the wrongful condition of *Many*. It is only by conceiving this difficulty as *temporarily* overcome, that we can comprehend a rëaction. There could have been no rëaction had the act been infinitely continued. So long as the act *lasted*, no rëaction, of course, could commence; in other words, no *gravitation* could take place—for we have considered the one as but the manifestation of the other. But gravitation *has* taken place; therefore the act of Creation has ceased: and gravitation has long ago taken place; therefore the act of Creation has long ago ceased. We can no more expect, then, to observe *the primary processes* of Creation; and to these primary processes the condition of nebulosity has already been explained to belong.

Through what we know of the propagation of light, we have direct proof that the more remote of the stars have existed, under the forms in which we now see them, for an inconceivable number of years. So far back *at least*, then, as the period when these stars underwent condensation, must have been the epoch at which the mass-constitutive processes began. That we may conceive these processes, then, as still going on in the case of certain "nebulæ," while in all other cases we find them thoroughly at an end, we are forced into assumptions for which we have really *no* basis whatever—we have to thrust in, again, upon the revolting Reason, the blasphemous idea of special interposition—we have to suppose that, in the particular instances of these "nebulæ," an unerring God found it necessary to introduce certain supplementary regulations—certain improvements of the general law—certain retouchings and emendations, in a word, which had the effect of deferring the completion of these individual stars for centuries of centuries beyond the æra during which all the other stellar bodies had time, not only to be fully constituted, but to grow hoary with an unspeakable old age.

Of course, it will be immediately objected that since the light by which we recognize the nebulæ now, must be merely that which left their surfaces a vast number of years ago, the processes at present observed, or supposed to be observed, are, in fact, *not* processes now actually going on, but the phantoms of processes completed long in the Past—just as I maintain all these mass-constitutive processes *must* have been.

To this I reply that neither is the now-observed condition of the condensed stars their actual condition, but a condition completed long in the Past; so that my argument drawn from the *relative* condition of the stars and the "nebulæ," is in no manner disturbed. Moreover, those who maintain the existence of nebulæ, do *not* refer the nebulosity to extreme distance; they declare it a real and not merely a perspective nebulosity. That we may conceive, indeed, a nebular mass as visible at all, we must conceive it as *very near us* in comparison with the condensed stars brought into view by the modern telescopes. In maintaining the appearances in question, then, to be really nebulous, we maintain their comparative vicinity to our point of view. Thus, their condition, as we see them now, must be referred to an epoch *far less remote* than that to which we may refer the now-observed condition of at least the majority of the stars.—In a word, should Astronomy ever demonstrate a "nebula," in the sense at present intended, I should consider the Nebular Cosmogony—*not*, indeed, as corroborated by the demonstration—but as thereby irretrievably overthrown.

By way, however, of rendering unto Cæsar *no more* than the things that are Cæsar's, let me here remark that the assumption of the hypothesis which led him to so glorious a result, seems to have been suggested to Laplace in great measure by a misconception—by the very misconception of which we have just been speaking—by the generally prevalent misunderstanding of the character of the nebulæ, so mis-named. These he supposed to be, in reality, what their designation implies. The fact is, this great man had, very properly, an inferior faith in his own merely *perceptive* powers. In respect, therefore, to the actual existence of nebulæ—an existence so confidently maintained by his telescopic contemporaries—he depended less upon what he saw than upon what he heard.

It will be seen that the only valid objections to his theory, are those made to its hypothesis *as* such—to what suggested it—not to what it suggests; to its propositions rather than to its results. His most unwarranted assumption was that of giving the atoms a movement towards a centre, in the very face of his evident understanding that these atoms, in unlimited succession, extended throughout the Universal space. I have already shown that, under such circumstances, there could have occurred no movement at all; and Laplace, consequently, assumed one on no more philosophical ground than that something of the kind was necessary for the establishment of what he intended to establish.

His original idea seems to have been a compound of the true Epicurean atoms with the false nebulæ of his contemporaries; and thus his theory presents us with the singular anomaly of absolute truth deduced, as a mathematical result, from a hybrid datum of ancient imagination intertangled with modern inacumen. Laplace's real strength lay, in fact, in an almost miraculous mathematical instinct:—on this he relied; and in no instance did it fail or deceive him:—in the case of the Nebular Cosmogony, it led him, blindfolded, through a labyrinth of Error, into one of the most luminous and stupendous temples of Truth.

Let us now fancy, for the moment, that the ring first thrown off by the Sun—that is to say, the ring whose breaking-up constituted Neptune—did not, in fact, break up until the throwing-off of the ring out of which Uranus arose; that this latter ring, again, remained perfect until the discharge of that out of which sprang Saturn; that this latter, again, remained entire until the discharge of that from which originated Jupiter—and so on. Let us imagine, in a word, that no dissolution occurred among the rings until the final rejection of that which gave birth to Mercury. We thus paint to the eye of the mind a series of cöexistent concentric circles; and looking as well at *them* as at the processes by which, according to Laplace's hypothesis, they were constructed, we perceive at once a very singular analogy with the atomic strata and the process of the original irradiation as I have described it. Is it impossible that, on measuring the *forces*, respectively, by which each successive planetary circle was thrown off—that is to say, on measuring the successive excesses of rotation over gravitation which occasioned the successive discharges—we should find the analogy in question more decidedly confirmed? *Is it improbable that we should discover these forces to have varied—as in the original radiation—proportionally to the squares of the distances?*

Our solar system, consisting, in chief, of one sun, with sixteen planets certainly, and possibly a few more, revolving about it at various distances, and attended by seventeen moons assuredly, but *very* probably by several others—is now to be considered as *an example* of the innumerable agglomerations which proceeded to take place throughout the Universal Sphere of atoms on withdrawal of the Divine Volition. I mean to say that our solar system is to be understood as affording a *generic instance* of these agglomerations, or, more correctly, of the ulterior conditions at which they arrived. If we keep our attention fixed on the idea of *the utmost possible Relation* as the Omnipotent design, and on the precautions taken to accomplish it through difference of form, among the original atoms, and particular inequidistance, we shall find it impossible to suppose for a moment that even any two of the incipient agglomerations reached precisely the same result in the end. We shall rather be inclined to think that *no two* stellar bodies in the Universe—whether suns, planets or moons—are particularly, while *all* are generally, similar. Still less, then, can we imagine any two *assemblages* of such bodies—any two "systems"—as having more than a general resemblance. Our telescopes, at this point, thoroughly confirm our deductions. Taking our own solar system, then, as merely a loose or general type of all, we have so far proceeded in our subject as to survey the Universe under the aspect of a spherical space, throughout which, dispersed with merely general equability, exist a number of but generally similar *systems*.

Let us now, expanding our conceptions, look upon each of these systems as in itself an atom; which in fact it is, when we consider it as but one of the countless myriads of systems which constitute the Universe. Regarding all, then, as but colossal atoms, each with the same ineradicable tendency to Unity which characterizes the actual atoms of which it consists—we enter at once upon a new order of aggregations. The smaller systems, in the vicinity of a larger one, would, inevitably, be drawn into still closer vicinity. A thousand would assemble here; a million there—perhaps here, again, even a billion—leaving, thus, immeasurable vacancies in space. And if now, it be demanded why, in the case of these systems—of these merely Titanic atoms—I speak, simply, of an "assemblage," and not, as in the case of the actual atoms, of a more or less consolidated agglomeration:—if it be asked, for instance, why I do not carry what I suggest to its legitimate conclusion, and describe, at once, these assemblages of system-atoms as rushing to consolidation in spheres—as each becoming condensed into one magnificent sun—my reply is that μελλοντα ταυτα—I am but pausing, for a moment, on the awful threshold of *the Future*. For the present, calling these assemblages "clusters," we see them in the incipient stages of their consolidation. Their *absolute* consolidation is *to come*.

We have now reached a point from which we behold the Universe as a spherical space, interspersed, *unequably*, with *clusters*. It will be noticed that I here prefer the adverb "unequably" to the phrase "with a merely general equability," employed before. It is evident, in fact, that the equability of distribution will diminish in the ratio of the agglomerative processes—that is to say, as the things distributed diminish in number. Thus the increase of *in*-equability—an increase which must continue until, sooner or later, an epoch will arrive at which the largest agglomeration will absorb all the others—should be viewed as, simply, a corroborative indication of the *tendency to One*.

And here, at length, it seems proper to inquire whether the ascertained *facts* of Astronomy confirm the general arrangement which I have thus, deductively, assigned to the Heavens. Thoroughly, they *do*. Telescopic observation, guided by the laws of perspective, enables us to understand that the perceptible Universe exists as *a cluster of clusters, irregularly disposed*.

The "clusters" of which this Universal "*cluster of clusters*" consists, are merely what we have been in the practice of designating "nebulæ"—and, of these "nebulæ," *one* is of paramount interest to mankind. I allude to the Galaxy, or Milky Way. This interests us, first and most obviously, on account of its great superiority in apparent size, not only to any one other cluster in the firmament, but to all the other clusters taken together. The largest of these latter occupies a mere point, comparatively, and is distinctly seen only with the aid of a telescope. The Galaxy sweeps throughout the Heaven and is brilliantly visible to the naked eye. But it interests man chiefly, although less immediately, on account of its being his home; the home of the Earth on which he exists; the home of the Sun about which this Earth revolves; the home of that "system" of orbs of which the Sun is the centre and primary—the Earth one of sixteen secondaries, or planets—the Moon one of seventeen tertiaries, or satellites. The Galaxy, let me repeat, is but one of the *clusters* which I have been describing—but one of the mis-called "nebulæ" revealed to us—by the telescope alone, sometimes—as faint hazy spots in various quarters of the sky. We have no reason to suppose the Milky Way *really* more extensive than the least of these "nebulæ." Its vast superiority in size is but an apparent superiority arising from our position in regard to it—that is to say, from our position in its midst. However strange the assertion may at first appear to those unversed in Astronomy, still the astronomer himself has no hesitation in asserting that we are *in the midst* of that inconceivable host of stars—of suns—of systems—which constitute the Galaxy. Moreover, not only have *we*—not only has *our* Sun a right to claim the Galaxy as its own especial cluster, but, with slight reservation, it may be said that all the distinctly visible stars of the firmament—all the stars Visible to the naked eye—have equally a right to claim it as *their* own.

There has been a great deal of misconception in respect to the *shape* of the Galaxy; which, in nearly all our astronomical treatises, is said to resemble that of a capital Y. The cluster in question has, in reality, a certain general—*very* general resemblance to the planet Saturn, with its encompassing triple ring. Instead of the solid orb of that planet, however, we must picture to ourselves a lenticular star-island, or collection of stars; our Sun lying excentrically—near the shore of the island—on that side of it which is nearest the constellation of the Cross and farthest from that of Cassiopeia. The surrounding ring, where it approaches our position, has in it a longitudinal *gash*, which does, in fact, cause *the ring, in our vicinity*, to assume, loosely, the appearance of a capital Y.

We must not fall into the error, however, of conceiving the somewhat indefinite girdle as at all *remote*, comparatively speaking, from the also indefinite lenticular cluster which it surrounds; and thus, for mere purpose of explanation, we may speak of our Sun as actually situated at that point of the Y where its three component lines unite; and, conceiving this letter to be of a certain solidity—of a certain thickness, very trivial in comparison with its length—we may even speak of our position as *in the middle* of this thickness. Fancying ourselves thus placed, we shall no longer find difficulty in accounting for the phænomena presented—which are perspective altogether. When we look upward or downward—that is to say, when we cast our eyes in the direction of the letter's *thickness*—we look through fewer stars than when we cast them in the direction of its *length*, or *along* either of the three component lines. Of course, in the former case, the stars appear scattered—in the latter, crowded.—To reverse this explanation:—An inhabitant of the Earth, when looking, as we commonly express ourselves, *at* the Galaxy, is then beholding it in some of the directions of its length—is looking *along* the lines of the Y—but when, looking out into the general Heaven, he turns his eyes *from* the Galaxy, he is then surveying it in the direction of the letter's thickness; and on this account the stars seem to him scattered; while, in fact, they are as close together, on an average, as in the mass of the cluster. *No* consideration could be better adapted to convey an idea of this cluster's stupendous extent.

If, with a telescope of high space-penetrating power, we carefully inspect the firmament, we shall become aware of *a belt of clusters*—of what we have hitherto called "nebulæ"—a *band*, of varying breadth, stretching from horizon to horizon, at right angles to the general course of the Milky Way. This band is the ultimate *cluster of clusters*. This belt is *The Universe*. Our Galaxy is but one, and perhaps one of the most inconsiderable, of the clusters which go to the constitution of this ultimate, Universal *belt* or *band*. The appearance of this cluster of clusters, to our eyes, *as* a belt or band, is altogether a perspective phænomenon of the same character as that which causes us to behold our own individual and roughly-spherical cluster, the Galaxy, under guise also of a belt, traversing the Heavens at right angles to the Universal one. The shape of the all-inclusive cluster is, of course *generally*, that of each individual cluster which it includes. Just as the scattered stars which, on looking *from* the Galaxy, we see in the general sky, are, in fact, but a portion of that Galaxy itself, and as closely intermingled with it as any of the telescopic points in what seems the densest portion of its mass—so are the scattered "nebulæ" which, on casting our eyes *from* the Universal *belt*, we perceive at all points of the firmament—so, I say, are these scattered "nebulæ" to be understood as only perspectively scattered, and as part and parcel of the one supreme and Universal *sphere*.

No astronomical fallacy is more untenable, and none has been more pertinaciously adhered to, than that of the absolute *illimitation* of the Universe of Stars. The reasons for limitation, as I have already assigned them, *à priori*, seem to me unanswerable; but, not to speak of these, *observation* assures us that there is, in numerous directions around us, certainly, if not in all, a positive limit—or, at the very least, affords us no basis whatever for thinking otherwise. Were the succession of stars endless, then the background of the sky would present us an uniform luminosity, like that displayed by the Galaxy—*since there could be absolutely no point, in all that background, at which would not exist a star.* The only mode, therefore, in which, under such a state of affairs, we could comprehend the *voids* which our telescopes find in innumerable directions, would be by supposing the distance of the invisible background so immense that no ray from it has yet been able to reach us at all. That this *may* be so, who shall venture to deny? I maintain, simply, that we have not even the shadow of a reason for believing that it *is* so.

When speaking of the vulgar propensity to regard all bodies on the Earth as tending merely to the Earth's centre, I observed that, "with certain exceptions to be specified hereafter, every body on the Earth tended not only to the Earth's centre, but in every conceivable direction besides." The "exceptions" refer to those frequent gaps in the Heavens, where our utmost scrutiny can detect not only no stellar bodies, but no indications of their existence:—where yawning chasms, blacker than Erebus, seem to afford us glimpses, through the boundary walls of the Universe of Stars, into the illimitable Universe of Vacancy, beyond. Now as any body, existing on the Earth, chances to pass, either through its own movement or the Earth's, into a line with any one of these voids, or cosmical abysses, it clearly is no longer attracted *in the direction of that void*, and for the moment, consequently, is "heavier" than at any period, either after or before. Independently of the consideration of these voids, however, and looking only at the generally unequable distribution of the stars, we see that the absolute tendency of bodies on the Earth to the Earth's centre, is in a state of perpetual variation.

We comprehend, then, the insulation of our Universe. We perceive the isolation of *that*—of *all* that which we grasp with the senses. We know that there exists one *cluster of clusters*—a collection around which, on all sides, extend the immeasurable wildernesses of a Space *to all human perception* untenanted. But *because* upon the confines of this Universe of Stars we are compelled to pause, through want of farther evidence from the senses, is it right to conclude that, in fact, there *is* no material point beyond that which we have thus been permitted to attain? Have we, or have we not, an analogical right to the inference that this perceptible Universe—that this cluster of clusters—is but one of *a series* of clusters of clusters, the rest of which are invisible through distance—through the diffusion of their light being so excessive, ere it reaches us, as not to produce upon our retinas a light-impression—or from there being no such emanation as light at all, in these unspeakably distant worlds—or, lastly, from the mere interval being so vast, that the electric tidings of their presence in Space, have not yet—through the lapsing myriads of years—been enabled to traverse that interval?

Have we any right to inferences—have we any ground whatever for visions such as these? If we have a right to them in *any* degree, we have a right to their infinite extension.

The human brain has obviously a leaning to the "*Infinite*," and fondles the phantom of the idea. It seems to long with a passionate fervor for this impossible conception, with the hope of intellectually believing it when conceived. What is general among the whole race of Man, of course no individual of that race can be warranted in considering abnormal; nevertheless, there *may* be a class of superior intelligences, to whom the human bias alluded to may wear all the character of monomania.

My question, however, remains unanswered:—Have we any right to infer—let us say, rather, to imagine—an interminable succession of the "clusters of clusters," or of "Universes" more or less similar?

I reply that the "right," in a case such as this, depends absolutely upon the hardihood of that imagination which ventures to claim the right. Let me declare, only, that, as an individual, I myself feel impelled to the *fancy*—without daring to call it more—that there *does* exist a *limitless* succession of Universes, more or less similar to that of which we have cognizance—to that of which *alone* we shall ever have cognizance—at the very least until the return of our own particular Universe into Unity. *If* such clusters of clusters exist, however—*and they do*—it is abundantly clear that, having had no part in our origin, they have no portion in our laws. They neither attract us, nor we them. Their material—their spirit is not ours—is not that which obtains in any part of our Universe. They could not impress our senses or our souls. Among them and us—considering all, for the moment, collectively—there are no influences in common. Each exists, apart and independently, *in the bosom of its proper and particular God*.

In the conduct of this Discourse, I am aiming less at physical than at metaphysical order. The clearness with which even material phænomena are presented to the understanding, depends very little,

I have long since learned to perceive, upon a merely natural, and almost altogether upon a moral, arrangement. If then I seem to step somewhat too discursively from point to point of my topic, let me suggest that I do so in the hope of thus the better keeping unbroken that chain of *graduated impression* by which alone the intellect of Man can expect to encompass the grandeurs of which I speak, and, in their majestic totality, to comprehend them.

So far, our attention has been directed, almost exclusively, to a general and relative grouping of the stellar bodies in space. Of specification there has been little; and whatever ideas of *quantity* have been conveyed—that is to say, of number, magnitude, and distance—have been conveyed incidentally and by way of preparation for more definitive conceptions. These latter let us now attempt to entertain.

Our solar system, as has been already mentioned, consists, in chief, of one sun and sixteen planets certainly, but in all probability a few others, revolving around it as a centre, and attended by seventeen moons of which we know, with possibly several more of which as yet we know nothing. These various bodies are not true spheres, but oblate spheroids—spheres flattened at the poles of the imaginary axes about which they rotate:—the flattening being a consequence of the rotation. Neither is the Sun absolutely the centre of the system; for this Sun itself, with all the planets, revolves about a perpetually shifting point of space, which is the system's general centre of gravity. Neither are we to consider the paths through which these different spheroids move—the moons about the planets, the planets about the Sun, or the Sun about the common centre—as circles in an accurate sense. They are, in fact, *ellipses—one of the foci being the point about which the revolution is made*. An ellipse is a curve, returning into itself, one of whose diameters is longer than the other. In the longer diameter are two points, equidistant from the middle of the line, and so situated otherwise that if, from each of them a straight line be drawn to any one point of the curve, the two lines, taken together, will be equal to the longer diameter itself. Now let us conceive such an ellipse. At one of the points mentioned, which are the *foci*, let us fasten an orange. By an elastic thread let us connect this orange with a pea; and let us place this latter on the circumference of the ellipse. Let us now move the pea continuously around the orange—keeping always on the circumference of the ellipse. The elastic thread, which, of course, varies in length as we move the pea, will form what in geometry is called a *radius vector*.

Now, if the orange be understood as the Sun, and the pea as a planet revolving about it, then the revolution should be made at such a rate—with a velocity so varying—that the *radius vector* may pass over *equal areas of space in equal times*. The progress of the pea *should be*—in other words, the progress of the planet *is*, of course,—slow in proportion to its distance from the Sun—swift in proportion to its proximity. Those planets, moreover, move the more slowly which are the farther from the Sun; *the squares of their periods of revolution having the same proportion to each other, as have to each other the cubes of their mean distances from the Sun*.

The wonderfully complex laws of revolution here described, however, are not to be understood as obtaining in our system alone. They *everywhere* prevail where Attraction prevails. They control *the Universe*. Every shining speck in the firmament is, no doubt, a luminous sun, resembling our own, at least in its general features, and having in attendance upon it a greater or less number of planets, greater or less, whose still lingering luminosity is not sufficient to render them visible to us at so vast a distance, but which, nevertheless, revolve, moon-attended, about their starry centres, in obedience to the principles just detailed—in obedience to the three omniprevalent laws of revolution—the three immortal laws *guessed* by the imaginative Kepler, and but subsequently demonstrated and accounted for by the patient and mathematical Newton. Among a tribe of philosophers who pride themselves excessively upon matter-of-fact, it is far too fashionable to sneer at all speculation under the comprehensive *sobriquet*, "guess-work." The point to be considered is, *who* guesses. In guessing with Plato, we spend our time to better purpose, now and then, than in hearkening to a demonstration by Alcmæon.

In many works on Astronomy I find it distinctly stated that the laws of Kepler are *the basis* of the great principle, Gravitation. This idea must have arisen from the fact that the suggestion of these laws by Kepler, and his proving them *à posteriori* to have an actual existence, led Newton to account for them by the hypothesis of Gravitation, and, finally, to demonstrate them *à priori*, as necessary consequences of the hypothetical principle. Thus so far from the laws of Kepler being the basis of Gravity, Gravity is the basis of these laws—as it is, indeed, of all the laws of the material Universe which are not referable to Repulsion alone.

The mean distance of the Earth from the Moon—that is to say, from the heavenly body in our closest vicinity—is 237,000 miles.

Mercury, the planet nearest the Sun, is distant from him 37 millions of miles. Venus, the next, revolves at a distance of 68 millions:—the Earth, which comes next, at a distance of 95 millions:—Mars, then, at a distance of 144 millions. Now come the eight Asteroids (Ceres, Juno, Vesta, Pallas, Astræa, Flora, Iris, and Hebe) at an average distance of about 250 millions. Then we have Jupiter, distant 490 millions; then Saturn, 900 millions; then Uranus, 19 hundred millions; finally Neptune, lately discovered, and revolving at a distance, say of 28 hundred millions. Leaving Neptune out of the account—of which as yet we know little accurately and which is, possibly, one of a system of Asteroids—it will be seen that, within certain limits, there exists an *order of interval* among the planets. Speaking loosely, we may say that each outer planet is twice as far from the Sun as is the next inner one. May not the *order* here mentioned—*may not the law of Bode—be deduced from consideration of the analogy suggested by me as having place between the solar discharge of rings and the mode of the atomic irradiation*?

The numbers hurriedly mentioned in this summary of distance, it is folly to attempt comprehending, unless in the light of abstract arithmetical facts. They are not practically tangible ones. They convey no precise ideas. I have stated that Neptune, the planet farthest from the Sun, revolves about him at a distance of 28 hundred millions of miles. So far good:—I have stated a mathematical fact; and, without comprehending it in the least, we may put it to use—mathematically. But in mentioning, even, that the Moon revolves about the Earth at the comparatively trifling distance of 237,000 miles, I entertained no expectation of giving any one to understand—to know—to feel—how far from the Earth the Moon actually *is*. 237,000 *miles*! There are, perhaps, few of my readers who have not crossed the Atlantic ocean; yet how many of them have a distinct idea of even the 3,000 miles intervening between shore and shore? I doubt, indeed, whether the man lives who can force into his brain the most remote conception of the interval between one milestone and its next neighbor upon the turnpike. We are in some measure aided, however, in our consideration of distance, by combining this consideration with the kindred one of velocity. Sound passes through 1100 feet of space in a second of time. Now were it possible for an inhabitant of the Earth to see the flash of a cannon discharged in the Moon, and to hear the report, he would have to wait, after perceiving the former, more than 13 entire days and nights before getting any intimation of the latter.

However feeble be the impression, even thus conveyed, of the Moon's real distance from the Earth, it will, nevertheless, effect a good object in enabling us more clearly to see the futility of attempting to grasp such intervals as that of the 28 hundred millions of miles between our Sun and Neptune; or even that of the 95 millions between the Sun and the Earth we inhabit. A cannon-ball, flying at the greatest velocity with which such a ball has ever been known to fly, could not traverse the latter interval in less than 20 years; while for the former it would require 590.

Our Moon's real diameter is 2160 miles; yet she is comparatively so trifling an object that it would take nearly 50 such orbs to compose one as great as the Earth.

The diameter of our own globe is 7912 miles—but from the enunciation of these numbers what positive idea do we derive?

If we ascend an ordinary mountain and look around us from its summit, we behold a landscape stretching, say 40 miles, in every direction; forming a circle 250 miles in circumference; and including an area of 5000 square miles. The extent of such a prospect, on account of the *successiveness* with which its portions necessarily present themselves to view, can be only very feebly and very partially appreciated:—yet the entire panorama would comprehend no more than one 40,000th part of the mere *surface* of our globe. Were this panorama, then, to be succeeded, after the lapse of an hour, by another of equal extent; this again by a third, after the lapse of another hour; this again by a fourth after lapse of another hour—and so on, until the scenery of the whole Earth were exhausted; and were we to be engaged in examining these various panoramas for twelve hours of every day; we should nevertheless, be 9 years and 48 days in completing the general survey.

But if the mere surface of the Earth eludes the grasp of the imagination, what are we to think of its cubical contents? It embraces a mass of matter equal in weight to at least 2 sextillions, 200 quintillions of tons. Let us suppose it in a state of quiescence; and now let us endeavor to conceive a mechanical force sufficient to set it in motion! Not the strength of all the myriads of beings whom we may conclude to inhabit the planetary worlds of our system—not the combined physical strength of *all* these beings—even admitting all to be more powerful than man—would avail to stir the ponderous mass *a single inch* from its position.

What are we to understand, then, of the force, which under similar circumstances, would be required to move the *largest* of our planets,

Jupiter? This is 86,000 miles in diameter, and would include within its periphery more than a thousand orbs of the magnitude of our own. Yet this stupendous body is actually flying around the Sun at the rate of 29,000 miles an hour—that is to say, with a velocity 40 times greater than that of a cannon-ball! The thought of such a phænomenon cannot well be said to *startle* the mind:—it palsies and appals it. Not unfrequently we task our imagination in picturing the capacities of an angel. Let us fancy such a being at a distance of some hundred miles from Jupiter—a close eye-witness of this planet as it speeds on its annual revolution. Now *can* we, I demand, fashion for ourselves any conception so distinct of this ideal being's spiritual exaltation, as *that* involved in the supposition that, even by this immeasurable mass of matter, whirled immediately before his eyes, with a velocity so unutterable, he—an angel—angelic though he be—is not at once struck into nothingness and overwhelmed?

At this point, however, it seems proper to suggest that, in fact, we have been speaking of comparative trifles. Our Sun, the central and controlling orb of the system to which Jupiter belongs, is not only greater than Jupiter, but greater by far than all the planets of the system taken together. This fact is an essential condition, indeed, of the stability of the system itself. The diameter of Jupiter has been mentioned:—it is 86,000 miles:—that of the Sun is 882,000 miles. An inhabitant of the latter, travelling 90 miles a day, would be more than 80 years in going round a great circle of its circumference. It occupies a cubical space of 681 quadrillions, 472 trillions of miles. The Moon, as has been stated, revolves about the Earth at a distance of 237,000 miles—in an orbit, consequently, of nearly a million and a half. Now, were the Sun placed upon the Earth, centre over centre, the body of the former would extend, in every direction, not only to the line of the Moon's orbit, but beyond it, a distance of 200,000 miles.

And here, once again, let me suggest that, in fact, we have *still* been speaking of comparative trifles. The distance of the planet Neptune from the Sun has been stated:—it is 28 hundred millions of miles; the circumference of its orbit, therefore, is about 17 billions. Let this be borne in mind while we glance at some one of the brightest stars. Between this and the star of *our* system, (the Sun,) there is a gulf of space, to convey any idea of which we should need the tongue of an archangel. From *our* system, then, and from *our* Sun, or star, the star at which we suppose ourselves glancing is a thing altogether apart:—still, for the moment, let us imagine it placed upon our Sun, centre over centre, as we just now imagined this Sun itself placed upon the Earth. Let us now conceive the particular star we have in mind, extending, in every direction, beyond the orbit of Mercury—of Venus—of the Earth:—still *on*, beyond the orbit of Mars—of Jupiter—of Uranus—until, finally, we fancy it filling the circle—17 *billions of miles in circumference*—which is described by the revolution of Leverrier's planet. When we have conceived all this, we shall have entertained no extravagant conception. There is the very best reason for believing that many of the stars are even far larger than the one we have imagined. I mean to say that we have the very best *empirical* basis for such belief:—and, in looking back at the original, atomic arrangements for *diversity*, which have been assumed as a part of the Divine plan in the constitution of the Universe, we shall be enabled easily to understand, and to credit, the existence of even far vaster disproportions in stellar size than any to which I have hitherto alluded. The largest orbs, of course, we must expect to find rolling through the widest vacancies of Space.

I remarked, just now, that to convey an idea of the interval between our Sun and any one of the other stars, we should require the eloquence of an archangel. In so saying, I should not be accused of exaggeration; for, in simple truth, these are topics on which it is scarcely possible to exaggerate. But let us bring the matter more distinctly before the eye of the mind.

In the first place, we may get a general, *relative* conception of the interval referred to, by comparing it with the inter-planetary spaces. If, for example, we suppose the Earth, which is, in reality, 95 millions of miles from the Sun, to be only *one foot* from that luminary; then Neptune would be 40 feet distant; *and the star Alpha Lyræ, at the very least*, 159.

Now I presume that, in the termination of my last sentence, few of my readers have noticed anything especially objectionable—particularly wrong. I said that the distance of the Earth from the Sun being taken at *one foot*, the distance of Neptune would be 40 feet, and that of Alpha Lyræ, 159. The proportion between one foot and 159 has appeared, perhaps, to convey a sufficiently definite impression of the proportion between the two intervals—that of the Earth from the Sun and that of Alpha Lyræ from the same luminary. But my account of the matter should, in reality, have run thus:—The distance of the Earth from the Sun being taken at one foot, the distance of Neptune would be 40 feet, and that of Alpha Lyræ, 159—*miles*:—that is to say, I had assigned to

Alpha Lyræ, in my first statement of the case, only the 5280*th part* of that distance which is the *least distance possible* at which it can actually lie.

To proceed:—However distant a mere *planet* is, yet when we look at it through a telescope, we see it under a certain form—of a certain appreciable size. Now I have already hinted at the probable bulk of many of the stars; nevertheless, when we view any one of them, even through the most powerful telescope, it is found to present us with *no form*, and consequently with *no magnitude* whatever. We see it as a point and nothing more.

Again;—Let us suppose ourselves walking, at night, on a highway. In a field on one side of the road, is a line of tall objects, say trees, the figures of which are distinctly defined against the background of the sky. This line of objects extends at right angles to the road, and from the road to the horizon. Now, as we proceed along the road, we see these objects changing their positions, respectively, in relation to a certain fixed point in that portion of the firmament which forms the background of the view. Let us suppose this fixed point—sufficiently fixed for our purpose—to be the rising moon. We become aware, at once, that while the tree nearest us so far alters its position in respect to the moon, as to seem flying behind us, the tree in the extreme distance has scarcely changed at all its relative position with the satellite. We then go on to perceive that the farther the objects are from us, the less they alter their positions; and the converse. Then we begin, unwittingly, to estimate the distances of individual trees by the degrees in which they evince the relative alteration. Finally, we come to understand how it might be possible to ascertain the actual distance of any given tree in the line, by using the amount of relative alteration as a basis in a simple geometrical problem. Now this relative alteration is what we call "parallax;" and by parallax we calculate the distances of the heavenly bodies. Applying the principle to the trees in question, we should, of course, be very much at a loss to comprehend the distance of *that* tree, which, however far we proceeded along the road, should evince *no* parallax at all. This, in the case described, is a thing impossible; but impossible only because all distances on our Earth are trivial indeed:—in comparison with the vast cosmical quantities, we may speak of them as absolutely nothing.

Now, let us suppose the star Alpha Lyræ directly overhead; and let us imagine that, instead of standing on the Earth, we stand at one end of a straight road stretching through Space to a distance equalling the diameter of the Earth's orbit—that is to say, to a distance of 190 *millions of miles*. Having observed, by means of the most delicate micrometrical instruments, the exact position of the star, let us now pass along this inconceivable road, until we reach its other extremity. Now, once again, let us look at the star. It is *precisely* where we left it. Our instruments, however delicate, assure us that its relative position is absolutely—is identically the same as at the commencement of our unutterable journey. *No* parallax—none whatever—has been found.

The fact is, that, in regard to the distance of the fixed stars—of any one of the myriads of suns glistening on the farther side of that awful chasm which separates our system from its brothers in the cluster to which it belongs—astronomical science, until very lately, could speak only with a negative certainty. Assuming the brightest as the nearest, we could say, even of *them*, only that there is a certain incomprehensible distance on the *hither* side of which they cannot be:—how far they are beyond it we had in no case been able to ascertain. We perceived, for example, that Alpha Lyræ cannot be nearer to us than 19 trillions, 200 billions of miles; but, for all we knew, and indeed for all we now know, it may be distant from us the square, or the cube, or any other power of the number mentioned. By dint, however, of wonderfully minute and cautious observations, continued, with novel instruments, for many laborious years, *Bessel*, not long ago deceased, has lately succeeded in determining the distance of six or seven stars; among others, that of the star numbered 61 in the constellation of the Swan. The distance in this latter instance ascertained, is 670,000 times that of the Sun; which last it will be remembered, is 95 millions of miles. The star 61 Cygni, then, is nearly 64 trillions of miles from us—or more than three times the distance assigned, *as the least possible*, for Alpha Lyræ.

In attempting to appreciate this interval by the aid of any considerations of *velocity*, as we did in endeavoring to estimate the distance of the moon, we must leave out of sight, altogether, such nothings as the speed of a cannon-ball, or of sound. Light, however, according to the latest calculations of Struve, proceeds at the rate of 167,000 miles in a second. Thought itself cannot pass through this interval more speedily—if, indeed, thought can traverse it at all. Yet, in coming from 61 Cygni to us, even at this inconceivable rate, light occupies more than *ten years*; and, consequently, were the star this moment blotted out from the Universe, still, *for ten years*, would it continue to sparkle on, undimmed in its paradoxical glory.

Keeping now in mind whatever feeble conception we may have attained of the interval between our Sun and 61 Cygni, let us remember that this interval, however unutterably vast, we are permitted to consider as but the *average* interval among the countless host of stars composing that cluster, or "nebula," to which our system, as well as that of 61 Cygni, belongs. I have, in fact, stated the case with great moderation:—we have excellent reason for believing 61 Cygni to be one of the *nearest* stars, and thus for concluding, at least for the present, that its distance from us is *less* than the average distance between star and star in the magnificent cluster of the Milky Way.

And here, once again and finally, it seems proper to suggest that even as yet we have been speaking of trifles. Ceasing to wonder at the space between star and star in our own or in any particular cluster, let us rather turn our thoughts to the intervals between cluster and cluster, in the all comprehensive cluster of the Universe.

I have already said that light proceeds at the rate of 167,000 miles in a second—that is, about 10 millions of miles in a minute, or about 600 millions of miles in an hour:—yet so far removed from us are some of the "nebulæ" that even light, speeding with this velocity, could not and does not reach us, from those mysterious regions, in less than 3 *millions of years*. This calculation, moreover, is made by the elder Herschell, and in reference merely to those comparatively proximate clusters within the scope of his own telescope. There *are* "nebulæ," however, which, through the magical tube of Lord Rosse, are this instant whispering in our ears the secrets of *a million of ages* by-gone. In a word, the events which we behold now—at this moment—in those worlds—are the identical events which interested their inhabitants *ten hundred thousand centuries ago*. In intervals—in distances such as this suggestion forces upon the *soul*—rather than upon the mind—we find, at length, a fitting climax to all hitherto frivolous considerations of *quantity*.

Our fancies thus occupied with the cosmical distances, let us take the opportunity of referring to the difficulty which we have so often experienced, while pursuing *the beaten path* of astronomical reflection, *in accounting* for the immeasurable voids alluded to—in comprehending why chasms so totally unoccupied and therefore apparently so needless, have been made to intervene between star and star—between cluster and cluster—in understanding, to be brief, a sufficient reason for the Titanic scale, in respect of mere *Space*, on which the Universe is seen to be constructed. A rational cause for the phænomenon, I maintain that Astronomy has palpably failed to assign:—but the considerations through which, in this Essay, we have proceeded step by step, enable us clearly and immediately to perceive that *Space and Duration are one*. That the Universe might *endure* throughout an æra at all commensurate with the grandeur of its component material portions and with the high majesty of its spiritual purposes, it was necessary that the original atomic diffusion be made to so inconceivable an extent as to be only not infinite. It was required, in a word, that the stars should be gathered into visibility from invisible nebulosity—proceed from nebulosity to consolidation—and so grow grey in giving birth and death to unspeakably numerous and complex variations of vitalic development:—it was required that the stars should do all this—should have time thoroughly to accomplish all these Divine purposes—*during the period* in which all things were effecting their return into Unity with a velocity accumulating in the inverse proportion of the squares of the distances at which lay the inevitable End.

Throughout all this we have no difficulty in understanding the absolute accuracy of the Divine *adaptation*. The density of the stars, respectively, proceeds, of course, as their condensation diminishes; condensation and heterogeneity keep pace with each other; through the latter, which is the index of the former, we estimate the vitalic and spiritual development. Thus, in the density of the globes, we have the measure in which their purposes are fulfilled. *As* density proceeds—*as* the divine intentions *are* accomplished—*as* less and still less remains *to be* accomplished—so—in the same ratio—should we expect to find an acceleration of *the End*:—and thus the philosophical mind will easily comprehend that the Divine designs in constituting the stars, advance *mathematically* to their fulfilment:—and more; it will readily give the advance a mathematical expression; it will decide that this advance is inversely proportional with the squares of the distances of all created things from the starting-point and goal of their creation.

Not only is this Divine adaptation, however, mathematically accurate, but there is that about it which stamps it *as divine*, in distinction from that which is merely the work of human constructiveness. I allude to the complete *mutuality* of adaptation. For example; in human constructions a particular cause has a particular effect; a particular intention brings to pass a particular object; but this is all; we see no reciprocity. The effect does not re-act upon the cause; the intention does not change relations with the object. In Divine constructions the object is either design or object as we choose to regard it—and we may take at any time a cause for an effect, or the converse—so that we can never absolutely decide which is which.

To give an instance:—In polar climates the human frame, to maintain its animal heat, requires, for combustion in the capillary system, an abundant supply of highly azotized food, such as train-oil. But again:—in polar climates nearly the sole food afforded man is the oil of abundant seals and whales. Now, whether is oil at hand because imperatively demanded, or the only thing demanded because the only thing to be obtained? It is impossible to decide. There is an absolute *reciprocity of adaptation*.

The pleasure which we derive from any display of human ingenuity is in the ratio of *the approach* to this species of reciprocity. In the construction of *plot*, for example, in fictitious literature, we should aim at so arranging the incidents that we shall not be able to determine, of any one of them, whether it depends from any one other or upholds it. In this sense, of course, *perfection* of *plot* is really, or practically, unattainable—but only because it is a finite intelligence that constructs. The plots of God are perfect. The Universe is a plot of God.

And now we have reached a point at which the intellect is forced, again, to struggle against its propensity for analogical inference—against its monomaniac grasping at the infinite. Moons have been seen *revolving* about planets; planets about stars; and the poetical instinct of humanity—its instinct of the symmetrical, if the symmetry be but a symmetry of surface:—this *instinct*, which the Soul, not only of Man but of all created beings, took up, in the beginning, from the *geometrical* basis of the Universal irradiation—impels us to the fancy of an endless extension of this system of *cycles*. Closing our eyes equally to *de*duction and *in*duction, we insist upon imagining a *revolution* of all the orbs of the Galaxy about some gigantic globe which we take to be the central pivot of the whole. Each cluster in the great cluster of clusters is imagined, of course, to be similarly supplied and constructed; while, that the "analogy" may be wanting at no point, we go on to conceive these clusters themselves, again, as *revolving* about some still more august sphere;—this latter, still again, *with* its encircling clusters, as but one of a yet more magnificent series of agglomerations, *gyrating* about yet another orb central *to them*—some orb still more unspeakably sublime—some orb, let us rather say, of infinite sublimity endlessly multiplied by the infinitely sublime. Such are the conditions, continued in perpetuity, which the voice of what some people term "analogy" calls upon the Fancy to depict and the Reason to contemplate, if possible, without becoming dissatisfied with the picture. Such, *in general*, are the interminable gyrations beyond gyration which we have been instructed by Philosophy to comprehend and to account for, at least in the best manner we can. Now and then, however, a philosopher proper—one whose phrenzy takes a very determinate turn—whose genius, to speak more reverentially, has a strongly-pronounced washerwomanish bias, doing every thing up by the dozen—enables us to see *precisely* that point out of sight, at which the revolutionary processes in question do, and of right ought to, come to an end.

It is hardly worth while, perhaps, even to sneer at the reveries of Fourrier:—but much has been said, latterly, of the hypothesis of Mädler—that there exists, in the centre of the Galaxy, a stupendous globe about which all the systems of the cluster revolve. The *period* of our own, indeed, has been stated—117 millions of years.

That our Sun has a motion in space, independently of its rotation, and revolution about the system's centre of gravity, has long been suspected. This motion, granting it to exist, would be manifested perspectively. The stars in that firmamental region which we were leaving behind us, would, in a very long series of years, become crowded; those in the opposite quarter, scattered. Now, by means of astronomical History, we ascertain, cloudily, that some such phænomena have occurred. On this ground it has been declared that our system is moving to a point in the heavens diametrically opposite the star Zeta Herculis:—but this inference is, perhaps, the maximum to which we have any logical right. Mädler, however, has gone so far as to designate a particular star, Alcyone in the Pleiades, as being at or about the very spot around which a general *revolution* is performed.

Now, since by "analogy" we are led, in the first instance, to these dreams, it is no more than proper that we should abide by analogy, at least in some measure, during their development; and that analogy which suggests the revolution, suggests at the same time a central orb about which it should be performed:—so far the astronomer was consistent. This central orb, however, should, dynamically, be greater than all the orbs, taken together, which surround it. Of these there are about 100 millions. "Why, then," it was of course demanded, "do we not *see* this vast central sun—*at least equal* in mass to 100 millions of such suns as ours—why do we not *see* it—*we*, especially, who occupy the mid region of the cluster—the very locality *near* which, at all events, must be situated this incomparable star?" The reply was ready—"It must be non-luminous, as are our planets." Here, then, to suit a purpose, analogy is suddenly let fall. "Not so," it may be said—"we know that non-luminous suns actually exist." It is true that we have reason at least for supposing so; but we have certainly no reason whatever for supposing that the non-luminous suns in question are encircled by *luminous* suns, while these again are surrounded by non-luminous planets:—and it is precisely all this with which Mädler is called upon to find any thing analogous in the heavens—for it is precisely all this which he imagines in the case of the Galaxy. Admitting the thing to be so, we cannot help here picturing to ourselves how sad a puzzle the *why it is so* must prove to all *à priori* philosophers.

But granting, in the very teeth of analogy and of every thing else, the non-luminosity of the vast central orb, we may still inquire how this orb, so enormous, could fail of being rendered visible by the flood of light thrown upon it from the 100 millions of glorious suns glaring in all directions about it. Upon the urging of this question, the idea of an actually solid central sun appears, in some measure, to have been abandoned; and speculation proceeded to assert that the systems of the cluster perform their revolutions merely about an immaterial centre of gravity common to all. Here again then, to suit a purpose, analogy is let fall. The planets of our system revolve, it is true, about a common centre of gravity; but they do this in connexion with, and in consequence of, a material sun whose mass more than counterbalances the rest of the system.

The mathematical circle is a curve composed of an infinity of straight lines. But this idea of the circle—an idea which, in view of all ordinary geometry, is merely the mathematical, as contradistinguished from the practical, idea—is, in sober fact, the *practical* conception which alone we have any right to entertain in regard to the majestic circle with which we have to deal, at least in fancy, when we suppose our system revolving about a point in the centre of the Galaxy. Let the most vigorous of human imaginations attempt but to take a single step towards the comprehension of a sweep so ineffable! It would scarcely be paradoxical to say that a flash of lightning itself, travelling *forever* upon the circumference of this unutterable circle, would still, *forever*, be travelling in a straight line. That the path of our Sun in such an orbit would, to any human perception, deviate in the slightest degree from a straight line, even in a million of years, is a proposition not to be entertained:—yet we are required to believe that a curvature has become apparent during the brief period of our astronomical history—during a mere point—during the utter nothingness of two or three thousand years.

It may be said that Mädler *has* really ascertained a curvature in the direction of our system's now well-established progress through Space. Admitting, if necessary, this fact to be in reality such, I maintain that nothing is thereby shown except the reality of this fact—the fact of a curvature. For its *thorough* determination, ages will be required; and, when determined, it will be found indicative of some binary or other multiple relation between our Sun and some one or more of the proximate stars. I hazard nothing however, in predicting, that, after the lapse of many centuries, all efforts at determining the path of our Sun through Space, will be abandoned as fruitless. This is easily conceivable when we look at the infinity of perturbation it must experience, from its perpetually-shifting relations with other orbs, in the common approach of all to the nucleus of the Galaxy.

But in examining other "nebulæ" than that of the Milky Way—in surveying, generally, the clusters which overspread the heavens—do we or do we not find confirmation of Mädler's hypothesis? We do *not*. The forms of the clusters are exceedingly diverse when casually viewed; but on close inspection, through powerful telescopes, we recognize the sphere, very distinctly, as at least the proximate form of all:—their constitution, in general, being at variance with the idea of revolution about a common centre.

"It is difficult," says Sir John Herschell, "to form any conception of the dynamical state of such systems. On one hand, without a rotary motion and a centrifugal force, it is hardly possible not to regard them as in a state of *progressive collapse*. On the other, granting such a motion and such a force, we find it no less difficult to reconcile their forms with the rotation of the whole system (meaning cluster) around any single axis, without which internal collision would appear to be inevitable."

Some remarks lately made about the "nebulæ" by Dr. Nichol, in taking quite a different view of the cosmical conditions from any taken in this Discourse—have a very peculiar applicability to the point now at issue. He says:

"When our greatest telescopes are brought to bear upon them, we find that those which were thought to be irregular, are not so; they approach nearer to a globe. Here is one that looked oval; but Lord Rosse's telescope brought it into a circle. . . Now there occurs a very remarkable circumstance in reference to these comparatively sweeping circular masses of nebulæ. We find they are not entirely circular, but the reverse; and that all around them, on every side, there are volumes of stars, *stretching out apparently as if they were rushing towards a great central mass in consequence of the action of some great power*."

Were I to describe, in my own words, what must necessarily be the existing condition of each nebula on the hypothesis that all matter is, as I suggest, now returning to its original Unity, I should simply be going over, nearly verbatim, the language here employed by Dr. Nichol, without the faintest suspicion of that stupendous truth which is the key to these nebular phænomena.

And here let me fortify my position still farther, by the voice of a greater than Mädler—of one, moreover, to whom all the data of Mädler have long been familiar things, carefully and thoroughly considered. Referring to the elaborate calculations of Argelander—the very researches which form Mädler's basis—*Humboldt*, whose generalizing powers have never, perhaps been equalled, has the following observation:

"When we regard the real, proper, or non-perspective motions of the stars, we find *many groups of them moving in opposite directions*; and the data as yet in hand render it not necessary, at least, to conceive that the systems composing the Milky Way, or the clusters, generally, composing the Universe, are revolving about any particular centre unknown, whether luminous or non-luminous. It is but Man's longing for a fundamental First Cause, that impels both his intellect and his fancy to the adoption of such an hypothesis."

The phænomenon here alluded to—that of "many groups moving in opposite directions"—is quite inexplicable by Mädler's idea; but arises, as a necessary consequence, from that which forms the basis of this Discourse. While the *merely general direction* of each atom—of each moon, planet, star, or cluster—would, on my hypothesis, be, of course, absolutely rectilinear; while the *general* path of all bodies would be a right line leading to the centre of all; it is clear, nevertheless, that this general rectilinearity would be compounded of what, with scarcely any exaggeration, we may term an infinity of particular curves—an infinity of local deviations from rectilinearity—the result of continuous differences of relative position among the multitudinous masses, as each proceeded on its own proper journey to the End.

I quoted, just now, from Sir John Herschell, the following words, used in reference to the clusters:—"On one hand, without a rotary motion and a centrifugal force, it is hardly possible not to regard them as in a state of *progressive collapse*." The fact is, that, in surveying the "nebulæ" with a telescope of high power, we shall find it quite impossible, having once conceived this idea of "collapse," not to gather, at all points, corroboration of the idea. A nucleus is always apparent, in the direction of which the stars seem to be precipitating themselves; nor can these nuclei be mistaken for merely perspective phænomena:—the clusters are *really* denser near the centre—sparser in the regions more remote from it. In a word, we see every thing as we *should* see it were a collapse taking place; but, in general, it may be said of these clusters, that we can fairly entertain, while looking at them, the idea of *orbitual movement about a centre*, only by admitting the *possible* existence, in the distant domains of space, of dynamical laws with which *we* are unacquainted.

On the part of Herschell, however, there is evidently *a reluctance* to regard the nebulæ as in "a state of progressive collapse." But if facts—if even appearances justify the supposition of their being in this state, *why*, it may well be demanded, is he disinclined to admit it? Simply on account of a prejudice;—merely because the supposition is at war with a preconceived and utterly baseless notion—that of the endlessness—that of the eternal stability of the Universe.

If the propositions of this Discourse are tenable, the "state of progressive collapse" is *precisely* that state in which alone we are warranted in considering All Things; and, with due humility, let me here confess that, for my part, I am at a loss to conceive how any *other* understanding of the existing condition of affairs, could ever have made its way into the human brain. "The tendency to collapse" and "the attraction of gravitation" are convertible phrases. In using either, we speak of the rëaction of the First Act. Never was necessity less obvious than that of supposing Matter imbued with an ineradicable *quality* forming part of its material nature—a quality, or instinct, *forever* inseparable from it, and by dint of which inalienable principle every atom is *perpetually* impelled to seek its fellow-atom. Never was necessity less obvious than that of entertaining this unphilosophical idea. Going boldly behind the vulgar thought, we have to conceive, metaphysically, that the gravitating principle appertains to Matter *temporarily*—only while diffused—only while existing as Many instead of as One—appertains to it by virtue of its state of irradiation alone—appertains, in a word, altogether to its *condition*, and not in the slightest degree to *itself*. In this view, when the irradiation shall have returned into its source—when the rëaction shall be completed—the gravitating principle will no longer exist. And, in fact, astronomers, without at any time reaching the idea here suggested, seem to have been approximating it, in the assertion that "if there were but one body in the Universe, it would be impossible to understand how the principle, Gravity, could obtain:"—that is to say, from a consideration of Matter as they find it, they reach a conclusion at which I deductively arrive. That so pregnant a suggestion as the one just quoted should have been permitted to remain so long unfruitful, is, nevertheless, a mystery which I find it difficult to fathom.

It is, perhaps, in no little degree, however, our propensity for the continuous—for the analogical—in the present case more particularly for the symmetrical—which has been leading us astray. And, in fact, the sense of the symmetrical is an instinct which may be depended upon with an almost blindfold reliance. It is the poetical essence of the Universe—*of the Universe* which, in the supremeness of its symmetry, is but the most sublime of poems. Now symmetry and consistency are convertible terms:—thus Poetry and Truth are one. A thing is consistent in the ratio of its truth—true in the ratio of its consistency. *A perfect consistency, I repeat, can be nothing but an absolute truth.* We may take it for granted, then, that Man cannot long or widely err, if he suffer himself to be guided by his poetical, which I have maintained to be his truthful, in being his symmetrical, instinct. He must have a care, however, lest, in pursuing too heedlessly the superficial symmetry of forms and motions, he leave out of sight the really essential symmetry of the principles which determine and control them.

That the stellar bodies would finally be merged in one—that, at last, all would be drawn into the substance of *one stupendous central orb already existing*—is an idea which, for some time past, seems, vaguely and indeterminately, to have held possession of the fancy of mankind. It is an idea, in fact, which belongs to the class of the *excessively obvious*. It springs, instantly, from a superficial observation of the cyclic and seemingly *gyrating*, or *vorticial* movements of those individual portions of the Universe which come most immediately and most closely under our observation. There is not, perhaps, a human being, of ordinary education and of average reflective capacity, to whom, at some period, the fancy in question has not occurred, as if spontaneously, or intuitively, and wearing all the character of a very profound and very original conception. This conception, however, so commonly entertained, has never, within my knowledge, arisen out of any abstract considerations. Being, on the contrary, always suggested, as I say, by the vorticial movements about centres, a reason for it, also,—a *cause* for the ingathering of all the orbs into one, *imagined to be already existing*, was naturally sought in the same direction—among these cyclic movements themselves.

Thus it happened that, on announcement of the gradual and perfectly regular decrease observed in the orbit of Enck's comet, at every successive revolution about our Sun, astronomers were nearly unanimous in the opinion that the cause in question was found—that a principle was discovered sufficient to account, physically, for that final, universal agglomeration which, I repeat, the analogical, symmetrical or poetical instinct of Man had predetermined to understand as something more than a simple hypothesis.

This cause—this sufficient reason for the final ingathering—was declared to exist in an exceedingly rare but still material medium pervading space; which medium, by retarding, in some degree, the progress of the comet, perpetually weakened its tangential force; thus giving a predominance to the centripetal; which, of course, drew the comet nearer and nearer at each revolution, and would eventually precipitate it upon the Sun.

All this was strictly logical—admitting the medium or ether; but this ether was assumed, most illogically, on the ground that no *other* mode than the one spoken of could be discovered, of accounting for the observed decrease in the orbit of the comet:—as if from the fact that we could *discover* no other mode of accounting for it, it followed, in any respect, that no other mode of accounting for it existed. It is clear that innumerable causes might operate, in combination, to diminish the orbit, without even a possibility of our ever becoming acquainted with one of them. In the meantime, it has never been fairly shown, perhaps, why the retardation occasioned by the skirts of the Sun's atmosphere, through which the comet passes at perihelion, is not enough to account for the phænomenon. That Enck's comet will be absorbed into the Sun, is probable; that all the comets of the system will be absorbed, is more than merely possible; but, in such case, the principle of absorption must be referred to eccentricity of orbit—to the close approximation to the Sun, of the comets at their perihelia; and is a principle not affecting, in any degree, the ponderous *spheres*, which are to be regarded as the true material constituents of the Universe.—Touching comets, in general, let me here suggest, in passing, that we cannot be far wrong in looking upon them as the *lightning-flashes of the cosmical Heaven*.

The idea of a retarding ether and, through it, of a final agglomeration of all things, seemed at one time, however, to be confirmed by the observation of a positive decrease in the orbit of the solid moon. By reference to eclipses recorded 2500 years ago, it was found that the velocity of the satellite's revolution *then* was considerably less than it is *now*; that on the hypothesis that its motions in its orbit is uniformly in accordance with Kepler's law, and was accurately determined *then*—2500 years ago—it is now in advance of the position it *should* occupy, by nearly 9000 miles. The increase of velocity proved, of course, a diminution of orbit; and astronomers were fast yielding to a belief in an ether, as the sole mode of accounting for the phænomenon, when Lagrange came to the rescue. He showed that, owing to the configurations of the spheroids, the shorter axes of their ellipses are subject to variation in length; the longer axes being permanent; and that this variation is continuous and vibratory—so that every orbit is in a state of transition, either from circle to ellipse, or from ellipse to circle. In the case of the moon, where the shorter axis is *de*creasing, the orbit is passing from circle to ellipse and, consequently, is *de*creasing too; but, after a long series of ages, the ultimate eccentricity will be attained; then the shorter axis will proceed to *in*crease, until the orbit becomes a circle; when the process of shortening will again take place;—and so on forever. In the case of the Earth, the orbit is passing from ellipse to circle. The facts thus demonstrated do away, of course, with all necessity for supposing an ether, and with all apprehension of the system's instability—on the ether's account.

It will be remembered that I have myself assumed what we may term *an ether*. I have spoken of a subtle *influence* which we know to be ever in attendance upon matter, although becoming manifest only through matter's heterogeneity. To this *influence*—without daring to touch it at all in any effort at explaining its awful *nature*—I have referred the various phænomena of electricity, heat, light, magnetism; and more—of vitality, consciousness, and thought—in a word, of spirituality. It will be seen, at once, then, that the ether thus conceived is radically distinct from the ether of the astronomers; inasmuch as theirs is *matter* and mine *not*.

With the idea of a material ether, seems, thus, to have departed altogether the thought of that universal agglomeration so long predetermined by the poetical fancy of mankind:—an agglomeration in which a sound Philosophy might have been warranted in putting faith, at least to a certain extent, if for no other reason than that by this poetical fancy it *had* been so predetermined. But so far as Astronomy—so far as mere Physics have yet spoken, the cycles of the Universe are perpetual—the Universe has no conceivable end. Had an end been demonstrated, however, from so purely collateral a cause as an ether, Man's instinct of the Divine *capacity to adapt*, would have rebelled against the demonstration. We should have been forced to regard the Universe with some such sense of dissatisfaction as we experience in contemplating an unnecessarily complex work of human art. Creation would have affected us as an imperfect *plot* in a romance, where the *dénoûment* is awkwardly brought about by interposed incidents external and foreign to the main subject; instead of springing out of the bosom of the thesis—out of the heart of the ruling idea—instead of arising as a result of the primary proposition—as inseparable and inevitable part and parcel of the fundamental conception of the book.

What I mean by the symmetry of mere surface will now be more clearly understood. It is simply by the blandishment of this symmetry that we have been beguiled into the general idea of which Mädler's hypothesis is but a part—the idea of the vorticial indrawing of the orbs. Dismissing this nakedly physical conception, the symmetry of principle sees the end of all things metaphysically involved in the thought of a beginning; seeks and finds in this origin of all things the *rudiment* of this end; and perceives the impiety of supposing this end likely to be brought about less simply—less directly—less obviously—less artistically—than through *the rëaction of the originating Act*.

Recurring, then, to a previous suggestion, let us understand the systems—let us understand each star, with its attendant planets—as but a Titanic atom existing in space with precisely the same inclination for Unity which characterized, in the beginning, the actual atoms after their irradiation throughout the Universal sphere. As these original atoms rushed towards each other in generally straight lines, so let us conceive as at least generally rectilinear, the paths of the system-atoms towards their respective centres of aggregation:—and in this direct drawing together of the systems into clusters, with a similar and simultaneous drawing together of the clusters themselves while undergoing consolidation, we have at length attained the great *Now*—the awful Present—the Existing Condition of the Universe.

Of the still more awful Future a not irrational analogy may guide us in framing an hypothesis. The equilibrium between the centripetal and centrifugal forces of each system, being necessarily destroyed upon attainment of a certain proximity to the nucleus of the cluster to which it belongs, there must occur, at once, a chaotic or seemingly chaotic precipitation, of the moons upon the planets, of the planets upon the suns, and of the suns upon the nuclei; and the general result of this precipitation must be the gathering of the myriad now-existing stars of the firmament into an almost infinitely less number of almost infinitely superior spheres. In being immeasurably fewer, the worlds of that day will be immeasurably greater than our own. Then, indeed, amid unfathomable abysses, will be glaring unimaginable suns. But all this will be merely a climacic magnificence foreboding the great End. Of this End the new genesis described, can be but a very partial postponement. While undergoing consolidation, the clusters themselves, with a speed prodigiously accumulative, have been rushing towards their own general centre—and now, with a thousand-fold electric velocity, commensurate only with their material grandeur and with the spiritual passion of their appetite for oneness, the majestic remnants of the tribe of Stars flash, at length, into a common embrace. The inevitable catastrophe is at hand.

But this catastrophe—what is it? We have seen accomplished the ingathering of the orbs. Henceforward, are we not to understand *one material globe of globes* as constituting and comprehending the Universe? Such a fancy would be altogether at war with every assumption and consideration of this Discourse.

I have already alluded to that absolute *reciprocity of adaptation* which is the idiosyncrasy of the divine Art—stamping it divine. Up to this point of our reflections, we have been regarding the electrical influence as a something by dint of whose repulsion alone Matter is enabled to exist in that state of diffusion demanded for the fulfilment of its purposes:—so far, in a word, we have been considering the influence in question as ordained for Matter's sake—to subserve the objects of matter. With a perfectly legitimate reciprocity, we are now permitted to look at Matter, as created *solely for the sake of this influence*—solely to serve the objects of this spiritual Ether. Through the aid—by the means—through the agency of Matter, and by dint of its heterogeneity—is this Ether manifested—is *Spirit individualized*. It is merely in the development of this Ether, through heterogeneity, that particular masses of Matter become animate—sensitive—and in the ratio of their heterogeneity;—

some reaching a degree of sensitiveness involving what we call *Thought* and thus attaining Conscious Intelligence.

In this view, we are enabled to perceive Matter as a Means—not as an End. Its purposes are thus seen to have been comprehended in its diffusion; and with the return into Unity these purposes cease. The absolutely consolidated globe of globes would be *objectless*:—therefore not for a moment could it continue to exist. Matter, created for an end, would unquestionably, on fulfilment of that end, be Matter no longer. Let us endeavor to understand that it would disappear, and that God would remain all in all.

That every work of Divine conception must cöexist and cöexpire with its particular design, seems to me especially obvious; and I make no doubt that, on perceiving the final globe of globes to be *objectless*, the majority of my readers will be satisfied with my "*therefore* it cannot continue to exist." Nevertheless, as the startling thought of its instantaneous disappearance is one which the most powerful intellect cannot be expected readily to entertain on grounds so decidedly abstract, let us endeavor to look at the idea from some other and more ordinary point of view:—let us see how thoroughly and beautifully it is corroborated in an *à posteriori* consideration of Matter as we actually find it.

I have before said that "Attraction and Repulsion being undeniably the sole properties by which Matter is manifested to Mind, we are justified in assuming that Matter *exists* only as Attraction and Repulsion—in other words that Attraction and Repulsion *are* Matter; there being no conceivable case in which we may not employ the term Matter and the terms 'Attraction' and 'Repulsion' taken together, as equivalent, and therefore convertible, expressions in Logic."

Now the very definition of Attraction implies particularity—the existence of parts, particles, or atoms; for we define it as the tendency of "each atom &c. to every other atom" &c. according to a certain law. Of course where there are *no* parts—where there is absolute Unity—where the tendency to oneness is satisfied—there can be no Attraction:—this has been fully shown, and all Philosophy admits it. When, on fulfilment of its purposes, then, Matter shall have returned into its original condition of *One*—a condition which presupposes the expulsion of the separative ether, whose province and whose capacity are limited to keeping the atoms apart until that great day when, this ether being no longer needed, the overwhelming pressure of the finally collective Attraction shall at length just sufficiently predominate and expel it:—when, I say, Matter, finally, expelling the Ether, shall have returned into absolute Unity,—it will then (to speak paradoxically for the moment) be Matter without Attraction and without Repulsion—in other words, Matter without Matter—in other words, again, *Matter no more*. In sinking into Unity, it will sink at once into that Nothingness which, to all Finite Perception, Unity must be—into that Material Nihility from which alone we can conceive it to have been evoked—to have been *created* by the Volition of God.

I repeat then—Let us endeavor to comprehend that the final globe of globes will instantaneously disappear, and that God will remain all in all.

But are we here to pause? Not so. On the Universal agglomeration and dissolution, we can readily conceive that a new and perhaps totally different series of conditions may ensue—another creation and irradiation, returning into itself—another action and rëaction of the Divine Will. Guiding our imaginations by that omniprevalent law of laws, the law of periodicity, are we not, indeed, more than justified in entertaining a belief—let us say, rather, in indulging a hope—that the processes we have here ventured to contemplate will be renewed forever, and forever, and forever; a novel Universe swelling into existence, and then subsiding into nothingness, at every throb of the Heart Divine?

And now—this Heart Divine—what is it? *It is our own.*

Let not the merely seeming irreverence of this idea frighten our souls from that cool exercise of consciousness—from that deep tranquillity of self-inspection—through which alone we can hope to attain the presence of this, the most sublime of truths, and look it leisurely in the face.

The *phænomena* on which our conclusions must at this point depend, are merely spiritual shadows, but not the less thoroughly substantial.

We walk about, amid the destinies of our world-existence, encompassed by dim but ever present *Memories* of a Destiny more vast—very distant in the by-gone time, and infinitely awful.

We live out a Youth peculiarly haunted by such dreams; yet never mistaking them for dreams. As Memories we *know* them. *During our Youth* the distinction is too clear to deceive us even for a moment.

So long as this Youth endures, the feeling *that we exist*, is the most natural of all feelings. We understand it *thoroughly*. That there was a period at which we did *not* exist—or, that it might so have happened that we never had existed at all—are the considerations, indeed, which *during this youth*, we find difficulty in understanding. Why we should *not* exist, is, *up to the epoch of our Manhood*, of all queries the most unanswerable. Existence—self-existence—existence from all Time and to all Eternity—seems, up to the epoch of Manhood, a normal and unquestionable condition:—*seems, because it is*.

But now comes the period at which a conventional World-Reason awakens us from the truth of our dream. Doubt, Surprise and Incomprehensibility arrive at the same moment. They say:—"You live and the time was when you lived not. You have been created. An Intelligence exists greater than your own; and it is only through this Intelligence you live at all." These things we struggle to comprehend and cannot:—*cannot*, because these things, being untrue, are thus, of necessity, incomprehensible.

No thinking being lives who, at some luminous point of his life of thought, has not felt himself lost amid the surges of futile efforts at understanding, or believing, that anything exists *greater than his own soul*. The utter impossibility of any one's soul feeling itself inferior to another; the intense, overwhelming dissatisfaction and rebellion at the thought;—these, with the omniprevalent aspirations at perfection, are but the spiritual, coincident with the material, struggles towards the original Unity—are, to my mind at least, a species of proof far surpassing what Man terms demonstration, that no one soul *is* inferior to another—that nothing is, or can be, superior to any one soul—that each soul is, in part, its own God—its own Creator:—in a word, that God—the material *and* spiritual God—*now* exists solely in the diffused Matter and Spirit of the Universe; and that the regathering of this diffused Matter and Spirit will be but the re-constitution of the *purely* Spiritual and Individual God.

In this view, and in this view alone, we comprehend the riddles of Divine Injustice—of Inexorable Fate. In this view alone the existence of Evil becomes intelligible; but in this view it becomes more—it becomes endurable. Our souls no longer rebel at a *Sorrow* which we ourselves have imposed upon ourselves, in furtherance of our own purposes—with a view—if even with a futile view—to the extension of our own *Joy*.

I have spoken of *Memories* that haunt us during our youth. They sometimes pursue us even in our Manhood:—assume gradually less and less indefinite shapes:—now and then speak to us with low voices, saying:

"There was an epoch in the Night of Time, when a still-existent Being existed—one of an absolutely infinite number of similar Beings that people the absolutely infinite domains of the absolutely infinite space. It was not and is not in the power of this Being—any more than it is in your own—to extend, by actual increase, the joy of his Existence; but just as it *is* in your power to expand or to concentrate your pleasures (the absolute amount of happiness remaining always the same) so did and does a similar capability appertain to this Divine Being, who thus passes his Eternity in perpetual variation of Concentrated Self and almost Infinite Self-Diffusion. What you call The Universe is but his present expansive existence. He now feels his life through an infinity of imperfect pleasures—the partial and pain-intertangled pleasures of those inconceivably numerous things which you designate as his creatures, but which are really but infinite individualizations of Himself. All these creatures—*all*—those which you term animate, as well as those to whom you deny life for no better reason than that you do not behold it in operation—*all* these creatures have, in a greater or less degree, a capacity for pleasure and for pain:—*but the general sum of their sensations is precisely that amount of Happiness which appertains by right to the Divine Being when concentrated within Himself.* These creatures are all, too, more or less conscious Intelligences; conscious, first, of a proper identity; conscious, secondly and by faint indeterminate glimpses, of an identity with the Divine Being of whom we speak—of an identity with God. Of the two classes of consciousness, fancy that the former will grow weaker, the latter stronger, during the long succession of ages which must elapse before these myriads of individual Intelligences become blended—when the bright stars become blended—into One. Think that the sense of individual identity will be gradually merged in the general consciousness—that Man, for example, ceasing imperceptibly to feel himself Man, will at length attain that awfully triumphant epoch when he shall recognize his existence as that of Jehovah. In the meantime bear in mind that all is Life—Life—Life within Life—the less within the greater, and all within the *Spirit Divine*."

The Power of Words

Oinos: Pardon, Agathos, the weakness of a spirit new-fledged with immortality!

Agathos: You have spoken nothing, my Oinos, for which pardon is to be demanded. Not even here is knowledge a thing of intuition. For wisdom, ask of the angels freely, that it may be given!

Oinos: But in this existence I dreamed that I should be at once cognizant of all things, and thus at once happy in being cognizant of all.

Agathos: Ah, not in knowledge is happiness, but in the acquisition of knowledge! In forever knowing, we are forever blessed; but to know all, were the curse of a fiend.

Oinos: But does not The Most High know all?

Agathos: *That* (since he is The Most Happy) must be still the *one* thing unknown even to Him.

Oinos: But, since we grow hourly in knowledge, must not *at last* all things be known?

Agathos: Look down into the abysmal distances!—attempt to force the gaze down the multitudinous vistas of the stars, as we sweep slowly through them thus—and thus—and thus! Even the spiritual vision, is it not at all points arrested by the continuous golden walls of the universe?—the walls of the myriads of the shining bodies that mere number has appeared to blend into unity?

Oinos: I clearly perceive that the infinity of matter is no dream.

Agathos: There are no dreams in Aidenn—but it is here whispered that, of this infinity of matter, the *sole* purpose is to afford infinite springs at which the soul may allay the thirst *to know* which is forever unquenchable within it—since to quench it would be to extinguish the soul's self. Question me then, my Oinos, freely and without fear. Come! we will leave to the left the loud harmony of the Pleiades, and swoop outward from the throne into the starry meadows beyond Orion, where, for pansies and violets, and heart's-ease, are the beds of the triplicate and triple-tinted suns.

Oinos: And now, Agathos, as we proceed, instruct me!—speak to me in the earth's familiar tones! I understand not what you hinted to me just now of the modes or of the methods of what during mortality, we were accustomed to call Creation. Do you mean to say that the Creator is not God?

AGATHOS: I mean to say that the Deity does not create.

OINOS: Explain!

AGATHOS: In the beginning only, he created. The seeming creatures which are now throughout the universe so perpetually springing into being can only be considered as the mediate or indirect, not as the direct or immediate results of the Divine creative power.

OINOS: Among men, my Agathos, this idea would be considered heretical in the extreme.

AGATHOS: Among the angels, my Oinos, it is seen to be simply true.

OINOS: I can comprehend you thus far—that certain operations of what we term Nature, or the natural laws, will, under certain conditions, give rise to that which has all the *appearance* of creation. Shortly before the final overthrow of the earth, there were, I well remember, many very successful experiments in what some philosophers were weak enough to denominate the creation of animalculæ.

AGATHOS: The cases of which you speak were, in fact, instances of the secondary creation, and of the *only* species of creation which has ever been since the first word spoke into existence the first law.

OINOS: Are not the starry worlds that, from the abyss of nonentity, burst hourly forth into the heavens—are not these stars, Agathos, the immediate handiwork of the King?

AGATHOS: Let me endeavor, my Oinos, to lead you, step by step, to the conception I intend. You are well aware that, as no thought can perish, so no act is without infinite result. We moved our hands, for example, when we were dwellers on the earth, and in so doing we gave vibration to the atmosphere which engirdled it. This vibration was indefinitely extended till it gave impulse to every particle of the earth's air, which thenceforward, *and forever*, was actuated by the one movement of the hand. This fact the mathematicians of our globe well knew. They made the special effects, indeed, wrought in the fluid by special impulses, the subject of exact calculation—so that it became easy to determine in what precise period an impulse of given extent would engirdle the orb, and impress (forever) every atom of the atmosphere circumambient. Retrograding, they found no difficulty; from a given effect, under given conditions, in determining the value of the original impulse. Now the mathematicians who saw that the results of any given impulse were absolutely endless—and who saw that a portion of these results were accurately traceable through the agency of algebraic analysis—who saw, too, the facility of the retrogradation—these men saw, at the same time, that this species of analysis itself had within itself a capacity for indefinite progress—that there were no bounds conceivable to its advancement and applicability, except within the intellect of him who advanced or applied it. But at this point our mathematicians paused.

OINOS: And why, Agathos, should they have proceeded?

AGATHOS: Because there were some considerations of deep interest beyond. It was deducible from what they knew, that to a being of infinite understanding—one to whom the *perfection* of the algebraic analysis lay unfolded—there could be no difficulty in tracing every impulse given the air—and the ether through the air—to the remotest consequences at any even infinitely remote epoch of time. It is indeed demonstrable that every such impulse *given the air*, must *in the end* impress every individual thing that exists *within the universe;*—and the being of infinite understanding—the being whom we have imagined—might trace the remote undulations of the impulse—trace them upward and onward in their influences upon all particles of all matter—upward and onward forever in their modifications of old forms—or, in other words, *in their creation of new*—until he found them reflected—unimpressive *at last*—back from the throne of the Godhead. And not only could such a being do this, but at any epoch, should a given result be afforded him—should one of these numberless comets, for example, be presented to his inspection—he could have no difficulty in determining, by the analytic retrogradation, to what original impulse it was due. This power of retrogradation in its absolute fulness and perfection—this faculty of referring at *all* epochs, *all* effects to *all* causes—is of course the prerogative of the Deity alone—but in every variety of degree, short of the absolute perfection, is the power itself exercised by the whole host of the Angelic Intelligences.

OINOS: But you speak merely of impulses upon the air.

AGATHOS: In speaking of the air, I referred only to the earth: but the general proposition has reference to impulses upon the ether—

which, since it pervades, and alone pervades all space, is thus the great medium of *creation*.

OINOS: Then all motion, of whatever nature, creates?

AGATHOS: It must: but a true philosophy has long taught that the source of all motion is thought—and the source of all thought is—

OINOS: God.

AGATHOS: I have spoken to you, Oinos, as to a child, of the fair Earth which lately perished—of impulses upon the atmosphere of the earth.

OINOS: You did.

AGATHOS: And while I thus spoke, did there not cross your mind some thought of the *physical power of words*? Is not every word an impulse on the air?

OINOS: But why, Agathos, do you weep—and why, oh, why do your wings droop as we hover above this fair star—which is the greenest and yet most terrible of all we have encountered in our flight? Its brilliant flowers look like a fairy dream—but its fierce volcanoes like the passions of a turbulent heart.

AGATHOS: They *are*!—they *are*!—This wild star—it is now three centuries since, with clasped hands, and with streaming eyes, at the feet of my beloved—I spoke it—with a few passionate sentences—into birth. Its brilliant flowers *are* the dearest of all unfulfilled dreams, and its raging volcanoes *are* the passions of the most turbulent and unhallowed of hearts!

Shadow: A Parable

Yea! though I walk through the valley of the Shadow.

—'Psalm of David'

Ye who read are still among the living; but I who write shall have long since gone my way into the region of shadows. For indeed strange things shall happen, and secret things be known, and many centuries shall pass away, ere these memorials be seen of men. And, when seen, there will be some to disbelieve and some to doubt, and yet a few who will find much to ponder upon in the characters here graven with a stylus of iron.

The year had been a year of terror, and of feeling more intense than terror for which there is no name upon the earth. For many prodigies and signs had taken place, and far and wide, over sea and land, the black wings of the Pestilence were spread abroad. To those, nevertheless, cunning in the stars, it was not unknown that the heavens wore an aspect of ill; and to me, the Greek Oinos, among others, it was evident that now had arrived the alternation of that seven hundred and ninety-fourth year when, at the entrance of Aries, the planet Jupiter is enjoined with the red ring of the terrible Saturnus. The peculiar spirit of the skies, if I mistake not greatly, made itself manifest, not only in the physical orb of the earth, but in the souls, imaginations, and meditations of mankind.

Over some flasks of the red Chian wine, within the walls of a noble hall, in a dim city called Ptolemais, we sat, at night, a company of seven. And to our chamber there was no entrance save by a lofty door of brass: and the door was fashioned by the artisan Corinnos, and, being of rare workmanship, was fastened from within. Black draperies, likewise in the gloomy room, shut out from our view the moon, the lurid stars, and the peopleless streets—but the boding and the memory of Evil, they would not be so excluded. There were things around us and about of which I can render no distinct account—things material and spiritual—heaviness in the atmosphere—a sense of suffocation—anxiety—and, above all, that terrible state of existence which the nervous experience when the senses are keenly living and awake, and meanwhile the powers of thought lie dormant. A dead weight hung upon us. It hung upon our limbs—upon the household furniture—upon the goblets from which we drank; and all things were depressed, and borne down thereby—all things save only the flames of the seven iron lamps which illumined our revel. Uprearing themselves in tall slender lines of light, they thus remained burning all pallid and motionless; and in the mirror which their lustre formed upon the round table of ebony at which we sat each of us there assembled beheld the pallor of his own countenance, and the unquiet glare in the downcast eyes of his companions. Yet we laughed and were merry in our proper way—which was hysterical; and sang the songs of Anacreon—which are madness; and drank deeply—although the purple wine reminded us of blood. For there was yet another tenant of our chamber in the person of young Zoilus. Dead and at full length he lay, enshrouded;—the genius and the demon of the scene. Alas! he bore no portion in our mirth, save that his countenance, distorted with the plague, and his eyes in which Death had but half extinguished the fire of the pestilence, seemed to take such an interest in our merriment as the dead may haply take in the merriment of those who are to die. But although I, Oinos, felt that the eyes of the departed were upon me, still I forced myself not to perceive the bitterness of their expression, and gazing down steadily into the depths of the ebony mirror, sang with a loud and sonorous voice the songs of the son of Teos. But gradually my songs they ceased, and their echoes, rolling afar off among the sable draperies of the chamber, became weak, and undistinguishable, and so faded away. And lo! from among those sable draperies, where the sounds of the song departed, there came forth a dark and undefiled shadow—a shadow such as the moon, when low in heaven, might fashion from the figure of a man: but it was the shadow neither of man nor of God, nor of any familiar thing. And quivering awhile among the draperies of the room it at length rested in full view upon the surface of the door of brass. But the shadow was vague, and formless, and indefinite, and was the shadow neither of man nor God—neither God of Greece, nor God of Chaldæa, nor any Egyptian God. And the shadow rested upon the brazen doorway, and under the arch of the entablature of the door and moved not, nor spoke any word, but there became stationary and remained. And the door whereupon the shadow rested was, if I remember aright, over against the feet of the young Zoilus enshrouded. But we, the seven there assembled, having seen the shadow as it came out from among the draperies, dared not steadily behold it, but cast down our eyes, and gazed continually into the depths of the mirror of ebony. And at length I, Oinos, speaking some low words, demanded of the shadow its dwelling and its appellation. And the shadow answered, "I am Shadow, and my dwelling is near to the Catacombs of Ptolemais, and hard by those dim plains of Helusion which border upon the foul Charonian canal." And then did we, the seven, start from our seats in horror, and stand trembling, and shuddering, and aghast: for the tones in the voice of the shadow were not the tones of any one being, but of a multitude of beings, and varying in their cadences from syllable to syllable, fell duskily upon our ears in the well remembered and familiar accents of many thousand departed friends.

Silence: A Fable

The mountain pinnacles slumber; valleys, crags, and caves are silent.

Listen to *me*," said the Demon, as he placed his hand upon my head. "The region of which I speak is a dreary region in Libya, by the borders of the river Zäire. And there is no quiet there, nor silence.

"The waters of the river have a saffron and sickly hue; and they flow not onward to the sea, but palpitate forever and forever beneath the red eye of the sun with a tumultuous and convulsive motion. For many miles on either side of the river's oozy bed is a pale desert of gigantic water-lilies. They sigh one unto the other in that solitude, and stretch towards the heaven their long and ghastly necks, and nod to and fro their everlasting heads. And there is an indistinct murmur which cometh out from among them like the rushing of subterrene water. And they sigh one unto the other.

"But there is a boundary to their realm—the boundary of the dark, horrible, lofty forest. There, like the waves about the Hebrides, the low underwood is agitated continually. But there is no wind throughout the heaven. And the tall primeval trees rock eternally hither and thither with a crashing and mighty sound. And from their high summits, one by one, drop everlasting dews. And at the roots, strange poisonous flowers lie writhing in perturbed slumber. And overhead, with a rustling and loud noise, the gray clouds rush westwardly forever until they roll, a cataract, over the fiery wall of the horizon. But there is no wind throughout the heaven. And by the shores of the river Zäire there is neither quiet nor silence.

"It was night, and the rain fell; and, falling, it was rain, but, having fallen, it was blood. And I stood in the morass among the tall lilies, and the rain fell upon my head—and the lilies sighed one unto the other in the solemnity of their desolation.

"And, all at once, the moon arose through the thin ghastly mist, and was crimson in color. And mine eyes fell upon a huge gray rock which stood by the shore of the river and was lighted by the light of the moon. And the rock was gray and ghastly, and tall,—and the rock was gray. Upon its front were characters engraven in the stones; and I walked through the morass of water-lilies, until I came close unto the shore, that I might read the characters upon the stone. But I could not decipher them. And I was going back into the morass when the moon shone with a fuller red, and I turned and looked again upon the rock and upon the characters;—and the characters were DESOLATION.

"And I looked upwards, and there stood a man upon the summit of the rock; and I hid myself among the water-lilies that I might discover the action of the man. And the man was tall and stately in form, and wrapped up from his shoulders to his feet in the toga of old Rome. And the outlines of his figure were indistinct—but his features were the features of a deity; for the mantle of the night, and of the mist, and of the moon, and of the dew, had left uncovered the features of his face. And his brow was lofty with thought, and his eye wild with care; and in the few furrows upon his cheek, I read the fables of sorrow, and weariness, and disgust with mankind, and a longing after solitude.

"And the man sat upon the rock, and leaned his head upon his hand, and looked out upon the desolation. He looked down into the low unquiet shrubbery, and up into the tall primeval trees, and up higher at the rustling heaven, and into the crimson moon. And I lay close within shelter of the lilies, and observed the actions of the man. And the man trembled in the solitude;—but the night waned, and he sat upon the rock.

"And the man turned his attention from the heaven, and looked out upon the dreary river Zäire, and upon the yellow ghastly waters, and upon the pale legions of the water-lilies. And the man listened to the sighs of the water-lilies, and to the murmur that came up from among them. And I lay close within my covert and observed the actions of the man. And the man trembled in the solitude;—but the night waned, and he sat upon the rock.

"Then I went down into the recesses of the morass, and waded afar in among the wilderness of the lilies, and called unto the hippopotami which dwelt among the fens in the recesses of the morass. And the hippopotami heard my call, and came, with the behemoth, unto the foot of the rock, and roared loudly and fearfully beneath the moon. And I lay close within my covert and observed the actions of the man. And the man trembled in the solitude;—but the night waned, and he sat upon the rock.

"Then I cursed the elements with the curse of tumult; and a frightful tempest gathered in the heaven, where before there had been no wind. And the heaven became livid with the violence of the tempest—and the rain beat upon the head of the man—and the floods of the river came down—and the river was tormented into foam—and the water-lilies shrieked within their beds—and the forest crumbled before the wind—and the thunder rolled—and the lightning fell—and the rock rocked to its foundation. And I lay close within my covert and observed the actions of the man. And the man trembled in the solitude;—but the night waned, and he sat upon the rock.

"Then I grew angry and cursed, with the curse of silence, the river, and the lilies, and the wind, and the forest, and the heaven, and the thunder, and the sighs of the water-lilies. And they became accursed, and *were still.* And the moon ceased to totter up its pathway to heaven—and the thunder died away—and the lightning did not flash—and the clouds hung motionless—and the waters sunk to their level and remained—and the trees ceased to rock—and the water-lilies sighed no more—and the murmur was heard no longer from among them, nor any shadow of sound throughout the vast illimitable desert. And I looked upon the characters of the rock, and they were changed;—and the characters were SILENCE.

"And mine eyes fell upon the countenance of the man, and his countenance was wan with terror. And, hurriedly, he raised his head from his hand, and stood forth upon the rock and listened. But there was no voice throughout the vast illimitable desert, and the characters upon the rock were SILENCE. And the man shuddered, and turned his face away, and fled afar off, in haste, so that I beheld him no more."

NOW THERE ARE FINE TALES in the volumes of the Magi—in the iron-bound, melancholy volumes of the Magi. Therein, I say, are glorious histories of the Heaven, and of the Earth, and of the mighty Sea—and of the Genii that overruled the sea, and the earth, and the lofty heaven. There was much lore, too, in the sayings which were said by the sybils; and holy, holy things were heard of old by the dim leaves that trembled around Dodona—but, as Allah liveth, that fable which the demon told me as he sat by my side in the shadow of the tomb, I hold to be the most wonderful of all! And as the Demon made an end of his story, he fell back within the cavity of the tomb and laughed. And I could not laugh with the Demon, and he cursed me because I could not laugh. And the lynx which dwelleth forever in the tomb, came out therefrom, and lay down at the feet of the Demon, and looked at him steadily in the face.

A Note About the Author

Edgar Allan Poe (1809–1849) was an American poet, short story writer, and editor. Born in Boston to a family of actors, Poe was abandoned by his father in 1810 before being made an orphan with the death of his mother the following year. Raised in Richmond, Virginia by the Allan family of merchants, Poe struggled with gambling addiction and frequently fought with his foster parents over debts. He attended the University of Virginia for a year before withdrawing due to a lack of funds, enlisting in the U.S. Army in 1827. That same year, Poe anonymously published *Tamerlane and Other Poems*, his first collection. After failing to graduate from West Point, Poe began working for several literary journals as a critic and editor, moving from Richmond to Baltimore, Philadelphia, and New York. In 1836, he obtained a special license to marry Virginia Clemm, his 13-year-old cousin, who moved with him as he pursued his career in publishing. In 1838, Poe published *The Narrative of Arthur Gordon Pym of Nantucket*, a tale of a stowaway on a whaling ship and his only novel. In 1842, Virginia began showing signs of consumption, and her progressively worsening illness drove Poe into deep depression and alcohol addiction. "The Raven" (1845) appeared in the *Evening Mirror* on January 29th. It was an instant success, propelling Poe to the forefront of the American literary scene and earning him a reputation as a leading Romantic. Following Virginia's death in 1847, Poe became despondent, overwhelmed with grief and burdened with insurmountable debt. Suffering from worsening mental and physical illnesses, Poe was found on the streets of Baltimore in 1849 and died only days later. He is now recognized as a literary pioneer who made important strides in developing techniques essential to horror, detective, and science fiction.

A Note from the Publisher

Spanning many genres, from non-fiction essays to literature classics to children's books and lyric poetry, Mint Edition books showcase the master works of our time in a modern new package. The text is freshly typeset, is clean and easy to read, and features a new note about the author in each volume. Many books also include exclusive new introductory material. Every book boasts a striking new cover, which makes it as appropriate for collecting as it is for gift giving. Mint Edition books are only printed when a reader orders them, so natural resources are not wasted. We're proud that our books are never manufactured in excess and exist only in the exact quantity they need to be read and enjoyed. To learn more and view our library, go to minteditionbooks.com